CAPTIVE

THIRD IN THE IMMORTALS OF INDRIELL SERIES

MELISSA A. CRAVEN

Praise for Immortals of Indriell

2016 RONE Award Winner – Best Book Cover
2016 YA Books Central Finalist for Best Indie
2015 Dante Rossetti YA Awards Finalist
2015 International Book Awards Finalist
2015 USA Best Book Awards Finalist

"Exactly who is the captive? That question keeps one guessing all the way through." Amazon reviewer ★★★★★

"This series is killing me! The Captive is just that good!" Amazon reviewer ★★★★★

"I have to admit I was disappointed at first, I wanted to know more about Allie and Aidan. My disappointment quickly changed as I was pulled in to the stories of Sasha and Quinn. Learning their part in all of this was fascinating." Amazon reviewer ★★★★★

"Brilliantly written. Leaves one emotionally raw and wanting more!" Amazon reviewer ★★★★★

"At first I was super angry that the Captive wasn't about Allie and Aidan But after the first 3 chapters, I was totally hooked! Ms. Craven has done it again and this one might be my favorite!" Amazon reviewer ★★★★★

"They get better and better!" Amazon reviewer ★★★★★

"This series is so different than any I've ever read and that's one of the things I love about it." Amazon reviewer ★★★★★

"I loved that Emerge wasn't the usual vampires, shape shifters and werewolves but an entirely new concept." Amazon reviewer ★★★★★

CAPTIVE: Immortals of Indriell Book 3

By: Melissa A. Craven

Midnight Hour Studio INC

Atlanta, Georgia

This book is a work of fiction. Names, characters, businesses, organizations, places, events and incidents either are the product of the author's imagination or are used fictitiously. Any resemblance to actual persons, living or dead, events, or locales is entirely coincidental.

For more information contact: Hello@Melissaacraven.com or visit the author's website at **Melissaacraven.com**

*Previously published as Emerge: The Captive (Immortals of Indriell Book 3) © August 28, 2017

Cover design by: Zoe Shtorm and Daqri Combs

Edited by: Chase Night of Story Taming and Robin Schroffel

Interior design by: @BooklyStyle

ASIN: eBook

ISBN: 9798687421317 Paperback

ISBN: 978-1-970052-12-1 Hardcover

First edition for print September 24, 2020

Printed in the United States of America

A FREE OFFER

In Captive, find out what happens when Quinn and Sasha are caught up in circumstances beyond their control. And then download your FREE copy of SCHOLAR and discover everything there is to know about the Immortals of Indriell. **Loyal subscribers will also receive bonus chapters and a short story.**

Visit **bit.ly/ScholarOffer** to download now

For my sister, Angela. My biggest fan—well, except for mom, she's kind of stalkery.

Thank you for your unwavering support and for being my sounding-board when my characters aren't behaving.

Also by Melissa A. Craven

Immortals of Indriell Series:

Emerge (Book 1) | Catalyst (An Immortals of Indriell Short Story) | Edge (Book 0) | Judgment (Book 2) | Scholar (An Immortals of Indriell Series Companion) | Volunteer (An Immortals of Indriell Short Story) | Captive (Book 3) |Assignment: An Immortals of Indriell Novella | Heir (Book 4) Betrayal (Book 5) | Runaway (Book 6) |

Proving (Book 7)

Queens of the Fae Series

Fae's Deception (Book 1)

Fae's Defiance (Book 2)

Fae's Destruction (Book 3)

Crimes of the Fae Series

Fae's Prisoner (Book 1)

Fae's Power (Book 2)

Fae's Promise (Book 3)

EMERGE
Family Tree

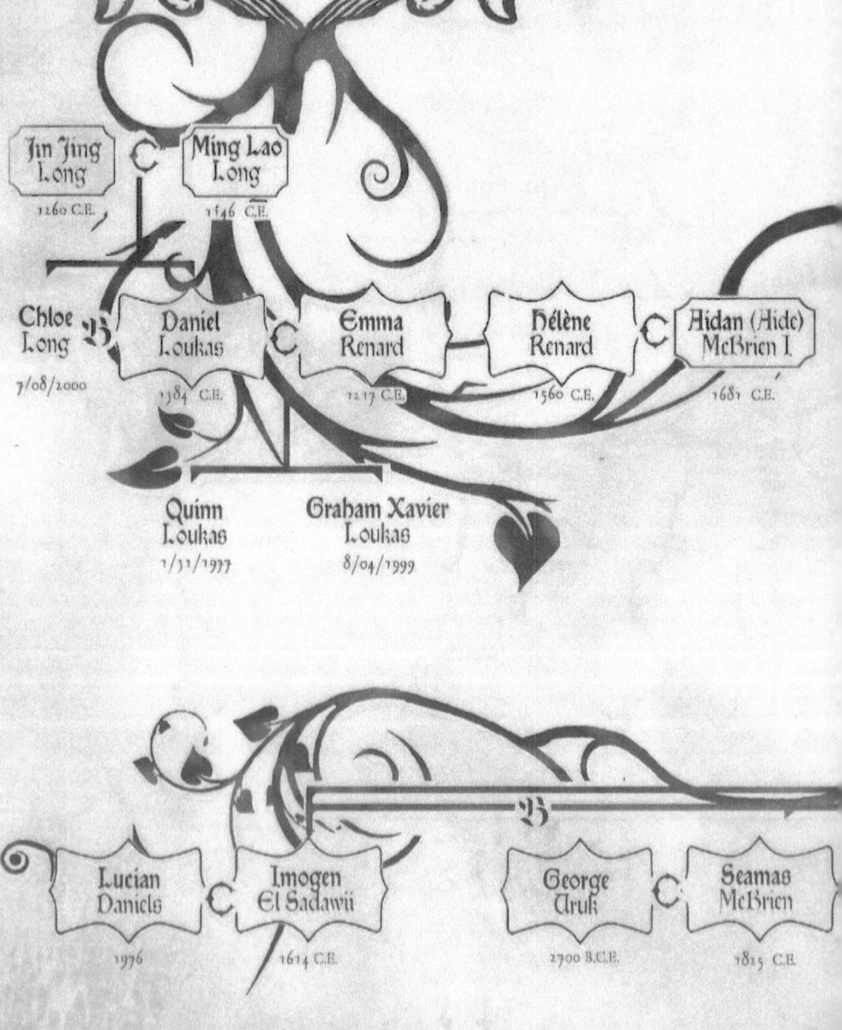

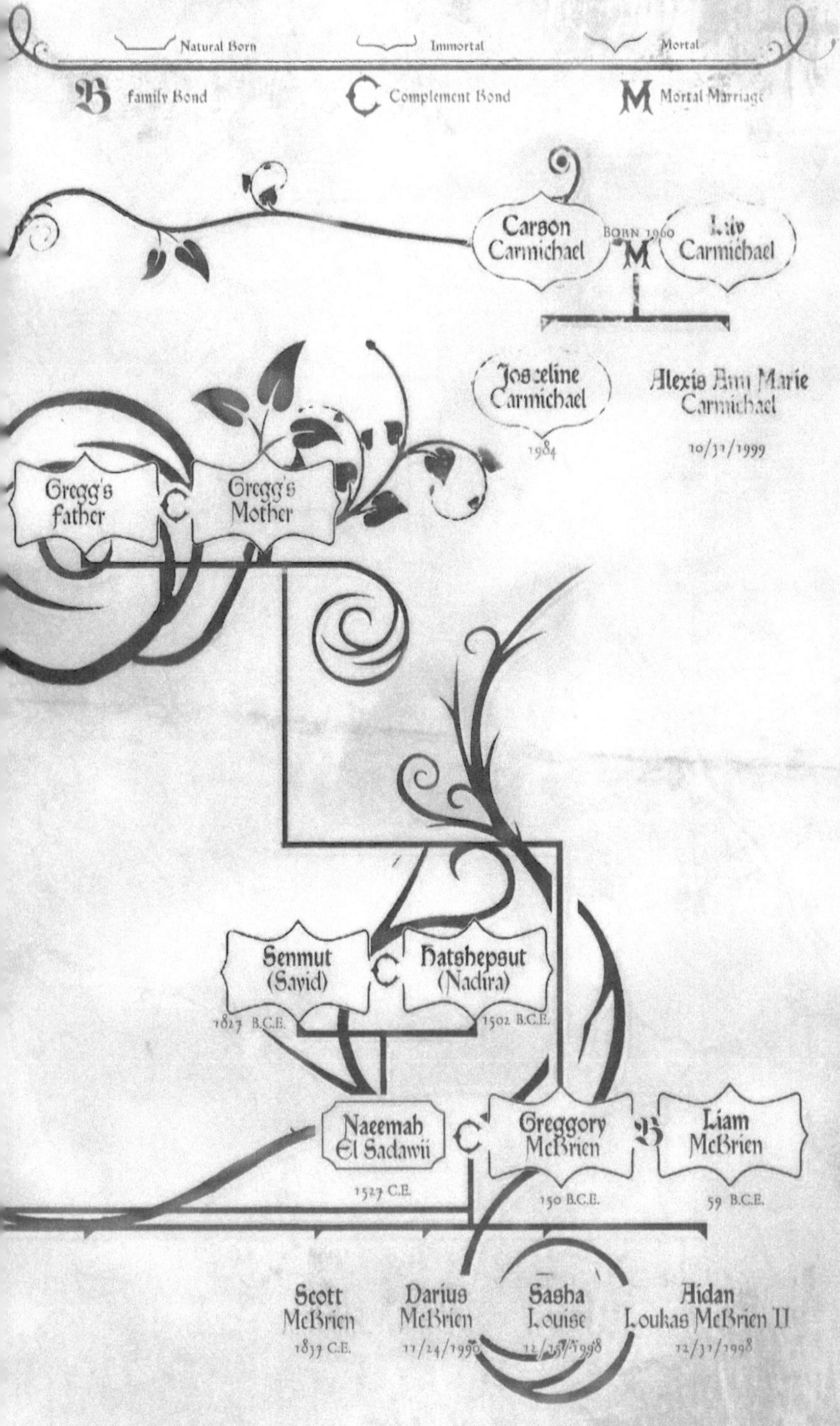

Natural Born
Immortal
Mortal
Family Bond
Complement Bond
Mortal Marriage
Carson Carmichael
BORN 1960
Liv Carmichael
Josceline Carmichael
1984
Alexis Ann Marie Carmichael
10/31/1999
Gregg's Father
Gregg's Mother
Senmut (Savid)
1827 B.C.E.
Hatshepsut (Nadira)
1502 B.C.E.
Naeemah El Sadawii
1527 C.E.
Greggory McBrien
150 B.C.E.
Liam McBrien
59 B.C.E.
Scott McBrien
1837 C.E.
Darius McBrien
11/24/1990
Sasha Louise
Aidan Loukas McBrien II
12/31/1998

RIGVEDA

"We have drunk Soma and become immortal; we have attained the light, the Gods discovered. Now what may foeman's malice do to harm us? What, O Immortal, mortal man's deception?"

—Rigveda 8.48.3

CHAPTER 1

Sasha: The Springtime Ball - Cleveland, Ohio

"You think Allie's face will freeze like that?" Sasha cheered with the crowd for their reluctant queen of the Springtime Ball.

"Is she pissed or excited? I can't tell which," Quinn said as he wrapped his arms around Sasha's waist.

"I'm going with sixty-percent pissed and forty-percent confused." Sasha leaned back against him, enjoying his closeness. *For however long it lasts this time.* They could never seem to get on the same page in their rocky relationship, but she couldn't imagine spending this night with anyone else. Even nearly a year after they ended their relationship ... again.

"Our Allie is really not the prom queen sort, is she?" Quinn laughed.

"There's something about those two together, though," Sasha said as her brother and her best friend stepped onto the dance floor.

"You think they'll ever figure it out?"

"They'll get there." Sasha smiled.

"Will we?" Quinn's breath was warm against her ear and his clean, masculine scent of birch and tea tree sent her pulse racing the way it always did when he was close.

"Of course we will." Sasha turned in his arms, the rush of all her old feelings coming back. Not that they'd ever really left. There was a time when she was convinced she would spend her life with her first love. Sometimes she still believed Quinn was her Complement and that the source of all their trouble was that they were just too young. Maybe they would be ready for it one day. She could wait.

"Dance with me?" Quinn asked, taking her hand in his.

They moved to the dance floor to join the crowd circling Allie and Aidan.

"Sometimes I wonder why we're so good together when we're not together," Quinn said, wrapping his arm around her waist.

"And so terrible for each other when we *are* together?" She added.

"We're ridiculous." Quinn twirled her around and dipped her until the tips of her hair brushed the floor. His smile was brighter than she'd seen it in a long time.

"We should see a shrink." She laughed, determined to enjoy the evening and not let their past drama spoil anything. "What made you ask me to the dance?" It was a risk. They'd both known going into this night that it would stir up a past probably best left buried.

"I made you a promise."

"That was ages ago, Quinn. I was just thirteen." She stared into his dark blue eyes, unable to believe he actually remembered a silly old promise from when they were kids.

"And seven feet tall with giant clown feet." His laughter rumbled in his chest as he held her a little too closely. "So worried no one would ever ask you to the junior ball because you were head and shoulders above the rest of us."

"Quinn Loukas, you take that back. I do not have big feet!"

"You grew into your height, Sasha. But you still have clown feet."

"You know I'm armed, right?" She scowled at him.

"Ah, you know you're gorgeous. Always have been."

"I'm glad you kept your promise ... and glad you finally got as tall as me."

"Walk with me?" He pulled her toward the gardens, away from the glittering dance floor. "I could do with a little quiet and some fresh air."

Sasha followed him through the double doors and into the chilly spring evening, wondering if her heart could handle it if they tried to go down that road again and failed.

"What are we doing, Sash?" Quinn sighed as they strolled along the winding pathway, avoiding the other couples seeking a quiet moment away from the revelry inside.

"Enjoying the ball. Let's not make it more complicated than that." Her heart wanted to gallop right over the cliff with him the way they always did, but her head cautioned her to take it slow. They'd hurt each other too many times to make the same mistakes again.

"The last thing I ever want is to hurt you. We suck at relationships, but 'just friends' ... it's not enough. I miss you, Sasha."

"I miss you too. But I ... won't go through that again—not until we're both ready to do it right. Let's enjoy tonight and not make any promises we can't keep."

They were always so drawn to each other like moths to a flame, but at the same time, they clashed like opposites. The constant battle of their relationship was exhausting. They were better as friends, but he was right, it wasn't enough.

"If tonight is all we have, then let's make it worth it." Quinn pulled her into the shadows, and the warmth of his cloaking gift enveloped them. In an instant they were wrapped up in their own little world, oblivious of anyone or anything going on around them.

When his lips found hers, it was like everything clicked into place and Sasha's world made sense again—in the way it only did when they were together like this. But *this* was never their problem. This was the one thing they were good at.

His hands slid down to her waist, his touch so familiar and, as it so often was with him, a little bit dangerous. Something powerful and angry fueled his power ... and his passion. With the vine-covered brick wall at her back, and the wall of Quinn's chest pressing against her, Sasha rushed headlong into all those old feelings. The concerns, the hesitations, all the reasons they shouldn't be doing this—she'd think about all those things tomorrow. But for this one night, she just wanted to focus on the boy she'd loved all her life. Consequences be damned.

"Sasha," Quinn whispered, his lips trailing down her throat. "I love you. That has never changed and it's the one thing you can always count on from me."

"I know. And I love you too. That's always been the easy part for us," she said, letting her hands wander over his shoulders.

"Sasha! Quinn?" Aidan burst into the garden. "We've got company." He whirled around, searching for them. "Where are you?"

"Here." Quinn gave Sasha one last kiss and stepped away, letting the illusion of their invisibility fall away.

"What kind of company?" Sasha asked, smoothing her hands over her dress, glancing around for mortal ears.

"Coalition." Aidan took off toward the edge of the gardens and through the gate leading into the alley. Quinn fell in right beside him as Sasha followed.

"I swear to God, you hurt my sister again and we're done," Aidan said.

Quinn nodded. He would take the threat seriously. It was just the kind of guy he was.

"How about you let me handle my own love life?" Sasha said. "We've got bigger things to worry about right now. What are we up against?"

"Allie and two Coalition. Front of the building." Aidan stopped short at the sound of gunfire as a bullet hit the brick wall behind him, just missing his head. Quinn pulled them behind the cover of the dumpsters.

"Aidan? What's going on?" Vince called in the darkness. "Where's Allie?" He ran to catch up with them. "Was that gunfire?" He joined them behind the dumpsters.

At the same moment, two Coalition men stepped into the alley from the rear of the conference center next door.

Sasha was on the verge of panic, but she looked to her brother for direction. Aidan was always quick to step into the leadership role. He would know what to do.

"Quinn, go after Allie, now," Aidan said. "Sasha, get past these thugs and circle the building. Get them to follow you. I'll handle Vince and meet you in the front in two minutes. Let's box these guys in."

"I don't need to be handled," Vince said. "But someone needs to tell me what's going on. Where is Allie?"

"Be careful, Sasha." Quinn turned and darted around the dumpsters, disappearing under the cloak of his gift.

Sasha ran straight for the men at the back of the alley, ducking under an arm and turning with a swift kick to disarm him. She fled down the back path along the rocky lakeshore, just beneath the gardens, hoping the men would follow her. Sasha was fast. She could easily outrun them and get back to Quinn before this turned ugly.

Just as she rounded the corner of the building, she heard another gunshot and chanced a glance over her shoulder to see the two men were trailing far behind. Sasha slowed, giving them the illusion that they might be able to catch her.

She circled to the front of the building and flung herself against the brick. The men following came flying around the corner a moment later. With them ahead of her now, she could finish boxing them in.

But the Coalition agents didn't seem to be looking for her.

"No," Sasha whispered as the men piled into a van.

"Nice!" Quinn's voice echoed across the empty parking lot. "Your aim sucks, Allie. How'd you manage that?"

"Progress under pressure, I suppose." Allie stepped up beside Quinn, facing the Coalition man in front of them. But they didn't see the van heading straight for their backs.

"Quinn!" Sasha shrieked at the same moment she heard Allie's anguished cry.

"Aidan! No!" Allie fell to her knees. "Aidan, please!"

"Allie! What's wrong?" Quinn shouted, not hearing Sasha's warning cry.

He didn't even see it coming. Leaning from the open door of the van, the Coalition man struck him with the butt of his knife and Quinn went down hard.

"No!" Sasha cried an instant later when the collar snapped around Quinn's throat.

She started running, heedless of her own safety.

"Sasha, no!" Graham crashed through the front door of the banquet hall and pulled her back into the shadows just as one of the Coalition cracked a bat across Allie's back. She looked like a broken doll, sprawled on the pavement as another man slipped a collar around her throat.

"Let me go, Graham!" Sasha struggled against him. "We have to help."

"The best thing we can do for them is escape the same fate so we can go after them later."

She knew he was right, but as she watched them heft Quinn's lifeless body into the van, she couldn't sit back and let it happen.

"Where's Aidan? We have to do something!" She jerked free of Graham's hold and ran, stumbling to her knees as the van's tail lights faded in the distance. There was nothing any of them could do.

"Quinn!" Her shrieks ripped from her throat like shards of broken glass.

"Sasha, get it together. My brother needs you." Graham grabbed her shoulders and pulled her to her feet.

"How did this happen?" She shook her head, refusing to believe Allie and Quinn had been taken.

"They must have followed us all afternoon. I'm pretty sure I saw those guys earlier today."

"The dove," she whispered. "This is my fault." Sasha's hands shook. Just that afternoon, she'd healed a bird with her gift. Right out in plain sight, too full of herself and her power to think that it could ever lead to this.

Sasha stood beside Quinn's brother in the deafening silence, too stunned to speak. *Did my arrogance just cost my Complement and my best friend their freedom?*

Chapter 2

Quinn: Summer - Atlanta, Georgia

"Time's up, brother. She's ready for him."

Quinn recognized the smooth-as-silk voice and knew it was a precursor to bad news. Nothing good ever came from Ryan Conner's visits.

"I see you came prepared," Michael replied, greeting his brother just outside Quinn's filthy cell. The Conners were the only people Quinn had seen in years. Except *her*. She visited often. *Too often.*

Quinn's head slumped against his chest as he dangled from the ceiling, the chains digging into his mangled wrists almost to the bone. He needed to take advantage of whatever reprieve he could get while the brothers bickered. He had no idea how long they'd had him like this. Days. Maybe a week this time.

After so many years, he missed his family. His friends.

Sasha. It was painful how much he missed her. Their last moments together haunted him. If he'd known it would be the last time he would see her, he would have made it count. He would have made promises. Plans. Plans for a future he no longer had.

As a captive of Soma, Quinn had two options. Submit to

Livia's will, immediately sign over the rights to his life and willingly become her slave. Or choose option B. Resist, and Livia would eventually break him anyway and he'd still end up a slave—against his will.

Give in. The errant thought was never far from his mind. To give them what they wanted—unfettered access to his power, his gifts, and his knowledge—would set him free from this torment in an instant. But Quinn would never willingly become a Soma slave. That left him with option B—resisting until she finally broke him. But breaking an Immortal was no simple matter. It would take more than just his desire for the pain to end. He would have to lose all hope and all ability to care about himself or anyone else. And that was why Quinn Loukas was no closer to breaking today than he was the day he arrived at Sterling Tower four years ago.

Or is it closer to five years now? He'd lost count, but he'd lasted this long. He could make it another day. *One more day....*

Liquid fire splashed across his back, shocking Quinn from his stupor and setting old wounds ablaze. The lashes never healed between sessions. Michael's magnetite-laced whip saw to that, and now the raw, infected gashes sizzled and bled anew. A second splash of Michael's special concoction—water mixed with alcohol and some sort of acid—peeled away what little new skin Quinn's ravaged Immortal body had been able to regenerate.

Raising his head, Quinn clenched his jaw shut, holding back the screams that burned his throat raw. With a glare, he met his jailor's gaze, his vision fading in and out of focus. He would not give the brothers the satisfaction of winning this struggle. Not today.

One more day.

"He's a stubborn son of a bitch. I'll give him that," Michael said, nodding at Ryan.

The two brothers looked nothing alike. Michael was blond and cruel, where Ryan was dark and indifferent. He held himself above the violence his brother dished out so eagerly.

"Lower him," Ryan said as he fiddled with a wooden box in his hands.

"You can do it where he is," Michael insisted.

"Lower him. I don't want his blood and grime on my new suit." Ryan brushed at his impeccably tailored jacket, cringing as he stepped into Quinn's dungeon-like cell.

"Fine, but make it quick." Michael flicked a switch on the gray brick wall and Quinn landed with a thud at Ryan's feet.

"Where do you want it?" Ryan nudged Quinn with the heel of his custom leather shoe, polished to a shine.

Quinn stared up at him in confusion. Then the metal rod in Ryan's hand suddenly glowed white hot and he understood. The brand. He'd seen it before. Quinn looked away, disinterested. He didn't care where they put it.

"If you don't tell me, I'll put it somewhere unpleasant."

Finally, Quinn gestured at the back of his shoulder so he wouldn't have to look at it. They could brand him like cattle but they would never own him.

The searing hot iron touched his skin, sizzling like steak in a skillet, and the screams finally came. There was only so much he could take. After all this time, why were they branding him now? Like it was only the beginning. Was this just another one of their tricks? *Like the white room?*

For so long, his days had been the same monotonous torture. Almost predictable. But Quinn knew from experience that sudden changes were never good. Whatever they had in store for him next, it wouldn't be an improvement to his current situation.

"We're done here." Ryan lifted the branding iron from Quinn's shoulder. "Never forget what that mark means, Quinn.

You belong to Soma. Whether you want to accept that or not doesn't matter."

Not for the first time, Quinn thought about giving them what they wanted. Submitting would be so easy and he had such little reason to keep fighting anymore. Quinn honestly didn't know if he had it in him to remain true to the person he wanted to be, or if he would finally succumb to the darkness he'd always known was inside him.

"Has he cracked at all?" Livia's cold voice pulled Quinn from his thoughts.

I hate that woman. His aching hands coiled into fists beneath him. He got to his feet, determined not to let her see him wallowing on the floor like an animal. Quinn's knees buckled the same moment he remembered the blistering burns on his feet. He settled for sitting on the floor with his back against the rough brick wall.

"Hasn't cracked yet, but he will," Michael assured her.

"You've wasted too much time already. Your methods clearly aren't working. Clean him up and bring him to my suite. It's my turn."

"Get him on his feet," Ryan said, snapping his fingers at the two goons who followed him everywhere.

Michael's version of cleanup was hosing Quinn off and sending him on his way in the same tattered t-shirt and jeans he'd worn for weeks. The gashes on his back oozed blood and pus, crusting over and making what was left of his shirt stick to his wounds. His shoulders were on fire now that his arms were free from the cuffs. He cradled his wrists against his chest, his stomach churning at the sight of the flesh hanging loosely around the bone.

As the guards shoved him out of the cell, the blisters on his feet burst, but Quinn was determined to walk out of this place on his own.

"Pick up the pace. I don't have all day," Ryan said.

Quinn's feet grew numb as he attempted to follow Ryan along the silent corridor. He made it about ten steps before he fell, his head cracking against the polished concrete floor. Ryan simply snapped his fingers and the two Soma guards jumped to pick him up. They dragged Quinn into the elevator and up to the top floor of Sterling Tower—Livia's penthouse suite—where Quinn had spent his first night at Soma with Santi.

Santi. He'd often thought about the girl who slept on Livia's floor, tethered to the Immortal who controlled her power. *Has she held on all this time?* Santi showed him the ropes that first night—what little she knew then. She was a volunteer. She came to Soma under false pretenses after an "interview" with Livia. He'd struck her as naïve, but he quickly saw how determined she was to survive this predicament on her own terms. He was both eager to see if she was still there and dreading it, hoping she'd been a figment of his imagination and not caught up in the horrors of this place.

"Liv's not going to go easy on you," Ryan said as the guards left them in the vestibule outside Livia's apartment.

Quinn sagged against the wall, smearing blood and grime on the expensive wallpaper. He'd likely pay for that once she saw the mess.

"Pain is the easiest and often most efficient route to forcing a new recruit to see that total submission is the only way. But for stubborn people like you, pain doesn't work. She will try other means to get what she wants. And she will get it. You need to ask yourself if it's worth the price."

"Worth it? My free will is worth enduring anything," Quinn said. It hurt to speak. He had distant memories of a broken jaw, but that was months ago. His face still ached—like there was permanent damage to the bones that had never healed properly. But if Ryan was right and the pain was at an end, Quinn could salvage what was left of his willpower and soldier on.

"My brother is talented in many ways. The reality of that is going to hit you hard, Quinn. She'll use that against you."

"Why bother with the pep talk?" Quinn glared at him.

"Not everyone here is as soulless as they may seem. Not even Livia. My brother ... he enjoys his job, but I find it disgusting." Ryan rang the doorbell and returned to the elevator.

"And your job? Do you find that disgusting too?"

"I find it bearable," Ryan said. "Good luck, Quinn. You're going to need it."

The elevator doors closed, leaving Quinn alone for the first time in ages. He turned at the sound of footsteps inside the apartment. The door cracked open, revealing a green-amber eye through the slit. *Santi. She's still here.* He had a sudden urge to hug her and weep on her shoulder. But as she opened the door, he saw how the years had taken their toll. Her face was gaunt with purple-black circles under her hollow eyes, like she hadn't slept since he'd seen her last. Santi was on the edge of losing her fight.

"Come with me. You don't have much time before she arrives." Santi pulled him inside and closed the door behind them. She limped as she hurried to the kitchen, dragging an elegant silver chain behind her. Santi's right foot was shackled, the magnetized metal rubbing her ankle raw, letting the poison leach into her bloodstream slowly. The angry scabs along her calf indicated she was rarely without the restraint. Her tether, anchored somewhere within the penthouse, extended and retracted with her movements. She seemed to have the run of most of the rooms, but he wondered how long she'd been cooped up in this apartment.

"This way. She wants you in the white room." She shoved a protein bar and a bottle of water into his hands and ushered him down the wide, white marbled hall.

"White room?" He halted. *I'm not going back in that room again.*

"*Muévete.* I'm supposed to get you settled before she gets here." Santi's voice was firm when it probably should have been desperate. From the looks of it, she'd embraced her position and accepted her life here. It was probably how she'd survived as long as she had.

"What's going to happen now?" he asked, choking down the protein bar, wishing he had ten more.

"That's not important." She turned to face him. "The reality of Michael's psychological mind games is going to hit you soon. And it's going to hit you hard. I'm sorry I don't have time to soften the blow, Quinn. How long do you think you've been here?"

"I don't know. I lost track of time years ago. I guess four years? Maybe five? What do you mean *think*?"

"You arrived here just three months ago." She held his gaze, willing him not to fall apart.

"Three months? That's not possible." Quinn grabbed the wall for support as his knees threatened to give out.

"Your memories of the last five 'years' are never going to leave you. You must find a way to live with it and not let the confusion overwhelm you."

"How do I get through it?" Quinn struggled to wrap his mind around the time screw. Logically, he knew it was possible for a psychological gift to affect him this way, but the experience of the last five "years" was so vivid. The memories were seared into his mind and he wasn't sure how to separate fact from that kind of fiction.

"Put it behind you. Pretend like you just got here. Everything from the last time you saw me to this very moment doesn't matter. It wasn't real, so suck it up and move on. It's the only way."

"It feels real." Quinn glanced down at his mangled hands. They were real enough.

"You've not healed from anything they've done to you, Quinn. That's not because of the magnetic weapons or your age. They've not given you time to heal. Think about it. How long has it been since Michael last flogged you?"

"Weeks. Maybe more than a month."

"Don't you think you'd have started healing by now? By the looks of it, it's only been a few hours."

Quinn nodded, staggering down the hall behind her. Inside he was reeling from the lightning bolt realization that it had only just begun. What felt like years of torture was just his initiation into Soma. That alone was enough to break him—which was exactly what they wanted, but Quinn made a habit of not giving them what they wanted.

"Deep breaths," Santi said softly, pausing in front of a closed door. "You don't have time to come to terms with it. Don't give them the satisfaction. Don't make it easy for them. You understand how her gift works, right?" She reached for his arm to give him some support.

"She's like a parasite." Quinn latched on to the change in subject like a lifeline.

She nodded, fumbling with a ring of keys. Her hands shook, but she managed to get the key into the lock. "She'll dig even deeper now. She'll want to understand every nuance of your gift she controls. She owns it. You won't have full use of your power as long as she's latched on to you. But you'll have some.

She'll keep you bogged down under the weight of her gift so you're almost useless. Her power works like a defense mechanism. If you attack her with one of your gifts, she takes control of it. You know that, but she's going to sift through your mind to see everything you're capable of. She'll discover things about your abilities that even you haven't discovered yet."

"She can tell what I can do? Everything?"

"Yes. You'll not be able to hide anything from her."

"I'm so screwed." Quinn followed Santi into the white room on shaky limbs. He stumbled, reaching for the doorway for support. He'd been here before—or at least a place just like it. He'd spent a year here. Tormented by the endless brilliance of white, never-ending daylight and the constant white noise that drowned out his screams. The monotony almost drove him into submission.

"It's not real. Whatever you're remembering, it's not real." Santi brushed her hand across his face.

Quinn nodded, taking comfort from her gentle touch. "It never happened?"

"Only in your mind," she said softly.

He closed his eyes, relishing her kind touch. He just needed a moment.

Finally, Quinn crossed the room to sit at the white table. He would wait for Livia's arrival and he would face whatever she had in store for him.

"She'll be here soon," Santi said. "She's going to push you hard today, but it's only to take advantage of your current state of mind. You can't let her win. You've lasted this long. If you can get through this, you'll stay here in the penthouse. With me. The painful part is behind you—physical pain, anyway. You've proven you can't be broken with a beating so she won't waste her efforts on that ... well, just that. This part is harder.

She's going to screw with your head and your emotions. But you just have to get through it."

"And after this?" Quinn gestured at the white room. "After tonight?"

"A reprieve." She smiled. "You'll enjoy it while you can, but it won't last. She'll try to win you over with a complete one-eighty, but it's false. Don't fall for it. Get through this and I'll patch you up. She should leave us alone tonight."

"You went through this? All of this?" Quinn took a moment to really look at the lovely Latina woman in front of him. Her chestnut brown hair fell in limp waves down her back. She was too thin but her petite frame still held a hint of the strength she'd once had.

"I've spent more than enough time with Michael," she said. "And Livia continues to find new ways to torture me. I can only take it one hour at a time. I can't ever think beyond that." She jerked her head toward the door. "She's coming."

Quinn heard Livia's unmistakable approach. She had a firm footfall. A no-nonsense, "don't waste my time or you'll wish you hadn't" attitude.

"I have to go." With that, Santi left him alone in the white room.

Quinn figured he had about thirty seconds to get his head on straight. He squared his stiff shoulders and shoved the whirlwind of conflicting memories out of his mind. He needed to focus if he was going to get through this. *Just one more day.*

Chapter 3

Sasha: Summer - Agra, India

"Sasha, are you coming to Quinn's vigil tonight?" Allie asked.

Sasha glanced over her shoulder to see Allie lurking in her doorway, sweaty and disheveled from her afternoon of training down in the courtyard with Aidan and Liam.

"No." Sasha's tone was unintentionally harsh. "You all might be ready to mourn Quinn's life, but I'm just not there yet."

All the blood rushed from Allie's face and Sasha winced at the hurt look in her eyes as she turned back to the corkboard wall. Sasha knew it wasn't fair to take her frustrations out on her best friend.

"I'm sorry, Allie." She sighed. "I didn't mean that. I'm just not ready to give up hope yet. This vigil ... it's too soon." She worked a piece of red yarn around a thumbtack in the wall and guided the thread to another thumbtack to link the two elements she was certain were connected, although she couldn't prove it. *Yet.*

"I don't think it's supposed to be about giving up." Allie flopped down on the corner of Sasha's bed, clearing a pile of her carefully documented notes. "It's not about that for me, anyway. I think this vigil-celebration thing is supposed to be about renewing our hope for whatever is ahead for him. It's not about moving on without him."

"You're right." Sasha nodded. In her heart, she knew Quinn's family wasn't giving up on him and never would. But they were keeping her in the dark and it seemed like they were no closer to liberating him now than they were when he was taken more than two months ago.

"What's all this?" Allie swept her hand across the bed, taking in the chaos that was Sasha's room. "It looks like you've been binge-watching old episodes of *Prison Break* on Netflix. If you've got plans to tattoo all this crap on yourself, please don't."

"You're not funny, mortal girl." Allie and her pop culture references usually went right over Sasha's head. "This is all my personal research on Quinn's situation. I can't sit back and let the adults do all the work. I need to do something, and I'm good at researching."

"Let me help," Allie said eagerly.

"You have to keep all of this stuff to yourself and not share with your little brain twin." Sasha gestured to Allie's forehead where her brother Aidan had taken up residence in Allie's telepathic mind.

"Let's just say I suddenly have the proper motivation to keep some of my thoughts to myself," Allie muttered.

Sasha's eyes widened in surprise. The last she'd heard, the two couldn't control the link they shared and were in each other's thoughts constantly. "I bet that's making him crazy."

"Well, it doesn't take much to send Aidan into a tizzy. Now tell me what you're planning. I have a feeling it has a kamikaze theme."

"I'm not planning anything." Sasha shot her a withering

look. "Just researching." Unfortunately, Allie was right. Sasha did have a plan and it was incredibly risky—but she wasn't going to be telling her friend anything about it. Sasha just needed to do *something*. The way she'd left things with Quinn haunted her. *What did that kiss mean?* They were headed for something just moments before he was ripped away from her. And it was her fault. *She* brought the Coalition's attention on them that night.

"Don't look at me like that, Sash. I know you. I know what Quinn means to you and I know sitting around waiting for something to happen is *killing* you. To be honest, it's killing me. So tell me what you know."

"What do you know about where he is?" Sasha asked.

"I know he's in Atlanta, and it doesn't seem like he's with the Coalition like we originally thought. At least not the normal Coalition. Livia's connected with them, but she was the one in charge the night we were taken, so I'm thinking he's still with her."

"He is. At least for the moment." Sasha passed her a stack of photos she'd managed to wrangle from Graham. Quinn's brother was busy with his own investigation and she'd been spending a lot of time chatting with him online while he was in the Azores with his family. They were helping each other fill in the gaps of missing information the adults didn't think they could handle.

Allie flipped through the photos, trembling at the sight of Livia, the woman who'd held her captive just a few weeks ago. Sasha felt bad. Allie didn't need another reminder of that awful night. She had been lucky to escape and Sasha knew Allie blamed herself because she was home now and Quinn wasn't.

"Do you know anything about her?" Allie asked. "They won't tell me anything."

"From what little I could find online, she runs a non-profit that caters to Immortals, called 'The Fold.' Their headquarters are based in Sterling Tower in Atlanta." Sasha turned her computer toward Allie. "That's the same building where Quinn is being held. That much I know from Mom."

"So if we know exactly where he is, why can't we just go in and get him?" Allie asked. "You can't tell me your family doesn't have the resources to make that happen."

Sasha shook her head. "The security in this place is like the Pentagon. You can't get in unless you have an appointment or you work there. Not unless you're a kid like Graham with more technologically advanced gifts. They run a program for kids who need the kind of training their parents can't give them. It's kind of like a boarding school for really talented kids."

"So why don't we dangle a carrot?" Allie leaned over Sasha's desk, scrolling through the website for the Fold. "Get one of us in there and we can figure out how to reach him."

"Dad refuses to even consider it. He's probably right. I'm getting a sinister vibe about this place, like it's a front for something else. Livia's affiliation with the Coalition doesn't give me the warm-fuzzies. Why would a woman advocating for young Immortals and their families secretly have one foot in the Coalition and make it a point of pride that they don't have a single tie to the Senate?"

"What does your dad say?" Allie asked.

"I haven't talked to him much since he left for Cleveland, but Dad won't tell me anything. I think he's worried I'll do something stupid." The family had spent weeks trying to find a way to get close enough to Quinn to act, but they refused to see the obvious. The best way into Sterling Tower was through the front door. If you were a young and gifted Immortal they would welcome you with open arms.

"And what exactly are you thinking? You wouldn't be Sasha if you didn't have a carefully articulated plan in place. With, like, pie charts and shit." Allie gestured at the wall to make her point.

"Nothing concrete at the moment." Sasha turned away, wincing at the lie. "I'm still researching, trying to find alternative ways into the building. And I'm convinced the Fold is connected with some rather ... corrupt organizations." She took a step back from her wall. "I'm missing something and I feel like it's staring me in the face." She glanced at Allie, hoping she wouldn't stop her from walking right through the front door of Sterling Tower, asking for help with her training. And once she was in, she could find Quinn and they could escape together.

"You're such a bad liar," Allie said. "I can literally see you plotting as we speak. So where is Quinn in this place? Probably not in a student dormitory?"

"No. He'd never cooperate, so he wouldn't be with the other kids who volunteer. He'd have to be in some kind of prison somewhere in the building."

"Sasha Louise El Sadawii McBrien. Don't you dare do what I know you're going to do," Allie said.

Sometimes it really sucks having a clairvoyant for a bestie.

"Don't you four-name me, Alexis Ann Mareé Carmichael. I'm not doing anything. I swear." *Yet,* Sasha added, silently begging Allie to look the other way.

"Please don't make us have to worry about two of you in there," Allie pleaded. "I don't think any of us could take it."

"I know." She did. She knew it would hurt the family if she acted rashly, but they didn't understand the pull she felt toward Quinn. It was like a fire, constantly burning in her veins. It was worse since his capture. Like he was calling her for help. She couldn't ignore that. She wouldn't.

"Hey, you two," Aidan said as he barged into the room without knocking, like the obnoxious little brother he was.

"Coming to the vigil?" he asked. "It's time."

"You guys go ahead without me. I'll be there in a little while." Sasha hated lying to them, but she couldn't face this vigil for Quinn. Not when she knew she could do something to help. Tonight would be the perfect night to slip away without anyone noticing. They wouldn't force her to join in the festivities, celebrating Quinn's life. They would all assume she wasn't ready and no one would bother her. By morning, when anyone thought to look for her, she'd be in Atlanta and well out of their reach.

"Hey kid," Imogen called as she knocked on Sasha's bedroom door.

"I'm not coming to the vigil, Gen." She dropped her duffel bag onto the floor and kicked it under her bed. It seemed she was wrong about the family leaving her alone, but she wasn't in the mood for Gen's sistering.

"I'm not here about the vigil. Mom and Gregg need to see you in their office. It's important."

"Dad's here? When did he arrive?"

"A few hours ago." Imogen looked worried.

"What's wrong? Is it Quinn?"

"No, this isn't about Quinn. It's the Senate. They're here and it's not good, sweetie. Clean this up before Mom sees it." She gestured at the photos and maps covering the surface of her bedroom wall. "Be quick about it. We don't have much time."

"Now you're scaring me." Sasha pulled a drape over the wall to conceal her investigation.

"They're here for you, Sash."

"Here *for* me?" *What could the Senate possibly want with me?* But her father's old worries suddenly seemed more than just his over protective parenting. Gregg had always suspected the Senate would use her for her gifts someday, but this was much too soon.

"Let's go." Imogen grabbed her hand and led her down the stairs to the common room and across the courtyard. Naeemah's office was on the opposite side of the huge villa they'd rented for the summer. Far enough away that any visiting Immortals would not be able to sense how many lived under Naeemah's care.

Sasha heard her father's voice long before they arrived at the office.

"We've been over this, Sloane. You're not taking over my daughter's training and that is final," Gregg said.

"And the Senate has been patient with you both, but Sasha is old enough now to handle the superior training we can offer kids like her."

"What?" Sasha came to a dead stop, looking at her sister for confirmation.

Gen gave her arm a gentle squeeze as she led her into their mother's office.

Sasha held her head high as she stepped into the room. She was the daughter of two influential Immortals and the granddaughter of an Egyptian pharaoh. She would not show weakness. She would not show fear. But Sasha's heart felt like ice in her chest.

Having the Senate take over her training had always been her greatest fear. Aidan was the rock star of the family—more powerful than just about anyone she'd ever met. Allie was right on his heels. But Sasha was a close third or fourth in that race. The Senate didn't know her brother or Allie existed—a fact neither of them even realized. Aidan came to the McBrien family as an infant. Gregg found him just after a storm when he was working in Ireland. Because their new son was so powerful, Gregg and Naeemah made the decision not to register him with the Senate—for this exact reason.

But Sasha wasn't so lucky. She came to the McBrien family when she was nearly five years old. For the first few years of her life, she'd lived in a mortal orphanage in Haiti. Her adoption was a public record and on file with the Senate. There was no hiding her existence. As far as the Senate knew, Sasha was likely the most promising Immortal of her generation.

"Mom, what is this all about?" Sasha's voice came out calm and formal. Regal, like her mother.

"Have a seat, Sasha. We will explain," Naeemah said.

"I'm not sure we can stop this from happening, sweetheart," Gregg said as he took her in his arms. She hadn't seen him in weeks. He was supposed to be in Cleveland. "We will be with you the whole way. They've agreed to let Imogen come with you." He gave her a level look but panic coiled in Sasha's chest.

"Go? Where am I going?" She sank into the seat her mother offered. All of her carefully laid plans started to crumble as she turned her attention to the two Senate representatives who had come to collect her. Sasha eyed the handsome young Indian soldier. He was about Imogen's age, maybe younger. Tall like Sasha, with a slim build. He was attractive, but in an unexpected way. Except for the livid tattoo marring his left cheek.

"Just give it to me straight." She was all but certain they were after her target ability. Sasha never missed a shot. No matter what, if she aimed while using her gift, she hit the mark. The ultimate recipe for the perfect sniper, a role Gregg had always prepared her for, but she never dreamed it would happen so soon.

"Jayesh Basu is an old friend," Naeemah said. "You can

trust him. I'm trusting him with my young daughter's safety and I know he will not disappoint me. Right, Jayesh?" Naeemah gave him her scariest look. Sasha had been on the receiving end of that look more than a few times and it never failed to scare her into total obedience.

"Of course, Naeemah. Your daughter's safety will be our number one priority." His words were meant to be soothing, but his tone said he wasn't thrilled to be here either.

"Anyone care to tell me what this is all about, or should I take a guess? I'm sure I won't need more than one."

"You're right, dear," the other Senate rep said in the most patronizing tone she could possibly muster. "It should come as no surprise to anyone here that the Senate has taken a special interest in your training."

"Please don't call me dear." Sasha shook her head in disgust. These people were taking her away from her plans. *I should have left for Atlanta yesterday.*

"I am Lieutenant Governor Sloane and I am here to tell you that your government has chosen you for a very special training program. Isn't that an honor?" She beamed at Sasha like she was talking to an eight-year-old.

"Not really," Sasha muttered.

"It is highly unusual for the Senate to take an interest in a child's training, but we believe you have such incredible potential, we'd like to offer you the full support of the Senate's resources. We have high hopes for your future, dear. We've hired a very special mentor to oversee your summer training. Think of it like an internship—a much-needed boost to your education."

"And what will I be learning?" Sasha crossed her legs and folded her hands in her lap to keep them from shaking.

"Jayesh is head of a special forces team employed by the Senate. Occasionally, the Senate must step into mortal affairs, and teams like Jayesh's typically handle those ... unseemly details. He is the absolute best of the best at what he does. He will be supervising your training in the ancient arts of the Chola assassins."

Sasha's pulse pounded in her ears. There was a huge difference between knowing this would happen one day and realizing it was happening right now.

"No," Imogen said softly. "We cannot allow this. Mother, she is too young. Jayesh ... we can't go back. I swore I would never return, and you want me to take my baby sister there?"

"She's not much younger than we were when we trained with the mother," Jayesh said. "She will be fine."

"We have to stop this." Imogen shook her head stubbornly. "There is no sense in doing this now. Wait until she is Proven. At the very least. She deserves that much."

"I'm afraid the Senate has spoken, Imogen," Lieutenant Governor Sloane said. "You know better than anyone what that means."

"Gen, please tell me what's happening," Sasha said. "So I can stop imagining the worst. I can't be an assassin. I'm seventeen years old. You know that, right?" Sasha turned to Sloane in desperation.

"They want you trained by the Chola," Imogen said. "This is serious. It's about them making an early investment in the future they have all planned out for you."

"You are nearly correct, Imogen, but do not make it sound like she doesn't have a choice about her future. While we may direct her training and offer her guidance, she will still be able to finish school with her friends and go to college wherever she likes. We simply feel Sasha's gifts are suited to this line of work and we would like to see her training reflect her strengths. But this is a one-time deal ... for now. When she has completed her training with Mother Raghavan, she will return home and continue her life as usual. If this summer goes well, we'd like to see her train one-on-one with Jayesh's team next summer before she pursues her college education. And over the intervening years until she reaches her Proving, we will offer her the special attention a girl like Sasha needs."

"And what if I don't want it?" Sasha leaned forward. "Does that even matter?"

"We simply want to give you the necessary tools to support the gifts you possess. Whatever lies in your future is your choice, but you will serve the Senate just as we all do. It is a privilege and a responsibility."

"A simple 'no' would have sufficed." Sasha sat back in defeat. This was happening whether she wanted it or not. "Where am I going?"

"You will travel with Jayesh to Tamil Nadu in southern India where you will spend six short weeks training with Mother Raghavan and her people until you become a Chola assassin—a title few are given the opportunity to earn."

"And what is the point of all of this?" Naeemah asked, her voice like the most corrosive acid.

"The point is to equip Sasha with the necessary skills to serve the Senate to the absolute best of her ability. Sasha is young, with many years ahead of her before she will be called upon to serve." She turned to Sasha, the syrupy-sweet smile slipping from her face. "But when you are called, you will be prepared."

"Prepared to kill mortals when and how I am told? Or do I get to voice my concerns as a non-violent person?"

"I would never have expected such resistance from a governor's daughter." Sloane wiped her brow nervously.

"Can you just answer my questions? Don't you think I deserve a little honesty?"

"This is no longer open for discussion," Sloane said in frustration. "When you are as talented as you are, sometimes you don't have the luxury of making your own choices!" She tucked her mousy brown hair behind her ear, biting her lip as if she regretted her outburst.

"Lady, if you intend to turn my child into a weapon, the least you can do is speak plainly and prepare her for what to expect." Gregg's voice was low and full of restraint. Sasha knew he was nearing the end of his patience.

"Thanks, Dad. I got this," Sasha said, leaning toward Sloane. "If you want to commandeer my gifts to serve your purpose, I understand it is our duty to serve the Senate in that capacity. But if you want me to cooperate and make this easy for you, then I suggest you do as my father said and speak plainly. Why now? Why not when I am Proven?"

Sasha wasn't certain, but she thought she heard Jayesh mutter something about the apple not falling far from the tree.

"A fair question," Sloane reluctantly agreed. "But I am not exactly ... prepared to give an answer."

"Then perhaps the Senate should send someone who is prepared, if they expect my blind cooperation?"

"Little Naeemah-ogen." Jayesh heaved a huge patronizing sigh. "Don't be a naive child. When you have a gift like yours, it should come as no surprise when people decide they are going to use you for it. Get used to it."

"I'm well aware of that eventuality." Sasha gave him her best glare. "I would just like a straight answer about why this has to happen now. I am seventeen years old. I accept the fact that the Senate will probably always have an interest in me and my gifts, but I also expect them to have enough respect for me and my family, who have served them well, to allow me a normal life for just a little while before making demands on my training."

"Couldn't have said it better myself." Gregg crossed his arms over his chest. "You will answer my daughter."

"Very well." Sloane sat ramrod straight in her chair. "The Senate has decided that you have been lax in your parental duties to your daughter." She lifted her chin as she met Gregg's glare. "You've allowed her too much freedom and not enough time to focus on her potential. Under your tutelage, her gift will never be of much use beyond target practice. We want to guide Sasha while this gift is still developing so we can help her shape it into much more than simple accuracy. We will not remove your daughter from your home. As long as you cooperate. But she will complete her training on our terms while she is still young enough to be molded into what we believe she can become."

If looks could kill, Lieutenant Governor Sloane would be nothing more than a pile of ash at Naeemah and Gregg's feet.

"It's okay, Mom. Dad. I think we can all agree that this is bullshit and I shouldn't have to do this. But we all know I can take care of myself. I'll be okay and I'll be home in six weeks." Sasha knew her only recourse at this point was to get this thing done and get back to the business of freeing Quinn. "When do I leave?"

"You have one hour to pack and say your goodbyes," Jayesh said. "But you will not tell anyone what you're doing. As far as your family knows, you're taking a clerical internship with the Senate for the rest of the summer."

Sasha snorted. There was no way her brothers would buy that. "Fine. I'll see you in an hour."

"Jayesh will escort you," Sloane said.

"No one enters our home at this time," Naeemah said. "Not even an old and trusted friend." She cast her eyes up at Jayesh, her gaze speaking volumes.

"We have reached the end of our patience and our hospitality." Gregg echoed his wife's decree. "We are governor of our region and we hold a position within the Senate community that demands respect as well as trust. My daughter will return to her room to pack and have a quiet moment to herself. Her sister, Imogen, will accompany her until they both return to this office in one hour. My wife and I will keep you company until then."

Chapter 4

Quinn: Summer - Atlanta, Georgia

"Quinn." Livia gave him a curt nod as she marched into the white room with a sour look on her olive face. She was as beautiful as she was terrifying. Her dark hair and high cheekbones hinted at her Arabic roots. Her silvery eyes, cold and unfeeling.

Quinn shook his head, remembering he didn't have the years of experience with her that he thought he had. He couldn't let that give him a false sense of confidence. It wasn't real.

"You're strong and you're stubborn, but make no mistake, I will break you." She sat in the chair opposite him, crossing her arms over her chest. "It's strange, but of all the scenarios Michael put you through, this room affected you the most. You don't respond to pain. It's like you expect it."

"I'm sure whatever else you have up your sleeve will be more of the same." Quinn sat back and met her piercing gaze. The hard chair against his back lit him on fire. "You will not break me." His voice wavered as he sat up straighter, the chair sticking to his wounds.

"You've either suffered a great deal in your life or you have the self-control and the pain threshold of a man a thousand years old. Which is it?" She leaned in closer, examining him like a bug under a microscope.

Quinn shrugged and gave her an empty look. He'd learned a long time ago that his future depended on his ability to harness his power—to never let it rule him. If Santi was right, Livia would know his secret soon enough. Quinn was an addict and his drug was his power.

Like most young Immortals, Quinn struggled with his gift. But it was different for him. He *wanted* to lose control. Wanted to let the power fill him until *it* controlled *him*. For those like Aidan and Allie, the struggle was simple. Maintain the upper hand. If they didn't, it meant a long road to recovery. For Quinn, the struggle was denying himself the thing he wanted more than his next breath. The seduction of his power lured him to the edge every time he used his gifts. He knew if he ever crossed that line and drew more power than he could reasonably maintain, the addiction would have him and there would be no coming back. He'd resisted the temptation every day since his first gift emerged.

The minute Livia discovered his addiction she'd have the means to manipulate him. She owned his cloaking ability. She could use it whenever and however she liked, but she channeled *his* power to fuel the gift. He trembled at the thought of how she might push him to the point of no return. With Livia at the helm, he would become the thing he hated most—a junkie monster too seduced by his own power to think of his actions and how they affected others. That was the secret to breaking an Immortal like Quinn. If he succumbed.

"You're a good guy, aren't you, Quinn?" Livia sat back and crossed her legs like she was just having a friendly chat. "Tell me about yourself. Your family."

He rolled his eyes. "Come on. I'm not that easy. At least buy me dinner first." His attempt at bravado would have been more convincing if he wasn't sweating and shaking from the intensity of his pain.

Livia reached for his hands. Her grip was strong and his wrists began bleeding again. He couldn't break her hold. He could feel her power slicing into him like a hot knife.

"You're a talented boy. You know very well by now how my gift works. You haven't been able to touch your cloaking gift since the night I forced you to come with me while your family chose to save the girl instead of you. What is she to them? She's not even family."

"She's family," he said through clenched teeth, praying she would release her grip soon.

"Tell me about her. Allie."

Of all the things he thought she might ask about his family, Allie was the last person he expected her to focus on. "She's no one. Just a girl." But he could see it in her eyes—Livia was obsessed. *It can't just be about Allie's power?* There had to be more to it than that.

"Bullshit. That girl is one of the most powerful Immortals I've ever met. Your family protected her and sacrificed you to save her. I want to know why."

"That's not how it went down, and you know it. You aren't going to plant that kind of doubt in my mind. My family came to rescue us both that night, and you were pissed you couldn't get out of there with Allie so you took me instead. Now you want to get to her through me and it's not going to happen, so just get on with whatever you have planned."

"Lead me to her and I'll set you free."

"No chance. I won't sacrifice her or my family to this place. You're stuck with me."

Livia's eyes narrowed. She tightened her grip and delved deeper with her gift, leaving him feeling naked and exposed. She could see everything. She would soon discover all of his secrets. He couldn't keep it hidden forever. That was all this was about. Michael's methods were all about delivering pain. Livia's methods were about raping his mind and leaving him helpless with nowhere to hide. She was about to see right through his walls to the root of his power and his addiction.

"I knew you were powerful, but this is too easy." She sat back with a smirk. "I've never seen an addict with so much restraint. Your cloaking gift alone makes you worth keeping, but I'm guessing you're good for much more than a fun trick. I know exactly how to break you now. All I have to do is give you exactly what you want. Let you get hooked on the use of your power and then deny you. The breaking will come with the first withdrawal symptoms. But I want to see what you can do first. No need to tell me all your secrets at once, Quinn. We have time."

She gripped his hands tightly, her gift lancing through him, searching for more of his secrets. Quinn went rigid, like a bolt of electricity shot up his spine. Livia was like a surgeon, cutting through the layers of his ability to see how it worked. It was nothing compared to everything else he'd been through, but it still had him clenching his jaw, and holding back a gasp of pain.

"Now that I have your full attention, tell me about the girl."

"Allie again?" Quinn bit back a moan of agony. He knew she didn't mean Allie this time. She was delving into his past, searching his memories without his permission.

"The brunette girl with the sweet disposition. What did you do to her?"

Quinn felt the first sting of tears burning his eyes. He would not let this woman make a mockery of his mistakes.

"You know I can look into your past whether you want me to or not, so just relax and let's see what we see."

Quinn resisted her push, but he was no match for her. Not

in his current condition. Before he knew it, he was falling into his memories with Livia at his side.

"Quinn?" Eva's soft voice made him cringe with regret, even after so many years. He sat under a huge oak tree with the young mortal girl he'd grown up with. Unshed tears burned his eyes like acid now as Livia stood by them, observing as the worst moment of his life was about to unfold. It wasn't enough to make him stand by and watch this happen again—no, Livia was going to make him experience it all over again.

"You're weird today." Eva gave him a quizzical look. She never pulled any punches, always saying exactly what was on her mind. She was the only mortal friend he'd ever had. He was so different now that he'd experienced his Awakening. He knew she couldn't see the stranger aspects of his appearance, but she sensed something was off.

"Did you get a haircut?" Eva asked. Her tiny hand looked odd against his larger one. Hers, smooth and unblemished, and his hard and calloused from years of training. She was slim and kind of geeky, with her nose always in a book.

"What are you reading?" Quinn asked, gesturing at the pile of books beside her.

"I'm catching up on my list of one hundred books to read in a lifetime. I'm almost done." She handed him *Hitchhiker's Guide to the Galaxy,* knowing it would be the one he'd choose anyway. "I'm on *Anthem* right now. Seriously, Why are you so ... bummed?" Eva set her book aside and gave him the kind of look that seemed to see right through him. "You're all tense and ... sweaty."

"I'm not, you little pest. Just read your book." He gave her a playful swat and leaned against the huge tree trunk. She was right—he was tense. He was still adjusting to all of the new sensations after his recent Awakening. He could feel his power swirling inside of him, like an icy storm filling his chest, eager to burst forth at any moment. The temptation to reach for it was already there, but it wasn't something he was capable of so soon. It took most Immortals weeks of practice before they could truly touch their power for the first time. He had nothing to worry about. He was just being overly cautious.

It wouldn't kill you to relax. Give yourself a break from all that self-control. It's not like you're actually going to touch your power or use a gift you don't even have yet. The voice was his—an echo of the thoughts whirling through his mind. *It's not a good idea, Quinn.*

You can feel it right there at your fingertips, man. It's so close and you're just going to sit there and read a book? The temptation was getting harder and harder to resist. His hands trembled and a bead of sweat rolled down his back. *I shouldn't have come here.* He ran a hand over his short-cropped hair, gazing down at Eva by his side. She was lost in her book already. He'd never known anyone who could fall into another world so quickly.

Go on. Touch her. The wayward thought sent him reaching for her hand without a moment's hesitation. It was like watching himself from far away and there was nothing he could do to stop it. His power filled him, urging him on like a siren's call.

Quinn, don't do it. Get a grip, man.

It's not going to hurt to just see what we can do. For once no one is watching and we can do what we want. He was losing it. The thoughts filled his mind like so many voices—like they weren't even his.

Control slipped away. The power raging inside him was intoxicating. He wanted more. Needed more. It wasn't supposed to be like this. Quinn spiraled out of control as he pulled on his power, taking in more than he could possibly understand how to handle, but he didn't care—it felt so incredible, like he'd never known what it felt like to be alive before this moment. He forgot about the book in his hand, about Eva, about everything, and let himself revel in the sensation of touching his power for the first time. He was so powerful, it was frightening. Nothing like Aidan would be, of course, but for just a moment, Quinn had an inkling of what it was like to be Aidan.

"Quinn?"

Eva's strangled voice pulled him back and he realized what he was doing.

"P-panic attack." She sat beside him, her hand in his, with a look of terror on her face. She couldn't breathe. He couldn't let go. His power was feeding off her fear. He'd never tasted anything so sweet.

No.

Yes, this is what we want!

No. Quinn battled against this new, darker side of himself, this monster that wanted Eva's sanity. Craved it like a drug. He would drive her mad if he didn't stop now.

You're not taking this from us! The insanity of his gift hissed in his mind.

With every ounce of willpower he possessed, he dropped her hand, forcing his power back into his core where he held it in a vise grip.

Eva coughed, wiping tears from her eyes. He stared at her in horror, uncertain of what he'd actually done. Her eyes were glazed, pupils dilated. She trembled beside him, but he couldn't risk touching her.

"Eva?"

She took a deep breath and clutched the blanket beneath her. "I-I'm fine. I think." Her voice sounded so meek. She gazed down at her hands in her lap, her shoulders hunched like she was trying to sink into herself.

Quinn stared at her but she was as still as a statue. He

reached for her when she started rocking back and forth, shaking her head. "Eva, please, what's wrong. Talk to me." She hadn't had a panic attack in years.

She snatched her hand away, muttering as she rocked.

"Eva? Talk to me, please?"

"It's always been so mild," she said.

"What are you talking about?"

"The panic attacks. My shyness with strangers. I have ... issues, Quinn. It's never been this bad."

Eva was always shy, keeping to herself and those she was most comfortable with. When they were kids, she'd needed speech therapy, but lots of kids needed that. But he'd never suspected she struggled with mental illness.

"Why didn't you ever tell me?"

She shrugged and rocked, refusing to look him in the eye. She didn't like to make eye contact. But Quinn was beginning to wonder if what he'd presumed as shyness was a sign of a much more serious condition. If that was the case, then what the hell had he just done to her? Had he made it worse? Was that even possible?

"Please leave," she said abruptly in a detached voice that didn't even sound like her.

"Let me help you inside, Eva." He stood and reached for her but she recoiled.

"Don't touch. I don't like people touching me. Please go, Quinn. I don't want you to see me like this. I'm barely holding it together."

Quinn turned from his friend, wondering if they'd ever be friends like they were. He'd done something to her. As he crossed the lawn in a daze, her manic screams echoed behind him. That sound would haunt him forever.

Quinn sat on his front porch with his head in his hands, wondering how he could have been so careless.

It's not our fault—it's just what we are.

"No. This is *not* what I am," he whispered, gripping the porch railing in his fist.

It's our nature. Get used to it.

"I will not be ... a monster who preys on the sanity of others." But that was the only way he could describe what happened with Eva. The lure of using his power had been so strong, he couldn't resist it. But even now, like a true junkie, he couldn't wait for another taste. *I can never let this happen again.*

But we will. It's what we do. It's who we are. You can't deny it or stop it.

"This is not my gift," he whispered into the silent afternoon. *My gift is not going to be this.*

Our gift is strong. We induce madness. You crave it already. We could feel that girl's sanity at our fingertips. We were almost there and you chickened out.

"Stop!" He leapt to his feet, his fists clenched as if to fight the half of himself he was now at war with. "I will never give in to this. I will not be a monster." He caught his reflection in the window and wondered if he wasn't the one losing his mind.

Chapter 5

Quinn: Summer - Atlanta, Georgia

"Did you even know what you'd done?" Livia's mocking tone almost hid the fact that she was impressed with what Quinn had been capable of such a short time after his Awakening.

"Not really." He shifted uncomfortably in his seat back in the white room.

"You are a talented young man." Livia released his hands.

Quinn hung his head in exhaustion. She'd made him relive every moment of the worst mistake of his life. Like he didn't already do that every single day. She made him listen to that voice again. The voice he'd conquered years ago.

"You have so much potential, Quinn. But you mistakenly believe your gifts make you a monster. You have an ability to induce madness. Can you not see how much of an asset that makes you in a place like this? You could go far if you allowed yourself to embrace your power for what it is. Your gifts don't define you. It's what you do with them that makes you who you are."

"That's rich coming from you." He'd heard those same words from his family for years, but from her, it didn't make any sense.

"It's my job to teach you not to fear this gift, but to use it as it was meant to be used. Don't hide it. Don't suppress it. That's weak. And you are not weak, Quinn."

"I will never use that gift against anyone. For any reason. Ever. Do what you will with me, but you will *never* defeat me on this."

"You're focusing on the gift as a weapon because that is how it manifested. Have you never thought about what positive things you might be able to do with it if you fully understood your gift? How you might be able to help those with mental illness?"

"No. It would mean unleashing this gift I've fought to control. I won't do that."

"Your gift could give you a unique understanding of the human psyche, but you have to master it, not suppress it. Suppressing it will keep the gift from developing."

"It will only develop into something worse." Quinn dug his heels in. He didn't want to hope that his gift could become something good. He'd longed for a gift like Aidan's or Sasha's. Something truly remarkable. But he seemed to only manifest gifts that fed his addiction and fueled the darkness inside him.

"Maybe I should just take it from you permanently since you clearly don't want it."

"It is my burden to bear, and I will not see it in the hands of an evil woman with zero moral compass."

"So naive. And so easy to read. Your moral compass is black and white. You haven't lived long enough to see the gray areas yet. But you will." She was back to looking at him like he was a science experiment. Something to deconstruct and reassemble to her liking. "Your tortured mind speaks volumes. I know exactly what to do with you now. You're the heroic type that will withstand anything we do to you. Pain won't work with you. Physical pain, psychological, emotional, you'll withstand it all because you think you deserve it. No, you need a different kind of coaxing."

Livia fixed him with her mesmerizing gaze, like a snake hypnotizing its prey. She clutched his forearms, her nails digging into his skin before he even realized she'd moved. She searched his mind, looking for his other abilities. He could feel her, sifting through his body without his permission. Anything she wanted to know about his power, she could find. She didn't need to torture it out of him.

He felt it the moment she discovered his gift for attracting metals and minerals from the earth. A harmless gift she discarded as useless. She moved on, digging deeper and deeper, looking for the thing he protected at the core of his being. The gift he never wanted her to find.

Quinn had spent every moment since that day with Eva learning how to control the power that fueled his gifts. The madness whispered to him constantly at first, enticing him to let it run rampant. The voice eventually quieted as he gained the upper hand, but it was always there, lurking just below the surface. Half the time he felt like he was losing his mind to the insanity of his own gift. His self-control was all he had.

The battle to control the power was just part of being an Immortal, but for Quinn it was a daily war against his very nature. If his family ever truly realized what kind of monster lay at the root of his power, they would be appalled. He could so easily find his home here at Soma with those like Michael and Ryan. It would take nothing more than letting nature take its course for him to become the person he was destined to be. He'd always known he couldn't resist it indefinitely. The pull was too strong. It was only a matter of time before the addiction won and everyone knew what he was: a weak junkie.

And Livia was about to become his dealer.

"Quinn?" She released him. "How do you do it?" Livia

shook her head. "How do you resist the lure of such a seductive power? You're persuasive. You can make people—Immortals even—do your bidding with just the power of suggestion. If you were a little older, and I didn't have control over you right now, you could just force me to let you go. You'd walk out of here without a backward glance. A free man. Manipulating everyone here to your will. You could be running Soma within a few weeks." Her laughter filled the stark room. "But you resist it? How noble of you."

"Go ahead. Mock me. Those who do not have such power can never understand the burden of it. It is not my right to control anyone. Even you. Just because I may have the ability to do it one day doesn't give me license to rule the world. These kinds of gifts aren't meant to be abused and should only be used when necessary. And only for the briefest of moments." Quinn sat back, clamping his mouth shut. There was no use trying to convince her she was wrong.

"Go on."

"No."

"You worry that you won't be able to live by the rules you were taught. That the gift will rule you." She shook her head, impressed. "There are other rules, Quinn. Especially for those like you. You are worth your weight in diamonds. I'm not sure I even want to let anyone else have you."

"To sell me like a pig at market, you'll have to break me first. And that's never going to happen."

"We will see about that." Livia stood and crossed to the door, gesturing for someone waiting in the hall to join them.

Quinn watched as a young girl stepped inside. Her thin arms crossed over her chest as the only protection she had against whatever Livia was about to do. She was a gangly thing. All arms and legs. As she came to stand at the center of the room, lifting her head in defiance. Quinn's heart filled with dread. This girl had been treated badly and she couldn't be more than thirteen.

"Stand there, Lennox." Livia gestured to a spot right beside her chair.

"What are you doing? Are you insane? She's just a little girl."

With a wry grin, Livia gripped the girl's arm tightly in one hand and dug her nails into his forearm with the other.

Quinn tried to stand as if he actually had the strength to help the girl, but a sharp tug gripped him in the gut and he fell back into his chair. He'd felt it many times before when Livia had used his cloaking gift. The first time was the night she took him from his family, shielding them with his gift as if it were her own. She'd worn him like a cheap suit that night. And now she was pulling on his power to remind him she was in control.

The surge of icy heat in his core surprised him. He hadn't felt this much of his power in a long time. In moments, Livia had driven him to his limit, and he realized what she intended to do. *She* wasn't going to hurt Lennox. She was going to make him do it, using his gift for madness as a weapon.

Livia would shape him into the image of what she thought he should be—if he allowed it. But he could fight her. He had to.

Just do it. It's our nature. The voice echoed in his mind. The voice he hadn't heard in years. He'd worked so hard to choke the life out of that voice. The sound of it reverberating through his head almost brought him to his knees.

You really didn't think you'd conquered us, did you?

Quinn put everything he had into resisting his desire to hurt the girl with his madness. But as Livia used her gift to force his hand, she soon had his power raging inside of him.

She's so tender and young! Let's make her scream! Just a little. Just a taste. And like the addict he was, Quinn found himself rationalizing the situation, taking one step toward giving in, and then another. He didn't have any control here. He was exhausted and at the end of his endurance. Livia would have her way one way or another. He had every reason to just let it happen. He didn't owe the girl anything.

Still, Quinn fought to take back the steps he'd lost. His mantra filled his mind, pushing the voice back into the darkness. *Just one more minute. I can last one more minute.* But he was fooling himself. He didn't have the stamina to battle the force Livia was pressing against him. Quinn watched like a spectator as his free hand wrapped around the girl's arm. The dam burst.

He looked away the moment Lennox screamed. Ashamed of his weakness.

"You will pay attention, Quinn," Livia insisted, forcing him to watch as the girl's eyes glazed at the touch of his sick ability. He felt her fear and her loneliness. Yet with that first taste, it was like the sweetest air. He wanted more. Quinn pushed the girl toward the brink of her sanity, forcing her to relive the worst moments of her life. He could see it in her eyes as she faced the reality of a world where no one wanted her.

"I'm not doing this!" He resisted Livia's influence, but Quinn couldn't seem to release his grip on Lennox. His gift was mesmerized by what he saw in Lennox's eyes.

Yes! Feel it, Quinn. Feel how strong her sanity makes us. Think of what we could accomplish if you stopped fighting us.

Physically, he wanted it. He wanted the feeling to last forever. The rush of blood through his veins. The way her madness caused his senses to awaken. He was flying high, his pain a distant memory. The ecstasy the girl's sanity gave him was like nothing he'd ever experienced. But logically, he knew he would never forgive himself if he didn't fight this. *I am not choosing to do this. This is her. Not me.*

Lennox screamed and the voice inside Quinn's head rejoiced, relishing her fear and anxiety. The more she screamed, the stronger he felt.

Quinn was more like himself than he'd been since the night Livia took him. *See? We make you strong. You need us. It's not our fault she chose an innocent.* For a brief moment, he found himself agreeing with the voice. That was when he knew he had to end it immediately.

"Stop!" He slammed his fist into the table, the pain instantly pulling him from the ecstasy of Lennox's insanity. He released his grip on the girl and she crumpled to the floor.

"Give in to me," Livia panted. She held her grip on him, still pushing him. "Give in to me and she goes back to her room now and this all ends."

"No." Quinn hung his head in shame, letting out a growl of frustration. He couldn't even look at Lennox. The tension in his body tugged at all of his injuries, splitting his back open again. His fists dripped blood onto the table and his peripheral vision went dark as the strength he'd gained from Lennox left him.

"Let's see what we can make her do then, shall we? I'm most interested in seeing more of what that twisted mind is capable of."

With an anguished roar, he leapt to his feet, breaking Livia's hold on him. He was closer than ever to submitting ... just to put a stop to Lennox's suffering. But it wasn't that easy. It went against everything he'd ever been taught. In a situation like this, Quinn was taught to fight. Period. Giving up was not an option. But in that moment, he would have done anything to end the girl's pain. It was the tiny voice in his mind that gave him the strength to continue—and it wasn't the voice of his insane gift.

Don't stop. I can handle it. We can't let her win.

He caught the young girl's gaze. There was no way she was old enough to have experienced an Awakening. But clearly, she was telepathic ... and clearly, Livia had no idea.

We defy her when we can and we suck it up and take it when we can't. She's not the monster she wants you to think she is. You'll win this battle. Just hang on a minute longer and she'll be the one to give in Let's call her bluff. Lennox looked so sweet and innocent but there was a fiery defiance there too. A backbone of steel. She didn't want to see him fail. Not for her.

"Sit down, Quinn," Livia snarled. "We are not done yet."

Chapter 6

Sasha: Summer - Agra, India

"Come. Now. We don't have much time." Imogen grabbed Sasha's hand and pulled her back through the house and up to her room.

"This isn't really happening." Sasha couldn't mask the tremor in her voice. She was scared out of her mind despite all her bravado back in the office. "They can't just swoop in here and take me like this! The Senate can require the assistance of any registered *Proven* Immortal. But I'm not Proven. I'm not even close to mastering my power yet."

"But you're powerful and they want you under their control while they can still get their hands on you. This isn't just about providing you the training they think you should have for your benefit. It's about keeping you under their thumb. Grooming you to be their creature. I imagine there aren't many who have the kind of ability you do and they're not going to let that slip through their hands. They don't care how this will affect you. They don't care that they've asked something of you that would make most Proven Immortals pause and question the validity of their request. They don't care. This is simply a means to test out the merchandise for the future." Imogen whirled around to face Sasha. "You're going to have to suck at this." She turned down a long hallway leading to their rooms, practically dragging Sasha behind her.

"I'm seventeen! Of course I'm going to suck at this. But how am I going to get through it, Gen?" The enormity of the last hour was sinking in. Sasha didn't have it in her to become an assassin. Yes, her gift was perfect for it, but she wasn't. And judging by her sister's reaction, the training would be brutal.

"We'll get through it together, Sasha. I will not leave you to do this on your own." Imogen shoved her through her bedroom door and closed it behind them. "Strip down to your under-things. We have work to do and not a lot of time to do it."

"What? I thought we were supposed to be packing," Sasha stammered as she watched her sister shed her sari and head coverings.

"We'll throw some clothes in a bag after we're done here. We'll have most of what we need when we get there. We have to arm ourselves now. Aide will be here in a minute so we need to hurry. Turn around."

Sasha did as she said, hurrying to finish before her uncle arrived.

"I've never had need to tell you of all my gifts, little sister. Only our mother, my husband and a few others know of the gift I'm about to use."

"What is it?" Sasha watched over her shoulder as Imogen reached for her power, her eyes simmering with rage and heat.

"It's an extension of my shielding gift. I'm going to protect you, but this is going to be uncomfortable. I'm sorry for the pain, but you cannot scream."

As Imogen laid her hands on Sasha's bare shoulders, fire lanced through her body, covering every inch of her skin. She gasped but managed to keep her voice in check. Her skin bubbled and shifted. It was agony like she'd never felt before.

Imogen's fire traced patterns across her skin, mimicking the Vedic designs of her sister's henna tattoos.

When Imogen released her, the liquid fire reverberated, causing Gen's body to glow red like her eyes until the smoldering heat faded and the same lines traced her arms and legs, settling into small patches of lace-like patterns.

Both women panted with the effort not to scream.

"What was that?" Sasha gazed down at the strange markings across her body. The henna tattoos her sister always wore were obviously not henna, but a physical mark of her power.

"A weave of protection only I can give you. When you are in danger, the patterns will move to shield you from any debilitating blow. We have no idea what we're walking into, Sasha. We cannot assume that they will keep their word and bring you home in six weeks. We have to be prepared to fight if it comes to that. And in the heat of the moment, if you're gravely injured, as young as you are, it could be the difference between failure and success. Escape or capture. The patterns will also warn you of the unexpected. If you feel them growing hot, be vigilant. There is no trace of my power in the designs and no one has ever suspected they are anything more than a henna obsession."

Sasha nodded, grateful for the added protection.

"Get dressed and make sure you cover every inch of those markings. Aide will be here shortly and we need to be ready."

Sasha retreated to her closet, pulling on a long blue skirt and tunic, carefully draping a blue and gold sari to hide the still-glowing marks from her sister's powerful gift.

Sasha wasn't naive enough to think she'd been given the whole story. But her family didn't trust the Senate. That was painfully clear now.

"You girls ready?" Aide asked with a soft knock on the door.

"Come in," Sasha said in a shaky voice, opening the door for her uncle.

"Is it done?" he asked as he stepped into the room.

Imogen nodded. "I've done all I can given the short time we have."

Of course, Aide would know what Imogen could do. His gift showed him exactly what an Immortal intended to do when wielding their power.

"Let's get you both armed, then." Sasha's uncle dumped a bag of weapons across the bed and Imogen went to work, using her signature gift to conceal them from the eyes of her enemies. And in this situation, the enemy was the Senate ... and the mentor they'd hired to train her.

Aide helped Sasha strap her concealed weapons across her back. The slim sword was a comfort. Just knowing it was there made her feel better about her situation now that she had the means to fight, whatever circumstances she might find herself in.

"What happens if they pat us down?" Sasha asked.

"They won't feel anything," Imogen said as she worked to arm herself. "When I shield something, I'm not just making it invisible, I'm also sending it to the ... to a special place, and only those with my permission can retrieve it. No time to explain now. Just know you'll never have to worry about getting caught with anything I've concealed."

"You'll be able to store your arsenal in your quarters when you get where you're going, but I want you to keep them on you until you arrive," Aide said as he strapped a thin-bladed knife to her upper arm, leaving the hilt accessible. She could slip her hand under her sari and up her sleeve to retrieve the knife in an instant.

"Don't go anywhere without ample protection. Just in case," Imogen added.

"We don't want to rock the boat until they show us they can't be trusted," Aide said. "But the instant the plan changes from what we've been told, we want you armed and ready to fight. And I'll be right behind you. I won't show myself unless I absolutely have to. My goal is to tail you and keep an eye on your activities and your movement. You will train in the south of India, but after that, we can't trust that they'll keep their word and bring you home. As soon as you've completed your training and you're on the move again, Liam will be able to track you with his gift. But if they've lied about anything, we'll know and I'll be close enough to react quickly."

Sasha nodded as her uncle holstered a pair of magnetized blades at her waist and looped her bow and quiver over her shoulder.

"You're ready for this, Sasha. They think they know what to expect from you but they don't have a clue how well you've been trained. We've kept your progress carefully guarded, which is probably contributing to their reasons for doing this. They believe we have neglected your training. Play their ignorance to your advantage. Don't let them see how capable you really are. Don't learn too quickly or too slowly. We need them to think that you're just not as talented as they thought."

"Be good, but not good enough. Got it." Sasha's pulse pounded in her ears.

"You take care of yourself out there. And don't forget, I will never be more than a day behind you."

"Thank you, uncle Aide." Sasha hugged him, laying her cheek against his chest, taking her last moments of comfort from her family. She was almost out of time and she still needed to talk to Aidan before she could leave. He had to keep working on the Quinn situation. She could trust him with her research.

"You have twenty minutes left. I suggest you go somewhere quiet and get yourself together. I'll be right behind you both." Aide nodded to Imogen and left them alone in Sasha's bedroom.

"You're packed. I found this under your bed." Imogen handed her the duffel bag she'd packed earlier. "At some point we're going to talk about where you thought you were going. Right now, I'm going to go tell my husband goodbye."

"I'm sorry, Gen." Sasha grabbed her hand. She hadn't thought about what this would mean for her sister.

"I'll come back for you in fifteen minutes and we'll head back to Mom's office. Go do whatever you have to do, and make it quick."

The second she was alone, Sasha got to work, taking down her corkboard wall behind the drape. She gathered the information into a folio and went in search of her brother. Part of her wanted to send it to Graham, but he was so young in so many ways. She didn't want to see him make a desperate move to save his brother. Aidan was a better choice. He loved Quinn as much as a brother could, and he was capable of taking over where she left off.

But can I really burden him with this?

As she headed along the main corridor, Sasha heard the sounds of the vigil. She'd forgotten about it. The rest of the family were oblivious of her situation. They were down in the courtyard, celebrating Quinn's life and drinking to his good health. She heard the unmistakable sound of Liam's song and covered her ears. She didn't have time to deal with the effects of his intoxicating gift. She needed to keep a clear head.

Sasha slipped her earbuds in and turned up the volume of a random playlist. She just needed to see if Aidan was at the vigil. She leaned over the balcony railing, peering down below at the revelry. Hélène and her children were there, along with Sasha's grandparents, Nadira and Sayid, with Seamas and George, Greyson and Naomi. Everyone currently in Agra had come out to hold vigil for the memory of Quinn. But Aidan and Allie weren't present. Which meant they had skipped out and were probably off somewhere flirting. *Or brooding.* They were both good at that.

It was apparent to everyone but Allie that they were mad for each other. Aidan would walk over hot coals for that girl and it freaked Allie out. Sasha wasn't sure how long she would be gone but she wanted to tell them how much they meant to her and how stupid they were for not being together when they had the perfect opportunity to be happy. *You guys don't know how much time you have to be together until it's gone.*

As Sasha headed back through the empty house, she heard Allie's laughter and followed the sound back to her brother's room. Their drunken laughter made her smile. They'd clearly taken advantage of Liam's song.

"Allie, stop. Please, baby, you're killing me," Aidan said, his laughter echoing down the hallway.

"What? Now you're com-com-plaining?" Allie hiccupped.

"You're drunk and this is not how I want this to happen, babe."

Good boy, Aidan.

"I am not drunk," Allie insisted. "Well ... I'm drunk enough to be brave enough to tell you this is what I want."

Ew, I do not need to be listening to this. Sasha tiptoed up to Aidan's door, trying not to listen. She'd wanted to leave her research for Aidan, and to tell them goodbye, but there was no way she was interrupting whatever this was.

"Allie, stop taking your clothes off. Please? Before I forget I have a conscience and stop trying to put them back on you."

All the nope. I definitely don't want to hear this.

"Don't be such a gentleman." Allie groaned. "You're killin' my buzz."

"This is going to happen for us, Allie. But it's going to happen when you're sober and honest with me about the thoughts you're hiding."

"I love you, Aidan." Allie suddenly sounded remarkably sober. "But there are things I'm not ready to talk about yet."

"You know I'm never going to let you forget you said that, right?" Aidan's voice softened. "But we will not be having a mortifying morning after of regret when you realize you threw yourself at me in front of everyone downstairs."

"Ugh." Allie snorted. "It's not like they don't know we're into each other."

"Did you forget you have a boyfriend back home?" Aidan asked.

"Um ... no," Allie said. "And I did *not* forget that he is coming for a visit soon."

"This is not how this is happening, Alexis Ann." He sounded sad.

God, he really does love her. Sasha looked down at the folio in her arms, trying to decide what her brother would do with it. *He'd walk right into Sterling Tower and sacrifice himself, the same as me.* Aidan wouldn't even think twice about it and Quinn would kill her for giving him the means to do it. Aidan was too powerful and too important to risk.

And Quinn would be the first to tell all of them to give up on him and go live their lives. She couldn't do that. She could never forgive herself for the things she'd done to cause this, but it was up to her to make the sacrifice. Quinn wouldn't want his best friends to hit pause on their own lives for the off-chance they might be able to help him when their parents couldn't even seem to do anything.

Sasha took a sheet of paper out of the folio and wrote her goodbyes to them both.

No time to explain. I won't be gone long. I love you both. Be happy.

Love Sasha.

She slipped the note under the door and darted down the hall to her bedroom. She quickly ditched her portfolio and notes in the back of her closet. *I'll be home soon enough.* Sasha would do this thing and get it done quickly, and then she would go to Atlanta and get Quinn out of Sterling Tower, one way or another.

"Remember, you have to convince them you are good, but not good enough," Imogen said as they headed back to Naeemah's office.

"Right, I need them to realize Mom and Dad have trained me well, but I'm just not as talented as they expected. I'll be intentionally mediocre at everything they're going to teach me and hope they decide I'm not worth the trouble and the effort."

"Mother Raghavan will see right through it, but Jayesh is the one we need to fool. It will save us from even more scrutiny from the Senate later. If they get an inkling of how talented you really are... Well, we don't want them to see you as an asset. You know how they use me. I don't want that for you."

Sasha nodded. Imogen was a high-ranking "freelancer" with the Senate. She didn't serve in an official capacity, but she was at their constant beck and call. Her shielding gift made her an important tool the Senate used freely and often. They sent her all over the world to conceal any trace of the Immortal world from prying eyes. Sasha suspected they had her do much more than just that.

If these people realized what Sasha could really do, her future would look much like her sister's. Not that Imogen had a bad life, but she could see the loss of her freedom taking a toll on her sister. They paid her well for her services to the Senate, but she was never given a choice.

Sasha stepped back into their mother's office, keeping her head held high. She could do this. In fact, the training might even help her in her plans to free Quinn. She would embrace the experience, learn what she could and get the hell out of there.

"All set to go, darling?" Naeemah smiled. It was her fake smile and her fake voice. Sasha realized she wasn't going to get a private goodbye with her parents. She swallowed her fear and nodded.

"I'm ready."

"Jayesh. Keep my daughters safe," Naeemah said. "You owe me."

Sasha glanced between her mother and the man in charge, wondering again what history lay between them.

"You have my word." Jayesh gave Naeemah a formal bow.

"It's been a long time, Jay. But I know the man you are deep down inside. Don't disappoint me."

Jayesh nodded and gestured for Sasha to say her goodbyes. "We must be going now. Make it quick. I have little patience for women's sentiments."

"Women's sentiments?" Sasha snorted. *What a douche.*

Naeemah eyed her as if to say that was the type of behavior Sasha did not need to engage in. Not with this man. She needed to keep her guard up and her tongue silent.

“I love you, Mom.” Sasha whispered as she hugged her mother. “I’ll be okay, Da.” She turned to Gregg, letting the childish Scottish sentiment slip out. “I know you’re probably ready to bring the building down around your ears, but I can do this.”

“I know you can, sweetheart. You just shouldn’t have to.”

“Be careful. Both of you.” Naeemah hugged her eldest daughter and watched them leave.

Sasha knew this was killing her parents so she put on a brave face and followed her sister from the room. It was time to get her head in the game if she was going to make it through this.

Chapter 7

Quinn: Summer - Atlanta, Georgia

"Get out of my sight. I don't want to see you again for the rest of the night." Livia's eyes smoldered with silvery-green fire as she shoved her chair back and retreated to the gym down the hall.

How could I do that to a kid? He watched in devastated horror as Santi gathered Lennox in her arms from where she lay sprawled on the floor. Foam oozed from her mouth and her breath was slow and labored.

I'm okay.

He didn't know how she was speaking to him like that at such a young age, but she'd assured him over and over that she could handle it. For the last hour, Livia had pushed him into using his persuasive gift to torment Lennox.

I'm a monster. He lay on the floor with his face buried in his hands, too ashamed to even look at Santi.

"*Muévete*, Quinn. We have to go."

Quinn managed to get to his feet and followed Santi down the hall. Her aura flickered with a golden light. Dim, but unmistakably there. She was using what little bit of her power she could to help Lennox, murmuring words of comfort.

"You'll be fine, kiddo. You're tough as nails."

The sound of Livia beating the hell out of a punching bag in the gym echoed across the silent penthouse. Quinn was just glad her fury was focused somewhere else for the moment. He didn't understand her reaction at all. He'd given her exactly what she wanted and now she was furious with him for what he'd done to Lennox.

I'm okay. Lennox's little voice was so weak and distant, but the kid was strong. She'd withstood more than a lot of people could. It spoke volumes about what she'd probably been through in her time at Soma. He wanted to go to her, to protect her, but he'd done this to her.

I'm okay.

No you aren't. But she couldn't seem to hear him.

Quinn dragged himself into the living room, every muscle screaming in protest. The fire in his core had finally grown cold as ice, leaving him weak and dizzy. He wanted to die. He would rather die a thousand deaths than to ever see a child hurt the way Lennox was—at his hand.

Not your fault.

"Will she be okay?" Quinn asked, his words crunching like gravel in his throat.

"She'll be fine. Len's tougher than she looks." Santi gestured for him to open the door, where Ryan waited in the vestibule to take Lennox off her hands.

Quinn hung his head. He'd fallen into a spiral of self-loathing and guilt like he'd never experienced before. He was still reeling from the sensation of so much time lost. Five years of memories that had never actually happened. Five years of hell he'd fought to survive, and it was all a joke.

"Come with me," Santi said as she closed the door behind Ryan. "Livia's furious, so we're going to lay low tonight. She'll be in the gym for hours before she retreats to her study for the night."

"Why is she so angry? I ... I gave her what she wanted."

"No you didn't. She wanted you to refuse to hurt Lennox. And she was going to demand your total submission and loyalty in exchange. I don't think she realized it was going to go that far. That you would call her bluff like that. She's mad at herself. Not you. Look at me, Quinn," Santi said softly.

He had trouble lifting his gaze to meet hers. He was so ashamed. He hadn't called Livia's bluff. He'd done what he wanted. Even now his gift hungered for more.

"Look at me." She lifted his chin with her fingertips. "That was not your fault."

He shook his head, the movement making him dizzy.

"Come on, big guy, I got you." Her slender arm wrapped around his waist, guiding him across the cool marble tile. "You've had enough for one day. It's time you rest."

Every inch of Livia's home was cold and hard, but not Santi. How had she managed to survive this place all these years?

"Not years," he mumbled.

"You'll struggle with that for a long time, but it will get better as more time passes. Let's get you cleaned up. You're a mess and you stink." She wrinkled her nose at him and he winced. When was the last time he had a shower? Weeks? Had it been a month?

"Hey," she said. "Remember what I told you before? It's not been as long as it feels."

"Right. What year is it again?"

"You haven't lost that much time, Quinn." She guided him into the enormous bathroom and helped him down to a plush covered bench at the center of the room, opposite the biggest tub he'd ever seen.

"You remember the night we met? When you first arrived at Soma?" She turned the tub faucets on and poured something medicinal into the water.

He nodded. It seemed like a lifetime since that night. He stared blankly at his surroundings, taking in the white-tiled bathroom—the sound of the water rushing into the tub. The warmth of the steam rising. Everything was so white it reminded him of that awful white room. He'd spent so much time there before.

"What is it with all the white in this place?"

"Look at me, Quinnton." She gripped his chin, forcing him to look into her green-amber eyes. "That was less than three months ago. Today. What happened with Lennox, that was just a few hours. You have to get past the time screw. They aren't going to wait for you to catch up."

"Three months. We talked today." Quinn nodded. He didn't trust anything about this place or his memories of it. But he trusted Santi. She was his lifeline right now.

"Michael's gift is psychological. He can trap you in the most frightening, awful places and make you think you've been there for weeks when it's only been hours. That's the way they get most of their captives to sign over their lives to Soma. When you come out of it and realize time has not passed the way it seems—that it's only just begun—it does something to most. Livia was so angry when you made it through without even cracking. That's why she did this to Lennox. She was punishing you for making her have to work for it."

"I did that to Lennox," Quinn said softly.

"No, you didn't. You cannot think like that or she will win. Look at me," she commanded. "Would you ever make a conscious choice to do that to a child?"

"No."

"Then it wasn't your fault. She forced your hand. Now stand up if you can manage it."

Quinn grabbed the edge of the bench, willing his legs to work.

"I've got you." Santi's voice was so calm and sure. And her hands against his tortured body were nothing but gentle. Kindness. He'd almost forgotten what that felt like. With his arm around her shoulders, he managed to get to his feet where he swayed, dizzy and disoriented.

"Don't lose your balance. If we go down, I'll never get you back up," she groaned under his dead weight.

"Sorry."

"Hold onto the wall if you need to." She reached for the hem of his tattered shirt and lifted it up over his shoulders. She couldn't quite get it over his head, even on her tiptoes.

"I got it." Quinn flung the remnants of his smelly shirt to the floor, but he flinched when Santi reached for the waistband of his jeans.

"Don't tell me you're shy?" The hint of her teasing tone made him smile. He hadn't smiled in ages.

"I don't know you." He shrugged. "And I'm not at my best at this particular moment."

"You don't have to impress me," she said. "If I thought you could get out of those awful clothes and into the bath by yourself without drowning, I'd leave you to it. But the second I turn away you're going down, you know that, right?"

"Probably, but I can handle my pants by myself, sweetheart. Turn around."

"Seriously?" Santi laughed as she turned away.

Quinn struggled with the zipper, but he finally shed his jeans and turned toward the welcoming bath.

"Hold on to me. I won't look." She offered him her shoulder to keep him steady as he climbed into the scalding hot water.

"You trying to boil me?" He winced at the sting of the water.

"Yes. You and I have to share the floor by Liv's bed and you reek."

"That's right. I remember that first night on her floor. She likes to keep us close and under the thumb of her power." Quinn eased himself into the steaming hot tub. The water turned milky-white with bubbles as the jets kicked on.

"Smells fruity."

"I put bubble bath and every kind of essential oil I could find in there. Lavender and eucalyptus to help you relax and ease your muscle aches. Lemongrass to cleanse your wounds, and the sweet orange oil is just to make you smell like a person again."

"Thank you." Quinn sat back against the edge of the tub, his back like a live wire in the hot water.

"I didn't see anything important, by the way. In case you were wondering." She winked as she knelt by the tub. The delicate chain of her tether was just long enough to reach him. He didn't like the glaring reminder of her captivity, but she seemed used to it.

She plunged a sponge into the water. "Lean forward."

He did, and she squeezed the sponge, letting the water cascade over his shoulders. Blood and dirt rolled off him, staining the water brown. He cringed. By the time this bath was over, his ego would be as bruised as his body.

"*Cálmate*. I've been right here. Many times. There is nothing to be embarrassed about."

With his hands clenching the side of the tub, dried blood and dirt ran down into the water.

"Put your hands in the water. It's going to hurt like hell, but you have to get them clean. Best just to get it over with."

He slipped his mangled hands beneath the water, hissing at

the sting. He clenched his eyes shut, trying to keep the tears back.

"May I touch you with my gift?" she asked as she continued washing his back and shoulders. "What little bit I can manage. It will give you comfort."

Quinn nodded. He recognized the flicker of her aura and her hands grew warm against his back.

"Just breathe. Relax, and give yourself a break, Quinn." Her gentle hands wandered across his shoulders and neck, filling him with a sense of calm. A moment of blissful peace and serenity washed over him, soothing his tortured mind. And then it was gone. But it was enough.

"Thank you." He rested back against the tub. "That was amazing."

"Not even a fraction of what I can really do."

"What did you do, just now?"

"I touched your soul." Her hands swirled in the water, lifting his hand to clean the wounds there. "It can be very invasive. I can tell a lot about a person once I've touched them with my gift. The touch is pleasurable, but I can use it to give pain too. I don't like doing that. I much prefer giving others a little moment of peace when they need it most."

"So you know more about me now?" Quinn frowned. He didn't like the thought of her seeing more about him than he wanted her to know.

"A little. But I would never go looking for information without your permission. Not that I can see much in my current state," she said bitterly.

"Tell me what you saw of me."

"You are a broody young man." She smiled. "Very hard on yourself. And you care so deeply for those you love. And ... you are an addict," she added softly.

"So you know I did exactly what I wanted to do when I hurt Lennox?" He pulled his hand away.

"No. I didn't see that. I saw a man with a difficult gift doing the best he can to control it. I saw bravery in the face of hell."

"And I saw nothing but weakness," Quinn said.

"I was there, you know?" she whispered as she dabbed the sponge over his chest. "These last months, I've been forced to watch you fight for your life like a useless voyeur. It's been part of my daily 'training,' and the only time I get to leave this house. I feel like I've been through it all with you."

His jaw clenched at the knowledge that she'd probably seen him cry for his mother.

"They are weak bastards who prey on the strong. We can't let them get to us or they'll make us into what they are. I refuse to let that happen. This is your new normal, Quinn. I'll give you tonight to get your shit together, but that's all the time you're going to get." She eased him back against the tub and moved to wash his blistered feet, her silky waves falling over her shoulder.

She looked like an angel. So serene and humble.

Quinn's eyes filled with unshed tears of anger and frustration. *I'm a total mess, falling apart right in front of her eyes.* But Santi had been on her own the whole time. She didn't have anyone to give her a pep talk. She just survived. Day to day.

"No. No more crying for your momma," Santi teased.

"You haven't met my mother." He smiled. "If I cried for her, it was because I knew she would burn this place to the ground and no one would escape."

"Sounds like my mom." Santi stood and held her hand out for him, turning her head away to give him privacy.

Quinn stood, letting the water roll off him, grabbing her hand for support. He stepped from the tub and took the towel she offered. “What about … Lennox?” He draped the towel around his waist and eased himself down onto the bench.

“Lennox will be fine.” Santi sifted through the linen closet, returning with first-aid supplies and a suture kit.

“She’s just a kid.”

“Can’t dwell on it or it will kill you. Len is special. She’s lived here most of her life.”

“She’s telepathic?”

“She talked to you?” Santi whirled around in surprise. “She must really like you.”

“She assured me that she was okay and it wasn’t my fault. It was like a knife in the gut every time she spoke to me. She couldn’t seem to hear me, though.”

“Lennox can only get a sense of what you’re thinking, but she only talks to the people she trusts.”

“She’s so young. She can’t be sixteen.”

“She’s thirteen.”

“Early Awakening?”

Santi nodded sadly as she stepped behind him, placing the suture kit on the bench. “Just recently. I was there. I helped her through it as best as I could, but it was awful.” She dabbed a numbing ointment over the deep cuts on his back. “They don’t know yet.”

“Livia? Hasn’t she realized?” Quinn didn’t think anything could get past Livia’s notice.

“No. Len was always going to be a powerful girl, but after her Awakening, when she should have been obviously stronger, the sensation of her power was about the same as before. I don’t know if she’ll ever be as powerful as she was supposed to be. We’re trying to shield her as long as we can. If they find out, she’ll go to market immediately and then she’ll never get the training she needs.”

“Who is ‘we?’” Quinn asked.

"Me and a few others who care," Santi said as she threaded a curved needle.

"She can recover. I've seen it." Quinn thought of Aidan's brother, Seamas and how little his early Awakening affected him now. It took him a few generations to get there, but it was possible to recover from the limitations an early Awakening could cause. Len needed the kind of training someone like Seamas could give her.

Quinn watched her reflection in the mirror as she moved around the bathroom. "You've grown more aware since the last time we met." She was more confident than he remembered. No longer the naive girl who'd volunteered to come to Soma, not knowing what awaited her inside.

"You opened my eyes to what was happening under my nose." She shrugged. "It's been a long three months since they took you away."

The pinch of the needle through skin didn't hurt, but the tug of the thread turned his stomach.

"I hate stitches," he murmured.

"What, you squeamish?" She laughed.

"Sewing me up like a pillow, it's just gross." He shuddered.

"Better get used to it, tough guy, You've got some deep cuts. They're not healing because of Livia's influence and you're still pretty young, too. Some of these are going to take a while."

"I'm twenty-thr—no. Wait. I guess I'm not. What month is it?"

"July."

"I guess I'm still just nineteen, then. Jeez, that seems so young." He winced at the sharp tug of her thread.

"Sorry. Almost done with the worst one. After all the time I've spent with Michael, I feel like I'm at least thirty, but I'm not much older than you."

They fell into a comfortable silence as she finished

stitching him up. Santi's gentle hands drifted over the dark bruise along his shoulder, rubbing a pungent ointment over the tender area.

"Frankincense, lavender and tea tree oil will help with soreness," she said. "The bruise will fade in a few days, but it should feel better by morning. Now let's see your hands." She sat beside him on the bench as she examined the damage to his wrists. "I don't think I can stitch this." She prodded the loose skin with a pair of surgical tweezers, pulling it back where it belonged. "I'm going to bandage this tightly and we'll see how it looks in a day or two."

Quinn yawned. He was so tired, he could feel it in his bones. He winced when Santi pulled his skin flat against his wrists and sprayed the area with antiseptic before she bound them with surgical tape and gauze.

His grumbling stomach broke the silence. His last decent meal was a distant memory.

"You're going to need your strength for what's next, Quinn." She met his gaze. "They won't stop until you're completely broken and you just don't care anymore. Don't let them win."

"They couldn't break me with pain, so what's next?"

"A nice break." She grimaced. "But don't let it fool you. They'll treat you like a human being just long enough to make you think it's all over, and then they'll turn on you."

"Build me up just to watch me fall again?" Quinn sighed. It would be better if they didn't bother.

"Come on, let's finish up here so we can get you fed before she's done in the gym. She doesn't like us underfoot. When she's home, it's best to just stay out of her way unless she needs something. If she gets annoyed, she'll lock you in the white room."

Santi covered his burned feet in ointment and wrapped

them in gauze. "Can you get dressed on your own now?" She handed him a set of folded sweats from the linen closet.

"I can manage." Quinn moaned as he stood.

"Just come out to the kitchen when you're ready." She left him to finish on his own.

Quinn felt a thousand years old as he struggled to put on a shirt and then hobbled down the hall, clutching the wall for support.

When he reached the kitchen, he collapsed on the nearest barstool. He needed food and sleep—and lots of it—to get his strength back. Then he could focus on getting his head on straight.

Santi moved around the kitchen like it was her own, the scrape of the silver chain around her ankle a reminder of her place in this household.

"What's with the chain? You try to escape?"

"No. I could break it without even trying. It's just meant to humiliate me and remind me that despite my stellar education and my lofty ambitions, I am nothing."

She served him a plate of lean chicken and steamed vegetables. No salt or butter, but it was the most delicious thing he could ever remember eating. It wasn't until he popped the last piece of broccoli into his mouth that he realized she hadn't eaten anything.

"You gave me your dinner didn't you?" His cheeks warmed in embarrassment. *Idiot.* She was obviously starving as well as sleep-deprived.

"You needed it more than I do."

"The kitchen must be stocked full. Why can't you help yourself?"

"She'll know. It's not worth it. Missing a meal won't kill me. I'll just sneak an extra protein drink before bed. She doesn't count those."

"Santi ... why are you doing this? Helping me? A place like this ... you have to look out for yourself first." He grabbed her hand and gave it a gentle squeeze.

"I need someone I can trust. I've been here for so long." Her voice shook. "Some days I feel like I'm going to lose this battle," she whispered. "When you were here last. Before they took you away. I drew so much strength from having you here. I want to repay that kindness."

"You need a friend, you've got one." He gave her a smile. "We're allies in this."

"Friends." She turned to the sink to wash the dishes.

Quinn limped to Santi's side, taking the dish from her. "You wash, I dry." He smiled down at her.

"She won't sleep tonight so she'll be in her study till dawn. We need to take advantage of the time and get some sleep while we can. She'll wake you in the middle of the night to reestablish her hold on your power. She'll do that frequently."

"How long does she have to be away before your power comes back?" Quinn returned the last plate to the cabinet and tossed the towel on the counter.

"The longest she ever left me was twelve hours." Santi grabbed a protein drink from the fridge, absently shaking it before she downed it. "I can start to feel my power around the ten- hour mark but I can never seem to grasp control away from her. I think the window is more like eighteen hours, but it might be different for everyone."

She tossed the empty bottle in the trashcan and led him to the bedroom. "You'll get used to the floor," she said as she made him a place to sleep at the foot of Livia's bed.

Quinn was too tired to care. The blankets were soft and the pillow was comfortable. They stretched out beside each other in the darkness. As his eyes grew heavy, Quinn reached for Santi's hand, grateful that he wasn't alone anymore.

CHAPTER 8

Sasha: Summer - Agra, India

As the private jet took off, Sasha still didn't know where they were going—only south to Tamil Nadu. It made her nervous, but she forced a bored expression on her face, tapping her foot irritably against the pale gray leather seat. The jet was definitely impressive, with a long, sleek sofa on one side and four luxurious reclining seats on the other. She'd caught a glimpse of a conference room in the back when she stowed her bow and arrow in the overhead compartment with her carry-on. That was after Jayesh's team searched them from head to toe. Imogen's concealment gift was way more impressive than Sasha had ever realized. It was fascinating to watch the guard's hands slide right through the weapons at her hip like they were made of vapor. It gave her comfort knowing she was prepared for anything—at least physically. Mentally, she wasn't prepared at all for what lay ahead of her.

Sasha watched Jayesh sitting opposite her now, poring over a stack of documents and speaking softly to the two soldiers sitting with him. The huge African men had joined them at the airport. They were both heavily scarred Immortals and spoke a dialect of French she had difficulty following. It was similar to

Haitian French and called to her roots. She wondered if the two men were from Haiti. *Or perhaps Africa?* African French would explain her struggle to follow their conversation.

Sasha's eyes widened in alarm as she realized what that could mean. Jayesh led a "special forces" team that they wanted her to become a part of in the future. He was overseeing her training to become an assassin. Sloane said he was "the best at what he did." *He's some kind of world-class assassin.* And his team was probably active on the African continent. Her family feared that Sasha would not be returned to them as promised when this was over.

Oh my God, are they going to take me to Africa? Her mind whirled with thoughts of warlords, jungles, drug smuggling and blood diamonds.

Sasha leaned over and whispered her suspicions to her sister.

"You could be right," Gen said. If it was possible, she looked even more uptight than when they'd boarded the plane.

Sasha watched Jayesh now. The moment they parted ways with Lieutenant Governor Sloane at the airport, his tune had changed. Apparently, he'd been on his best behavior for her parents. Now he was a smug son of a bitch, barking orders and ignoring Sasha and Imogen completely. Dressed in faded black fatigues, he was certainly handsome and every inch a soldier, but his attitude ruined any chance of them getting along the minute he opened his mouth.

Sasha concentrated on their hushed conversation, trying to decipher enough of their French to get the gist of what they were discussing. She continued gazing out the window, feigning boredom, catching bits and pieces as they spoke. It was mostly about Jay's low opinion of the "brat" he was forced to babysit. But they seemed to be discussing a contingency plan for after this was all over.

Sasha just wanted this thing done as quickly as possible. She was determined to get back to her plans and if that meant learning the subtle art of killing people, then she would do it. It didn't mean she actually had to implement those skills.

She had an insane desire to prove herself worthy of the task they were giving her. A desire to prove herself to the prick sitting opposite her now. But she didn't want the Senate to come for her again anytime soon. She had to botch this somehow. She had to dance along the razor's edge of good, but not good enough. She had to convince Jayesh that she was too young, too immature and too inexperienced for this.

"Come, let's get this over with," Jayesh said, standing and motioning for Sasha and Imogen to follow him to the conference room at the back of the plane. Sasha followed quietly, unsure of what to expect from his sudden summons.

"Sit," he commanded. His tone was one of a superior officer addressing the lowest of his soldiers.

Sasha took her seat beside Gen in one of the black leather chairs at the obsidian conference table.

Jayesh leaned over her. "We have a few things to get straight," he said. "The Senate wants you here. I do not. They want you trained to become a member of my team. I do not. They want you to be the Senate's representative on my team. I do not." He slipped into the seat opposite her, keeping his gaze level with hers.

"Then we can agree all around." Sasha leaned forward, not dropping her gaze from his. "I don't want to be here either, but it looks as if neither of us has a choice. So I don't know what you expect me to do about it."

"I expect you to do what you're told, complete the training to the best of your ability and stay out of my way. I am not your babysitter. I am not your mentor. I am only here because the Senate would place you on my team and under my protection. I can't stop it, but I can make damned sure you won't be a liability to the rest of my team, if and when you do join us."

"I assure you I will not need babysitting," Sasha said calmly.

"Whatever, angel." His lip curled into a sneer. "Call it whatever you want. I'm not your handler. For either of you." Jay gave Imogen a look of equal disdain.

My sister could fry you on the spot, dude. Don't be an ass. Sasha gave him a withering glare.

"Please," Imogen interjected. "My sister is young. I'll ask that you show her a little respect since she's been asked to do something no one her age should ever have to do. I would suggest that you give her an explanation of what to expect next."

"Fine." Jayesh crossed his arms over his chest. "We will land in a few hours along the southern coast of India. We will travel into the rural countryside to one of the most ancient regions of the country. Your training will begin at dawn the day after we arrive. You will train for six weeks. It will be brutal. Mother Raghavan will oversee everything while we are there. When she deems you have successfully completed your training, we will leave and I will return to my team, who are currently ensuring the peaceful transfer of power in a war-torn African country. I should be there now. But instead I've been conscripted to babysit a pampered tween with an attitude problem."

"I'm not the one acting like a child," Sasha said.

"We are done here, angel. Go back to your seat, I have important work to do while I still have the chance to do it." Jayesh shouted for his soldiers to escort the sisters back to their seats. He rattled off something in his unfamiliar French dialect. Something about "keeping the brat away from him for the rest of the flight."

"You will speak to her with—" Imogen began, her eyes blazing in fury.

"I got this, Gen," Sasha said calmly.

"Need I remind you that I have little patience for questions and prattle?" Jayesh said.

"First. You're a dick," Sasha began, deciding she was going to make his life difficult at every possible interval. "Second. Don't *ever* call me 'angel' again. My name is Sasha and you will use it. You don't know me, so don't judge me. Third. I am Haitian born and my native tongue is French so you should watch what you say when you think you're having a private word with your men. I don't care if you have a low opinion of me and my ability to embark on this training I never asked to do. And fourth. Tell me—and tell me now—*exactly* what this training will entail."

"Ask your sister, angel. She's been through it," Jayesh said, nonplused by her demands. "The Senate seems to think you're capable of hitting the most impossible targets. That's the only thing about you I'm interested in."

Sasha sat back in a huff. She could land any shot as long as she made a connection with the target. She had to see it with her gift. When that happened, she could shoot with her eyes closed and still see the target in her mind. But that didn't always happen, particularly when she was anxious or stressed.

"You won't be joining my team until I have a complete understanding of your gift."

"Why do you care? You've made it perfectly clear that you don't want me on your team."

"I don't want an untested girl on my team. But if your gift is as good as they say, I'll get over that. We're done with questions." Jayesh rose and left them sitting at the table alone.

"He *is* a dick," Imogen muttered.

"What was he like when you knew him before?" Sasha asked.

"He was always a jerk and rather full of himself, but we were friends." Imogen shook her head in confusion. "That man ... he's not the man I remember."

Sasha watched the landscape roll by, her eyes glazing over, lost in the turmoil of her thoughts. This country was so beautifully ancient. She could feel the history in her bones. She might not have been born of her mother's body, but Naeemah's lineage was still rooted in her blood through the bond that made them mother and daughter. This was her mother's country.

Sasha prided herself on her ability to rise to any occasion and bend circumstances to her will, but she was losing her confidence. Lately, each time life threw a curveball at her, she just fell apart.

She sat quietly beside her sister in the back of the large black SUV. They had arrived at a rural airport in Tamil Nadu in the early evening and were traveling to some temple in the middle of nowhere. As they neared the Nigiri hills, a fertile valley rich in vegetation, lying between the Eastern and Western Ghat mountains, Jayesh slowed the vehicle and turned onto a winding path through the foothills.

"We're nearly there," Imogen whispered. She'd been quiet and tense in the hours since they left the airport.

"How long ago did you train here?" Sasha asked.

"Another lifetime." Imogen smiled. "It is not a bad place. There are things about the mother and the Chola Valley temple. Things I cannot tell you until we are there. It will be hard. You will suffer. But you will find good in what the mother can teach you. She is hard, but she is also kind."

"And I have you," Sasha said.

"Exactly. A friend was not a luxury I had the day I entered the temple grounds."

"You made one while you were there," Jayesh said quietly from his perch behind the wheel.

"True enough." Gen nodded, but Sasha wasn't so sure these two counted each other as friends any longer.

"We hike the rest of the way," Jayesh announced, pulling the SUV to the side of the road. His soldiers were still with them and would be returning to nearby Coimbatore to wait for them.

Sasha grabbed her duffel bag, careful to keep her concealed bow secured by the handles. With a deep sigh, she followed Imogen and Jayesh into the rolling hills of the fertile valley. Steps rose along the slope, following a path that led to the higher hills in the distance.

The light grew dim in the twilight evening as Sasha stepped up one crumbling stair after another. Her brow beaded with sweat and her heart hammered in anticipation. After hours of hiking with her somber companions, she couldn't take the silence anymore.

"You know, your tension isn't really giving me the warm fuzzies about where we're going," Sasha said as they crested yet another hilltop. The temple still wasn't visible. But this hilltop was different from all the others lying behind them. As she took a final step up, Sasha entered an ancient, crumbling pavilion.

The structure was weathered and worn, but the mosaic floor was beautiful. Bright blue and green tesserae tiles blended with warm yellows and reds to paint a linear path, like a threshold across the center of the pavilion. The way Jayesh and Imogen stood hesitantly on this side of the mosaic line made Sasha think it really was a threshold. That once they crossed it, there would be no turning back.

"What is the significance of this place?" Sasha asked in a more reverent tone as she joined them.

"The Chola Valley. This place. This experience. It will change you," Jayesh said, his tone soft as his mind drifted to some past memory. With a deep breath, he took a step forward —his eyes closed and a grimace on his face.

"It is time, sister. I am so sorry for this. All of this," Imogen whispered as she took Sasha's hand and stepped across the threshold into the Chola Valley below.

Chapter 9

Quinn: Summer- Atlanta, Georgia

"Wake up," Livia's tone was flat and hollow, rousing both Santi and Quinn out of a dead sleep.

Her power seared along his spine like a white-hot poker. Through all his time at Soma, Quinn had grown accustomed to the experience of Livia exerting her dominance over him again and again. This time, for a single instant, he could almost grasp hold of his gift. But before he could find purchase, the moment was gone and he was cowering on his side, gasping for breath. He slammed his fist against the floor, oblivious of the blood seeping through his bandages.

He watched helplessly as she did the same to Santi.

"Selena was called away so you're working at the Fold today, Santi." Livia turned without another word and retreated to the fortress of her office for the night.

"Is it always like that?" Quinn rolled over to find Santi scrubbing at tears of frustration.

"Sometimes are worse than others. Depending on her mood."

"What does she mean, you're working at the Fold?"

"That's what Sterling Tower's all about," Santi said dryly.

"The Fold is the public face of Soma. A squeaky-clean non-profit organization dedicated to helping Immortal families through tough times and training young and talented Immortals when their parents don't have the means to teach them. It's everything Livia wants the world to see. And it's a big fat lie. Behind it all is Soma and the Coalition. You'll see the Coalition running in and out of the building, working hand in hand with Soma, doing Livia's bidding. She has some kind of agreement with them."

"So what does the Fold do?"

"Lures young kids and their families into Soma so they can cherry-pick from the most talented of our generation. I suspected it when I came here looking for a job but I was desperate. And too naive to realize the Fold is just another resource they use to fuel their slave market. She'll have me spend the day working with the kids on the lower level. Kids like Lennox. They grow up here not knowing they'll end up sold to the highest bidder if they're talented enough. The ones who aren't will end up with the Coalition."

Quinn wasn't sure why he did it, but she'd shown him such kindness when he was at his lowest, and she had a difficult day ahead of her. He wrapped his arms around her, taking solace in her warmth, and they slept like that until Livia sent one of her minions to wake them at an ungodly hour.

"This way to my office."

Quinn reluctantly followed the young Soma agent along a stark white hallway in the early morning light. Dressed in clean clothes but still feeling like a wreck, Quinn grappled with the old memories that had haunted his dreams. Memories of Sasha and their last moments together before he was ripped away from her. All this time and he still wondered what that last kiss meant.

It was only three months, Quinn. Not years.

"In here," the man said, stepping aside and gesturing for Quinn to enter the small training room. "You're my responsibility now. I have to get you back on your feet, fit and strong and healed from the mess Michael put you through. I'm the good guy here, so this will be easy. Take a seat."

Quinn sat on one side of the long white desk near the door. The room was sparse and white, like everything in Soma seemed to be. Silver gym equipment lined the wall, and a wide white mat ran down the center of the room. Training weapons hung on the walls. It vaguely reminded him of his mother's office at home. But her rooms were warm and inviting and they reflected her life and her personality. This cold, clinical room had all the elements for training a young Immortal, without the warmth of home.

"I'm James, by the way." He sat opposite Quinn, offering his hand.

Quinn eyed him warily. He wasn't prepared to trust anyone in this place, but James seemed like a decent enough guy.

"Relax. I couldn't care less about the Soma agenda. I'm here to do a job I was never given any choice but to do. I'm in the same boat as you. I'm just the result of what happens when you agree to their terms and sign on the dotted line. You and Santi are the result of ... resisting the inevitable." James pointed to the Soma brand on his neck. "At the end of the day, we all wear the mark of a slave."

"I won't sell out," Quinn muttered.

"Have you eaten?" James asked.

"No."

"I'll order brunch brought up from the dining hall." He

tapped a message into his phone. "For now, let's have a chat." James crossed his legs, with a notepad in his lap. He looked every bit the psychologist or counselor, although he was quite young. Not much older than Quinn or Santi.

"Oh, God. You're a shrink?" He almost laughed at the absurdity of it. They wanted to fix what they'd damaged.

"Definitely not," James said dryly. "They don't care that much about our mental health. And they definitely never let me go to college. I barely qualified as a high school grad. No, I'm just here to get you back on track, Quinn. This doesn't have to be difficult. And if you listen to nothing else I say, listen to this. Enjoy your reprieve while you can. This part is a cakewalk compared to what you have behind you and in front of you."

Quinn took a deep breath, preparing himself for a sermon about how wonderful Soma was and how good life could be if he'd just drink the Kool-Aid.

"Let's just focus on your immediate future." James sat back in his chair. "You've been through hell your first few months here. You lasted a lot longer than most, which tells me you are incredibly strong of will. Michael's tactics are base and cruel. His tactics are not mine. While you are here with me, you will work out. Regain your strength. You will eat well and you will sleep soundly. We want you to recuperate. You've earned it."

"You want me healthy and happy so you can push me back down when I least expect it?"

"We're only talking about your immediate future. I am not privy to whatever happens to you when you leave me."

Quinn twisted in his seat, looking over his shoulder at the door. He could sense her. The tug of her control was always there, but he knew she was coming and he knew she was furious.

"Yeah. She's mad as hell." James winced, glancing at the door just before Livia barged in, the door rattling on its hinges.

"Livia." James stood to greet her but she swept past him, dropping a pile of photos on the desk in front of Quinn.

"We have a problem." She took James's seat. "Whenever we remove a young Immortal from their home, the families tend to take the hint and walk away when they realize the kids are better off with the kind of training we can provide. Occasionally, a family will attempt to negotiate the release of their loved one, but rarely does a family challenge the Fold the way yours has."

"Are you that deluded or are you just stupid?" Quinn leaned forward, ignoring the way James tried to cover his laughter with a coughing fit. "Do you really think what you did qualifies as 'removing me from my home?' What are you? Immortal Social Services? If you think they're going to let me go that easily, you don't know a thing about family."

"I hate families," Livia sighed. "Yours has been poking around for weeks, but today ... this man had the nerve to pay me a visit." She pulled a surveillance photo from the stack and Quinn's heart skipped at the sight of a familiar face. Liam. He technically wasn't family, but he'd always been like an uncle to Quinn and Graham.

He shrugged as if to say he didn't know the man in the photo.

"He made an appointment with one of my assistants. Apparently he's interested in purchasing a commercial space on the first floor of Sterling Tower. He wants to open a bar, of all things. He pitched it as a means for the Fold to gather useful information on those Immortals who come and go in Atlanta. I met with him briefly. He didn't mention you, of course, but my sources tell me he is connected with the governor's family in your region. He's obviously using this scheme to get close to you. Who is he? I don't like the way he looks at me."

"What do you want me to say, Livia? Maybe he just has a crush on you," Quinn said.

"There have been others. A lieutenant governor of your region has approached Soma—a Greyson Hauser. He claims the governor there is interested in our next auction and would like to start the paperwork to join our exclusive and private organization. Who is the governor to you? Are they your parents? Friends of your parents?"

"I've never met the governor," he lied. He wouldn't sell out Gregg and Naeemah like that. "If they're interested in joining your secret club, it's not because of me. Maybe they want to buy a servant? I hear she's an awful cook. Burns everything." Quinn shook his head, thinking of the way Naeemah always burned the bread. Every. Single. Time. He'd give anything to be home now, not complaining about her cooking ever again.

"Your family is hunting for information and it will lead to nothing good. For you. Or them."

She slid a photo across the table and Quinn's mouth went dry at the sight of Graham. It wasn't just seeing his brother that sent Quinn into a panic. It was seeing where his brother was. The time stamp on the photo was just a few days ago. Graham sat on a bench in a park. Piedmont Park, just below Sterling Tower. Graham was in Atlanta. Quinn did his best to seem disinterested in the photo of his brother sitting on a bench, casually texting on his phone—but Quinn knew better. Graham could hack the Pentagon from his phone and make it do a little dance for his entertainment. Graham was trying to get to him and it crushed something inside of him. *Forget about me, little man, I'm not worth the risk.*

"Your brother?" Livia said. "I can just imagine what he's up to. He has that techie look about him, doesn't he? You know we love our techies around here, right? They fetch such a spectacular price at market. We prefer kids like Graham. Kids who don't have access to the kind of training they need to understand their more modern gifts. He'd be a perfect fit for Soma."

"Lay a hand on him and I will end you." Quinn's eyes blazed in fury. She was right. Graham was a technological genius who had only scratched the surface of what he would one day be capable of. His training was often unproductive and frustrating for him because their parents didn't know enough about his type of gift. But they were making an effort to get him the help he needed. Quinn would die before Livia ever laid a finger on his brother.

How did he manage to slip away from Mom and Dad? And why? If Quinn knew anything about how his family would react after his capture, it would be to get Graham and the other kids out of the country as fast as possible. Graham should be in the Azores with their parents by now. But Graham was sneaky. He could easily ditch the family and hop a plane to Atlanta to check out Soma and return without their ever noticing his absence. Their mom was probably a mess anyway. *And Dad....* Quinn couldn't fathom what his dad must be thinking. All his years in a Coalition prison only to lose his son to something even worse? They couldn't know much about Soma yet, but by the looks of it, they were all busy doing their homework, looking for an opportunity to make a move.

"A kid like that could bring a fortune. And this one? She's beautiful." Livia slid another photo from the pile.

A girl with sun-kissed caramel skin stared back at him and Quinn's heart stopped in his chest. His eyes starved for the sight of her.

"She's not nosing around our front door, but she's asking too many questions and seems quite determined to find you. But we're keeping her busy."

What is Sasha doing in the jungle? It was obvious from the selfie that she was far from home, laying on a mat beside a man teaching her how to use a sniper rifle. The brilliant smile that lit her face told him she was in her element. But there was something wrong. The light in her eyes was different. There was something incredibly sad there. Like she wasn't the girl he remembered. The man beside her had a faded tattoo on his face and the two looked far too friendly for Quinn's comfort. *They look happy.* Jealousy coiled like a snake inside him. Even after that last night together, Quinn and Sasha had no claim on each other. They'd set each other free more than a year ago. He'd done enough to hurt her over the years, but he didn't want to see her anywhere near this man.

What have they pulled her into? The time stamp was from just a few weeks ago.

"Who are all of these people, Quinn?" Livia gestured at the photos piled on the desk.

"I'm not telling you anything, Livia." Quinn heaved a deep sigh of despair. The only thing he could do for Sasha and his brother was to keep his mouth shut. Wherever Sasha was now. Whatever they had her doing, there was no way Greggory McBrien didn't have a tail on her. Livia could threaten all she wanted. He was calling her bluff and praying to God he could count on Gregg to keep Sasha and Graham safe.

"She's your girlfriend, right?" Livia gave a disgusted snort. "She was your date to the little school dance that night, wasn't she?"

"We've hooked up on and off over the years, but she means nothing to me," Quinn said, the lie tasting like ash on his lips. Sasha meant the world to him. He'd gladly stay here if it meant keeping her safe.

"I'm keeping her close for the moment. Just remember that." She fanned out the images of his family in different parts of the world. Liam and Darius meeting with a Soma rep in Chicago. Graham, all on his own just across the park, right here in Atlanta. Sasha in some distant corner of the world. The photos of his mother standing watch on the rooftops just a few buildings away—each one was like a knife in the gut. His father, looking older than he remembered, clearly following Ryan along the streets of some foreign city. Gregg. Naeemah. His grandparents. Everyone he loved was looking for him and he wanted nothing more than for them all to give up and let him go. He wasn't worth the risk.

"I want names, occupations and abilities, right now." Livia placed a pen and a sheet of paper in front of him. "Who they all are and what they do."

"So you can go after them? Not a chance." Quinn folded his arms across his chest and sat back.

"Then your girlfriend will wind up right here with you." Livia tapped the picture of Sasha. "The Senate has taken an interest in her training and have hired my people to do it. When it's done, she's supposed to go home, no damage done. But I'm intrigued by the intel I've received about her. I'd love to bring her in, but if you tell me who these people are, she'll get to go back to her life. Otherwise, you can make room for her between you and Santi."

"You can't cheat, Livia. You can't break me this way and you know it," Quinn said. "I know how it's done and this isn't it. You want to blackmail me by threatening the people who mean the most to me, fine. But we both know I'm never going to submit willingly and you can't take shortcuts to break me. Breaking an Immortal's will requires a hell of a lot more than breaking their heart or scaring them into it. You have to damage me beyond repair. You have to earn it, and this is a cheap shot." Quinn shoved the pile of photos across the table.

This was all a game to her. This whole thing with the photos was just one more ploy to crush him. It might work for some, but he'd spent half his life training for this and he knew not to fall for it.

"You're an intelligent guy, Quinn." Livia sat back with a smile and something that almost resembled respect in her eyes. "You've been trained well. Not many kids your age are even aware that an Immortal can be broken, much less understand how it's done. I walked into a goldmine the night I came for the redhead and came away with you instead."

"Well, you'll have to do better than 'good cop, bad cop.'" He cast a glance toward James, who had stood silently beside Livia throughout their exchange.

"But your brother is a problem." She pulled the photos of Graham from her stack. There were dozens. Graham at the airport, stepping into an Uber cab. Graham at the park. Graham at a coffee shop with his laptop out, talking with another Immortal boy about his age. Whatever he thought he could discover by coming here, it wasn't worth it.

"He's an annoying little punk." Quinn smiled. "But you should know, he's damaged goods. He has a deformed foot and he walks with a limp. Surely your people followed him long enough to notice that. His deformity limits him in a lot of ways." It was a lie. Graham was born with a twisted foot, and he did walk with a limp, but it never slowed him down. If anything, it somehow made him faster. Once that kid started running, few could catch him.

"That's the thing about the techies. They're the new scholars. They don't need to be particularly gifted fighters. Your brother shows up again and he's mine."

"You're daring. I'll give you that," James said as he collected the scattered photos from the table after Livia had gone. "Most wouldn't risk raising her ire like that. Well done."

"You're encouraging me to piss off your boss?" Quinn tried not to look at the photos. He didn't want James to see how much they affected him.

"Livia's not as bad as she seems. She wants you to believe she's evil incarnate, but she has a heart buried in there somewhere. It peeks out from time to time. It's good to see someone stand up to her. And for the record, you were right. This was just a scheme to get you to stumble. It's hard work breaking an Immortal. It'd be a lot easier for her bottom line if she can get you to sign your life away. Like me. But you don't want to be me."

"You sure you want to be telling me that?" Quinn watched the stocky man thumb through the pictures of his family. His life. Everything that had ever mattered to him. "Aren't you on her side?"

"James is on whatever side benefits James." He sat back down. "But make no mistake, Quinn. I'm a Soma slave just like you. This your brother?" he asked.

Quinn nodded.

"He's a cutie. It's reassuring to see a young gay Immortal with such talent. I hear he's pretty impressive. Let's hope he stays far away from Soma ... and Amrita."

"My brother's not...." Quinn paused and took another look at Graham with another boy at a cafe.

"That is most definitely a date," James said.

Quinn smiled. Graham had changed in the months since Quinn's capture. He was leaner, taller and looked like the constant worry wasn't letting him get much sleep. But it was clear there was something Quinn had missed about his little brother. "I'll be damned." He leaned over the photos, trying to see what James saw.

"Missed that, did ya?" James chuckled. "Families usually do."

"How can you tell by looking?"

"You can't see gay, you idiot. I just have a way of seeing things others can't. Your brother has accepted who he is but he doesn't want to come out until you return. He doesn't want to move on without you. Coming out was easy for me. I didn't have a family to worry about."

Quinn ached inside. He wondered how long Graham had known? If he worried about telling their parents. Quinn wanted to be there for his brother. To help him through whatever his future held, but he wasn't sure he'd ever get that chance.

"Dammit." Quinn sighed. "I'm going to miss everything."

His eyes burned and his throat tightened. He missed his brother so much. Quinn hadn't always been the protective big brother he was now. When he was nearly three and Graham first joined their family, Quinn was insanely jealous of the little blond boy who looked more like their French mother than Quinn ever would. It took Quinn a long time to understand that his parents didn't see color when they looked at their two sons—one dark and one fair. They simply saw their children. In time, Quinn reciprocated the brother bond Graham offered so freely, and he too stopped seeing color when he looked at his family.

"Yes, food's here." James stood to greet the delivery person from the dining hall. "This is getting a little too real for me. Why don't we dial it back a bit and just eat? I'm starving." James set the lunch trays on the table.

"There's a cafeteria here?" Quinn looked down at the tray

in front of him. It was very institutional. Like a school. *Or a prison.*

"The dining hall's two floors down, near the big gym. You can go any time you want, unless you're on a particular diet."

"Like a starvation diet?" Quinn dropped his sandwich, thinking of Santi and that god-awful chain around her ankle.

"Yeah, that would do it. You should know you shouldn't try to sneak Santi food. You'll just make it worse."

Quinn nodded, hating the idea of contributing to her suffering.

"So what were you saying about Amrita before?" Quinn asked, looking for a chance to talk about anything else. He'd heard of the underground Immortal club that traveled all over the world. He and Sasha used to talk about going if it ever came close enough to Cleveland for them to slip away for a night of fun.

"Surely you've heard of it?" James said. "Every kid our age is dying for a chance to go to Amrita."

"Yeah, but you just associated Soma with Amrita."

"They are one and the same, Quinn. Think about the meaning of the two words. Both are used in the *Rigveda*. 'Amrita' means 'immorality' in Sanskrit. But in the *Rigveda*, Amrita is a drink that was said to bestow immortality. The drink has also been referred to as Soma in other Hindu texts. Indra, the god of heaven, and Agni, the god of fire, drank Amrita to attain their immortality, after which they said:

"We have drunk Soma and become immortal; we have attained the light, the Gods discovered. Now what may foeman's malice do to harm us? What, O Immortal, mortal man's deception?"

"Clever. It's an obvious connection in a way most of us would overlook," Quinn said.

"My gut tells me Amrita is going to Cleveland in a few

months. You better hope your friends are smart enough to stay away."

"There's no way they'd risk it." Quinn shook his head. "Not after all this. They aren't that stupid." *I swear, Aidan, I will rip your head off so they'll have to feed you through a straw if you're stupid enough to take them to Amrita.*

"The redhead will be there," James said, trying and failing to act casual.

"What? How do you know?"

"I see things." James shrugged, fiddling with his food. "Most of the time it's nonsense. My clairvoyance is mild and not remotely dependable. The Soma powers don't put much stock in what I do. And ... I may make it a point to appear as useless as I can possibly be. But I see important events and people. Your redheaded friend is everywhere I turn. I see her, I dream about her. She smells like apples and soot ... and rage. That girl's anger scares the hell out of me. Whatever's coming for her isn't good. She'll be at Amrita. But that's all I know."

If Allie was going to be there, the others would be too. They had to know it was dangerous. Why would they risk it for a party? Quinn's mind whirled with the possibilities of what they could possibly be thinking. *Graham was just here snooping around—talking with other young Immortals. Does he know Amrita is connected with Soma? Are they going because they think in some twisted way they can help me?*

"You say you only see important events and people?" Quinn asked. There was something James wasn't telling him. Or maybe he really didn't know. If he grew up here... if Soma didn't see his gift as valuable ... maybe they neglected something they should have paid much more attention to.

"I see the big things. Events I rarely understand until after they've happened, so I'm not much use." James shrugged uncomfortably.

"What you see ... do you happen to feel a compulsion to write it down or draw it after?"

"That's a very specific question." James gave him a wary look. "Why would you ask that?"

"I think your gift is much more valuable than you let on, James. And I think you know it. This place. They focus on flashy new gifts that we've never seen before. But an ancient gift ... a gift we haven't seen in centuries, they wouldn't know what to do with it."

"What is it you think I can do?" James frowned. "I've never been very powerful. Not measured against the likes of you or Santi. What I do...." He shrugged. "It's just doodles and nonsensical poetry."

"It's prophecy." Quinn leaned toward him, keeping his voice low. "The last known prophet died centuries ago in Europe when she and her Complement were murdered by the Coalition. Burned at the stake for sorcery and witchcraft."

"How could you possibly have figured that out in the two minutes we've talked when I've spent half my life hiding it?" James paled in the bright fluorescent lights of the training room.

"I've always been an avid student of Immortal history. I've been lucky enough to have access to the kind of history lessons I imagine wouldn't be important here. And I have a particular interest in ancient powers that don't exist anymore. Call it a hobby."

Quinn liked to read about people with useful gifts, but he also like to read about Immortals who struggled with an addiction like his. He was always searching for a precedent. Someone like him who had figured out how to use their gifts for good without succumbing to the addiction. He'd read everything he could get his hands on and never found a single person like him who hadn't turned into an evil son of a bitch.

"Prophets often spoke of seeing only the most important events and people in their visions or dreams," Quinn explained. "And it is the nature of prophecy to only be understood after the events have occurred. Interpreting prophecy is an exercise in futility ... unless you have access to the prophet delivering the prophecy." Quinn leaned back in his seat, convinced he was right about James. "If they ever realize what they have in you, say goodbye to your cushy job."

James swallowed, staring out the window as he considered what Quinn said.

"Whatever you're seeing about my friend, please don't tell anyone," Quinn asked in the silence.

He wasn't sure how Allie qualified as someone important—other than the fact she was one of the two most powerful Immortals of their generation. He had no doubt that Allie and Aidan would be important someday, but right now they were just kids. What could James possibly see about them that would inspire prophecy? Prophecy concerning an underground Immortal nightclub?

"It seems I have a vested interest in keeping that secret now more than ever," James said softly.

Quinn felt bad about exposing James's secret like that. But he was certain he was looking at the first prophet of their generation. Prophets were only born when the world had need of them and they were often abused for their power. James really needed to get as far away from Soma as he possibly could. He needed a proper mentor to teach him and help him prepare for his Proving.

"You've just been teaching yourself? Running on instinct?"

James nodded. "It's my only option. "If they knew...."

"Can I really trust you?" Quinn knew Livia wanted to get her hands on Allie and the rest of his family, but he wasn't sure he could trust James to keep the little information he had about Allie to himself.

"You think I'm the enemy," James said. "But I don't offer information to Soma unless they ask, and when they do, I'm intentionally vague. It's saved me from a worse fate than this cushy job. I'll be at Amrita. I always have to go. Apparently I'm a good recruiter. I'll make sure we don't recruit your friends. They'll be fine."

"Can you give her a message?" Quinn asked. "The redhead." It was a reckless request but he was desperate.

"Depends on the message."

"Tell her they need to forget about me. I don't want any of them looking for me anymore. It's too risky. Tell her ... tell her I'm okay and I'm handling it."

James nodded. "I can respect that. I'll see she gets the message. And don't worry. You can trust me, Quinn."

"Please don't make me regret it," Quinn said.

"You just concentrate on not giving Livia a reason to go after Graham, and I'll handle keeping her away from the redhead. I may not be a hero, ready to die vanquishing the evils of Soma, but I'm also not an asshole."

CHAPTER 10

Sasha: Summer - The Chola Valley Temple

Sasha stared up at the early evening stars as she stepped over the mosaic threshold at her feet. Something about crossing into the valley had both Jayesh and Imogen visibly anxious.

"There is no turning back now," Jay whispered. "We are here for the duration."

"How did ... what is this?" Sasha screwed her eyes up against the blazing afternoon sun. "Oh!" she gasped as the Chola temple appeared in the valley below. The sun shone brightly when only a moment ago it was nearing nightfall.

"Give us a minute, Jay," Gen whispered as she took Sasha's hand. "Welcome to the Chola Valley."

Hidden far from mortal eyes and nestled in a verdant green valley, the temple had a timeless quality about it. Like something from the ancient past, but at the same time, it was in pristine condition. Towering gatehouses stood at the north and south ends of the walled structure, each at least eight stories high and carved with intricate patterns of relief sculpture. The gatehouses at the eastern and western walls were half the size. The gardens within the temple walls bloomed bright, with trees and bushes shielding the inner wall that housed the temple.

Fifteen stories of carved stone stood at the center of the grounds, surrounded by four quadrants of smaller temples and pavilions with cloistered paths connecting the walkways.

"Time is different here, Sasha," Imogen said gently. "There is no rhyme or reason to it. While six weeks will pass at home, for us, it could feel like months or even years here. Mother Raghavan is gifted in many ways. She will teach her students what they need to learn in the time that is needed for them to learn it. The outside world and the river of time is of no concern to her. While we are here, it will be like stepping into the past. The days will blend together and you will lose all sense of time."

"And how long were you here before?" Sasha was almost too afraid to ask.

"I was gone from my home only a few months," Imogen said.

"But it seemed longer?"

"Nearly a decade by my count," Jayesh answered, staring across the valley. "But it could have been longer." He shrugged. "It takes as long as it takes."

Sasha sank to her knees on the steps. *I can't do this.* Even if was only six weeks of her life at home, she wasn't sure she could live through the months and years it could be for her in this place. She was already so anxious to get this business behind her.

"How could you not tell me?" Sasha glared at her sister.

"One must come to the mother in ignorance. Many do not realize how this place works until they leave and return to their own time. It was a necessary deception, sister. Take comfort in knowing your life is on pause until you learn what is needed from the mother."

Sasha's feet felt heavy as she followed her sister. With every step she walked farther away from her goals. "I can leave at any time, though, right?" But she was afraid she wouldn't like the answer to her question.

"We may leave only when the mother believes we have each learned what we came here to learn," Imogen said, her eyes filled with tears. Sasha realized how long Imogen would be away from her husband, Lucien. The separation could feel like an eternity for her.

"Each of us?" Sasha glanced at her sister and the silent man who stood just ahead of them. "I am the one here to learn."

"Oh, she'll have something to teach us all," Jayesh said bitterly. "If it's one thing the mother does well, it's teaching those who don't want to be taught." He hefted his bag up onto his shoulder. "She will not allow our departure until she believes we are ready."

"Gen ... I'm so sorry," Sasha whispered.

"Do not be sorry, sister. I would never let you do this alone. We will learn together, but you must understand, it will take longer if you do not embrace this experience."

"Then we should go meet this mother and get on with it. I have important things to get back to at home." Sasha took a step forward.

Jayesh groaned. "We're going to be here forever."

Sasha gazed up at the stone walls as they approached the northern gate. The silence was deafening and it struck her that this was a place only ghosts haunted.

"We must go to the main temple to request an audience with Mother Raghavan," Imogen explained. "She'll be expecting us."

"She'll make us wait," Jayesh said.

"Are there other people here?" Sasha asked.

"Many are here, seeking wisdom from the mother, although it will seem deserted to us," Jayesh said. "There are ... many layers of this place. We will never cross paths with anyone outside our own time."

Jayesh led them to the temple at the center of the complex.

Sasha's eyes were huge as she tried to take it all in. *It really is like stepping out of time.*

"Come, please. The mother will see you." The voice caught Sasha by surprise; she didn't see or hear the man approach from the garden path behind them. With her sense of hearing as sharp as it was, the sensation of having someone surprise her from behind was a strange one.

"Do not worry. Brother Raj has trained here all his life," Imogen whispered. "He is like a ghost. He travels the shadows on silent feet."

Sasha nodded as they followed the monk along the path to the center of the complex. The temple cast them in shadow as Sasha gazed up. Each level grew smaller as the structure rose to its highest peak. Statues of men and women stood twisted into the most impossible contortions, wielding sharp-bladed weapons and shields. Trumpeting war elephants and pouncing tigers, carved in relief, seemed to leap from the building.

Hundreds of steps rose from the garden path up to the great stone building. Sasha took them slowly, warmth spreading from the roots of her hair, standing on end, all the way to her toes. But it wasn't from the heat of the day. It radiated from the marks left by Imogen's protection. A warning that she was in danger. She shared a nervous glance with her sister. Gen took her hand and gave it a gentle squeeze. "It is just the unnaturalness of this place causing you distress. Nothing to worry about."

Sasha wasn't so sure about that as she stepped into the coolness of the temple vestibule. The shade was refreshing after their long climb up the pathway, but the atmosphere here gave her a creepy vibe.

Brother Raj led them to a small antechamber to wait. "Please rest. The mother will be with you shortly." He bowed as he left them. Silken pillows rested on the cool stone floor, surrounding a table of refreshments. Braziers burned at the entrance, filling the room with a cloying incense.

"It could be a while," Imogen said, taking a seat at the table.

Sasha sat beside her and fidgeted with the fringe on the corner of her pillow.

"Meditating would help speed this along," Jayesh said. "The mother will not join us until we are all in the right frame of mind."

"You are right. As long as we are tense and uneasy—and impatient," Gen added with a nudge to Sasha's side, "we will be here for a long time."

Sasha meditated regularly with her family. It was part of their daily training and she knew she needed it now.

"Fine." Sasha found a comfortable position and began the breathing exercises that would help her find peace within her mind. She had to leave all her baggage at her feet and focus only on her mind and her body, letting the tension and fear fall away.

When she opened her eyes, the sun was setting for the second time that day. She heard the soft shuffle of footsteps along the stone corridor behind her. The immense lifeline of the mother washed over her as she came to greet her guests. *She might be the oldest Immortal I've ever met. Even older than Grandmother Nadira.*

"You are welcome here, Sasha El Sadawii, daughter of the most honored Mughal empress and sister of Rani."

Sasha glanced at her sister at the mention of the unfamiliar name.

Imogen's only response was to stand and bow to the ancient guru.

The mother was old, but her features were still smooth, giving her an ageless appearance. She walked with a cane, but didn't seem to need it. Her long hair was swept up in a no-nonsense bun at the nape of her neck, a few wispy strands escaping to frame her face. Her robes were plain and well worn. She was exactly what one would expect of a guru living in an ancient Hindu temple in the valley of the Ghat Mountains. And Sasha was pretty sure that was what the mother wanted her to think.

Sasha rose to greet the woman. She may not want to be here. This might be the last thing on earth she ever wanted to do, but this woman deserved her respect.

"Thank you, Mother Raghavan." She gave a curt bow. "It is an honor to meet you."

"You are like your noble sister. In some ways. In others, I think you may be even more stubborn." She gave her a sly wink. "Come, let us speak of your training."

"Jayesh." The mother nodded as he rose to greet her. "It is good to see you again, although I fear circumstances have chased all your hard-learned lessons straight from that stubborn head of yours." She rapped her cane against his forehead. "We will help you find your way again, dear boy." She gestured for them all to return to their seats and eased herself down onto a cushion with aid of her cane.

"You are all here because the Senate wishes me to teach young Sasha the old ways. You both know I cater to no government—I merely humor them. I have invited you here because you each possess a spark of the ancient power within you—most strongly in our young charge." She bowed her head reverently to Sasha. "Lessons will be learned. Fears will be confronted, and you will leave here with the knowledge you need to face what comes for you next. It will take as long as it takes. Tonight you will feast and rest, for tomorrow you will need your strength."

Mother Raghavan snapped her fingers and a host of robed attendants rushed in with the evening meal, placing trays of clean and wholesome foods on the table before them.

"May I ask what you will be teaching me, Mother?" Sasha spoke with respect, unsure if she was even allowed to ask questions.

"I will not be teaching you, Sasha. Another student needs my attention." She glanced at Imogen with a knowing smile. "I will oversee your training, but another will be your guru while you are here."

Jayesh's shoulders slumped as he took a long gulp of his wine. "She means me." He slammed his cup down, gesturing for a refill.

"You are correct, Jayesh. While you are here, you must take on the responsibility of teaching this young woman. We will meet at dawn in the eastern gardens each morning to discuss your progress."

Sasha didn't think it could get any worse, but every time she thought she had her head wrapped around this newest chapter of her life, the knife twisted as a reminder of how little she knew. She couldn't imagine anything worse than Jayesh as her trainer.

"And what will I be learning?" Sasha asked.

"While you are here you will master the art of *kalaripay-attu*, an ancient martial art taught in three stages. Tomorrow at dawn you will begin with *meithari*, stage one of *kalaripayattu*. Jayesh will explain now."

"Of course," Jayesh said. His tone was respectful, but his body language made it clear he wasn't amused. "*Kalari* means 'training ground' and *payattu* means 'fight.' Stage one of *kalari-*

payattu is called *meithari* and is simple enough, yet it can be the most difficult aspect of training for both the teacher and the student. *Meithari* focuses on physical exercise that will prepare the body for the later stages of training. You will engage every muscle and every joint from head to toe to ensure you are flexible and strong enough for the difficult forms that will come later. The *kalari* forms can be complex and will require your complete focus. We will work them every day, through each phase, until you have perfected them all." He sounded as if he'd swallowed *Teaching Kalaripayattu for Dummies*.

"The second component of *meithari* is focused on the mind. The ideal student will achieve balance between the strength of the body and the strength of the mind. Deep meditation and focus is no doubt already part of your daily routine. But during *meithari* the teacher and the student must achieve a pure relationship of trust and devotion to each other. We must find our balance before we can continue to the second phase, called *ankathari*. You will not learn what *ankathari* means until we have both mastered our roles during *meithari*."

We're never going home. Sasha felt her old life slipping away from her faster than she could blink. *It takes as long as it takes.* She would be here only six weeks, but she still had to live through however long that might be in this place. It could feel like years. *Quinn.* The thought of leaving him to whatever hell he was going through shattered something inside her. The days and months, maybe even years, ahead with her hands completely tied, unable to do anything to help him. The thought of experiencing something so profound without him left her feeling sad and hopelessly lost.

"No tears, my dear," Mother Raghavan said, her voice full of sympathy. "Your life lies just beyond the threshold of this valley, right where you left it. Your time here at the temple will only make you stronger so you can face what is coming with the experience you need to achieve what has been set before you."

Sasha got the sense that the mother wasn't just talking about the Senate's well-laid plans for her future.

"Embrace this experience and it will go quickly. Resist it and you could be here for a very long time. Either way, it takes as long as it takes. It will be up to you and your teacher to make this a success."

Sasha nodded, drying her eyes. She would do this. She would find a way to get along with Jayesh.

"We will talk each evening as the sun sets over my gardens. I will wait for you there." She gestured at the head monk waiting to take them to their rooms. "Rabishan will see you to your dormitories."

"Yes, mother," Sasha murmured, bowing her head as the mother left them for the evening.

"Please don't make this difficult," Jayesh and Sasha said at the same time after Mother Raghavan's footsteps faded in the distance.

CHAPTER 11

Quinn: Fall - Atlanta, Georgia

"Why are you so twitchy?" Santi scowled at Quinn across the kitchen island.

"I'm not." Quinn fidgeted with his breakfast. It always bothered him to eat in front of her, knowing she was never getting enough.

"You're like a five-year-old messing with his cereal. Eat and get out of here. You know Livia's a stickler for the schedule. And God help you if you mess up Lennox's day. She'll tear your face off."

"I'm going." Quinn drained the last of his juice and went to rinse his dishes. He hated making Santi clean up after him.

"You know you're sweating, right?" She frowned up at him, checking his forehead.

"I'm just ... off today, I guess." He grabbed her hand and gave it a squeeze, leaving her to her chores.

He caught a glimpse of himself in the foyer mirror on his way out of his penthouse prison. He looked like shit. He felt weird, too. Like a newly Awakened kid on the cusp of touching his power for the first time. He hadn't felt like that in ages.

It wasn't that long ago, Quinn. Just a year ago his last gift had manifested, but with four unique gifts in his arsenal, it wasn't likely he'd ever have to go through that again.

Quinn stepped onto the empty elevator to make his way down to the training center. His life had settled into a new normal over the last few weeks and it surprised him how easily he had slipped into the routine of Soma. After a morning with James, they'd hit the gym to work with Lennox. He knew Livia only had them working together so he would get attached. That way, when she was ready to remind him who was in charge and what she wanted from him, she could use Lennox against him and it would hurt that much more.

Lennox came to Soma before she could even remember living anywhere else. Ryan found her wandering around the first floor lobby. She couldn't have been more than two at the time. James suspected her parents feared raising a child as powerful as Lennox would likely be. To Quinn, she wasn't much more than average. But to those who hadn't grown up with someone like Aidan, in a family as powerful as theirs, he supposed Lennox could seem intimidating--especially to a young couple. They probably thought they were leaving her with people who would see she was trained properly. But they couldn't have known they were sentencing her to a cold and clinical life that would never be her own.

"You're late," James said the moment Quinn arrived at the enormous training center where counselors worked with the Soma kids in residence. These kids were slated to hit the slave market in a few years and few of them realized it. Most of them came to the Fold for help and, in exchange, they'd lost their freedom. There were other kids, in a different part of the building, who hadn't made it this far in yet. They lived in dormitories and thought they were lucky to be accepted into the program.

"Sorry. I'm not feeling up to my usual today," Quinn said.

"Had a bad night." His dreams were leaving him restless. He dreamed of home almost every night he slept now. It was getting easier to remember he'd only been at Soma a few months, but he still missed his home and his family as if he hadn't seen them in years. The ache of missing Sasha haunted him. So many times, he woke in a sweat after chasing a phantom of her through his dreams, reliving those final confusing moments with her. That last dance. Their last words to each other. The kiss. He'd wake up wondering what that kiss meant to her. What it meant to him now that he felt like he had five years' distance from that night. Other times, throughout his day, he would get an overwhelming sense that she was in trouble and needed him. The separation from her was almost worse than anything he'd suffered at Michael's hand.

"You're training with Lennox this morning."

"What, no pep talk today?" Quinn gave his trainer a shove.

"You don't listen to anything I say anyway." James returned the shove with a grin.

"What's with the change in my schedule?" Lennox burst through the door looking like a street urchin, with her ratty hair in a messy braid over her shoulder and a smear of blood on her chin. "I have training at eleven on weekdays, not nine." She didn't like it when her routine changed without notice. She was a mouthy little kid with a tough skin. She needed it, living at Soma.

"Have you been fighting again?" James frowned down at her.

"Isn't that what we're all here for?" She crossed her arms.

"Depends. Were you the bully in whatever scrape you've gotten yourself into now?"

"No comment." She wiped the dried blood off her chin.

"We're working out, and then you and Quinn are going to spar," James said.

Lennox wrinkled her nose at that. "He's a *giant* ox. You want him to put me in the infirmary?"

"My aunt isn't much bigger than you and I spar with her all the time," Quinn said, thinking of Chloe. Her Awakening would have happened recently. The realization that he'd missed it and hadn't even realized knocked the wind out of him. *I'm missing everything.*

"She's just a little older than you are." His voice took on a softer tone.

"You have an aunt who's younger? That's weird." Lennox dropped into the chair beside him.

Quinn glanced up at James, wondering for the millionth time if he could trust him. He didn't want these people knowing more about his family than they should. "My father is her much older brother. She's only fifteen ... *sixteen now* ... and she's an incredible fighter—even if she is small."

"She's fifteen and she trains? I guess I thought kids got to have an actual life outside this place." Lennox frowned.

"She goes to school and she has friends but we all train every day, pretty much like we do here." Quinn sat back and pressed his lips together as if to stop the flow of words. He didn't want to be the reason Soma went snooping around his family any more than they already had.

"She has friends, though, so it has to be better than this place." Lennox picked at a rip in her jeans. "So what, you're going to kick my butt today?"

Quinn glanced back at James, wondering what his agenda really was.

Don't worry about James, Lennox said in her peculiar way. *He's just doing what he's told. He never tells them anything important and they don't push him. We can trust him. He's just lazy, that's all.*

Quinn laughed at the kid's honesty, wondering if James knew about Len's situation.

"Quinn's going to work with you for a while," James said. "Just routine training, like always."

"For what purpose?" Quinn asked, though he was certain today was just meant to give them another opportunity to connect now so Livia could use it against him later.

"Well, I'm not the best sparring coach and our little Len has some ... personality conflicts with some of the other trainers." He gave her a patronizing look.

"My personality is just fine. I can't help it if everyone else sucks." Lennox shot him a glare.

She's a mini Allie. Quinn shook his head at the painful reminder of his friend.

"How about you show Lennox how someone small can take down a bigger opponent?" James suggested.

"Come on, squirt." Quinn forced a smile for the angry little girl beside him. He might as well make this fun for her. She got precious little of that living here. "One of these days you're going to grow into those limbs of yours." He crossed the gym to one of the free mats.

"You sayin' I'm short?" Lennox bit back.

"I'm saying you're going to be tall ... eventually, but right now you're all arms and legs, so I'm going to show you how to use that to your advantage."

"How?"

Quinn crouched low. "Come at me in an offensive strike."

Lennox charged at him like an ox ten times her size.

"Good." Quinn moved in a defensive sidestep, watching how Lennox responded, changing direction effortlessly. "Now use the span of your arm's reach to overwhelm me as you come in for your first strike. You can easily reach my right shoulder and my left knee at the same time; use it to tip my balance and take me down."

Quinn let her move in, showing her how to grasp him behind the knee and put all her energy into throwing him off-balance, using his weight against him.

The first time he went down, she kicked him for added measure.

"Sorry!" She reached to help him up. "I got excited."

"Len's a kicker. Better watch out," James said dryly.

Quinn worked with her for most of the morning, under the careful watch of James—Livia's eyes and ears. No matter what he said, at the end of the day, that was his job.

Lennox knew how to fight dirty, but her training was far behind what Quinn would have expected for someone her age.

"You're fast and you have a good sense of how to move in a fight against someone bigger, but you don't have to resort to cheap shots." He rubbed his shin where she'd kicked him again.

"I find it quite satisfying." Lennox laughed as she danced around him, eager to go again.

Quinn shook his head; the smile on his face felt foreign to him.

"Why do I hear laughter when I should hear fighting?" Livia asked from the observation deck above the gym. She stared down her nose, trying to give them her resting bitch face, but even Livia couldn't help smiling at Lennox when she was clearly having fun.

"Did you see me flip this big ox?" Lennox asked.

"I did." Livia nodded. "It seems he's taught you a few new tricks. Care to try them out on me?"

"Bring it on, Liv." Lennox grinned as Livia came down the stairs to join her on the mat.

Quinn couldn't help but gape in surprise at the way Livia responded to Lennox—like a for-real, actual nice person.

Tossing her a bo staff from the weapons wall, Livia faced off with the girl, barely half her size but Lennox was determined to beat her. She moved fast and was a pro with the bo staff, but Livia kept her on her toes.

It was good to see Lennox enjoying herself, but it was bizarre seeing Livia act like a real person. When Lennox rushed in to grab her by the knee, Livia hadn't expected it and went down like a ton of bricks. But she was ready for Len's signature kick to the ribs and grabbed the girl's foot, bringing her down beside her with a laugh.

"What have I told you about kicking?"

"Don't be so predictable." Lennox giggled.

Quinn couldn't believe what he was seeing. Livia clearly loved that little girl. It didn't make any sense how she could use her like she had.

"That's enough fun for today," Livia finally said. "I have work to do. Bring her home with you tonight, Quinn. We're having dinner in the penthouse. This one is too skinny. I don't think they feed her enough in the dining hall."

"I don't like the dining hall. Not since they took out the sundae bar."

"From what I hear that was the only thing you'd eat." Livia winked as she turned to go.

"Did she just wink?" Quinn looked to James for confirmation. "Or am I hallucinating again?"

"As difficult as it may seem, Livia isn't completely heartless. She just has a demanding job she never really signed on for. Kind of like most of us here at Soma. She's hard. She expects obedience and she has little patience for anyone other than Lennox, but she's not pure evil."

"I wouldn't believe it if I hadn't seen it with my own eyes."

"Hey, Len, clean up here and put your weapons away. We'll meet back in my office in five," James instructed.

"Don't we have people for that?" She scowled at the mess of weapons and towels on the gym floor.

"Len." James sighed.

"Fine, I'm going." She stalked off with a huff.

"It's Lennox," James said, lowering his voice. "She's a special kid. Everyone loves her. Even Livia."

"Her life is so cold and monotonous. Kids like Lennox don't belong here."

"She doesn't know any better, Quinn. Sure, she wishes for a life outside of Soma, but you can't really miss what you never had."

Quinn eyed his trainer. He wasn't so sure James knew any better either.

"I'm starving," Lennox said as they stepped into the penthouse foyer. "Something smells amazing."

Quinn was hungry too, but he was anxious to see Santi again. His training sessions were running longer and longer, and she rarely got to leave the apartment. They never had much time to talk privately anymore. Only on the nights they slept when Livia didn't. And even then, Santi was often too tired to talk much. He found himself missing her during the day and then feeling guilty about it when he inevitably thought of Sasha and the growing distance between him and the girl he'd loved most of his life.

"I made your favorite, *chica*." Santi smiled as she set the table, her chains suspiciously absent.

"Spaghetti and meatballs?" Lennox grabbed a seat at the table set for four.

"With lots of garlic bread," Santi said.

Quinn gave Santi a perplexed look. This had all the

makings of a family dinner and that didn't bode well for any of them. This had to be some kind of attempt to disarm him—a false sense of peace that could shatter at any moment.

Santi shrugged, moving to pour iced tea into the glasses.

"Dessert?" Lennox asked.

"Sundaes." Santi winked. Her eyes were dark. She hadn't slept a full night in months. Nor had she eaten more than a meal of bland chicken and steamed vegetables since he arrived. It was enough to sustain a mortal, but the limited diet was taking a toll on her Immortal body.

"You had to cook all of this?" he asked as she placed a huge bowl of pasta and meatballs on the table with a basket of cheesy garlic bread. Her hands shook from the effort to restrain herself.

"Every delicious-looking bit." Santi sighed.

"Dinner ready?" Livia asked as she swept in from her office with a look of grim determination on her face and a tumbler of whisky in her hand. "I'm starving," she said as she sat down at the head of the table and nodded to Santi to serve them.

Quinn sat across from Lennox, fuming as Santi served each of them before she could join them. Lennox chattered away, but even her anxious rambling couldn't mask the sound of Santi's rumbling stomach. On most nights they each fended for themselves. Quinn usually ate in the dining hall downstairs with James so he wouldn't have to eat in front of Santi.

"This is bullshit, Liv," Quinn finally said when Santi sat down beside Lennox to a plate of brown rice and canned tuna. The whole thing was barely three bites.

"It's fine, Quinn. Just eat," Santi insisted, but he could see the longing in her eyes. Mind games were the way of life around Soma, but this he couldn't stand. Watching her needless suffering when he knew she was a breath away from giving up. It was too much.

"Just let her eat, Liv. Please?"

Lennox nearly dropped her fork. "You don't let Santi eat?" *That is totally messed up.* She glanced at Quinn in uncertainty.

"Hush, Len. It's okay. I'm just on a special diet. I made this for you, so I want you to enjoy it," Santi said.

"Let her eat," Quinn demanded.

"What's with not letting her eat?" Lennox said. *You don't understand, Quinn. Livia doesn't like doing this to people. She has to.*

"That's enough, Lennox," Livia said. "Santi knows her diet will improve when her behavior does." Livia narrowed her eyes at Quinn. Gone was the Livia he'd seen that afternoon. Her armor was firmly back in place.

"This is sadistic, even for you. Can't you see she's never going to fall for your stupid games? She will never agree to a life of slavery."

"Slavery?" Lennox's eyes widened in alarm. *Who's a slave? You guys?*

Quinn glanced at the brand on her ankle and wished he could crawl into a hole and disappear. *She doesn't even know she's a slave?*

"You don't know what you're talking about, Quinn." Livia's voice held an edge of warning for him to shut up.

"Well, I won't sit here and watch you do this to her." Quinn stood up to leave, not sure which "her" he was more incensed on behalf of—Santi or Lennox.

"You will sit here and have dinner with us and you will enjoy it," Livia demanded. Her tone said Santi would pay the consequences for his outburst if he didn't sit down immediately.

"It's fine, Quinn. Please, just sit and eat," Santi begged.

With a curt nod at his seat, Livia told him she would let it go if he obeyed. It was lenient for her in the extreme and it was the best outcome he could hope for at this point.

With a shaky breath, he sank back into his seat and nearly laughed. Out of the corner of his eye, he saw Lennox wrapping meatballs and pasta into her napkin and shoving it into the pockets of Santi's cargo pants. He was pretty sure by the hint of a smile on Livia's face that she knew exactly what Lennox was up to.

What? Starving's no joke, man. Lennox passed him the parmesan cheese with a smirk.

CHAPTER 12

Sasha: Summer - The Chola Valley Temple

"This is it?" Sasha swept the narrow room with her eyes, looking for the rest of it.

"The student must focus on the lesson," Brother Rabishan said. "You will find everything you need here."

"Yes, thank you." Sasha set her duffel bag on the edge of the small cot. She couldn't call it a bed since she was pretty sure it had been made at a time when people were much shorter than her five-foot-ten-inch frame.

The cold stone floor was covered in brightly colored rugs, and the window would give her the early morning sun. A small cabinet housed the traditional clothes she would be expected to wear while in residence. All her size. Like they'd known months ago that she would be arriving today.

That's exactly it, Sasha. In the real world they probably found out yesterday, but who knows how long that gave them to plan for her visit here.

It wasn't a sleeping night for her, and she wasn't sure she would have been able to settle down even if she was tired.

Sasha ultimately spent her first evening at the Chola temple, alone in her Spartan dormitory, reviewing every last detail of Quinn's situation in her mind. She didn't need her corkboard wall—she remembered everything. And thinking about Quinn kept her from thinking about tomorrow.

She missed him terribly. No matter how good her intentions were, Sasha just kept making Quinn's situation worse. The kiss that she still wasn't sure about had flustered Allie when she ran into them in the gardens that night. To avoid interrupting them, Allie had circled the building instead, and that sent her right into the hands of the waiting Coalition—who were there because they'd seen Sasha heal that dove just hours before. And now this. She'd waited one day too long to act, and now she was stuck in this time screw with her hands tied and no way to help Quinn at all for the foreseeable future.

"Midnight snack?" Imogen stuck her head into the room after a soft knock on Sasha's door.

"I'm always down for snacks." Sasha smiled.

Her sister brought in a tray of fruit, hot tea and some kind of nutty bread.

"Let's get our plan in place for tomorrow."

"We have a plan?"

"We need a plan, Sash. Jay's going to take over your training. We will be separated, since the mother wishes to teach me something while I am here," she said bitterly. "We need to decide the best ways for you to learn what you must, but not too quickly. Or too well."

"I don't like the idea of us being separated," Sasha said, taking a bite of warm bread and butter, fresher than anything she'd ever tasted before.

"He's made certain assumptions about you so I think we should play into his expectations. For now."

"Act like a brat and only learn the lesson after I've driven him to the complete edge of his patience?" Sasha suggested.

"Exactly. You're going to be stuck in the *meithari* phase for a while, so you two are going to have to find a way to be friends, which is going to make it difficult for you to keep up the necessary deceptions. You should be cautious of Jay, but you need to trust him as your teacher. He is a good man but he has ... issues that have nothing to do with his ability to be a good instructor."

"I don't trust him," Sasha said. "There's something he isn't telling us."

"Let him have his secrets. It doesn't matter. It's in his best interest to teach you well. His attitude toward you now is his armor. It's his way of keeping people from getting too close. He's a career soldier. I've seen it before with others like him. He keeps everyone at a distance because his life belongs to those he works for. He doesn't have anything else. Give him some time to learn how to talk to a seventeen-year-old girl."

"What history do you two have?" Sasha asked. "You weren't, like ... romantically involved, were you?"

"No, nothing like that. We spent a lot of time here together a lifetime ago. We became close friends. But when we left the mother, we went our separate ways. I made positive changes after I learned to let my past go. Jayesh seems to have gone right back to the life he was trying to escape when he came here in desperation. I think coming back has thrown his failures in his face, so try to remember that he is also here to learn whatever the mother hopes to teach him. You cannot know how difficult his private time with her is for him.

"But there is something odd about this arrangement, isn't there?" Sasha asked. "Sloane was obviously a Senate rep through and through, but Jay strikes me more as a ... mercenary than a loyal Senate soldier."

"That's what we can never forget. Jay is a hired gun and his loyalty is questionable. We don't have the whole story from either side so you must be extremely careful about what you reveal to him."

"I'll just distract him with my brattyness." Sasha grinned.

"Don't lay it on too thick, sister. We want to get out of here eventually."

"I'm aiming for somewhere between annoying and uncooperative, dialed in at about seventy percent of my capability. At the end of the day I'll get the lesson so we can move on. I just want him to have to work for it enough to know he never wants to work with me again."

"That's the dream." Imogen smiled. "Let's just hope it doesn't take years here to accomplish it."

When Jayesh came for her shortly after dawn, Sasha was prepared to make him wait.

"Almost ready!" she called as she rushed around her dormitory to finish dressing. She wore loose-fitting linen pants and a matching tunic. The yellow fabric and golden embroidery made her skin glow like polished bronze. She struggled to lace the embroidered belt around her waist as she hunted for the matching slippers. She wore her dark curly hair in a messy bun on top of her head, letting a few curls escape to frame her face.

"Took you long enough," he said when she finally answered the door still holding her belt and her shoes. "Hurry up. We're behind schedule." His traditional white linen trousers fit him like a glove and the long sleeveless over tunic fell to his knees, and had a deep embroidered V-neck. A golden armband cuffed his tattooed bicep. With his feet bare and his ensemble topped with an actual turban, Jayesh looked like he'd stepped straight out of the Mughal Empire of the sixteenth century.

"I didn't realize we had a schedule. Maybe you should try slipping an itinerary under my door since I don't read minds.

What are we doing this morning?" She attempted to find a civil tone as she continued to fumble with the belt.

"We will be training in the northwest pavilion." He turned her around abruptly and tied the belt for her. "Finish pulling yourself together and meet me there in fifteen minutes." He stepped down the long stone corridor without another word.

Sasha darted back into her room to grab her sunglasses and overtunic and headed down the hall to her sister's dormitory.

"Phase one of irritate Jayesh was a smashing success without even trying," Sasha said as she stepped into her sister's rooms—which were hella more comfortable than her tiny closet. "Hey, no fair—this is an apartment."

"I am a veteran of the temple, sister. Believe me, I did my time in the dormitories. How did you manage to irritate him so quickly?"

"Breathing? I don't know." She shrugged, flopping down onto the bed beside her sister. "You're meeting with Mother Raghavan later this morning, aren't you?"

"I am." Imogen sounded nervous.

"Any idea what she thinks you need to learn?"

"Not the first. I imagine she sees something I don't. For a woman who lives outside of time and away from the happenings of the world, she is remarkably informed about the current climate of the Immortal world."

"You'll tell me about your lessons later?" Sasha asked.

"If I can. Now you'd better run along. Don't keep Jayesh waiting too long."

"I'm going. See you tonight."

"Be careful, Sasha."

"You too. I know you're here because of me, but I want you to know I'm here for you too, sis."

"Thanks, Sash. That means a lot."

Sasha made her way along the labyrinth of corridors and

into the bright sunshine of the temple courtyard. She headed for the northwest quadrant to meet Jayesh at the largest pavilion there. The gardens were in full bloom and the fragrant flowers calmed her in a way only nature could. Sasha had such a close connection with the earth and an even stronger bond with its creatures. The gardens would be a perfect place for her to train and meditate—if she and Jayesh could get past their differences.

The pavilion was almost primitive, built of stone and carved with Vedic figures and patterns. Dozens of columns held the pavilion aloft, each draped in billowing silk in oranges and yellows to match the warm earthen tones of the landscape. Inside, the shade was cool and the light dim. Torches burned along the stone walls on either end of the structure, and incense burned in braziers near the entrance. *This place really is like taking a trip back in time.* It was so untouched and innocent in a way. But Sasha had no doubt that many Immortals had come here to face their demons.

The training room had seen much use. Swords and shields hung on the walls at opposite ends of the pavilion. Practice weapons were stacked on shelves along with staves of varying lengths. The western wall was open to the gardens, sheets of silken fabric tied back against the pillars.

Jayesh stood at the center of the room, shirtless and moving through a sequence of *kalaripayattu* forms. His strong shoulders strained against the movements.

"Take those idiotic glasses off. They are an outside distraction," Jayesh said as he slipped his tunic back on.

Sasha was more than a little disappointed when his abs disappeared behind his shirt. He was a dick, but at least he was pretty to look at—until he opened his mouth.

She left her slippers at the threshold of the pavilion—it was considered holy and she wasn't the disrespectful teen he thought she was. She hung her sunglasses and the flowing orange silk vest she wore over her tunic on the pegs at the entrance.

Crossing the room, Sasha thought of all the ways she could make this difficult for him, but in this place, with so much history and atmosphere, her palms itched to get started. For the first time she felt her interest stirring, wondering what she would learn while in this sacred place.

"What's on the agenda for today?" she asked, taking her usual student's stance in front of her teacher. She wasn't used to training with strangers. It left her feeling awkward.

"You will touch my feet as a sign of respect when you enter these training grounds." He stood ramrod straight, waiting for her to comply.

Sasha was no stranger to martial arts training and she was familiar with most customs of respect. She had no doubt what he said was true, but there was no way she was touching his feet.

"How about we don't and say I did?" Sasha gave him a curt bow instead.

"We will abide by the Chola customs while we are here." He returned her bow with a level stare.

"I don't think so." She lifted her chin. "You're demanding it as a sign of submission when it should be given in respect."

"Just sit already," Jay barked in his military tone and her back was immediately up for the second time in as many minutes.

"Say the magic word." She put just the right amount of angst into her request. "I am not one of your soldiers. At least not yet."

"I don't need the attitude, Sasha. We're never going to get anywhere if you don't show some respect."

"Quite frankly, if the *kalaripayattu* guru and his student are supposed to have a close relationship of respect and friendship, *you* are the one giving attitude. I'm just following your lead," she said as she took a seat on the stone floor, gesturing for him to join her.

"We will begin our first lessons of *meithari* tomorrow." He took his seat opposite her. "Today, I would like to take the opportunity to get to know you. Or rather, your gifts," he amended. "You will not be permitted to use them during our sparring sessions until we reach the second stage, *ankathari,* but as your mentor during this time, I need to have a thorough understanding of all your gifts."

"Absolutely not. When it comes to my gifts, my sister is my mentor while we are here," Sasha said. "I do not know you. I trust you to teach me *kalari,* but you've given me very little reason to trust you blindly where my gifts are concerned. We can discuss my targeting gift, but that is all. The rest of my abilities are mine to protect. Until you show me you are worthy of my trust, I'll be keeping them close to the belt. To do otherwise goes against everything I've ever been taught."

"Fine. We will begin with your targeting gift. That's the most interesting thing about you anyway," Jayesh muttered. "Clearly, it is going to take a miracle for us to achieve the kind of relationship that will get us out of this place."

"I did not ask for this," Sasha said. "You are blaming me because you find yourself in this place you hate. That is not my fault. I wasn't given a choice."

Jay stood and crossed the room. His shoulders tensed and his footsteps heavy as he paced. "This is hopeless."

"It doesn't have to be. If you will *just* meet me halfway...."

"My mind is on the mission I should be preparing for. My team needs me in Africa, yet I am here. With you. My job there ... it means something to me, Sasha. I'm not just a hired gun. I know the Senate wants you trained in a way that will only strengthen the future of my team, but I have never been a patient man. There are things I need to be doing, and training a sixteen-year-old child isn't one of them."

"I'm seventeen," she corrected him. "And there are other things I should be doing than wasting my time here with you."

"Shopping with your friends for shoes?" Jay turned to face her with a sneer. "Snapchatting your life away?"

"Go ahead. Judge me one more time." Sasha stood to face him. "Paint me with all the stereotypes of my generation. Don't attempt to actually get to know me so we can get out of here anytime soon. Go ahead. Keep acting like a dick and see how long we'll be stuck in this time screw."

"Please tell me what important things we are pulling you away from, angel?" he snapped as he crossed his arms over his chest. "Tell me what you have going on in your life that is more important than a nation of people at war, suffering under the rule of a brutal dictator? I'm listening."

"My Com—" Sasha's hands clenched into fists at her side. "...The boy I've grown up with and loved my entire life is a captive of the Coalition. He was taken from his family because of me." Her tone was low and full of all the loathing she felt for Jayesh and his assumptions as well as for herself and her failures. "He is suffering because I wasn't there for him. I was leaving for Atlanta. Before you came for me, I was going to go find him. I was going to help him escape, or at least be with him as a support. And then *you* showed up on *my* doorstep and now we are here and Quinn is still in Atlanta where no one can reach him."

"What did you think you were going to accomplish by going there, Sasha?" The critical tone in his voice vanished, replaced by one bordering on kindness.

"The people who have him seem to attract people like me. Young and talented Immortals. I was going to walk through the front door of Sterling Tower and ask for help with my training. It was a good plan. I could have gotten close enough to help him. To help our family with the knowledge they need to free him."

"It wouldn't have worked," he said softly.

"How do you know?" she fumed.

"Trust me. I know. You'd never reach him that way. Put it behind you and let your family take care of Quinn while you take care of yourself. I need you to have your head in this, Sasha. Fully in this ... or we are going to fail."

"Let's just get back to training. I'm in the mood to punch things."

"We will meditate first. Then we will have lunch and discuss my plan for your training. We will have time for *kalari* tomorrow."

"We have to make the most of our time here, Jayesh. We should train and not let the days slip past us."

"When I was here before, the best I was able to calculate, time passes at a rate of one day to every couple of hours outside. Sometimes, when we aren't learning what we came here to learn—like now, because we are both sucking at the first lessons of *meithari*—it's more like a week here is an hour at home. We have all the time in the world to get this done, Sasha. Somewhere along the way, we will become friends. It is the nature of this place. Follow me." He stepped through the giant pillars and down the crumbling stone steps into the sweeping gardens below.

Sasha followed him down the steps, too irritated to truly appreciate the beauty of the temple gardens.

"Together or separate?" Jayesh asked.

"Let's not push our luck on the first day. I'm going over here," Sasha said, leaving Jayesh to find his own quiet corner to meditate.

Sasha stomped along the garden path, her blood pounding in her ears.

"Sasha?" Jayesh called behind her. "Just ... give me time to find my footing. I wasn't expecting any of this."

"You think I was?" She winced at her sharp tone. "Perhaps we both need a good minute to ourselves."

"Perhaps," he agreed. "Come find me when you feel you have found the right frame of mind."

Sasha walked along the dirt pathway to one of the many small alcoves. Short shrubs grew around a natural fountain where flowers floated in the breeze along the water's surface. She knelt on the moss-covered cobblestone and focused her gaze on the flowers. Meditation was as much a part of her life as her daily training was, but for the first time in ages she couldn't seem to ground herself in the moment.

She continued to stare at the flowers floating on the surface of the murky green water until all other thought left her. With a deep breath, she relaxed each part of her body, from her toes, all the way up to her neck and shoulders. Jayesh was the source of all her current stress and anxiety and she needed to learn to interact with him in a positive way. As long as they affected each other negatively, their training efforts would be futile.

With a last look at the beauty of the paradise around her, Sasha closed her eyes and began to breathe, focusing on the way the air filled her lungs and how her diaphragm moved with each breath. She felt the rise of her chest, the brief pause before exhaling. She counted on each exhale, clearing her mind of all negative energy.

The longer she focused on her breath, the more relaxed she became, until she even forgot to count her breaths. She was no longer aware of her tension or her anxiety. It was only Sasha and the air in her lungs. The point where her breath entered her body and exhalation a beat later.

When she opened her eyes again, she wasn't sure how much time had passed, but she felt better. Still, she wasn't ready to go back to Jayesh yet. She needed a moment to reflect on the source of her negative emotions. It was easy to blame him. But at the end of the day, Jayesh was just trying to do his job.

Sasha stood, ready to return for the remainder of their session. She had demanded Jayesh meet her halfway while her own feet were planted firmly in place. If she wanted to get back to her life, back to her family, and back to saving Quinn, she would have to take a step toward Jayesh.

As she walked through the garden, she had no sense of how long she'd meditated. It could have been hours or minutes. Judging by the rumbling of her stomach, it had been hours. The disoriented feeling of not knowing how much time had passed was alarming.

She found Jayesh back in the temple, moving through the *kalari* forms she would soon learn. She recognized some of the familiar movements from her Kung Fu training and hoped it would help speed things along.

He stopped when he saw her standing at the entrance to the pavilion.

Sasha swallowed her pride and crossed the room. She knelt and touched his feet.

"I am ready. Are you?"

CHAPTER 13

Quinn: Fall - Atlanta, Georgia

Quinn wandered along the familiar grassy slope. His dreams were restless, and he often found himself dreaming of home. But this version of his home was different. A gloomy cloud hung over the hillside near Sasha's house. They'd grown up on this hillside, playing with their siblings. Quinn stood rooted to the spot, alone. The pull of home was so intense he almost couldn't breathe. But this wasn't home. Not really. It was a creepy substitute of the home he remembered.

He walked through the tall grass, yellowed and dying. The purple clouds hung low on the horizon and the roar of the waves breaking against the rocks far below the cliffs sounded like the crash of cymbals. The echo tinny and unnatural. He walked right up to the edge of the cliff, so focused on his misery and homesickness he almost didn't see the person waiting for him there.

"What is this place?" Santi asked, turning to face him.

"Home." He shrugged. "Or something like it, I guess."

"Show me?" She smiled, taking his hand and pulling him away from the precipice.

As they turned, the landscape changed and Quinn stumbled at the sight of his house. They were no longer on the hillside. Now they walked hand in hand across the wide lawn to a ghostly replica of his childhood home. The two-story California Craftsman was his father's pride and joy. He'd done much of the restoration work himself. All dark wood, natural stone and exposed joists with a subtle hint of Asian influence in the low rooflines and surrounding gardens. With the warm light glowing from within, it was all too much for Quinn. The surge of homesickness brought him to his knees. He could hear the faint sound of Graham's laughter and their father yelling for them to come inside.

"You grew up here?" Santi asked, kneeling beside him. "It's beautiful."

"I spent my whole life here." He nodded, staring at the vision before him. "It's just a house, I know, but it's been so long ... I miss it so much. The thought of never returning...." He shook his head.

"I know how much our childhood homes mean to us," she whispered. "It's why I volunteered—back when I thought I was applying for a job as a Soma agent." She laughed bitterly. "I wanted to save my family home from foreclosure. I can't even remember the last time I saw it. It's been so long. But I saved the house. It seems silly now. A pile of bricks and mortar isn't a home."

"It's the people inside that matter." Quinn stood, draping his arm around her waist as they crossed the front porch to the swing where his mother and father spent so much time together in the evenings. They never got into the bad habit of watching television or pursuing solitary endeavors. No, his parents still sat on the front porch swing in the summers, laughing and talking until the evenings grew late. He and Graham used to tease them about it, but Quinn would give anything to sit on this swing with his dad and have one of their philosophical discussions. "I don't know if

I'll ever get to go home again. If I'll ever escape the clutches of Soma. I'm not even sure I *could* go back to the way it was before."

"You're not a kid anymore, Quinn." Santi slid closer to his side as they rocked the swing into a slow rhythm. "Michael ... and Soma took that from us. But we'll get out and we'll move on with our lives, and someday we'll find a place to call home again. Do not lose hope. Not yet."

He didn't know where the feeling came from, but Quinn had an overwhelming urge to kiss her. But even in his dream, he couldn't do that to Sasha. Not with the way they'd left things. The guilt would crush him. But in the short time they'd known each other, with their shared circumstances what they were, Santi had become the best part of his world. He liked where they were heading, but at the same time he didn't know how to move on from Sasha. Or if it was even fair for him to consider loving someone else. In the chaos of his mind, his time with Sasha felt like the ancient history of first love.

Santi seemed to respond to his reservations, leaning her head against his shoulder, content just to sit quietly with his arm around her. She saw him so clearly, it was often disarming. All his life, his friends and family only saw what Quinn wanted them to see—the façade he wore to hide the severity of his addiction. But Santi saw through him, right down to his soul, and she still liked what she saw.

"You are thinking big thoughts," she whispered, reaching to stroke the crease of his brow. The clean scent of her like lavender and citrus. In Quinn's dream, Santi was relaxed and free of the chains that bound her to Livia's home. In his dream she was happy.

"Santi? What's your real name?" Quinn frowned down at her. He'd never asked and it felt wrong not knowing her real name.

"Santi," she said, her chin lifting stubbornly.

"What's it short for?"

"Santi is short for my father's surname, Santiago."

He could tell by the way she fidgeted with her hair that she wasn't about to tell him her full name because it was something completely dreadful.

"Come on, spill it. I won't tell anyone."

"Of course you won't tell anyone, because there is nothing to tell."

"So you're trying to tell me that your mother named you Santiago and didn't bother to give her beautiful daughter a real name?" He pulled her closer, but still she refused to budge. "Fine, I'll just call you Mark." He laughed at the look of horror on her face.

"You will call me Santi, like everyone else."

"I'm not everyone else. Please? Let me know your name?"

"It's Carmina María Sofía Delgado Santiago," she said in a rush.

"Wow, that's a mouthful. But it's beautiful."

"It's ridiculous."

"I like it. I'm going to call you Mina."

"I can live with that." She rested her head against his shoulder. "It's better than Mark."

"All those names have to mean something special." He rested his head against hers. "Tell me about them."

"My great-grandmother, Carmina, who I never met, was a Tikal queen in fifth-century Guatemala. She died right before I was born. My mother's name is María Lucia Delgado and her mother's name is Sofía Rose. I'm the only natural born child in a family of ancients so they named me after all the important women of our line."

"But you call yourself Santi? Why?"

"It's my father's name. I've always been so much like him, they used to call me little Santi and it stuck."

They fell silent in the gentle breeze, enjoying the peaceful moment together. For the first time in ages, Quinn was truly at rest.

There was something eerie about this dream. It called to the power deep within his core—the power he couldn't touch without Livia's permission. But his chest burned with the icy stirring of his gift. He needed to wake up, but he was reluctant to let go of this time with Santi.

"We need to leave." Santi's eyes grew wide in alarm. "We can't be here. We need to wake up. Now, Quinnton."

His eyes flew open in the darkness and his body pulsed with the stirring of his power—a sensation he hadn't felt this strongly in ages. *A new gift?* That couldn't be. Quinn already possessed a multitude of gifts and never anticipated having another. *But what is it?* What could have emerged, pulling him out of a dead sleep?

He stared down at Santi, her head pillowed on his chest and her arm around his waist. In his sleep, he'd held her close. They always went to sleep in their respective beds, but throughout the night, they would inevitably drift toward each other and woke up in each other's arms more often than not.

She gasped and her eyes snapped open. "Quinn?" Her head came up as she searched his face. "What is this? You have to get a grip on it. If she senses...." But Livia's heavy footfall pounded down the hallway from her office.

"She already knows." Quinn sat up, taking a deep breath to release the power he should not be wielding. Not without Livia's permission. *But if it's a new gift, will she have the same kind of control?*

"Santi, I suggest you get back to sleep," Livia said as she

stepped into the bedroom. "Ryan will be here soon to wake you up."

Santi scrambled back to her pallet.

Quinn slammed against the floor as Livia's controlling gift swept through him. She had a piece of him already, but he wasn't about to give her another. He would cling to his remaining gifts until his last breath.

The white-hot heat of her gift stole the air from his lungs. She wrestled for control, proving her dominance once again as she searched his mind and his body for the source of this new gift.

"Do not think to fight me now." The look on her face said it all. Out of nowhere, Quinn had developed a new gift and she had no more clue what it was than he did.

"Hide it." Livia stood to her full height over him, shoving him back against his bed, her face now a calm mask obscuring her emotions.

"What?" Quinn couldn't quite process what she was saying. It was a warning. Not a threat.

"Keep this to yourself and do not make a spectacle of it." Her voice was low but her meaning was clear. She didn't want the knowledge of his new gift to leave this room. "I won't interfere with this. Whatever it is, it needs to evolve naturally... but make no mistake—I'm watching you."

Quinn gaped up at her.

"Don't look so surprised." She smiled and handed his pillow back to him. "I'm not a monster of my own making, Quinn. Even I rebel in my own way ... when it suits me. And it suits me to keep you close and protected from the prying eyes of Soma ... and my father. Why do you think I keep Santi locked in this house?" With that cryptic warning, Livia turned and left Quinn in a turmoil of confusion.

He was pretty sure he'd just gotten a glimpse of the good

Livia. The Livia who didn't like what she did. And like the others said, she wasn't all bad.

"I do not understand that woman."

"What was that place, Quinn?" Santi asked with a yawn.

"What place?" He crawled back into his bed and curled up next to her, eager for a chance to rest peacefully beside her for a little longer.

"Your home. Kelleys Island. The swing. Where were we?" she asked.

"That was my dream." He looked at her with a sense of growing dread.

"I was there with you, Quinn. That wasn't just a dream." She turned in his arms, nuzzling into his chest. She was so exhausted, her eyes were already drooping. "Whatever it was, it was nice."

"Rest while you can, Mina," he whispered. He would let her sleep as long as she could. But Quinn wasn't sure he ever wanted to sleep again.

It can't be that. The gift was rare. A relic of a dead world. The gift of dreamwalking hadn't manifested in centuries. He needed to get out of Soma more than ever now. He would need his family to get through this. To be a dreamwalker without a mentor could be a disaster for him and anyone he touched in the dreamworld.

CHAPTER 14

Sasha: Summer - The Chola Valley Temple

It turned out Jayesh wasn't quite as Zen as Sasha. Weeks later and he was still a closed-off prick, but they had at least reached a place where they could work together, despite the tension between them.

He's still blaming me, Sasha thought as she moved through the *kalaripayattu* forms beside him. She matched her movements to his, bending her body and flexing her muscles as he guided her through the poses. The exercise felt good. With each passing day she was becoming more limber and her joints more flexible. She knew it would benefit her later to get these movements perfected now. Once she began active sparring with Jayesh she would be glad she had.

They worked well together during these moments. *During these silent moments.* It was only when they had to communicate with words that things started to fall apart.

"Time to go." Jay clapped her on the shoulder just as she moved into the last position, causing her to stumble.

"Where're we going?" She crossed the pavilion to gather her sunglasses and slippers, adding an indigo silk headscarf to protect her from the sun. But Jay was already halfway up the path to the northern gates and she had to jog to catch up with him.

"Higher ground." He pointed across the grassy valley up to the wilder terrain toward the Ghat Mountains in the distance.

"How far do the temple grounds reach? I mean, the mother's influence?" Sasha asked.

"Many, many miles in each direction," Jayesh said. "All the way to the Arabian Sea to the west and to the far reaches of the valley to the east. North over the high mountain peaks and south to the foothills where we entered the valley."

"And mortals can't wander into this region?"

"They can. But they see only the temple ruins when they come. The mother's influence makes them wary of this place, though. Whenever they do venture close, they never stay long."

They hiked in silence. Sasha struggled to keep up with him in her inappropriate-for-hiking slippers. She had often thought about continuing her bratty behavior over the last weeks, but she'd decided to take the first steps toward cutting the bullshit. They might not like each other, but if they were going to get anywhere, they had to put their mutual dislike aside. Still, Jayesh seemed to be finding it difficult to remember how to *not* be an asshole.

"Seriously, where are we going?" Sasha finally asked after they crested yet another hill.

"We're here," Jayesh said, pointing at the sheer cliff below and the rough terrain of the mountains in the distance.

Sasha crossed to the cliff edge to scan the view. Rocky mountains rose in the distance and trees grew in patches of jungle-like forests, interspersed with grassy plains. As she turned, she saw that the temple monks had traveled ahead of them and set up a clearing for target practice. There were various weapons spread out on a makeshift table, but Sasha only had eyes for the beautiful piece of machinery calling her name.

"Can I, please?" She brushed her fingertips over the cool metal surface of the sniper rifle. "This is a Barrett M107A1?" She leaned down to get a good look at it. "This thing is badass. I can't wait to shoot it. Look at this!" She picked up the shell ammunition. "This a .50 Cal, long-range armor piercing round!" She held up the five-inch bullet that looked more like a tiny missile.

"Uh, yeah. I think so." Jayesh tried to hide his surprise at her enthusiasm.

"Can-I-Can-I-Can-I?" Sasha danced in place; she couldn't wait to try it.

"Not yet." He turned her away from the pretty gun. "Lunch first, and then we start small."

Refreshments waited for them in the shade of a canopy where the temple monks relaxed. Jayesh offered her a cool drink.

"You've been busy." She accepted the drink, wondering when he'd arranged this. "What am I shooting?" She scanned the horizon, expecting to see long-range targets in the distance.

"Over here," Jay said. "Like I said, we're starting small."

An array of clay birds sat in a basket beside the table along with a simple bow and a quiver of arrows.

"No." She shook her head. "No, no, no. Jayesh, you cannot dangle a Barrett M107A1 with *armor-piercing* rounds in my face and then put a bow in my hand. It's not cool, man. *Not* cool."

"Show me you can hit a moving target first and then we'll move up to the big guns."

"You were informed what I can do with my gift, right?"

"I'm not interested in seeing anything flashy, angel. I just want to see if you can hit the broad side of a barn, and then we'll talk."

"Ugh! Enough with the 'angel' crap. It's insulting. And what makes you think I can't hit the broad side of a barn?"

"You wouldn't be the first young Immortal to disappoint. Your generation is all talk. Special snowflakes with 'unique and astounding abilities' and your parents have stoked your egos into thinking you are more capable than you actually are. I'd rather see for myself if you can really do what I've been told you can."

"I'm shooting that gun before we leave today. That's like giving my brother a Stradivarius and telling him he can't play it."

"I don't know what that means, but show me you can follow directions and we'll see about having a demonstration later."

"I don't need a demo. Me and guns, we're friends."

"Lunch, Sasha. Eat something and then we'll get to the fun stuff. I promise."

"Fine." She took a seat under the shade of the canopy and helped herself to the buffet the monks had spread out for them. "What do you need to see from me?"

She couldn't show him how good she really was, but she needed to show him enough to put an end to his doubt.

"Arrows." Jay slid the bow over to her side. Except it wasn't the kind of bow Sasha was used to training with. It was a rudimentary sapling bow. The most un-gun-like thing Jayesh could possibly find. But Sasha could shoot anything, and as long as her gift connected with the target, her aim was infallible.

Don't get cocky. That was what he expected. She selected an arrow from the quiver and strung the bow. Her gift never missed, but she could. If her head wasn't in it and her gift failed to connect, she could miss the easiest shot. She had to walk a dangerous line today. She had to be good. But she couldn't be too good. She had to fail at the right moments. She had to have her head on straight and her gift under her firm control. And that required a level of focus and calm she did not currently have. And Jayesh knew it. He was testing her.

"Just need a minute to get my focus on." She stepped into the sunlight.

Sasha walked up to the edge of the cliff, taking a moment to really see the world stirring to life all around her. She smiled, closing her eyes as her conscious mind sought the wildlife lurking just out of sight. The Senate might demand the use of her target ability. That was all they could see when they looked at her. But they didn't need to know all the cards she carried. Sasha drew strength from nature. She was in her element here in the wilds of ancient India. As she focused on the untouched world around her, she'd never felt more alive. For a moment, she put herself in their place. She soared with the birds, experiencing the joy of their flight. She ran with the predators deep in the forest, thrilling at the exhilaration of the hunt.

When she opened her eyes, returning to herself, she'd found her center. The animal kingdom never failed to set her at ease. With a deep breath, Sasha notched an arrow along the bowstring and took aim at the sky. When she was ready, Brother Raj would launch the clay target over the cliffside and she would have mere seconds to connect with the target and take aim.

Jay was giving her an easy first shot and she needed to make it.

"Ready," she said.

The monk flung the clay bird into a high arc, giving her plenty of time to call the target with her gift. She felt it, stirring low in her chest, the icy burn of her power as familiar as her next breath. Her eyes followed the clay bird's flight. The breeze stilled as she searched for the break in the air, the tiniest indication that told her when to release the arrow. She took a breath. Counted down slowly in her mind, keeping her focus on the target. As it began to fall, arcing back toward the ground, Sasha's breath caught in her throat and the world went silent when she released the arrow.

She didn't need to look. She knew exactly where her arrow would pierce the clay bird.

"What's next?" she asked. "More birds?"

"Take a few more shots with the bow," he replied. "But let's see how you do with multiple targets."

"Nice shot, Ms. Sasha," Brother Raj said.

"Thank you." She bowed respectfully to the monk. "Let's go with three birds this time and give me about five seconds between each."

"Two birds. Ten seconds," Jayesh corrected. "We're starting slow, Sasha. I know you can do much more with your gift. This isn't about you showing off. It's about me seeing your gift in action."

"Did I complain?" She raised her brow but he didn't acknowledge her question. "No, I didn't complain because I get it, Jayesh. I'm not an idiot." Sometimes the man made her want to break things with her fists. She could feel her pulse pounding in her veins.

You're supposed to be Zen, Sasha. This is not good for my blood pressure ... or my gift. Her gift came to her only when she was in a meditative state, and for it to work properly, she had to push everything else away.

It took her a moment, but she found her center and didn't miss a single shot with the bow. When she moved on to the handguns and multiple targets, Jay asked her to hit one specific target of the three or four birds the monks pitched for her. It was elementary stuff, but she waited as patiently as she could.

"Give me something a little harder this time?" She set her handguns down and traded them for the repeating rifle.

"Hit all five this time," he said, nodding to the monks to set her targets in motion.

Sasha took aim and sighted down the first clay bird, taking them each in rapid succession.

"Very good."

Sasha was surprised to hear real praise coming from him.

"Good enough to test drive the big gun?" she asked.

"One shot."

"Yes!" She watched eagerly as Jay rolled out a rubber mat and moved the enormous weapon to the ground, just at the cliff edge. She waited impatiently for him to sight down a target.

"Come, let me show you." He gestured for her to lay beside him on the mat.

She listened carefully as Jayesh demonstrated how to use the high-powered lens to zero in on the steel plate target he'd set up more than two thousand yards away.

"I put a block of ballistics gel behind the plate so we can see how clean a shot you can get from here.

Sasha laughed as she switched places with him.

"What's so funny?"

"This is so not how I thought I'd be spending my summer."

"You're a little bit of a weirdo, aren't you? Most girls your age get excited about fancy shoes and boys, right?"

"Don't get me wrong, Jay. I like shoes and boys, probably even more than most girls, but guns are my jam." She smiled as she positioned herself behind the lens to get a feel for the weapon.

In that moment, as much as she wanted to succeed, she knew she needed to miss the shot. Jayesh needed to be reminded that she wasn't infallible. That someone her age couldn't be trusted behind a sniper rifle when the situation was real.

"Take a breath and focus," Jayesh said, his hand at her back to steady her. "When you're ready, pull the trigger and be prepared for the recoil. It's going to kick like a bull."

Sasha felt a flutter in her chest at his nearness.

He smells nice. The errant thought sent a spike of dread through her. Jay was certainly attractive, but she did not need to be crushing on her trainer. Especially not the arrogant jerk laying beside her. *What's wrong with me?* Guilt sent her reeling. She owed Quinn more loyalty.

Sasha took a deep breath, letting her emotions take precedence over her gift. She aimed, waited for the subtle warning of her gift to pass and fired.

"You missed," Jayesh said.

She wasn't certain how he would react when she missed the first time, but the chill of his tone terrified her.

"Why did you miss?" he asked. "I was told you never miss."

"I never miss the target when my gift is engaged. Sometimes my focus is off, and I don't connect with the target. When that happens, I can miss."

"Explain." He stood with his arms behind his back, watching her like a predator waiting to pounce on its prey.

Sasha rose to face him. "Sometimes I just don't feel it, Jay." She shrugged. "There is no other explanation."

"That isn't good enough, Sasha. You must practice until there is no room for error."

"Which is exactly what my training has been about in the two years since my Awakening. I had this ridiculous notion that I would have all this time to master this gift. I guess I'm expected to perform well beyond my years, then?"

"Yes, you are young." He stood ramrod straight in front of

her. "But you need to accept that the Senate will demand perfection. Explain."

"When I'm in that moment, right before I take a shot, I need to be centered. I need to be calm and I need to feel it when my gift engages with the target. When that happens, I will not miss."

"And if you're in a situation where it is impossible to be calm and serene? I need to understand every aspect of your gift before I can ever trust you to join my team. You will tell me what it takes to make your gift work when it matters."

"*You* need to trust *me*?" Sasha glared, her eyes simmering with rage. She'd had enough. "You. Trust. Me?" She leaned in to him. "What about me trusting you? You arrogant ass. Do you think for one moment that I'm stupid enough to trust you with the knowledge of every nuance of my gift when we live in a world that teaches us the exact opposite? You think my mother didn't teach me to guard the secrets of my power with my life? You trained with her. You know her ways. Do you really think Naeemah El Sadawii would teach me to give in so easily just because someone older and stronger tells me I'm supposed to trust him when he hasn't even earned it? This goes against every fiber of my being. And you want to be able to trust me? Trust is a two-way street, Jayesh. I'm not one of your soldiers. I'm not even out of high school yet. I know you need to trust my gift, but you need to back the hell off and show me you're worth trusting."

Jay took a step back, his face pale in the heat of the day. He clearly wasn't accustomed to anyone standing up to him the way she continuously did.

"Of course. You're right." He nodded absently. "You are so young. I know this is difficult." His voice sounded distant as if he hadn't heard a single word she'd said. "You will continue to practice on your own here for the rest of the afternoon. I—I want you to feel at ease when you practice and clearly my presence is affecting you negatively. I will leave you to it."

With that, Jayesh turned and walked away.

"What just happened?" Sasha asked.

"It appears the young man isn't prepared to take on the role of teacher yet," Brother Rabishan said, watching Jayesh disappear into the valley. "It's a shame. We were having fun."

"I don't know what that was, but something spooked him and it wasn't me going teen brat on him."

"Perhaps you are simply more than he expected," Rabishan said, shaking with laughter. "But you are absolutely right, young Sasha. He must earn your trust if he expects you to fully commit to becoming a Chola assassin. I'm afraid you two are going to have to find a way to become friends if you are ever to move forward."

"I have enough friends, thanks," Sasha muttered.

CHAPTER 15

Quinn: Fall - Atlanta, Georgia

"What is *with* you two?" Livia threw her hands up in disgust. "You have the chance to use each other to make your own situations better, but you're so concerned about the other, you're torturing yourselves for no reason. It's just prolonging the inevitable and making this harder than it needs to be."

"It's called being a decent human being," Santi said. "You must have missed that lesson growing up."

"Well, being a decent human being never got me anywhere." Livia shoved her hands into her boxing gloves, a sure sign she was annoyed. Quinn just hoped she'd vent her frustrations on the punching bag instead of his face. One hit and he would go down like a sack of rocks.

Quinn flexed his shoulders, trying to work out the ache in his back. He was so hungry and exhausted from Livia's demented schedule he wasn't sure how he was still on his feet. His reprieve had been short and sweet, and now he was caught up in Soma's newest torture scheme.

Every morning for the last month, Livia delivered Quinn to the entrance of Soma's version of the Yard. A ten-thousand-square-foot warehouse connected to Sterling Tower via an underground tunnel. The warehouse was the result of a myriad of gifts, much like the Yard was at home. When stepping into the warehouse for the first time, Quinn felt like he'd stepped through a portal to another realm. The forest was unlike anything he'd ever seen, dense and dark with menacing plant life that grew quickly and crept along the ground in an unnatural way. The whole place was unnatural. From the wildlife lurking in the darkness, right up to the sheer mountain peak hidden among dark, swirling clouds.

Each morning he was given the same task: run to the top of the mountain to retrieve a two-hundred-pound log waiting for him there. If he dropped it on the way down, he had to start over. The old Immortal who lived in the warehouse was responsible for the landscape, which changed constantly from one week to the next. The terrain grew more challenging each week and the log became heavier and more difficult to find. The expanse of wilderness inside the building defied the laws of physics, but the old Immortal's ability was extraordinary. Quinn had five hours each day to complete the task. If he failed, Santi was sent to Michael for the night while Quinn was given a feast and a full night's sleep. He rarely failed.

But failure was the whole point of the impossible exercise. They were supposed to fail, but neither of them could face what that failure meant for the other. So Quinn spent his days running up the mountain and back down as fast as he possibly could. Every day he dropped the log at Santi's feet with barely a moment to spare, his clothes drenched in sweat and his heart racing in his chest. It was her job to return the log to the top of the mountain each afternoon. If she failed, Quinn was sent to Michael for the night while she got to feast and rest. She rarely failed, but when she did, Michael made sure it was the worst night of Quinn's life.

After Quinn completed his daily task he trained with Livia

in her private gym in the evenings. She spent hours pushing him further and further into his addiction, keeping him dancing on the cusp of going too far.

And on the nights when he'd failed his task, he had to see the fear in Santi's eyes when Michael came to collect her. The food tasted like ash and he tossed and turned the whole night worrying about her. On the nights when they were both successful, Santi and Quinn spent a quiet night together on the wide balcony that ran the length of the penthouse. They weren't allowed to eat or sleep, but they found solace in each other.

"Hold my bag, Quinn. I need to hit something."

"Liv, what you need is a good, long talk with a therapist," he muttered as he took his place behind the punching bag.

"Quinn's got jokes." Livia laughed, landing her first strike, leaving him breathless.

His time at Soma had taught him one thing: Livia was merciless, but that wasn't the real Livia. He suspected she had no idea who she really was.

Quinn let out a grunt when her foot connected with the bag. He stood, clinging to the punching bag so he didn't fall over. An outsider might wonder what had her so furious, but he knew. She hated watching them struggle. She hated doing this to them. Deep down, she wanted them to take turns failing so at least one of them would get a good meal and some much-needed rest. Livia didn't understand how they could care so much about each other in such a short time that they would be willing to kill themselves every day just to see that the other didn't have to suffer at Michael's hand.

"Tell me why you make this so difficult," Livia said as she flew into a high kick.

That was the thing about Livia. When she got frustrated, she didn't immediately lash out in anger like Michael did. She backed away and dropped the facade, carefully considering her next move, always trying to understand their point of view. Like now. In moments like this, he almost liked her. The Livia he first met was the type to do something extreme to get their attention. To remind them who was in charge. But as the weeks went by and they continued their "training," she was becoming less of a monster and more of a person with a very demanding job. Her job just happened to be bringing them to heel, and neither Santi nor Quinn were making it easy on her.

Did I just feel bad for her?

Livia launched into a complicated sequence of kicks and strikes, taking her frustrations out on the bag.

"The momentary comfort of food and rest just isn't worth putting him through that," Santi said. "But that's the point, isn't it? We're not supposed to enjoy those things. It's a double-edged sword. I screw over my friend, I get food and sleep, but I don't enjoy it because I screwed over my friend. Put yourself in my place, Liv."

"I'm trying to."

"Then put your mother in Quinn's place and ask yourself if you wouldn't race up and down that mountain even harder than we do if that was all it took to keep her away from Michael ... or your father."

"I see," Livia said, her brow furrowed in concentration. "But she's my mother. You two aren't anything to each other."

"Haven't you ever had a friend you cared about?" Quinn asked.

"Sure, but I wouldn't give up a good meal for them." Livia landed another kick.

"Then you don't understand people at all." He winced at her punch. He cared more for Santi than he was ready to admit, even to himself, but there was no way he was going to be responsible for allowing Michael to lay one hand on her. Not as long as it was in his power to stop.

"Love?" Livia sneered. "Love only causes problems. Look what it's doing to you two."

"That's not what's happening here." Quinn flushed. "And it's none of your business."

"I'd say we're more in the heavy *like* phase at the moment, but it works the same for helping you understand, Liv." Santi shot Quinn a wink. "When you care about someone, you don't put your own needs before theirs."

"Even if it's pointless? You guys think you're holding out—that you'll manage to gain your freedom from this place. But it's a pipedream. It's time you both accept it and start looking out for your own interests. Soma is your life. My father will never let you leave."

"Your father. You talk about *your father* like that's supposed to scare us when it doesn't mean anything. We don't know anything about him." Quinn was sick of her empty threats and punishments one moment and then in the next, she really seemed to be trying to understand them. Livia was an impossible woman.

"Quinn, you remember the night I took you from your family?" She jabbed a right hook, landing her punch and whirling a round house kick a little too close to his face for comfort.

"Uh, yeah, that kind of thing stays with you, Liv."

"Then you remember how I told you if you proved to be loyal and useful, that life with the Coalition didn't have to be the atrocity you've been raised to believe."

"Well, this isn't the Coalition, is it?" Quinn snorted in disgust.

"Isn't it?" Livia cocked her head.

"What are you saying?" Santi asked. Her chain rattled

across the floor as she reached for a bottle of water from the fridge. Not for herself or for Quinn, but for Livia, because it was her job to anticipate everything Livia ever needed before she needed it.

"Soma *is* the Coalition, my little darlings." She waved the water away, turning instead to throw another round of punches and kicks.

"It's obvious you have some kind of deal with them. You have Coalition agents running in and out of this place," Santi said. "But they still act independently. They couldn't possibly be under complete Immortal control."

"My father—my *Immortal* father—is Marcus Servius. Also known as the reigning *mortal* Marches, Marius Von Essen IV, among his many other aliases. Head of the Coalition. Leader of the Margrave council. The fools haven't realized they practically worship the very thing they profess to hate. They follow him like blind sheep—the same man who has led them for nearly three hundred years. Marcus infiltrated the Coalition in the fifteenth century. He established himself and our family as a Coalition dynasty, making himself his own heir generation after generation. Eventually he created the Margrave and turned the Coalition into what it is today. Without him, they would still be the same mindless, unorganized zealots they were when he found them." Livia kicked the bag, sending Quinn staggering across the room to land on his back.

"Immortals have controlled every aspect of the Coalition as you know it. When I said it doesn't have to be the terrible thing you heard horror stories about growing up, I meant it. You are on the right side of things. You two are strong. You have useful abilities. I will break you if I must, but it would be so much easier if you'd join me as allies. Surrender your unconditional loyalty to me, to Soma and the Coalition, and I can protect you as part of my personal team and household. This exhausting game we're playing, it could all end right now." She turned to gauge their reactions.

It was an offer she'd never extended before. An offer many in their shoes would leap to take.

"I'd rather not have to destroy you to gain your allegiance," Livia added.

"No," Quinn and Santi said in unison. They didn't even need to discuss it. "You're asking us to betray our own kind—our families. It's just not an option. This...." Santi gestured to the whole of Soma. "This is not how you earn a person's allegiance."

Quinn nodded in agreement as he sat up, but his voice caught in his throat. Something oppressive crashed into him. A presence unlike any he'd ever experienced threatened to suffocate him. He couldn't seem to get back on his feet or catch his breath.

"What's the matter with you now?" Livia said. "I couldn't have hit you that hard ... shit." She turned toward the door. "He's here. Ummm ... hide. Now!" She tugged her gloves off and dumped half the contents of the water bottle over her head. "On the balcony. Quick."

She heaved Quinn up to his feet and ushered them toward the back of the gym and onto the balcony beyond the open glass partitions. She frantically shoved them against the brick wall.

"Here. Get down and keep quiet. He'll take you from me if he senses your strength. You don't want that."

"What's going on?" Santi demanded.

"Please, Santi. Hide," Livia begged as she broke Santi's restraints, sending the chain retracting back into the wall.

It was so unlike her it startled Quinn. The silvery ice of her eyes warmed into green fire as she stepped back inside, returning to her punching bag.

He pulled Santi down to the cool slate floor, crouching in

the corner. He couldn't fathom why Livia wanted them to hide from the Immortal who'd just entered the building and was on his way up to the penthouse. But if his ancient lifeline was any indication, simply hiding was not going to shield them from Livia's father. Quinn pulled an oversized wicker lounge in front of them, praying she wouldn't do what he knew she was about to do.

"Won't he sense us?" Santi whispered.

"She has a plan for that and I'm sure it involves me," Quinn said. "Lay down here beside me, Santi." Quinn maneuvered their position until they were both laying on the floor behind the lounge, peering through the bottom of the glass partition. From their vantage point, they had a good view of the gym where Livia was busy beating the hell out of her punching bag as if she'd spent the afternoon working out at home alone.

“Stay quiet and do *not* fight me on this, Quinn. I'm honestly trying to help you,” Livia whispered as she backed away from the bag, glancing in their direction. Her power charged through him like a kick from a bull. Whatever control she'd exerted over him before was nothing compared to the force she pressed against him now.

“What's happening?” Santi reached for him when he cried out. Her hands fluttered over his face, searching for something she could do.

“She's using my gift to shield us.” Quinn managed to get the words out, but between his fear of Livia pushing him too far and the arrival of the oldest Immortal he'd ever sensed, he was a total wreck.

“Is it ... her father?” Santi's voice was almost inaudible as she shrank against him, pulling his arms around her, trying to make herself as small as possible.

Quinn nodded, holding on to Santi as tightly as she clung to him. Their lives depended on remaining silent. If Livia's father sensed them, it wouldn't bode well for either of them. If Quinn hadn't seen it with his own eyes, he wouldn't believe it, but Livia was protecting them. She drew on his cloaking ability like a leech, taking everything she could from him to shield both Santi and Quinn, not just from her father's sight, but from sensing their Immortal presence—something Quinn himself could not do with his own gift. He'd often suspected he would be able to do that eventually, but it was decades beyond his current ability.

"Where are you?" The curt voice reached them from the penthouse living room. Livia's father didn't deign to shout for her, but his urgency was clear.

"In here, Father," Livia called in such a calm voice, Quinn would never suspect she was in the midst of using her power in such a way. "I've just been working out," she said, dabbing a towel over her brow to mop up the "sweat" from her workout. "I thought we were meeting at the restaurant later. I'm sorry, I wasn't expecting you." Her tone was respectful and polite but there was no warmth there for the man who'd raised her.

"It's urgent." Her father marched into the gym like he owned the place—which he probably did.

Quinn and Santi peeked through the window, watching with bated breath.

"Can I get you a drink? You look like you could use one. Let's go to my office and sit." Livia tried to direct him out of the room and away from her two charges, but the ancient Immortal just sat on the weight bench in his Italian suit and waved his bodyguards away, gesturing for them to close the door behind them.

"This must be bad," Livia said dryly, crossing her arms over her chest.

"She's escaped."

"Who? Mother?" Livia frowned.

"No, of course not. Your mother is safe at home."

"Still in her gilded cage?" Livia sank to the floor opposite her father.

"I don't have the patience for that old argument, Livia. We have much more important issues to discuss than where I allow your mother to spend her time."

"You must mean the queen, then? She's escaped?" Livia asked in surprise. "She's been your most prized captive for two thousand years. How on earth did she manage it?"

Santi frowned up at Quinn in confusion, and he shrugged in response. They couldn't possibly be talking about the queens of Indriell. They all died ages ago.

"That is not important right now," Livia's father said, his voice like acid.

"Mother let her go, didn't she. What did you do to her?" Livia stood up like a shot, facing her father with a riot of emotions flitting across her face. Fear, intimidation and fury.

"Despite what you think of me, I only have your mother's best interest at heart. She means more to me than you will ever know, but yes. I did have to punish her for her transgressions against me."

"Where is she?"

"That is why I am here. You will lead the hunt for the queen."

"Not the damned queen! Where is my mother?"

"Porcia is fine, but you'll not see her again until you have returned Alísun to me. Your mother's visitation privileges have been revoked for the time being."

"She isn't a child you can just ground to her room when she displeases you. She's a powerful ancient and you treat her like her only role in life is to amuse you ... and obey your every decree."

"Livia, stay on point." His eyes flickered with impatience.

"Fine. You want my team to lead the hunt for an eight-thousand-year-old queen of Indriell? It's impossible." Livia took a deep breath, squaring her shoulders and looking her father in the eye.

Most young Immortals in her shoes would cower and hang their heads in the presence of such an ancient. Her bravery in the face of her father's ire said more for her character than anything Quinn had witnessed from her since his arrival at Soma.

Livia continued to draw on Quinn's power, pulling him into that dreaded danger zone—the imaginary line in the sand where he stopped using his power with care and started using it for pleasure.

We like her at the helm. She gives us a taste for freedom. The voice of his gift hissed in his mind. The voice he hadn't heard in years. It was a warning signal that he was reaching the point of no return. He needed Livia to stop pushing him—now. Or it was going to be too late for Quinn.

"No," he begged, trying to resist Livia, but she wasn't having it. She took what she needed to shield them, sending him racing for the edge of his endurance.

Quinn groaned in frustration. The taste of so much power coursing through his body lured him in. It didn't matter that he wasn't in control—that she could do whatever she wanted with him. He wanted this.

Yes! That's right, Quinn, his gift agreed. *Just let go. Let us have this. It's what we need.*

No. I can't do this again. But the more he focused on the power raging inside of him, the more he wanted to fall down the rabbit hole. He wanted nothing more than to give in to the urge—to use again. The temptation was always there. But no matter how far Livia pushed him before, he'd always fought to stay in control. But in that moment, he was more afraid of what would happen if he gave in to the addiction than what Marcus would do if he discovered Livia's prized pupils.

Soft hands cupped his face. "Stay with me, Quinnton," Santi whispered in his ear, pulling him back into the moment with her. "You're okay. Let her do what she needs to do. I won't let you give in to the addiction. Focus on me."

"Santi." He pressed his face into her hair, too ashamed to meet her gaze.

"Look at me, Quinn." She tilted his face toward hers. "It doesn't define you and it doesn't lessen the person you are in here." She tapped his forehead. "I've seen power like yours before. I've seen the strength it takes to resist the temptations. You're a rock. You don't have it in you to fail. Focus on me and we'll get through this together. One breath at a time."

His lips found hers and he held on to her, letting her be the rock he needed in that moment.

"And how shall I find her?" Livia demanded. "I have nothing to go on and since you will not let me speak with Mother, I can't know what the queen might be thinking. Who she will seek? Where she will go? She has been a captive for two thousand years. This modern world will frighten her."

"I've been told she plans to go back to where it all began," her father said.

"What does that even mean? Where do I start? My team is good. But we've always focused on the younger generations. The best, brightest and youngest. That's what you've always wanted for Soma—an army of the most technologically advanced Immortals on earth. We rarely hunt anyone more than a few decades old. You're setting us up for failure. I don't do failure, Father. You know that. So tell me what I need to know."

"She will seek her Complement. Together they will 'return to where it all began.' That is the key to finding them."

"Her Complement? I can't recall who he was." She frowned.

"Every Immortal on the planet knows of Alexander, but when asked, they can't recall a single detail about him. Hunt for Alexander. When you find him, you will find Alísun."

"Alexander? The Scholar?" Livia gaped. "You expect me to find a man who refuses to be found? A man half our world is convinced is a myth and the other half believes is a joke?"

"The Scholar is a useless old loon with a flair for the dramatic. Find him. Find him before she does and he will lead you to her. They aren't smart enough to stay away from each other. Not after two thousand years apart. Their weakness is their bond."

"But isn't that the weakness of all Complements? In your estimation, at least?" Livia's mocking tone could cut glass.

"The Complement bond is our greatest weakness, child. The need for that other person drives us to do stupid things. In Indriell we never recognized the bond. Not among the nobility. Until Alísun's mother, Eiselynn, betrayed me and bonded with that commoner, Ian. That was the day our world began to fall apart. The royals messed with the natural order that day. It led to the Great War and sullied the power for us all, yielding the world to the mortal masses. I will see order restored. I will see the royal line extinguished. It is time."

"As you have reminded me constantly for the last decade," Livia muttered.

"My gift lives again, my child. I can feel it. The ancient royals have done everything in their power to shield their line from me, but I will find the boy from Alísun's prophecy. I set the task to you more than a decade ago and you've failed time and again to bring him to me. He will be approaching his Awakening soon if he hasn't already. It is vital we find him before his gifts fully manifest. This setback with the queen must be resolved straightaway. I want you back in the field, tracking this royal offspring who had the audacity to be born with my gift."

"This *boy* you seek, Father ... will you just take what belongs to you and leave him to rot?"

"I will drain him, and when given the chance, I will see him dead. The Indriell line will end with him and those bonded to him through birth or other means. A new order will arise from the ashes of their dead kingdom. It is long past time Immortals stopped hiding. Alísun gave our world away, but we will take it back before the mortals destroy it like the cockroaches they are."

"And Lord Teigan will rise again to take the throne for himself," Livia whispered.

"You mock me, but the world will know me as the Lord Teigan again when I shed the name Marcus Servius. And I will reward you for all your hard work, my daughter. See you don't betray me and you will rise with me."

"If things had gone the way they should have, you wouldn't have risen to power as Eiselynn's consort all those years ago. *She* was destined to be queen and ruler of Indriell and *you* were meant to be nothing more than powerful DNA to pass on to her daughter. Can't you let it go and ... I don't know, live your life for once? Or let those around you live theirs?"

“Eiselynn was weak. I was chosen as her consort because I could rule in a way she couldn’t. The queen’s council was on my side and she swayed them back to hers. I will have what the *Enlightened* failed to give me. And this time I will win. You are part of my master plan, my darling girl. The world will be your oyster. I will lay it at your feet one day soon. See that you do your job. Find Alexander and you will find the queen. If you cannot deliver them both to me, collared and on their knees, bring me Alexander and I will use him to manipulate her.”

"Who is Alexander?" Livia asked, shaking her head in confusion.

"This will be impossible if you do not focus, Livia." Marcus heaved a great sigh of impatience. "Alex is the Scholar. His gift will make you forget everything you know about him as quickly as you remember it. You have to resist his influence."

"How do you expect me to find a man I keep forgetting exists?"

"He is a scholar. He is weak. You and your team can overpower him if you can get close enough. Get to him before the queen does. If she finds him first, I will be displeased. The queen is a prophet, a psychic and a warrior. You and your team have no chance against her. Get to the Scholar and she will show herself. She will sacrifice herself to save him the life she has known under my care."

"And how do you propose I do that? Approach the Scholar when he can see me coming?"

"Jayesh will be arriving shortly to help. Let his gift do the work for you. But my sources tell me you have a talented young man with a gift for invisibility. I suspect you are shielding this boy from me even now. Your eyes give you away, my dear. I know how you keep your most difficult children close, yet the house is empty except for you and I—but you wield your power as if surrounded by enemies. Use Jayesh to stay a step ahead of Alex and then use the boy to trap him. She will show herself. Bring the queen to me. And then, for God's sake, finish breaking the boy. You're dragging your feet with this one and that girl you've insisted time and again is useful. Do with her what you will, but I'll expect you to either prepare the boy for market or train him to join my staff."

"I'll see him sold to the highest bidder before I'll ever hand him over to you."

"Still money in my pocket, my dear. Either way, it is your choice." He stood to leave.

"What of my mother?" Livia demanded.

"Porcia is at home where she belongs. Comfortable, surrounded with everything she could ever want."

"Except the freedom to come and go as she pleases?"

"Until I reunite with my gift, it is not safe for her to be out in the world. She will have her freedom one day. She understands that."

"She hates you for it, but she loves you enough to allow you to have your way. She will eventually tire of it." Livia shook her head in disgust.

“I believe you have a mission to plan, daughter.”

“Of course, Father.”

“Then I will see you when you get back. Call in any of the reserves you need. My resources are at your disposal, as always. Jayesh has just completed a mission for the Senate, in some godforsaken corner of Africa. He'll be back home soon. You two can make quick work of this problem if you'll stop bickering like spoiled siblings long enough to work together. I expect to see the queen back where she belongs. Immediately.”

Quinn and Santi sat in stunned silence for a long time after the ancient left the building, clinging together as they watched Livia resumed her stance at the punching bag. She drew on Quinn's power until he was a breath away from losing control. Santi's constant murmurs of encouragement kept him grounded.

With a last resounding kick, Livia burst the bag, the sandy contents running out like time from an hourglass, falling to the pristine white floor. Her shoulders sagged and she let out a deep breath, releasing her hold on Quinn for the moment.

His breath rattled in his chest, and Santi had to help him up.

"So now you know," Livia muttered as they joined her. "I'm just as trapped as you are. But my father is deluded enough to think that because he doesn't brand me with his mark that it doesn't make me his slave. Come with me; we need to meet with my team to discuss our plan. I'll need you both for this mission. We leave tomorrow night."

Chapter 16

Sasha: Summer - The Chola Valley Temple

"Stubborn, arrogant ass!" Sasha paced along the edge of the fountain, waiting for Mother Raghavan to join her for their evening walk through her private gardens.

"What has you so frustrated this evening, Sasha El Sadawii?" the mother asked, surprising Sasha with her silent footsteps. "No doubt, Jayesh again?"

"The man is impossible to work with, mother." Sasha sighed. "Every time it seems we are making progress, he pulls away and we're back at square one again. I've tried, mother. I've really tried to make this work, but I'm afraid we're just spinning our wheels."

"Come, child. Let's walk in silence for a while. When you find you can again see the beauty of this world, rather than the turmoil of your own thoughts, we will talk."

Most of her evenings with Mother Raghavan began this way. Sasha linked her arm through the mother's and walked beside her. Fuming.

For a moment, she'd thought she and Jayesh were finally getting somewhere. *And then he freaked out on me when I missed the shot. And then I freaked out on him.* Since then, he'd kept his distance. Even during their shared training sessions, he was distant and aloof.

"We're going nowhere fast."

"Still not seeing the beauty of the garden?" The mother chuckled softly. "So caught up in your own mind."

Mother Raghavan's private garden was a veritable Eden on earth. Sasha knew she should be focused on the flowers blooming with their fragrant perfumes. The colorful fish in the murky ponds. The ancient statues capturing the most impossible of the *kalari* forms. The majestic trees towering over them. The squish of the moss-covered stones beneath her feet. This oasis should be the one place where she could leave all thoughts of Jayesh behind.

But still she itched to wrap her hands around his throat.

With her next step, Sasha took a breath, exhaling deeply, focusing only on the act of breathing. She felt her pulse return to its normal rate and the tension finally left her body.

"Much better," Mother Raghavan said, patting Sasha's hand where it lay tucked against the crook of her elbow.

"I am sorry, mother. I should not bring my tension and anger into this sacred place of peace."

"Nonsense. This is what our evenings together are for, Sasha. You do not need me to tell you how well you are doing with the physical aspect of *meithari*. You are a born martial artist. You've trained all your life. This is all second nature to you."

"Then why are we still stuck in phase one? I'm going crazy with the sameness of every day."

"*Meithari* is the most important phase of your training here, child. It is the first stage because in some ways it is the hardest. The rest will come in time, but you will never succeed without *meithari*."

"Maybe I'm just not getting the lesson, mother."

"Perhaps you should try to see things from his point of view, rather than your own," the mother suggested as they walked.

"He treats me like a child."

"You are a child, dear. As much as it might seem like an insult, it is not. It is simply the truth."

"Then what am I missing?"

"Jayesh has never known the kind of life you have. A family who loves you. Wealth. Status. Friends. Stability. Jayesh's life has never really belonged to him. I believe he struggles to communicate with you because he simply does not understand how to talk to you. He's made assumptions about who you are because your life is completely foreign to him."

"That doesn't give him a license to react the way he does."

"It doesn't?"

"I've given him no reason not to trust me," Sasha said.

"You haven't?" The mother gave her a knowing smile. "When you missed your target, what were you doing to give Jayesh cause to react so harshly?"

I was deceiving him.

"He doesn't know you missed the shot on purpose," Mother Raghavan said. "The dear boy is not that perceptive. He is simply worried about what it will mean for you if you cannot meet the Senate's expectations. It is his responsibility to make you a success."

"I need to fail at this, mother. I am not ready to become a Chola assassin." *If we ever get through the training.*

"And have you given it a moment's consideration that Jayesh might agree with you? That he might not want to be the one to turn you into an assassin? That he might see you as an innocent girl he doesn't want to corrupt?"

"No." Sasha sighed.

“Have you considered that he is waiting for you to give him your trust? That he might be on your side in this mess?”

“No.” Sasha suddenly felt exactly like the child she was.

“You fear if you show him what you are truly capable of that he will betray that knowledge to the Senate and they will continue to demand your services even though you are not yet Proven.”

“Yes.” Sasha nodded. “I can’t risk it. I don’t want my life to belong to the Senate before I’ve even had a chance to live it.”

“A valid fear. But you are holding Jayesh accountable for a betrayal he hasn’t yet committed.”

“You are right.” Sasha laughed. “You usually are.”

“Come now.” The mother hugged her. “I’m not suggesting you reveal all of your deepest secrets to a man you’ve only just met. I’m simply suggesting that you meet him halfway. Isn’t that what you expect of him?”

“Yes, ma’am.” Sasha nodded again. The mother was right. How could she expect Jayesh to trust her if she was the one deceiving him at every possible turn?

“You will dust yourself off and try again, yes?”

“Yes, mother. I will.”

CHAPTER 17

Quinn: Fall - Atlanta, Georgia

"What do we know about the Scholar?" Livia demanded, staring at each member of her team in turn. They were few. Just Livia, Michael and Ryan, Quinn and Santi, and a woman named Selena.

They each were there for a reason, but Quinn and Santi seemed to be the only ones who would rather not be. The rest of the group ignored them as they sat at the edge of the room, trying not to get in the way. It was early evening and Livia planned to leave the following day, but they still didn't know where they were going.

"He was last seen in Viña Del Mar along the coast of Chile," Selena offered. "But he's been on the move. Spotted in different parts of the world. Cape Town, South Africa; Nigeria, Egypt and the Sudan." Selena scanned through her notes. "He's randomly showed up in rural Scotland and all across Eastern Europe. Then he had a really good time in the cafes of Amsterdam for a few days before heading off to the Philippines, Brazil, and back to Egypt, Indonesia, New Zealand and finally ended up in Sydney, Australia, just a few days ago." Selena let her notes fall to the table.

"Any idea where he is headed next?" Livia asked.

"No. But I would love the opportunity to collect his gift." Selena rubbed her hands together eagerly. "Can you imagine all that knowledge? I'll make a fortune!" Selena's gift allowed her take a gift from one Immortal and bestow it to someone else —usually the highest bidder.

"His gifts would melt your brain," Livia said. "Try it and I'll snap you like a twig." She gestured for her team to join her around the conference table inlaid with a map of the world in black onyx against a sea of white marble.

"We need to know where he'll show up next," Livia continued. "He and the queen will have a rally point. We need to figure out where that is."

"Where and when was she captured?" Ryan asked.

"She was taken somewhere in Africa in 259 BCE, and spent some time in a Coalition prison in Carthage before my father liberated her in 30 BCE. She's had no contact with the Scholar in all of that time, but a credible source says they intend to 'go back where it all began,'" Livia said. "But the start of what?" She glanced around the room, looking for answers.

"They would have needed a rally point that would stand the test of time," Michael said. "Maybe they meant the beginning of civilization? Somewhere in Mesopotamia?"

"Or did she mean the beginning of Indriell? It is believed Indriell was located near Egypt," Ryan offered.

Quinn listened as they threw out different suggestions. All useless. There was something to be said for his education. He knew volumes more than they did on the subject of Immortal history. He just wasn't sure if he should help them or let them hang themselves with their own ignorance. But he desperately needed this chance to get out of Sterling Tower. Nothing else mattered beyond this opportunity to escape with Santi. If a queen of Indriell still lived, he didn't want to be responsible for her capture. But if it got him out of Soma, it could be worth the risk.

These guys have zero chance of success anyway. They don't know what they're up against.

"Quinn, Santi? What do you know?" Livia demanded, snapping her fingers for them to join the discussion.

Quinn stood with a sigh. He would never forgive himself if this led to terrible things for the queen or the Scholar. He glanced down at Santi and she gave him a shrug as if to say they didn't really have a choice.

"What does your teaching tell of the last Indriell queen?"

"She was the best of them all. And if she still lives, I wouldn't underestimate her," Quinn said.

"Where would she go after she dismantled Indriell?"

"It depends on where you believe Indriell once existed. When Queen Alísun banished the first mortals, she laid waste to the entire realm and sent the remaining Immortals to the far corners of the world. She left no trace of her kingdom. Some believe Indriell must have existed around Mesopotamia because that is the cradle of all civilization, but the earliest known civilizations emerged around 3200 BCE. We've existed since long before the mortal cradle of life." Quinn moved a stone marker to modern-day Mesopotamia, placing it at the center of Eastern Turkey, Syria and Iraq before continuing.

"During the banishment, Alísun sent her mortal subjects as far away from Indriell as possible. Some believe she couldn't have sent them very far because that kind of travel wasn't possible back then, but this was during a time when most still wielded the pure power. They could do more than we can ever dream. Some believe they traveled the world much as we do today. Not in airplanes, but through other fast means of transportation fueled by the power. It is possible the queen did send them to the ends of the earth, but wherever they ended up, it took centuries for those mortals to figure out how to exist on their own. The banishment is believed to have occurred sometime around 5000 BCE. So what happened to those mortals in the nearly two millennia intervening? Did they stay wherever she sent them? No. They were nomads. They went where the food was. So if mortal civilization emerged in Mesopotamia and Egypt, how far did they travel from their original location?"

Quinn had the whole room's attention as he paused to take a breath.

"Immortal records indicate the first mortals were sent across two oceans before they reached the queen's destination. Then, for nearly two thousand years they wandered, so it is safe to assume some of them ended up in Egypt while others drifted to Mesopotamia." Quinn placed markers on the map at both areas of the world. "Scholars have suggested that the two oceans they crossed were the South Atlantic and the Indian oceans, and the original banishment took them to India along the Arabian Sea." He placed stone markers on each.

"How do we know this is accurate information?" Michael asked.

"It's accurate," Quinn said.

"Have you spoken to these *scholars*?" he replied with a sneer.

"I have."

"The scholars do not mix with the rest of us. They keep to their own. How can we trust this boy?" Selena asked.

"How do you know this information, Quinn? Tell me," Livia demanded.

"My great-grandparents are scholars. That is all I will say." Quinn folded his arms across his chest and refused to speak further about his grandmother's parents.

"Go on," Livia said.

"If they ended up in India and crossed two oceans to get

there, Indriell couldn't have existed on the same continent, right?" Quinn removed the marker representing the nation of Indriell in the Middle East, and placed it off the map. "Indriell wasn't just a small city-state with a single thriving city as most believe. It was the seat of the world and it was enormous. But there were earthquakes in the Great War. Massive ones that probably changed the map of the world, making this nothing more than an educated guess." He gave Livia a hard look to make sure she understood his words shouldn't be taken too literally.

"So where was it?" Livia asked.

"South America."

"Where in South America?"

"The entire South American continent was likely the nation of Indriell and it was nothing even remotely resembling what it is today."

Santi nodded. "It's true. The Mayan Immortals have records that would confirm much of what Quinn is saying. We believe the Maya just didn't go very far after Indriell was destroyed."

"But the Scholar has been in Chile for years," Selena said.

"He already went back to where it began." Quinn nodded, looking at the map again.

"So they could both be heading there now, and all his travels recently have just been a ploy to throw us off his trail?"

"The Scholar is said to be something of a trickster," Quinn said. "He likes messing with people. And let's never forget he has the knowledge of the world at his fingertips. He has constructed the history of ... everything. He's leading you on a goose chase. He's going to meet his wife where it all began—where Indriell fell and the banishment happened. The banishment caused many of the issues our world still struggles with today. They are circling back to where that struggle began. The banishment probably happened somewhere along the coast of Brazil. They traveled across the South Atlantic Ocean around the Cape of Good Hope and across the Indian Ocean to their new home."

"So where is he going? Where are they meeting?"

"He is going back to Indriell, where he's been all along, but he's not going to Chile." Quinn studied the map, recalling everything he could from his history lessons. "Rio de Janeiro." He tapped the coastline of Brazil, placing a new marker on the port city. "That is my best guess of a landmark they would both remember that would still be visible after so much time. It didn't become Rio until the sixteenth century, but port cities like that have always existed in some capacity. The statue of Christ the Redeemer atop Mount Corcovado has only been there for the last century, but it could be a good meeting place, don't you think? That is just a guess, though." Quinn stepped away from the table, praying Livia would buy it. It was a good guess, but he had no real reason to suspect that was where they were going. He just needed Livia to buy it long enough to get them out of Sterling Tower.

"Wow," Santi breathed. "That just happened."

Quinn looked around the room at all the blank-staring faces and wondered if he'd overdone it on the history lesson.

"Have his movements suggested that is where he is headed?" Livia asked.

Ryan nodded as he checked the dossier on the Scholar's movements. "It's possible."

"It's as good a place to start as anywhere," Livia sighed. "Let's get some rest and we'll reconvene in the morning to go over our most recent intel. We'll be on our way—somewhere—by tomorrow afternoon. You two are with me." She nudged Quinn and Santi out of the room and away from the prying eyes of the rest of her team.

"It's getting late." Livia checked the time as they headed back to her penthouse. "Go nuts in the kitchen. You both have my permission to eat whatever you want. But I would suggest you stick to foods that will give you the most energy. Then get some sleep. Both of you. You're going to need it."

As soon as they entered the foyer, Livia retreated to her study to continue planning their mission, and Santi made for the kitchen at once. She was trembling at the mere thought of a good meal. As she put water on to boil, she struggled with a box of pasta.

"Sit, Mina," Quinn said. "It's my turn to cook for you. What do you want?"

"I want *all* the carbs." She reached for a bag of Cheetos from the pantry along with a jar of peanut butter. "Cheesy pesto pasta with a big juicy steak and lots of garlic bread with cheese. And for dessert I want chocolate cake and ice cream."

"And when you puke it all up at three in the morning?"

"Then I'll go for round two. *Muévete, mija,* I'm starving here. Literally." She snapped her fingers and Quinn poured the pasta into the boiling water.

"Get the bread," he called over his shoulder. "The good stuff."

"This?" Santi held up a loaf of French bread from the pantry.

"Yeah." He grinned.

"How much you want?" she asked.

"All of it, baby. I've been dreaming about bread."

"On it!" She grabbed a tub of garlic butter from the fridge and began slicing up the loaf.

Quinn busied himself with making a spice rub for the steaks as Santi slid a pan of buttered bread into the oven. "I'll make all of your requests, but we have to go slow and eat small portions. You haven't eaten well in months and you need fuel to get you through whatever we're about to face. We do not need to be sluggish." Quinn turned to get fresh cilantro and lime from the fridge. "Santi?" His laughter caught in his throat. "What the hell are you eating, babe?"

"Don't knock it till you try it." She dipped another Cheeto into the peanut butter jar.

"That is disgusting."

"Pasta?" She smiled, urging him to get back to work. "It smells good. Where did you learn to cook? Your mom? She's French, right?"

"Yeah, but she was a terrible cook. She could bake the most amazing cakes and pastries, but real food was her Achilles heel. I learned from my dad, actually. We pretty much all had to learn how to cook in self-defense. Mom's idea of a meal was to take all the leftovers from the fridge and make a casserole. She thought if she put enough cream sauce and cheese on it, we wouldn't notice the taste."

"Don't talk about your family in past tense, Quinnton. You'll see them again," she whispered softly as she retrieved the bread from the oven.

"I know. It's just easier not to hope. How do you like your steak?"

"Bloody and juicy."

"Coming up in three minutes." Quinn served them each a small portion of pasta and when the steak was perfectly seared, he split it between them and took his seat beside her. He was so hungry, his hands shook when he lifted his fork.

"Go slow," she murmured. "I don't want you to get sick after so many weeks of bland food and not nearly enough of it."

"We eat this, wait twenty minutes and if we don't puke, we go for seconds?" Quinn asked. "Like maybe some rice and beans, something with protein and carbs?"

"I think there's a deep dish pepperoni pizza in the freezer." She grinned.

"On it." Quinn hopped up to put the pizza in the oven.

"You thinking what I'm thinking?" she whispered as she piled the last of her pasta onto a slice of garlic bread.

"If we have a chance, we have to take it," Quinn said just as carefully. No matter what happened or where they ended up, they had to be prepared to run at a moment's notice.

"But Lennox?" Santi's eyes watered. "I can't leave her."

"We can come back for her. She's fine here for the time being. My family will help. We'll buy her if we have to," he said.

"Can you do that?" Her eyes widened in surprise. "It would be millions."

"It's doable." Quinn didn't want to talk about money when he knew her family struggled with limited resources. "We'll never be able to help her as long as we're stuck in this place. James too." He liked the selfish bastard and wouldn't think of leaving him behind, especially considering what he was hiding about his gift for prophecy. If they could escape, Quinn would do his damnedest to bring Soma down and free all the slaves harbored behind that brand.

CHAPTER 18

Quinn: Fall - Atlanta, Georgia

"What?" Livia snapped as she answered the phone.

Quinn stirred restlessly on the floor at the foot of her bed. He was a light sleeper, waking the second the phone rattled on Livia's bedside table. Santi still slept soundly at his side. It was the first full night in months that she was allowed to sleep without interruption and he didn't want to disturb her.

"He's *where*?" Livia snarled.

Quinn shook his head, clearing the cobwebs from his mind. He'd dreamed of home again. His chest burned with the ache of his power. He entered the dreamworld almost every night he slept now. He was almost certain he was a dreamwalker, but without a mentor who could confirm it, he couldn't be sure. He wandered aimlessly most nights, among the memories of his home, sometimes venturing to places he'd never been. It was usually an eerie place filled with the whisper of voices. He always hoped to see Santi there again, but he hadn't been able to find her since that first time.

Other nights, Quinn could sense the unrest of the dreamworld. The echo of screams from the deep recesses of some nightmare. It was a dangerous, ancient and mysterious place. He needed guidance. Someone who knew how to navigate the dreamworld safely. He was afraid of what he might do in his naïveté. Since his Awakening, whenever Quinn used any of his gifts, he felt the lure of the addiction taunting him. It was worse with his gifts for madness and persuasion. Less so with his cloaking gift and his ability to call the elements from the earth; but it was always there, lurking just below the surface. But when he was in the dreamworld, he hardly felt it at all. He could feel the power coursing through him—the power that allowed him to enter the dreamworld—but he didn't feel the temptation to use more than he needed. It filled him with hope that he might finally have an ability he could use in a positive way.

But when he returned to the waking world, inevitably embracing his power, the addiction hit him with its full force.

"*Cálmate,* Santi whispered as she rubbed the tension from his shoulders. "Take a deep breath and leave the dreams behind," she whispered in his ear, her voice sleepy and content ... for the moment.

"I should throw you back into Michael's dungeon and forget about you." Livia's cold tone sent chills down his spine. "You think you can spout a fancy history lesson and send us to South America chasing our tails?" She kicked him in the ribs as she marched to her closet, tossing her fatigues and weapons onto the bed.

"What are you talking about, Liv?" Quinn rubbed his hand over his ribs, wincing at the sting. Even in her bare feet, it was like getting kicked by a horse.

"Our target has been spotted," she said, jerking on her black leggings. "Up, both of you. Let's move."

"Who's the target again?" Santi yawned.

"The Scholar," Quinn said. "I told you Rio was a guess, Livia. Where was he sighted?"

"Your guess was shit. You weren't even close. And if I find out you were bullshitting me, you and your friends will pay for it. I'll drag every member of your family here and brand them myself." Her breath came in ragged gasps as she shoved her knives into their sheathes in her boots. "To make matters worse, the intel came from my father. We completely missed the Scholar's activity over the last twelve hours."

"I was making an educated guess based on loosely documented history that your target is responsible for writing. That's all." Quinn stood, grabbing his jeans from the small chest where Livia let them keep the few things they had.

"Let's go. My office downstairs. Now. We're briefing the team and then we're leaving." Livia slipped a pair of slim metal collars into the hook on her belt. Those collars were intended for at least one of the oldest Immortals still living. But for the moment, they were a reminder of how easily she would use those collars on Quinn and Santi if they displeased her.

"Well, where is he?" Quinn asked again.

"Cleveland." Livia shot him a glare, waiting to see his reaction at the news of where they would be heading in just a few hours.

"Cleveland?" His heart thumped in his chest at the thought of going home. *Why is the Scholar in Cleveland?*

"This has something to do with your family. I don't know why or how, but I just know it."

"I honestly have no clue why the Scholar would be meeting his Complement in Cleveland. If the queen said she was going back to where it all began and she's been confined for the last two thousand years, I just ... I honestly don't know how that connects, Liv."

"What the hell is he doing in *Cleveland?*" Ryan said the moment they walked into Livia's office.

"Show me the photos," Livia barked.

Quinn and Santi watched from the sidelines as Ryan and Michael spread photos across her desk. In every image of the Scholar, he was on display, loud and proud. Like he knew Livia was looking for him and he was saying, "Come and get me."

Quinn hid his smile. He recognized where the Scholar was. He stood at the center of the sloping green lawn of Edgewater Park, his dark, silvery hair gleaming in the sunlight. He was an average-looking man, seemingly in his early fifties. He was muscular and mostly fit, except for the slight paunch around his middle. He wore a bright red Hawaiian shirt, khaki shorts and flip-flops. And he was busy flying a white kite, emblazoned with a green dragon. He looked like nothing more than a retiree having a fun day at the park. The man was taunting Livia—and it was working. The tension in the room mounted with her every breath.

"You should probably see this too, but it's going to piss you off," Ryan said as he turned his computer screen toward her. "Remember I'm just the messenger here."

He hit play and Quinn watched over Livia's shoulder at the bad karaoke montage. The Scholar was singing at a club in Cleveland. He'd changed every song lyric just enough to get his point across. He knew she was looking for him and he wanted her to know he was waiting for her. He obviously held no lasting fear that she would actually manage to catch him.

"This is on YouTube?" she sneered.

"Yes. It has about half a million hits, but people seem to be forgetting about it as soon as they see it."

"He's deranged."

"I like him." Quinn grinned as the Scholar butchered the lyrics of an old country song.

"He has that, I-don't-give-a-shit vibe that old people have sometimes." Quinn laughed as the Scholar's voice warbled from the speakers.

"Turn this bullshit off," Livia snarled.

"There's more," Michael said as he slid a stack of new photos across the table. "The queen just booked a flight from L.A. to Cleveland for tomorrow."

Quinn gazed over her shoulder at the images of the queen.

"What?" Livia looked at him.

"Nothing." Quinn murmured as he took in the silvery-blond woman with the gray eyes. The family resemblance was subtle, in the shape of her face, the sprinkle of freckles across her nose and the curve of her mouth. The woman looked like an older, blond Allie.

Allie's a royal? As soon as the thought entered his mind he knew he had to protect Allie's identity with his very life if he had to. The royals *were* returning to where it all began. They were rallying around their bloodline. A person, not a physical destination. A person they intended to protect. A person Livia had already shown way too much interest in.

"You've seen her?" Livia demanded.

"No." Quinn shrugged. "Just wanted to see what an ancient queen looked like. She's really Alísun? Never thought I'd see an Immortal so old."

"Bullshit. You know something. Tell me."

"Liv, I've never seen this woman in my life. I can't tell you anything I haven't already."

Livia snapped her fingers and in the next instant, Ryan had Quinn's arms behind his back, and Selena had Santi face down on the table with a magnetized knife to her cheek.

"Livia, I don't know anything, I swear," Quinn insisted. He

wouldn't let them ruin Santi's face. He knew she wouldn't care. But the magnetic poisoning would scar her for life. He'd seen enough of those scars to know they came with just as much emotional pain as physical. He couldn't do it to her. The scars around her ankle already caused her enough pain.

"You took one look at the queen and something clicked. I want to know what you've discovered and I want to know now."

"I told you. I was just curious," Quinn said.

"Michael, go get Lennox."

Blood dripped down Santi's face. The jagged cut from Selena's knife traced her hairline from her temple down to her collarbone.

"Don't do it, Quinn," she whispered. "It's just my face. It's nothing."

Lennox whimpered, crouched in the corner of the room where Michael held her in thrall, caught up in some horrific experience she didn't deserve.

"Don't keep making me hurt them, Quinn." Livia's voice held a touch of the pain she never let them see. The pain of caring for the people enslaved to her. "He *can't* be stopped. Do you even know what that means? Marcus will torment my mother. Punish her for my failures if I don't give him what he wants. She's the only family I've ever had. He'll keep me from her until I lay the queen at his feet." The defeat in her voice showed him she was genuinely terrified of what her father would do to her mother if this mission wasn't a success.

"Fine," Quinn sighed in frustration. "I don't know why. I promise, I have absolutely no idea ... but I think their rally point is Allie."

“What *is* it with that girl?” Livia muttered.

Quinn didn’t think Livia had put the pieces together yet, but she was a smart woman. She would figure it out, and when she did, she would want Allie more than ever.

“What are we doing, Liv?” Ryan asked.

“We’re going to pay a visit to Quinn’s hometown. Let’s go.”

CHAPTER 19

Sasha: Meithari - The Chola Valley Temple

"Get dressed," Jayesh said.

Sasha blinked in the early morning light. Her limbs felt heavy and her eyelids were like lead. The last months of heavy training kept her on the brink of exhaustion.

It's not months. Not really. She was beginning to understand how the time screw worked here. She'd wake in the mornings to an identical dawn every day, followed by an identical, perfect sunset over the mother's gardens every evening. She enjoyed her talks with the mother. But each day bled into the next so it started feeling like one really long, monotonous day on endless repeat. Her body felt the passage of time. It should be fall by now, but it was still the height of summer. That was a physical reassurance that her life back home wasn't speeding along without her.

And they still hadn't moved on from *meithari* yet. Despite the mother's advice, Sasha found it difficult to give Jayesh her blind trust. She knew she needed to meet him halfway, but she had a visceral need to protect herself from his potential betrayal.

"What do you want from me, Jay?" She rolled over to stare

at him where he stood in her doorway, dressed in his typical linen trousers and sleeveless tunic; his golden armbands glinting in the early light.

She rarely saw him outside of their daily training. Not since that day on the cliffs when she went off on him. That was months ago. Since then, he'd been methodical in her training, and never let their conversations drift away from the lessons. He withdrew from her almost completely for days at a time, barely speaking to her at all. And then other times, when he praised her progress or they laughed at some shared joke, she could almost swear they were becoming friends. Sasha feared they would never get through *meithari* and they would be stuck here forever.

"Just get dressed and meet me in the courtyard."

"We going somewhere?" She hoped he wasn't in the mood for more target practice. She was getting bored with spending so much time shooting at clay birds and grass bales. He'd made a point to make target practice part of her regular routine, but he rarely accompanied her and she hadn't seen the beautiful sniper rifle since that first day.

"Yes. We're taking the day off." He glanced at her nervously.

"Why?" She sat up and looked at him like he had three heads. Jayesh didn't believe in taking time off.

"Do you trust me?" He gave her a rare smile.

"No," she said honestly.

"That's why." He nodded as if she'd confirmed something important. "Dress comfortably. We'll be riding a long way."

"Where?" she asked.

"It's a surprise." He winked and left her staring after him.

"Did he just smile?" Imogen asked as she came into Sasha's room bearing a breakfast tray. It was their morning ritual to sit and talk over breakfast before they each left for training.

"He did. Freaky, right? It seems we're taking the day off."

"What's going on with you two? Any progress?" Imogen asked. The dark circles under her eyes worried Sasha, but Gen refused to talk about her training with the mother.

"No. Not since I yelled at him." Sasha crossed her arms over her chest.

"Well, maybe this is him trying to move past that?"

"It's creepy," Sasha said. "But I will do what I can to help us move forward."

"The mother is expecting me or I would come with you. But quite frankly, you two have got to learn to communicate better, so this could be a good thing," Imogen said.

"I still don't trust him."

"He is not a bad man, Sasha. He's just a very hard man to know. Help him. It may not seem like it, but he is trying."

"Maybe I'm a hard woman to know," Sasha muttered.

She made her way to the courtyard, munching on the last of her buttered toast.

"Where are we going?" she asked, surprised to see it was just Jayesh waiting for her in the dusty courtyard and not the host of Chola monks who accompanied them wherever they went.

Jay stood waiting with a huge basket and canteen as they walked along the garden path to the eastern gates. "Do I need to explain what a surprise is?"

Sasha stopped suddenly when she heard the trumpet of an elephant. Her smile spread wide as she rushed through the gates.

"He's beautiful!" She beamed at the enormous elephant waiting to take them wherever Jayesh had planned. "Hello, Kandula," she murmured as the elephant sniffed her with his elaborately painted trunk. She traced the Vedic patterns along his trunk, reaching up to pat his face.

"How did you know his name?" Jayesh laughed.

The elephant, Kandula, had told her his name. Sasha had never felt comfortable revealing her special connection with animals to her teacher. She decided then that she would show Jayesh today, but not here.

Kandula gazed at Sasha with trust and an eagerness to take her wherever she needed to go. *Animals are so much better than people.* Sasha could give them her unfailing trust and they returned it without guile, secrets or manipulation. Kandula offered her a step up, lifting his back leg. Sasha hopped up and held on with a squeal as he lifted her all the way up to his back, where she scrambled up the length of him, like she rode elephants all the time.

"Done this before?" Jayesh smiled.

"Never." She sat carefully where Kandula told her to sit. When she gave a second thought to the ethics of using such a beautiful creature as a beast of burden, he assured her it was his pleasure to take her on her journey to the sea.

Jayesh is taking me to the sea? But Kandula quickly reminded her that *he* was the one taking her to see the leaves. Sasha gave him a playful pat on his enormous head and decided it was not a good idea to argue with the sage wisdom of elephants.

Sasha only half listened to Jayesh as he climbed up behind her. She was enjoying her chat with Kandula far too much. As they made their way across the rolling hills, Sasha learned Kandula was a young bull with a pretty mate and a newborn calf. He and his mate worked for the monks, but were always treated with reverence and given the run of the valley that was their home. Kandula and his mate came when they were called, but otherwise they were free.

"You aren't listening to a word I'm saying," Jayesh said.

"Oh, sorry." Sasha winced. She was bad about that. She

often forgot that humans tended to treat animals like part of the scenery when to Sasha they were part of the conversation. "I'm just enjoying the ride."

"I thought you might like to get out of the temple for a break. We've been working so hard these last months; I know I'm starting to go stir crazy with the routine."

"It's like living the same day on an endless loop," she agreed.

"With no end in sight for the two most stubborn people on the planet."

Sasha laughed. "It's frustrating how we both know what we need to do to get out of here, yet we both refuse to do it."

"Maybe we deserve this place."

"Wait. Stop." Sasha felt the stab of pain in Kandula's front foot. Before she gave it a second thought, she slipped down the elephant's left side, just catching his offered foot as he lowered her to the ground.

She patted Kandula along his trunk.

"What are you doing, Sasha? Be careful. He could trample you," Jayesh called from above.

"He won't." She dismissed Jay's concerns as she rounded to Kandula's right side, telling him to lift his injured foot.

The great elephant snorted his dismissal, claiming it was nothing to concern herself with.

"You have a rock in your foot, Kandula. I can feel how much it pains you and you're not walking another step until I get it out."

Kandula grunted at her.

"I am not a silly human. You're a silly elephant. Now give me your foot." She gestured for Kandula to lift his foot high while she prodded the area between his toes, looking for the culprit. She knew she looked like a madwoman, having a one-sided argument with an elephant.

"I see it," she murmured, grabbing the knife sheathed at her hip. She dug the offending rock from his foot, checking for cuts or any sign of blood. All the while, Kandula protested her fussing. She laughed at the way he looked at her like she was some strange bug on the end of a stick.

"All better?" She smiled as the elephant wrapped his trunk around her shoulders, sniffing her hair.

Without comment, Jayesh tossed her an apple, which she gave to Kandula for a treat.

"So now you know," Sasha said as she took her place back up in front of Jayesh.

"Now I know." He chuckled as they set off across the open valley. "You must lead an interesting life, talking to animals."

"They're easier than people. They trust me and can sense I understand them and they never fear me. Most creatures are eager to offer me help when I need it because I do the same for them."

"You shouldn't be here, Sasha," Jayesh said softly.

"I know." She reached to pick a flower from a low-hanging vine, tucking it behind her ear.

"You should be training to become a woman who inspires peace. Instead they push you into a life of war and death."

"Who knows, maybe I can do the world some good ... staring down the barrel of a sniper rifle."

"Hang on to the girl you are, Sasha. Don't let them beat it out of you."

Sasha found herself wondering what Jayesh was like before life had beaten him down into the jaded man she was just beginning to get to know.

"So Kandula here told you where we're going?" he asked in a cheerier tone.

"His thoughts are somewhat confusing since animals don't

think with words. I saw something about the sea and then something about going to visit leaves."

"Good boy, Kandula." Jayesh reached to rub his big, floppy ears. "He hasn't given away the surprise yet."

"He likes you," Sasha said.

"Does he, now?"

"He likes me better, though."

"You are a rare girl, Sasha El Sadawii. A lot like your mother. And your sister. But you have your own mind."

"So what's the deal with you and the women of my family? If you don't mind sharing."

"I met your sister here when we both trained as you are doing now. We did not get along at first, but we grew to become friends."

"Perhaps history repeats itself?" Sasha said softly.

"Perhaps. Perhaps I struggle to relate to such terrifyingly strong women. In my experience, the strongest women are the ones who routinely try to put a knife in my back."

"The women of my family are not like that, Jayesh."

"A lesson I've had to learn three times now." His warm breath brushed against her shoulder as he laughed. "I am nearly three hundred years old, Sasha, and I've had precious little time at peace. Doing what I do … makes it difficult for me to trust people. But I am trying."

"And I am trying not to make it too difficult for you. My position is frightening, Jayesh. I'm only trying to protect myself and at the same time, accomplish this impossible training at an impossible age."

"I know. And I understand. I really do."

"So you knew my mother, how?" She glanced over her shoulder.

"You will have to ask Naeemah about that someday."

"Ew." Sasha shuddered. She couldn't picture her mom with

Jayesh—not in a million years, but that had to be why no one wanted to tell her how he knew her mother.

"Get your head out of the gutter, Sasha. She was significantly older than me when we met. I knew her when I was even younger than you are now. She was my mentor ... for a time. That is all."

"Then what's the secret?"

"Maybe I knew her during a time of her life she might not be very proud of, and if she wants to tell you about that, it's her right as your mother to do that if and when she chooses."

"Ooooh, you knew Mom during her dark century?"

"Is that what she calls it?" Jay laughed. "I can't imagine she would tell you much about those days."

"Nope, not even a little bit. My brothers and I only know that she's never told us a single detail about her life after she left the Shaolin temple in 1635 and before she arrived in Europe in 1735. It's like she didn't exist for one hundred years. When did you say you met her?"

"I didn't." She caught the white of his smile over her shoulder.

"Well, if you're about three hundred and you knew her at my age...."

"I met your mother in 1729 when I was fourteen years old."

"Tail end of the dark years? I'm intrigued."

"And you will continue to be intrigued because it is not my story to tell."

"You're no fun."

"Says the girl riding through the Indian wildlands on my elephant."

"Kandula begs to differ," she said. "He is his own elephant and belongs to no one. It is his choice to take the pretty lady on this journey."

"Touché, Kandula." Jay laughed. "But it was my idea to

take the pretty lady on an adventure today." He leaned over and patted Kandula's head. "The way the wildlife flocks to you is simply astounding." Jay gazed around, taking in the hesitant animals in the trees.

"You noticed? They usually don't come close enough for most people to realize." It was never in an obvious way, but wherever Sasha went, the animals came out to see her.

"They trust you. And they're insanely curious about you. I think if you were alone here, they would come right up to you."

"Some would, but the larger predators would keep their distance."

"I bet a visit to the zoo with you would cause a ruckus."

"I hate the zoo. The animals are so sad. It breaks my heart."

"It breaks my heart to be doing this to you, Sasha," he said after a long pause. "You're a sweet girl with a bright future. You don't need to get mixed up in ... politics."

"With my gift I knew it was coming, Jay," she said softly. The concern in his voice cracked a little bit of that hardness in her heart toward him. He did care. "I thought I had a few more decades to prepare for it, but I knew it was coming."

"You know they're ... they're not going to lose your number after this. No matter how much you try to hold back what you can really do."

"Maybe.... And maybe they'll hear I'm not very good at this. That I'm a nature-loving, non-violent person who isn't cut out for the work they have planned for me. And maybe they'll be inspired to wait until I'm Proven to continue this kind of training."

"It is likely the Senate will receive a report suggesting just that when we are done here."

It was a shame it had taken them this long to have a real conversation. *Maybe that's what today is supposed to be about.*

"Look." He pointed. "We're almost there."

Sasha gazed along the horizon—green as far as she could see. The hint of salt in the air told her they were near the coast.

"The mangrove forests?"

"I thought you might like to explore the canals with me. We can't go far, but I came here before. It was an escape from the monotony of the training grounds."

"Do we have a boat?"

"We do. And a feast." He thumped the picnic basket behind him.

The mangrove trees seemed to grow straight out of the water, their gnarled root systems spreading like a spider's web in every direction. Clusters of trees stood like islands in the blue-green water, creating a maze of canals as far as she could see. Sasha was eager to go exploring with Jayesh and make some memories about her time here in the Chola Valley that didn't involve her training.

"Here we are," Jayesh said.

"Kandula, my friend, will you be all right without us?" Sasha asked. She laughed at his response a moment later. "He plans to play in the canals while we eat. He wishes to wash off this silly paint the monks insist on decorating him with."

"We will go exploring after we eat. And then Kandula can take his bath." Jayesh slipped to the ground, taking Sasha's hand to help her down.

Her breath caught when his hands wrapped around her waist and he sat her down beside him. She looked up at him and he reached to brush the loose curls from her face. She smiled, feeling at ease with him in a way she never had before.

"You are a beautiful girl." He seemed startled that he'd spoken out loud.

Sasha flushed, dropping her gaze. There was no doubt Jayesh was handsome. *I could get the biggest mad-crush on this jackass of a man.* But he was substantially older, even though he looked no more than twenty-five.

"I know I don't look much older than you, but this is not a good idea, Sasha," he said softly, echoing her thoughts exactly.

"I didn't say anything," she whispered.

"You said it with your eyes." He smiled. "They are very expressive. You've managed to cut me with them on multiple occasions."

"Then don't look at me the way you're looking at me." She grabbed the basket he handed to her.

"Like what?"

"Like I'm not your student and you aren't a million years too old for me."

"I am not that old. But I am too old for you."

"Then we agree on something at last." She laughed. "You are very handsome and it's not out of the realm of possibility in another time or place. But here, today, I want nothing more than to be your friend, Jayesh. That is all." She reached for his hand.

"You are still looking at me like you do not think I am too old for you." His hand wrapped around hers with a squeeze.

"A girl can look, can't she?" Together they turned to the path leading down to the canals.

"I'm guessing you're starving. I've rarely seen you stop eating since we arrived." Jay walked beside her.

"Funny guy. I guess you're too old to remember the gnawing hunger that never goes away at this age."

"It is a rather distant memory, but I'm hardly *old*, Sasha."

"I have brothers about your age."

"Tell me about your family?" Jayesh asked as he spread a rolled carpet on the ground beside the canals.

"I have three older brothers, two brothers-in-law and one younger brother who's worse than all the others combined about pulling the overprotective bullshit. And two uncles too. And then there's Quinn. He's not like a brother, but we grew up together. His little brother *is* like a brother, though."

"That's a lot of brotherly types you've got surrounding you." Jayesh laughed. "Makes dating hard, I bet."

"Oh, I can handle the McBrien boys." Sasha sighed. She missed them all so much. Especially Aidan and Darius.

It was nice, sitting in the warm afternoon sunshine, talking about normal life stuff with Jayesh.

"So Quinn's the boyfriend?"

"No, not for a long time. These days we're just friends." She reached for the picnic basket to distract herself from thoughts of Quinn and the overwhelming guilt she felt for flirting with Jayesh.

"But you think he is your Complement?"

"I do. Or ... I did. I don't know, honestly. There's a big history there. When we're together, we make each other miserable and we fight constantly. When we're not together, we can't stand to be apart. It's frustrating and confusing."

"He's a big part of your life."

"There's this overwhelming pull I feel for him. A fire in my veins that's always there. I used to think that meant we were Complements, but I don't really know anymore." She thought about that last kiss before he was ripped away from her, still not sure what it meant or if she even wanted to go down that road with him again. It only ever led to heartbreak. "I just know I have to help him, and being stuck here with my hands tied is making me crazy."

"You have to promise me, Sasha. When we leave this valley, you cannot go looking for him." Jayesh frowned. "It will do him no good."

"I can't face a future without Quinn in it." She shrugged.

"No matter what he is or isn't to me. I'll do whatever I have to do to help him."

"These people ... there is likely much more to them than you could ever know. You should let his parents decide the best course of action."

"I know. I just ... I have to do something."

"When we get through this, I will do what I can. I know all sorts of sordid people in the seedy underworld of Immortality. I'm sure I can find a safe way for you to help Quinn."

"You'd do that?"

"If it keeps you home where you belong and not out trying to get yourself locked away in a cell right next to him, then yes. I will see what I can do."

"You're not so bad, Jay." Sasha smiled, her hopes soaring at the thought that he might be exactly what Quinn needed.

"Well, you've turned out to be a good student and not nearly as annoying as I thought you'd be." He gave her a wink and she threw her almonds at him.

"What's with the face tattoo?" she asked. She'd been curious about it since she met him. "That has to have an interesting story behind it." The black lines were faded with age, and she couldn't quite make out any distinctive shapes.

"It does." His smile was forced.

"Maybe you'll tell me about it one day?"

"I hope never to speak of such things with you, angel."

It was the first time, "angel" wasn't an insult.

CHAPTER 20

Quinn: Fall - Atlanta, Georgia

"Sit," Livia barked. "Don't get in the way, and don't even think about wandering off when you think I'm distracted. It doesn't work, so don't try it."

Santi and Quinn took their seats at the back of the private jet in a secluded alcove set apart from the rest of the team. The white leather double seat was roomy and comfortable, with footrests and a television on the opposite wall. A fully stocked bar and kitchenette occupied the other side of the aisle.

"Nice digs," Santi said as she took the window seat.

"I hate flying but I could get used to this." Quinn sat beside her. He could still see what was going on with the other passengers beyond the curtain, but this was definitely where they stuck the captives.

"The seatbelts have locks," Santi whispered. "Look, the headrests have places to hook into a collar. That's so messed up."

"Still a better way to travel than the way I arrived at Soma."

"Didn't you fly? This is Livia's plane. It goes everywhere she does."

"Yeah, I flew. With the luggage."

The jet was small but luxurious. Livia sat up front in the lounge with her team, preparing for takeoff. The flight attendant took their drink orders while the pilot did her final preparations.

"It's about time you showed up," Livia called as a passenger boarded in a rush at the last minute. "I was hoping to leave without you."

"Hello to you too." The voice wasn't a familiar one. Quinn leaned into the aisle to see who had joined them.

"Come. We don't have long to brief you." Livia snapped her fingers.

"Did you forget how to say please?" the man asked. "I don't want to be here any more than you want me to be here, Liv. I was actually in the middle of something important."

"I didn't call you here. You're free to go back to whatever third-world hellhole you crawled out of."

"We both know I'm not. He wants me here, so I'm here. Deal."

"Then stay out of my way, and remember this is my mission. Not yours."

"It's my job to make sure this is a success. You know you need me, so let's play nice and get the job done so we can go back to pretending the other doesn't exist."

"That's the dream." Livia turned back to the small conference table with the other members of her team.

"It's him," Quinn whispered, clenching his fists in his lap. He recognized the man with the face tattoo. The man from the photo with Sasha. Without thinking, he slipped out of his seatbelt.

"What have you done with Sasha?" Quinn said in a dangerously controlled voice as he made his way down the aisle. "Where is she?"

"Quinn, get back to your seat," Livia demanded.

"Quinn?" The man gave him a once-over. "Yeah, she talked about you." He nodded. "Way too much talking, that one."

"Jayesh, don't bait him," Livia said.

"What have you done with her?" Quinn took another step forward, itching to put his hands around the man's throat.

"You don't want to know," Jayesh said. "Let it go, man."

Quinn lunged at him, but Michael had him flat on the floor with a knee in his back before Quinn's fist could make contact with Jayesh's face.

"Get him back to his seat," Livia snapped.

Michael and Ryan dragged Quinn to the back of the plane and belted him in.

"You get up again and you're going skydiving without a chute," Michael said.

Quinn watched helplessly as the man who'd held Sasha's freedom in his hands went back to the conference table.

"What was that about?" Santi asked, trying to loosen his death grip on the armrest.

"A few months ago, Livia showed me a photo of that guy with Sasha." Quinn's nostrils flared in anger. "He was in charge of some kind of special training she was conscripted into by the Senate."

"The Senate?"

"Exactly." Quinn turned to meet her gaze. "Why would a Soma agent be working for the Senate? He was teaching her how to use a sniper rifle. Livia threatened to have her brought here after her training was completed. If I submitted and signed over my life to Soma, Sasha was supposed to go home none the wiser. But I called her bluff." Quinn shook his head in disgust. "I knew ... I thought Sasha's father would travel to hell and back to keep her safe."

"You care about her a lot, don't you." Santi's voice held a hint of uncertainty.

"I do. She's ... Sasha." He couldn't find the right words to describe what she meant to him. "If anything happens to her ... if that man hurt her in any way, I will never forgive myself."

"You love her?"

"I do. I always will. But we aren't good for each other. We've both known that for a long time, but it's still always been more than just friends with us."

"I see." She stared at her hands in her lap.

"It's confusing when you have feelings for two people at the same time," Quinn said softly, taking her hand in his. "And it's not fair to you or to Sasha."

"Me?" Santi whispered.

"You know I care about you." Quinn gave her hand a gentle squeeze. "But the way I left things with Sasha...."

"You don't have to explain."

"But you'll understand more than anyone, Mina." Quinn smiled. "The night Livia took me, Sasha and I were right in the middle of starting things up again after we'd broken off our relationship the year before. And then we were torn apart. To her, that is all still a fresh wound. To me ... it's ancient history. It still hurts. I still love her in the way you always care about your first love, but this distance ... this whole experience ... you ... it's all moving me in a different direction. Sasha will always be special to me. I suppose it's a sad and bittersweet thing when you realize it's time to move on from that first love."

Santi nodded. "I know you don't want to see her mixed up in all of this. We need to see if we can talk to Jay. He's a good guy. When he wants to be."

"You know him?"

"Yeah. He and Livia don't get along because Jayesh is her

father's man. Marcus sends him to help her when he doesn't think Livia can handle something on her own. She takes offense to it, so they butt heads like siblings vying for daddy's attention."

"Does he outrank Livia?"

"No. He's a slave like the rest of us, but he has the old man's ear. They've been together most of Jay's life. I think he and Livia grew up together. They're about the same age."

"Can he be trusted?"

"I think so. It's no secret Jay prefers not to have anything to do with Soma. He keeps himself separate from all of this, working in different parts of the world whenever Marcus hires him out. But he's broken. He doesn't care about much. He's cold and calculated. Kind of goes through the motions of whatever's expected of him. He doesn't have much patience for chitchat. He's a career soldier. Does what he's told."

Quinn laughed at the thought of this guy with Sasha. "She probably made his life a living hell."

Quinn caught Jayesh's eye and thought he saw a subtle nod, as if in agreement.

"Sir, let me get that for you." The flight attendant tried to intercept Jayesh at the entrance to the alcove where Santi and Quinn sat.

"I can make my own drink, thanks." He stepped around the young man, closing the curtain in his face.

Jayesh shot them a warning look to keep silent, peering over the curtain to see if Livia was watching.

"I have maybe five minutes before she get suspicious," Jayesh said almost inaudibly. "I left Sasha safe with family a few months ago, but she's drawing too much attention to herself. How do I get her to stop trying to find me? She's refusing to let me walk away without an argument."

"She's safe?" Quinn rested on the edge of his seat.

"Yes. But if she doesn't stop asking questions about both of us, she's not going to be."

"That's Sasha," Quinn said.

"She is ... very special to me." Jayesh busied himself making a drink and a sandwich. "But this life." He gestured toward Livia and the others. "I can't ever let this place touch her any more than it already has."

"Then you need to do whatever you have to do to get her to forget about you. Simple as that."

Jay nodded, taking a bite of his sandwich. "She's not making that easy."

"Sasha is a force to be reckoned with," Quinn said. "Have you ... is there anything going on with you two?"

"Not like that. I'm too old for her, and I'm not a free man. But we are close. I don't want to hurt her."

"She cares about you?" Quinn asked.

"I believe she does." Jay nodded. "Although I don't know why."

"You're going to have to break her heart. Tell her whatever she needs to hear to keep her from coming after you because she will not rest if she feels like you've abandoned her. She's not going to let it go."

"Just like she hasn't let go of you. Did you know she was planning to show up at Sterling Tower to volunteer?"

"Someone needs to superglue her ass to the floor." Quinn sighed.

"She might slit my throat for this." Jay smiled, but there was something in his eyes. Something like heartbreak. "But I'd rather have her angry at me than hurt."

"If you care about her at all, you do not want to see her

wearing the Soma brand. You know how badly they would want someone like her. They would mold her into something she's not cut out to be. Cut her loose, Jayesh, because if she winds up at Soma, I'm coming for you."

Jayesh nodded. "I'll put an end to her questions. If that means she never thinks about me again, all the better."

"See that you do it soon."

"I promised her I would help you, but I can't do much considering how closely tethered Livia is keeping you. The fact that she has you out of Sterling Tower at all surprises me. She would normally never risk it unless she was certain of your loyalty, or she'd managed to break you. If you have the opportunity to run, you take it. I'll do what I can to give you the time you need to get away, but she will retaliate so you need to be prepared for a fight."

With that, Jayesh left them.

"He cares," Santi said. "That is a good sign."

"How so?" Quinn asked.

"It means he isn't broken anymore. He's found his way back, and it sounds like Sasha's the reason. She must be incredible."

Quinn smiled. "Leave it to Sasha to unbreak an Immortal."

Santi stared out the window at the carpet of clouds just below them. "Do you think we have a chance, Quinnton?" she whispered.

"Maybe, but this is the only one we're going to get, so we better make it count."

"I can't wait to see my family."

"I know you want to see them again, but if we can actually do this, I don't think we should go back to Atlanta. It's too dangerous."

"I know." Santi sighed. "I can send for them once I get settled somewhere."

"You'll come with me back to my family. They will protect us and they'll get your family out of Atlanta."

"You want me to come home with you?" She gave a hesitant smile.

Quinn took her hands in his. "Santi, I want you with me wherever I go."

Chapter 21

Quinn: Fall - Cleveland, Ohio

Cleveland was covered in a blanket of fog when they stepped off the private jet at Burke Lakefront Airfield. The small airstrip was bordered by Lake Erie on one side and the bustling city center on the other. As they waited for their driver to pull up on the tarmac, Quinn caught sight of the Rock & Roll Hall of Fame and the Cleveland Browns' Stadium nearby. The nostalgic feeling of homecoming burst inside him. Freedom was at their fingertips and Quinn was anxious to get away. Returning to Soma was just not an option.

"Pull it together, people!" Livia screamed after a nasty couple of minutes when none of them could remember why they were there. "I will dedicate the rest of my life to tracking down your Complements just for the pleasure of killing every single one of you if you don't focus, now!"

Quinn didn't believe they would actually find the Scholar. Every time they made a decision, half of them forgot what they were doing. Michael had spent most of the flight replaying the Scholar's YouTube video because he couldn't remember he'd already seen it. But Livia somehow managed to stay focused and refused to forget. She had eyes and ears stationed all across

Cleveland, reporting in at different intervals. If the Scholar showed his face anywhere, she would know well before her sentries forgot to make a report.

Quinn and Santi piled into the back of the limo with Livia, Michael, Ryan, Selena and Jayesh. He wasn't sure where they would go, but Quinn knew this city like the back of his hand. Wherever they ended up, he would have the hometown advantage on his side.

"We'll get settled at the hat factory tonight and see what the surveillance reports yield. Then we'll make our moves tomorrow," Livia said.

"Hat factory? Really?" Quinn scowled at her.

"Yes. I believe you're familiar with the place?"

Quinn had spent one of the worst nights of his life in that old warehouse—right before Livia stole him away from his family.

"Jayesh keeps it concealed for our use. Once we're holed up there, the Scholar won't be able to locate us."

"So I can thank you for all this?" Quinn shot a glare at the man who'd made his capture possible so many months ago. If Jayesh's gift hadn't blocked Liam's, his family would have found them sooner and Quinn would likely be home now. *And Santi would be here alone.* He glanced at her beside him. If he had to do it all over again, he wouldn't change anything.

"My deepest apologies," Jayesh said, absently staring out of the window.

"If we can all remember to stay on point, we will maintain the upper hand," Livia said. "With Jayesh, we'll be working a few steps ahead of the Scholar. We will get between him and the queen, attempt to take them both if we can, or settle for the Scholar if we can't."

"They're ancients, Liv," Quinn said. "Don't forget there are things about them you won't know."

"I know how to use people against each other, Quinn. Your only job here is to stand on the sidelines, keep your mouth shut and hand over your gift when I have need of it."

"Well, good luck with that," Quinn muttered. She was walking right into the Scholar's trap and she was either too arrogant to realize it or too desperate to care.

"We've been discreet," Livia said, flipping through the surveillance reports on her lap. "And we have certain abilities at our disposal that will protect us, so stop bothering me with your needless concerns."

Quinn snorted in disgust. They had no idea who they were dealing with.

"You have something to say?" Livia demanded. "Something an untested child would think of that we haven't?"

"You are hunting the Scholar and you haven't got a clue what that man is capable of. He sees you coming. They both do. If anyone is in control of how this is going to go down, it's them. Not you."

"How so?" Ryan asked. "We've covered everything."

"Doesn't anyone study history around here?" Quinn shook his head in disgust. *I should just let them hang themselves.*

"Out with it or we'll be back to carving up Santi's face and other parts of her I'm sure you quite enjoy."

"Stop making idle threats and just do it already," Santi said. "Maybe I'll fetch a big price at market if you make me look scary enough. Or better yet, I'll end up in the clearance bin and all your efforts to break me will be for nothing. I like that idea. Let's do it."

"Santi. Stop baiting her. Please." Quinn sighed, turning to face Livia beside him. "You are tracking the man who has shaped every aspect of our history, Livia. He's practically omniscient."

"No one's omniscient."

"He's older than dirt. Nothing dates back as far as the Scholar. History calls him a ghost. He sees everything of importance and he records it. When Caesar was stabbed twenty-three times on the Ides of March, Alexander was there. When Carthage was sacked, Alexander was there. When the Twin Towers fell, he was there. He doesn't need to be physically present to see the most important moments in history. Just as his psychic wife sees the future in her prophecies. You can't surprise a man like that. Not an ancient with power you can't even fathom. He has the upper hand, and he will keep it."

"You've been listening to too many myths. Alexander is not the all-powerful presence he would like you to believe he is. At the end of the day, he is just a man. Jayesh will stay five steps ahead him and warn us when trouble is coming. He will conceal our headquarters so we can continue our surveillance undetected. And your gift, my little darling, will get me close enough to collar him, so I can touch him with Santi's gift to discover what I need to know to find the queen."

"Alexander will not be so easily affected by my gift," Santi said.

"Maybe if you were wielding your gift, but I will be using it for you and I have a much better sense of what your gift can do."

"Why not go after the queen directly?" Selena asked. "She's the one Marcus wants. At least we can remember who she is," she muttered.

"The queen is a prophet and a warrior. The Scholar is a couch potato. Alísun would see us coming through her gift and we'd never be able to touch her. But as Quinn said, the Scholar's gift only shows him the most pivotal moments in history. Important events and people that shape the world to come. He will not see a couple of insignificant slaves until it is too late.

We will not be a blip on his radar. Not until it is too late for him."

"I didn't say 'only.'" Quinn sighed, but Livia wasn't listening.

Shadows threw them into darkness as the limo entered a long, crumbling tunnel.

"What is this place? Driver, where have you taken us?" Livia demanded.

"I think it's the old subway tunnel under the Detroit-Superior Bridge," Quinn said, looking around. "It's been closed for decades."

"You should listen to the boy. He's the smartest one back there," the driver said as he lowered the privacy window.

"Alexander?" Livia's face flushed at the sight of the man she was supposed to be hunting.

The Scholar sat in the front seat wearing a chauffeur's hat with dark sunglasses, torn jeans and a Darth Vader t-shirt with the slogan, "*Use the Force, Harry.*"

"You wanted to speak with me?" He eyed her over his sunglasses. "You could have just called, my dear."

"Jayesh, what have you done?" Livia snarled.

"Oh, no, the boy's done his job," Alexander said. "But I've been working double time to make him forget his own name."

"How did you find us?" Livia asked.

"You forget ... I am much more than a scholar. I am the father of all scholars who have come after me. I am an ancient with omniscient access to all of history. Even history in the making. Even history made, say, a couple of hours ago." He checked his Apple Watch. "Things like mundane flight manifests. Public record, you know. I knew you were coming the moment your pilot filed her flight plan. You young people forget to use your brains and rely too much on your gifts."

"Out." Livia snapped her fingers and everyone exited the vehicle.

It was time. She would do what she came here to do, and Quinn would slip away with Santi before Livia even realized what happened. He had the advantage, too. He knew exactly where to go where she would never find them.

"You two, stay with me. I don't want any bullshit from you, Quinn. Lennox is my insurance policy. You try anything, you even think about running, and she pays the price."

Quinn didn't buy her threat. Livia loved that little girl and she wouldn't follow through with it—especially if he wasn't there to see it carried out.

Livia shoved Santi ahead of her, keeping them in her sights, daring them to step a toe out of line. Her team lined up in the darkness of the old subway station. The Scholar stood alone. They had him surrounded, but he gazed around like he was meeting old friends for brunch.

"Lovely to meet you all," he said, with a beaming smile.

Ryan and Michael lit the flashlights on their phones, washing them all in the dim blue LED light.

"Such a wonderful invention." Alexander gestured at the smartphones. "I've always found it miraculous how my mortal children have managed to thrive without the use of the power that was once a natural part of the world they inherited. Their ingenuity is simply marvelous. Don't you think, Alivia?" He turned to face her, not bothering to cast a glance in the others' direction. He was in control here.

"It's *Livia*." The color drained from her face at the mention of the name.

"No. It isn't. You were named Alivia, after a distant relative on your mother's side, but how could you know that? Leave it to Marcus to give you a Roman name. Livia it is, then." He nodded. "You won't find Alísun here, dear. My wife sees you coming before you've had your morning tea and biscuits."

"You're the one we want anyway," Livia said. "For the moment."

"Who is this 'we?'" He frowned. "It seems most of your team has wandered off."

Quinn had watched them each drift away as if some pressing task had just occurred to them. First Selena and Ryan, and then Jayesh, with Michael right behind. They were now busy scouring the tunnel, taking pictures and measurements, murmuring about how perfect the place was for hosting Amrita.

Livia's hand hovered near her hip, a finger tracing the lines of the intricate collar at her belt.

"You could try it, but I think you'll find me difficult to collar, my dear."

"He's crazy," Livia muttered.

"I like him." Quinn grinned.

"Listen, Alexander. We have dozens of agents in the surrounding area. If you run, we will catch you."

"Oh, dear me, no. I'm afraid I haven't run in years." He patted the small swell of his protruding belly. "But I have my reasons for meeting with you today. Tell me, what is your despicable father up to these days? I'm afraid Teigan and I never got along well when he thought to court my mother-in-law all those years ago. Eiselynn was a clever girl to turn away from him when she did. Caused all sorts of problems we're still dealing with, but she was a wise girl nonetheless."

"If you're so all-knowing, then you should know exactly what he has planned for you and your wife. None of which is of any concern to me or my team," Livia said.

"Of course not. Your only concern is for your mother. Porcia. I was always fond of her, but the dear girl was most unfortunate to find herself in league with one such as Teigan. Something happened to him during the Great War. He's gone a bit squirrely if you ask me."

Livia began to speak, but her voice fell mute and her movements grew sluggish.

"Ah, much better." Alexander smiled. "Now then, Quinnton, isn't it?" He turned to face Quinn and Santi, the only two who hadn't wandered off. "We have much to discuss, and very little time to do it."

"I'm sorry, sir?" Quinn frowned, confused.

"It is time to go, my boy. You and your pretty friend. We have about ten minutes to get out of here or we're all toast." He ushered them along the tunnel, back to the entrance. "Well, you two more than me. I may have bluffed a bit back there. I make a habit of running when cornered. I'm a scholar, not a fighter. Come, let's go, shall we? Come, come. Quickly."

"The car?" Santi tried to turn back.

"Leave the car, darling. It won't run long without this thing anyway." He held up a torn radiator hose. "And to be honest, I'm not the best driver."

Quinn gaped at the kooky old man before Santi grabbed his hand and tugged him along. "This is our chance. We have to take it now."

"How do you know my name?" Quinn asked as they followed Alexander up to the street entrance.

"Well, Quinny, my boy, it seems you are close with someone who means a great deal to me and my lovely wife. Several someones, in fact. I've kept a close eye on you recently. Livia was right when she said I see important people and events that shape our world, but she was wrong to assume you are not one of those important people. You and Santi both—and that unfortunate boy back there. But he'll have to figure that out on his own. None of you are insignificant. You are all vital to the future of the Immortal world. But you have *got* to get out of this snare you're currently in. Take yourselves and run. Now. It's the only chance I can give you, though I fear it might not be enough."

"Why did you lure us here? If you knew Livia was coming for you, why did you let her close in on you?"

"Why? For this moment right here, son. You want to escape, don't you? Listen, interpreting the future is a terrible business, Quinnton. It's just not my bag." The Scholar laid a strong but finely wrinkled hand on his shoulder. "Deciphering prophecy takes more patience than I've ever had. That's why I've always left it to my wife, my daughters and granddaughters. In this instance I am but a messenger. We are headed for dark times, and circumstances must play out in our favor. What happened here today was just a bit of fun for this old man." Alexander ushered them up the stairs to the street.

"I brought you two here right now for this moment. This is the stuff that makes history, Quinn. Have you learned what you need to know to face the future as the man you should be? Or are you still running scared from your tired old fears? Maybe I thought you needed a kick in the pants. Eh? Your new gift. It is exactly what you think it is, but you have to get a grip on it soon, my boy. It's important. There is another dreamwalker who will teach you. He will find you soon. Trust him. He is worthy." Alexander clapped him on the back and turned to Santi.

"What does all that even mean?" Quinn struggled to decipher the old man's babble.

"You'll figure it out. Santi, dear girl, he's going to need you to give him a push. You get out of Soma soon. If not today, then as soon as you can manage it. Take the prophet and the little one and you get yourselves out."

"How?" Santi asked, but the old man just shrugged and

gave them a wink before he turned and blended into the crowded street.

"That was like meeting Dumbledore. Come on," Santi said. She squinted into the sunlight. "Where are we?"

"Just a few short steps away from freedom." Quinn grinned. "Let's go." He grabbed her hand and darted across the Superior Avenue traffic.

"How far?" Santi asked.

"Two blocks up Huron Street to Terminal Tower." If they could get there before Livia recovered from whatever Alexander had done back there, they could disappear forever.

Santi kept up with him as they ran along the busy street. The city teemed with people heading to work, going on about their lives, oblivious of the fact that Santi and Quinn were running for theirs.

"Almost there." Quinn pulled her along behind him as they darted through the glass doors of the tower entrance.

They took the steps two at a time down the escalator until they reached the underground train station.

"She'll be recovering soon," Santi said, her voice full of fear and dread.

"Maybe Jayesh will buy us a little more time like he promised."

Santi nodded as they approached the busy train platform.

"A train isn't the answer. We need to disappear. She has people everywhere."

"We're not getting on a train." Quinn pushed through the crowd of morning commuters. It would be nearly impossible, not to mention foolish, to go where he was about to go with so many mortal eyes on them, but he was desperate.

"Here." He jumped off the train platform and reached to help her down. Stay against the wall and follow me." He slid along the concrete wall heading into the darkness of the

Terminal tunnel where the trains turned around in a loop to head back in the direction they came. Santi didn't ask questions; she just followed.

In the darkness, Quinn found the crevice in the wall and opened the panel to reveal an analog keypad. He prayed he could figure out the code to the secret tunnel to the island. He tried a few different sequences but the door didn't budge. His father monitored the access codes at all entrances leading to the underground. He tried every imaginable date, anniversary and password he could remember, but nothing worked. Then he entered the date of the day he joined his family when he was just a baby. The thick concrete wall slid open. It seemed his father had been thinking of him.

"Let's go."

"What is this place?" Santi whispered.

"It leads to Kelleys Island, straight into the underground facility there. We'll be home in a few hours. It's a long way ... and there may be some swimming involved if it's flooded."

"Swimming? Are you serious? This goes under the lake?" She followed him into the darkness. When the concrete wall slid shut behind them, he knew they were home free.

"Do you feel it?" Santi asked.

"She's furious." The tug of Livia's gift was pulling them back. She was livid, and if she ever found them, they would regret this moment with every breath Livia allowed them to take. "We have to keep going, Mina."

Santi nodded and they headed into the darkness of the tunnel. The farther they went, the darker it grew. It would be black as night a mile in and it was over twenty-five miles to the crypt. They'd be at it for several hours, but Livia wouldn't be able to reach them now. They ran into the darkness like a horde of demons chased them.

CHAPTER 22

Sasha: Ankathari - The Chola Valley Temple

"Are you ready for this?" Imogen asked as she brushed Sasha's hair.

Sasha glanced nervously out of the window of her sister's bedroom. The sun seemed to be setting at an accelerated rate—to the time of her heart hammering in her chest.

"No. Not even a little bit. I'm terrified."

"I wish I could prepare you for what to expect during your first night of *ankathari* but you have to go into this completely naive."

"Mother Raghavan says if I live to be ten thousand, tonight will still be the most difficult night of my life. What am I supposed to do with that?"

"Take it moment by moment. One breath at a time. Midnight will be here before you know it and it will be over."

"Until tomorrow, when I have to do it all over again."

"It will never be as bad as the first night. You and Jayesh have worked so hard to get here. This is progress. Try to hold on to that thought if you can."

Sasha closed her eyes as her sister finished securing her hair back with a black silk scarf.

She was right. Sasha and Jayesh had made so much headway in the weeks since that day at the mangrove forest. He was still the most obstinate man she'd ever met, but they were friends now. There was mutual respect between them.

Now when Sasha entered the training grounds and she knelt to touch her teacher's feet, it didn't feel like she was giving him the upper hand the way it once had. After months of struggling, they'd finally found their way through *meithari* and it was time to move on. Though she knew very little about what she would face tonight.

For months, she and Jayesh studied the *kalari* forms, sparring together in the evenings. Sasha felt stronger than she ever had before. Now it was time to put all of that training into practice. At sunset tonight, she would enter the place between the outer and inner walls of the temple grounds. There she would face whatever obstacles Jayesh and the mother had planned for her. She would not be free to return to the safety of the temple until the stroke of midnight.

"You are ready for this, sister. Remember, your mind will be your biggest obstacle tonight."

Sasha nodded and crossed the room to the bench where her weapons lay. Dressed in simple black robes with a golden embroidered belt, she looked every bit the assassin straight out of some fantasy tale. The slim blades hooked at her waist were the only protection she would have tonight. Mastering the assassin's blade was the whole point of *ankathari,* and once she did that, she would earn the Chola blade for herself.

"It is time," Imogen said. "I will be here for you when you return. You will rest in my rooms tonight."

"Gen ... thank you for being here with me. I know the separation from your husband is killing you. But ... I love you."

"I love you too, little sister. Be brave."

Sasha made her way to the western gate alone. She needed a moment to collect her thoughts.

This is just another obstacle between you and your goals, Sasha. Get it done and move on.

"I don't know who's more nervous—me or you," Jayesh said as he greeted her at the gate.

"Definitely me. I'm the one walking into this with no idea what's coming."

"You can do this, Sasha. I'll be right here the instant midnight strikes."

"I'm scared," she whispered, taking his offered hand. Just a few months ago she'd never have admitted her fears to Jayesh. They'd come a long way.

"Drink this. It is part of the ritual." He handed her a chalice filled with spiced wine.

Sasha nodded, taking a deep breath. She gulped the wine and stepped through the gates into the growing darkness between the walls of the temple grounds.

The acrid smoke smelled of sulfur and heat, tickling her nose as she made her way along the perimeter of the interior wall. Everything looked different at night.

"Don't lose your way," she muttered, keeping her eye on the temple entrance.

Familiar voices echoed behind the swirling clouds of smoke. Sasha wasn't sure what to expect of this night, but she knew it would be dangerous.

"Aidan?" She whirled around in the unnatural darkness. Her mind was playing tricks on her. Sasha blinked, shaking her head to clear the confusion. She drew her blades and turned in a slow circle, struggling to remember how she came to be in this strange place.

"Sasha?" Aidan called from beyond the veil of fog and smoke.

Sasha stumbled toward the sound of her brother's voice. She heard them all. Her mother, her father. Chloe, Allie, and her brothers. Everyone who had ever mattered to her whispered in the darkness.

"Sasha?"

"Quinn?" Her voice caught in her throat as he came to her through the swirling fog. He was a shadow at first, but she'd know him anywhere. Sasha nearly threw her weapons down in her eagerness to reach him. Touch him. Feel his arms around her again just to know he was real.

"I've missed you so much." Her tears fell as the gaping hole Quinn had left in her life began to diminish at the mere sight of him. "How did you find me here? I don't even know where here is." She couldn't remember what brought her to this temple. She struggled to even remember her own name. The only thing she knew for certain was that she loved Quinn, but she had to get out of this place with or without him.

Pain surged through her and she reached to grasp her head. "Quinn, please. We have to get out of here. It's not safe." But he stood with his back to her.

Sasha touched his arm and he turned on her, brandishing his sword. His dark blue eyes were vacant and cold. She reeled back but the bite of steel against her cheek brought a rush of blood. She cupped her face, astonished that the boy she loved could ever hurt her.

"Please, Quinn? It's me. It's Sasha." She reached for him again but the scent of first blood seemed to energize him and he brought his weapon down on her again. Sasha reacted quickly, blocking his aggressive strike with her blades.

"Why do you push so hard, Sasha?" Quinn growled. "I don't love you."

"Quinn, please. Don't do this," she cried as she fought him off, trying not to let him corner her against the wall.

She had to save him from this madness. Her mind was a whirl of confusion, but her body fell into the *kalari* forms seamlessly. She moved with instinct, twisting her body into the familiar defensive movements. As the minutes dragged into hours and still he pursued her, Sasha's limbs grew heavy and weak. *I'm running out of time.* She couldn't remember why, but an overwhelming sense of urgency filled her. She had to get out of this place. Now.

"Snap out of it!" She ducked his sword and rushed to his side, hoping her touch or the sound of her voice could bring him back to himself. "This isn't you. We've loved each other our whole lives!" But Quinn didn't care anymore. His blade sliced through her robes, connecting with her flesh. The action shattered something inside her.

It took her far too long to realize the only way out of this nightmare was to kill the boy she loved. He was too far gone. He was going kill her. *I can't let that happen. I have an important job to do.* Although she couldn't remember what that job was.

With a heartbroken sob, Sasha stopped fighting defensively and began pushing her attack.

"Don't make me do this," she begged when she had him cornered, but he wouldn't back down. He never spoke. He just continued his single-minded pursuit.

Sasha's cries bounced off the temple walls, the echoes filling the night as she brought her blades to his throat.

"Sasha?" Quinn finally looked at her in confusion. His blue eyes warmed with recognition and she hesitated.

But his smile was one of triumph and not the smile she

remembered from the boy she was once convinced was her Complement.

"No!" Sasha's voice broke in anguish as she screamed and brought her blade across his throat. The dagger he was about to plant in her side clattered to the ground. The spurt of his warm blood sprayed her face and covered the front of her robes.

Sasha stumbled back, dropping her weapons, letting Quinn's lifeless body slump forward.

"I killed him!" she shrieked into the swirling clouds of smoke.

She stared down at her bloody hands, wondering how they could betray her. Violent tremors racked her body as she backed away from Quinn's still form. "I killed him," she whispered, dropping to her knees.

"What have you done?" Aidan's shadow loomed over her.

"I had to do it, Aidan." She scrambled through the dirt as he closed in on her. "No. Please. Don't." She cringed as he pulled his sword from the sheath at his back. A dagger in one hand and his favorite sword in the other, her brother—her best friend—stalked her. His eyes glowed in fury.

"How could you do it, Sash? You're supposed to love him. What's wrong with you?" Aidan hauled her up from the ground and had his dagger at her throat before she could blink.

Once again, her body reacted in a way that defied what her mind wanted. Her bloodied blades glinted in the moonlight as she twisted out of his grip and turned them on her brother. She danced on silent feet, never letting her opponent touch her. It was easier this time, moving through the motions of the fight as her mind disconnected from her body until she felt like a spectator—a soldier following orders they didn't understand.

"No, Aidan. Leave, please just leave," she begged.

"You killed my best friend!" His accusing stare cut her to the core.

"He was going to kill me."

"Then you should have died! You obviously deserve it. While he's been out there fighting for his life, what have you been doing, Sasha?"

"I, I don't know! I can't remember!" she sobbed.

"You've been off flirting with your trainer while the boy you profess to love has been tortured and enslaved. You were supposed to be helping him escape!"

"I know. I know—that's why I have to get out of here. It's important, Aidan."

"It's too late, Sasha. You killed him." Aidan's eyes blazed in fury. "There is nothing more for you to do. I wish Mom had left you to rot in that orphanage where she found you." He raised his sword to run her through.

She couldn't look into those eyes anymore. She flew into a whirling kick to disarm him. Sasha raised her daggers for the killing blow, plunging both blades through her brother's chest.

Sasha threw her head back and a scream like a wounded animal ripped from her throat.

"You killed my son?" Their mother drifted through the smoke, staring at Aidan's still form, blood pooling beneath him. "He was right. I should have left you in that orphanage the day I found you. It should be you dead on the cold ground. Not him. He was my favorite. My precious son."

"No. Mom. Please. I'm so sorry," Sasha wailed, but Naeemah lunged at her with a knife.

"Momma, please don't." Sasha dropped her weapons to the ground, too heartbroken to fight her own mother. "Mom!" Sasha's voice shook as she raised her arms, deflecting Naeemah's blade with her bare fingers. "Please," Sasha whimpered, her arms a bloody mess from her mother's knife.

"You will pay for the life of my child." Naeemah stalked her.

"I have an important job to do," Sasha insisted. She reluctantly retrieved her weapons. She would rather die than be forced to kill her mother, but Sasha's work wasn't complete. She had a mission. She would not fail.

"You? You're nothing. Nothing at all next to my powerful son. Is that why you killed him? Petty jealousy?"

"No, Mother," Sasha said calmly. "I loved him like my own twin." She gave herself over to the fight, letting her body perform the job her mind couldn't fathom.

Naeemah's body joined Aidan's. The bodies continued to pile up as Sasha fought the people she loved most in this world. They kept coming for her and her sense of urgency to escape grew with each opponent she faced. Her brother, Darius. Her father. Uncles. Imogen. Allie. Chloe. Graham. Everyone she'd ever loved came for her, spouting the most terrible lies as they tried to kill her. So many times, Sasha wanted to give up and let them have her. But her body refused to fail the mission that had been set before her.

She stumbled in the darkness, her arms slick with the blood of her family. Her voice broken from the screams that tore her throat raw until it bled.

As the smoke began to clear, Sasha fell in a heap among the bodies she'd slain. The ground still warm with their blood.

She stared up at the moon, her energy spent. She watched the clouds scuttle across the sky. The cool breeze chased the scent of sulfur away, replacing it with the scent of flowers.

"The gardens are so pretty at night."

"Shhh, angel." Jayesh stood over her now. "You're okay; it was just the wine. Come back to me, Sasha." He pulled her to her feet, gently slapping her face, but she couldn't see past the visions of her dead family.

"I killed them." She swayed on her feet.

Jayesh swept her up in his arms. "It's alright," he whispered. "It's over now."

"I killed Quinn. I love him. I should have let him kill me and then none of this would have happened. They'd all be safe. Why did I do it, Jayesh? Why? Am I a monster?" Her voice cracked as she sobbed into his shoulder.

"No, angel, you're not the monster here. I am for making you do this."

Sasha's head throbbed as the effects of the wine began to wear off in the hours just before dawn. She stared at the ceiling as Imogen lay beside her, stroking her hair, still damp with sweat and blood.

"It wasn't real?" she whispered.

"No, sweetie. They were phantoms, conjured by one of the monks in residence here. The wine causes the confusion. It makes you forget everything except the need to fight for your life. To respond as you have been trained."

"In my mind ... they were all mortal and I really killed them. Our family." Sasha sniffed back a fresh wave of tears. "I just don't understand. Why? What was the point?"

"This is what it means to become an assassin, Sasha. You must experience this night again and again and again. You will face those phantoms, forgetting you've done it before. Forgetting your immortality. Forgetting theirs. You will fear death. Theirs as well as your own. Every single night until you can survive the experience without an emotional response. You will kill your family and those you love over and over and over until you learn to shut off your emotions and follow the instincts of your body, leaving the madness of your mind behind you. When you can walk out of the experience on your own two feet, you will have conquered *ankathari* and can move on to the final phase of *verumkai*."

"How many times did you kill our mother?" Sasha whispered.

"I slayed our mother's phantom more than one thousand times," Imogen said sadly.

Sasha buried her head on her sister's shoulder and sobbed.

"Sasha, you need to eat. You're getting too thin," Jayesh said.

"I'm not hungry." She shoved the plate of fruit away. Even the sight of it made her sick.

"You need your strength for tonight."

"Please don't remind me." Her eyes filled with tears. Perhaps some people were built for this kind of training, but Sasha wasn't one of them. It was more than she could bear.

"Have you been sleeping at all?"

She shook her head. "Every time I close my eyes I see them. Dead or dying. Blood everywhere. I can't do this, Jayesh."

"We have to get through this. We've come this far."

"We? What do you mean, *we*? I'm the one down there every night, killing my family."

"And I'm the one watching you do it, Sasha. I'm the one forcing you to drink the wine every night. You don't remember, but some nights I have to pour it down your throat." His voice shook as he slammed his fist against the stone pillar. "And I'm the one who carries you out of there every night. *I'm* doing this to you. And if it were up to me, I'd end it now. But I am powerless against this. I'll never be able to convince the Senate that just because your ability is attractive to them, it doesn't make you a born assassin. They don't care. I'm afraid we are stuck here until we can both get through the night without cracking.

Do you even know how many times I've pulled you out of there simply because I couldn't bear to watch you scream for another minute?"

"We've done this for eighty-seven nights in a row and it's not getting any easier," she whispered. "If anything, it's getting harder. What am I doing wrong? How do I make it through the night when the wine makes me forget, makes it seem like the first time all over again?" Her eyes brimmed with the tears she couldn't seem to stop. Sasha had never been a crier before, but her experience with *ankathari* had broken something inside her.

"You have to find your determination. You have to fight and keep fighting. It doesn't end when I carry you back to the temple. The fight is right now and you're losing it. You have to eat. You have to sleep. You have to keep your body strong. You have to train in the mornings and you have to slay the phantoms each night. You have to forget who they represent. You need to learn to see them as faceless strangers. And one day it will get a little easier. And the next. And the next. And eventually you will conquer your mind as well as your body."

Sasha swiped at her tears. "This is so messed up, Jay. I just want to break things, I'm so angry and so *sick* of feeling like this."

"Yes. Get angry, Sasha. You should be angry. Channel that rage into getting through this."

Sasha reached for the bowl of fruit. She'd thrown up almost everything she ate lately. But he was right; the only way to end this was to get through it.

"Don't let me wallow, Jay. Keep me moving forward. Please. Whatever it takes."

"You have my word." Jayesh took her hand in his. "We will take this one day at a time ... together."

CHAPTER 23

Quinn: Fall - Cleveland, Ohio

The darkness made it worse than it actually was. And the sound of water rushing through the tunnel miles ahead didn't bode well for the second half of their journey. The flooding was bad this time of year, when the lake was at its highest. They might have to swim a good part of the way.

"I need to rest," Santi said. "Just for a minute."

Quinn nodded, slipping to the muddy ground. Livia's power pulled harder and harder with every passing minute. It was like she was sucking the life right out of them. He wasn't sure how they were going to make it. For the last hour Quinn had struggled with the overwhelming urge to turn back.

"I feel sick," Santi said. "I'm not sure I can go on. She's too deeply ingrained in me."

"I knew it would be hard, but I didn't anticipate this." Quinn reached for her hand in the darkness.

"Whatever happens, you have to keep going. You have to get away. If I can't do this...."

"Shhhh, Mina. We'll do this together. By tomorrow I'll be showing you the Yard, where Livia can never touch us."

"What's the Yard?"

"It's a huge cavern deep under the lake. My mother and grandmother and some of their friends turned it into a terrarium like the warehouse back at Soma, but I promise there are no mountains there to climb. It's amazing, Santi. It's filled with warm sunshine, cool breezes, and birds chirping."

He winced at the thought of those birds. Sasha had called them there years ago. She'd raised them and ferried the old ones out every few generations when the young ones ventured out of their nests. He would have to figure out how to deal with his feelings for Sasha and his feelings for Santi. It was impossible to go through something like they had and not be forever bonded by the experience. But he had so much history with Sasha. *How can you be in love with two people at the same time?* After so much time, and after everything he'd been through, Quinn wasn't the same person he'd been the night of the Springtime Ball. But there was still a part of him that would always be in love with Sasha.

And then there's Jayesh. Jealousy ripped through him at the thought of all the time Jay had spent with Sasha.

"Sounds beautiful," Santi whispered.

"You'll love it," Quinn said, putting his warring thoughts of Sasha aside.

"I'm not going to make it, Quinn. I'm not strong enough. Not anymore. Maybe if I hadn't been with Livia as long as I have. But she owns me. She'll always own a piece of me. I can feel her draining me, pulling me back. Already my feet itch to do her bidding."

"We can push through it, Santi. Don't give up on me now."

She drew in a ragged breath that sounded more like a death rattle.

"I'm coming," she whispered. "I'll be right behind you. If I fall back, you have to promise you'll keep going, Quinnton. You're stronger than you know. You're stronger than she knows.

She's been pushing you for months but you've held your ground. You can do this. If she pulls me back, it'll be okay because you'll be free and you'll come for us. Promise me? Promise me you won't quit?"

"I promise. Come on. Let's keep going." He offered her his hand. There was no way he would let her give up.

"I'm right behind you. For as long as I can."

"Just ... don't give up, Santi. I need you. I can't go back to my old life. Not without you. My family ... they'll expect me to go back to how it was before and I just can't face that. Not alone."

"We'll do it together," she promised.

They continued on in the darkness, their steps echoing all around them. Quinn fell into a steady pace, but his mind whirled with thoughts of Livia and how badly he wanted to return to her side. He fought the urge with every breath. With each step he took, Livia pulled back, reeling him in like a fish on a line. He grew foggy and disoriented and wasn't sure how long he'd stumbled through the shallow water rushing around his knees, nor how long ago Santi had succumbed and left him in the darkness to return to their master.

When he realized she was gone and he was alone, he sobbed. Quinn couldn't fathom not having her near. But he knew he couldn't turn back. He had to keep going. For both of them. He had to keep his promise.

The water churned around his shoulders, forcing him off his feet. His chest ached with the icy burn of his power. Livia was furious with him, but she would take it out on Santi. Every step he took would bring her more harm. But he had to keep going. His arms sliced through the water and he gasped for each breath as it rattled in his lungs.

He wasn't sure when he started drawing on his power. Livia's hold on him was slipping. He had more control than he'd had in months. He struggled with the seduction of it, cautious not to fall into the temptation now, at the worst possible moment.

As the tunnel began to rise, Quinn emerged from the muddy waters, dragging one foot in front of the other. He drew on the strength of his power to keep himself moving forward, but the battle he was currently fighting against Livia had him dangerously close to the limits of his addiction.

More. We need more.... The voice of his gift echoed in his mind. *To resist her we need more power. Give us control.*

"No! I am in control," Quinn shouted into the darkness, his voice reverberating back to him.

Then go back to the bitch. She owns you.

"I'm not going back," he argued with himself. But he was about to cross a line he swore he never would. If he was going to make it, he had to use the full force of his power.

"I have to do it now if I'm going to beat her." He could do it just this once.

Yes! Just this once.

Livia still pulled him and he resisted her with each step, but each step took him closer to giving in to the voice in his mind. The voice that told him it was okay to take a taste of that much power. Just this once.

But it wouldn't be once.

All his life, Quinn had only allowed himself to take small steps with his gifts. Only the smallest taste of the power that fueled them. His progress was slower because of it, but he never trusted himself to tempt fate. It would be too easy to take one step too far.

I would rather be a reluctant slave to Soma for the rest of my life than to give in to my power and become the thing I hate most.

Quinn stumbled to his knees. He was so close, he could see

a faint light up ahead. If he could make it into the crypt, he could get help. He just needed someone to keep him from turning around long enough to outlast Livia's strength and break her hold on him. He imagined it would be like going through detox, but if he made it home, he would have the help he needed to defeat her.

Getting to his feet, Quinn started to run. The darkness was fading quickly. When he fell again, he crawled. He was almost there. He could almost touch it—the smooth concrete wall separating him from freedom.

Where is the mosaic floor? The arches? The tunnel ended in an arched chamber that led to other parts of the crypt.

Quinn sank to the floor as he realized that somewhere along the way he'd turned back. He was staring at the concrete wall at Terminal Tower. Right back where he started—and Livia was just on the other side of the door.

Chapter 24

Sasha: Ankathari - The Chola Valley Temple

"Why do you think *ankathari* affects you so?" Mother Raghavan asked as Sasha walked beside her. "You stare at this lovely garden with vacant eyes as if this experience has broken you."

"It has," Sasha said, taking the mother's hand. "I am not built for this."

"And why do you think that?"

"The Senate sees nothing beyond my abilities that, to them, make me the perfect assassin, but they are overlooking this whole other side of me, mother. The nature-loving young woman who talks to animals, heals and protects them. The peace-loving girl who abhors violence of any kind." Sasha's voice shook with the threat of tears. "I've slayed the phantoms of my family one-hundred and fifty-nine nights. This experience is killing that side of me, and it breaks my heart and wounds my spirit. I fear it will ruin me."

"Take the Senate out of the equation. They do not matter." Mother Raghavan stopped and turned Sasha toward her, wiping the tears from her eyes with a weathered thumb. "They are simply the force that brought you here, but this experience is not about them or what they foresee for you. The Senate is remarkably blind when it comes to these things." She grasped Sasha's hands.

"I fail to find the good in this experience, mother," Sasha whispered, helping the mother down onto the bench that overlooked the western garden wall. It was their favorite place to watch the sunset.

"You must find the lesson. In here." She tapped Sasha's forehead with the tip of her cane. "And in here." She placed her hand over Sasha's heart. "The outside world is of no concern."

"Becoming a Chola assassin will make me harder and unfeeling when I'm faced with a difficult fight. I could almost accept that if I thought I could return to my old self in other ways."

"But this isn't about returning to your old self, Sasha. You left that girl behind the moment you stepped into this valley. Find a way to use this experience to improve yourself and you will leave this place a stronger and better woman because of it."

Sasha tried to focus on the mother's lesson, the thing she'd been trying to beat into her since the beginning of *ankathari*, but Sasha couldn't see beyond her desire to get this all behind her and move on. *Maybe that's the problem.*

"I am such a fool." Sasha laughed. That was exactly the problem.

"Why do you say that?" the mother asked.

"I'm the girl with the plan. The girl who always knows what she wants and how to get it. I bulldoze through life, making things go *my* way. I'm a fool, mother." She looked at the wise old guru with a hesitant smile. "I've been trying to do that here. But that's not what life is about, is it?"

"You're getting the lesson." She nodded. "Go on."

"I've always faced life with a checklist." Sasha shook her head. "A list of all the things I'm going to do and exactly how

I'm going to accomplish them. Finish school, go to college with Quinn, double major in graphic design and marketing. Get my MBA and start my career with a stellar internship. I figured by the time I landed my first real job, Quinn and I would be ready to get married or at least live together and buy a house. We'd spend a good long time with just the two of us, working hard to make our fortune. Then in a century or two we'd retire and raise our family, devoting all our time to training our children. But it's all so ... childish." Sasha laughed again. "Did I really think it would be that easy? That life wouldn't throw an unexpected tragedy or obstacle in my way that would send my carefully built house of cards crumbling into the dirt?"

"How do you feel about that realization?" the mother asked.

Sasha stared at the setting sun. "A little bit like I just grew up. Disappointed that it took me this long to get the lesson. And ... it feels quite freeing, to be honest. I think I've known for a long time and I've just been too stubborn to admit it to myself, but Quinn and I just aren't right for each other. I love him. I always will. He means the world to me and I'll always fight for him. He was my first love, but I can't force something that just isn't there. The distance I've had from him here has helped me see that."

"There are a lucky, rare few who are meant to have two great loves in their lifetime," the mother said. "It can be difficult coming to terms with how to love them each in their own way. I have no doubt that you will discover how to love Quinn in a way that is healthy for you both."

"That is a comforting thought," Sasha said. "He has always been larger than life to me. We put labels on people. Friend, boyfriend, family, lover.... Quinn has never been just one of those things. He is all of them. And none of them. I don't know where he fits into my life anymore, but I know he is and always will be as important to me as my next breath."

"But Quinn is not the lesson you are learning in this moment. This is about you and you alone. So what is it? What will you carry away with you tonight as you face your battle with *ankathari*?"

"My life will never be predictable and under my complete control. I need to be ready to roll with the punches. I have to be willing to alter my plans even if it means my life might not look anything like I intended. And I need to be okay with that. I need to accept the fact that some things are beyond my control. Becoming a Chola assassin was never in my plan. That is the Senate's plan for me. But I need to decide how I will use this experience for myself because that *is* within my control."

"Well done, Sasha."

"There's just one thing." Sasha smiled. "How do I do that?"

The mother chuckled, squeezing Sasha's hand with affection. "Take it one moment at a time and I am confident you will figure it out."

"Thank you, mother. You have been a source of great inspiration." Sasha bowed her head in respect.

"The sun is setting, dear one. It is time."

"Sasha?"

"Quinn?" Sasha turned in the swirling cloud of fog and smoke, the scent of sulfur threatening to suffocate her.

How did I get here? The confusion sent her stumbling toward the sound of Quinn's voice. She needed to see him. Feel his arms around her and know that he was real and not just a figment of this awful nightmare.

He stood in the moonlight, his shoulders hunched as if he

had the weight of the world on his mind.

"Quinn? Is it really you?" Sasha couldn't remember the last time she'd seen him. She couldn't even remember how they'd arrived at this temple. But she felt a driving need to escape.

He turned on her, his eyes a smoldering fire of power raging inside of him.

"No. Quinn, you didn't." Sasha took a step back. "You couldn't have." But the man facing her now was not the boy she loved. He'd succumbed to the addiction of his power. This was the evil that Quinn had always feared lurked inside him. The fear she'd dismissed time and again because in her mind there was nothing Quinn couldn't conquer.

"You should run," Quinn said as he raised his sword.

But Sasha refused to leave him like this. No matter what life threw at them, she would always stand with him.

"And *you* should be afraid." Sasha pointed her twin blades at him. She would not let the madness take him.

As Quinn charged her, she stood her ground, hating the thought of hurting him but determined to help him find his way back.

"Sasha, don't do this!" Aidan cried from the darkness. "He is our friend."

"Stay out of this, brother." Sasha met Quinn's attack, but it wasn't Quinn.

She twisted her body into the defensive forms she couldn't remember learning, but found herself with the upper hand against this faceless phantom that had worn Quinn's face just a moment ago. She kept her head, letting her body respond to the fight as she studied the way the phantom moved. This was not Quinn. She'd sparred with him since she was a child and her father first put a bo staff in her hand. She knew how Quinn moved, and this was not him.

"I never loved you," the phantom said, his voice full of

loathing.

"You're wrong. Quinn has always loved me. But it's time for us both to move on," Sasha replied in a level voice, thrusting her blade into his side. She let him drop to the ground without shedding a single tear.

Sasha turned in the grim darkness, seeing the others circling in the shadows of the temple wall.

Her mother and father, her brothers. Even Jayesh. They each taunted her with the most hateful lies, but it wasn't them. Not really. These were her demons, wearing the faces of those she loved most. Saying the things she feared the most.

The worry that Quinn did not love her the way she loved him. That she was no longer certain how she felt about him.

That her brother resented her place within their family.

That her mother loved Aidan more because he was so special.

That her Scottish father would have preferred a daughter more like him physically rather than in personality alone.

That her friends only tolerated her because she was Aidan's sister.

That Jayesh would leave and she would never see him again.

"I'm right here!" she screamed. "Come and fight me if you dare." She pointed her blade at the ground, determined to conquer her demons once and for all.

She faced them each in turn, slaying the faceless phantoms. Quieting their hateful lies. Because they were lies. Her fears were unfounded but they were part of her. She had to accept that it was okay to have doubts about herself. That it was okay for her to not be perfect, because she wasn't. Far from it. Sasha simply needed to do the best she could with the challenges life presented her.

As her brother Darius fell to join the others, the moon burst through the clouds, bathing the temple grounds in light. As the smoke cleared, Sasha turned toward the gates and walked all the way back to the temple on her own, shrugging off the effects of the wine that made her forget.

"You did it." Imogen ran to meet Sasha along the path to the temple.

Sasha fell into her sister's arms, exhausted from her final battle of *ankathari*.

"You are a rare person, Sasha El Sadawii." Imogen guided her up the steps to join the mother at the temple entrance.

"Greetings, dear Sasha." The mother bowed low when they joined her. "You have survived one hundred and sixty nights of sheer agony." She took Sasha's weapons from her. She didn't need them for practice anymore. "But you have succeeded and earned the blades of the Chola for yourself." The mother nodded at Jayesh, who stood by, waiting to honor his student with her reward.

"Thank you, Mother Raghavan." Sasha bowed.

Turning to Jayesh, Sasha knelt before him, touching his feet with the deepest respect. She could not have survived this experience without him.

"Well done, Sasha," Jayesh murmured as he pulled her to her feet. With a flick of each dagger, he sliced open her cheeks, bathing her new blades in her own blood. The ritual complete, Jayesh tucked the weapons of the Chola assassin into her belt.

The metal was milky white and the hilts were black obsidian, unlike anything Sasha had ever seen. She would wear them always. She'd earned those blades with a piece of her soul.

Jayesh gave her a level look to remind her they were not done yet. "We begin the final stage of *verumkai* tomorrow."

Chapter 25

Quinn: Fall - Atlanta, Georgia

"Dad, please ... stop," Quinn sobbed.

"How could you bring those people here, son?" Daniel's voice rose in anger to match the crack of the whip against his son's back. "How could you risk exposing your brother to Soma?"

"I'm sorry. I was just trying to get home. I needed help." Quinn's wrists ached from the shackles that bound him to his cell in the crypt.

"Well you've risked the safety of everyone we love. And we can't allow that." Daniel's whip ripped across his back once more. "You're going to have to go back."

The disappointment in his father's voice broke something inside him.

"You should have stayed in Atlanta," Daniel said sadly as he released the chains holding his son suspended from the brick wall.

Quinn crumpled in a heap on the dirty floor.

"You'll stay here and think about what you've done." Daniel left him alone in the darkness of the cold crypt. "And then we're taking you back. You don't belong here anymore."

Quinn curled up and cried himself to sleep.

He stared up at the odd yellow sky. The puffy white clouds were edged in gold and the warm breeze across the lake lifted his spirits. For the first time in ages, Quinn felt free.

He sat on the rocks beside the still waters of Lake Clara Meer and stared up at Sterling Tower, trying to remember how he'd gotten here.

The unreality of this place bothered him. It was too quiet. Piedmont Park was never quiet.

It's the dreamworld. The thought brought clarity to his mind as recent events began to slide into place. He was back in Michael's dungeon as punishment for his escape attempt.

"Michael's learned some new tricks." Using the faces of his family to punish him cut Quinn deeper than anything else could.

"But Michael doesn't know I can come here."

Quinn stood, staring across the lake. Livia had to know he was a dreamwalker by now, but she'd wanted this gift to develop naturally. *Why wouldn't she warn Michael not to let me sleep? She can't be protecting me. Not after I tried to escape.*

"No. She's not *letting* me sleep." Quinn paced along the water's edge, trying to put the pieces together. "I'm so sleep deprived I've finally collapsed." But she would have put him in a magnetized cell, specifically so he *couldn't* enter the dreamworld.

"She's underestimating me." Quinn stopped his pacing.

Livia was a pro at working with young Immortals with new gifts. Young Immortals far less powerful than Quinn. She wouldn't anticipate that he was even capable of fully entering the dreamworld yet, or that he would even know what to do if he happened to stumble his way into it.

"That's where you're wrong, Liv. I know exactly what to do." He turned and walked back up the path to the bridge. The Scholar had told him there was another dreamwalker here. Someone he could trust. He just had to find him.

Quinn walked halfway across the city before he realized he could simply think of a place and he was there. With the whole wide world of dreams at his fingertips, he didn't even know where to begin to look for a man he knew nothing about.

But before he could think of a plan, he was back in the waking world and under Michael's influence.

"I need more time." Quinn cursed his Immortal body for its ability to go days without rest.

In the weeks since his escape, he'd spent every possible moment in the dreamworld. It gave his mind a break from the torment his body was experiencing. But he was never there long enough to find the man he sought.

Sometimes Quinn heard voices, but he quickly learned not to follow them. The few times he had, he found himself caught up in the random nightmares and dreams of others. Quinn was working completely on instinct. It was much too dangerous to experiment with this gift. So he simply waited and observed, moving on only when the dreamer was safely enveloped in a dreamless sleep.

He avoided the temptation to follow the voices, but it was especially difficult when he recognized someone he loved. He often heard Allie and Aidan. But he could never seem to find them. Whenever he went looking for them, he inevitably ended up walking the cliff sides of Kelleys Island just as he did now.

"I should have turned around." He sat down in the tall grass, resting his arms on his knees as he gazed across Lake Erie to the city skyline in the distance. *When I realized I was back at the train station and not at the crypt, I should have turned around and kept fighting.* But in that moment, he'd fought as hard as he could. There was no other choice but to open the door and return to Soma.

With a last look at the home he loved, Quinn got to his feet and headed back down the hillside, eager to get away. He couldn't stand the sight of home for another second.

"Stay where you are!" A voice echoed like a boom from the sky. Quinn halted, looking up in confusion, unsure if he should show himself or leave this place immediately.

"Quinn? Wait!" a man called just as he hurried back into the cover of the forest.

How does he know my name? He turned back to see the man appear along the path behind him. The enormity of the man's lifeline threatened to send Quinn running in the opposite direction.

"I can help you." The man stood at a safe distance.

He was almost as ancient as the dreamworld, but Quinn was wary of trusting anyone who just happened to find him.

Quinn found his voice. "How do you know my name?"

"A friend sent me to find you."

"You're a dreamwalker?"

"So you do know what this place is. Very good, Quinn."

"Who are you?"

"My name is Navid." He closed the gap between them, offering his hand. "Let's have a chat, shall we?"

Quinn nodded. He had nothing to lose.

Navid gripped his shoulder and Quinn felt an odd lurching sensation in his stomach.

He stumbled over the uneven ground. They were in a

forest of ancient redwoods, the sky blocked by the enormous canopy arching overhead.

"Have a seat." Navid gestured at a fallen log that looked like it had served as a seat for an eternity of conversations. "You are the first new dreamwalker in a very long time. You need me, Quinn; this place is dangerous. There are others here who can't be trusted."

"How can I trust a random stranger?" Quinn hesitated to sit.

"It seems you are close with someone who means a great deal to me and my lovely wife. Several someones, in fact." Navid smiled.

"You've been talking to Alexander." Quinn laughed, finally taking a seat beside Navid. "He said the same thing when I met him recently. I still don't know what it means."

"He is a wise but confusing man. He has briefed me on your situation."

Quinn wanted to trust the dreamwalker but he wasn't sure if he should. It felt like Navid was only giving him half of the story.

"You're having a rough time of it, Quinn," Navid said softly. "If I could free you from Soma, I would do it in an instant. But I am afraid you're going to need to get yourself out of there. And soon. The best way I can help you is to mentor you here in the dreamworld. But like anyone, I have my limitations. My gift only allows me to stay here for a short time, so I cannot linger here long."

Quinn nodded, staring absently at his hands. "Can you show me how to reach someone in their dreams?" If he could somehow contact Sasha or even Aidan, he could get the help he needed.

"You are not ready for that yet. It is not wise to leave your own dreamscape until you come to understand this world better. When you visit your home here, you are venturing far too close to another's dreamscape, and that is very dangerous. I need you to stay away."

"So I can't reach my family?" It seemed his last hopes were fading quickly. He should have known not to expect so much from such a new gift.

"I'm afraid not. They are too far away. As young as you are, close proximity is needed to pull a dreamer into your own dreamscape." Navid squeezed his shoulder in sympathy. "But there are other ways this gift can help you. We just need to find the right way."

"So, if someone I needed to talk to was close enough, I could bring them here?"

"Yes. I believe you have already done that with your friend, Santi. Just remember rule number one: Do not ever leave your own dreamscape. No matter what."

"How do I know when I've left it?"

"As long as you ignore the voices that can lure you into other dreams, you will remain safe in your own little world."

"I've followed the voices a few times but I made sure to just observe until I thought it was safe to leave the dreamer in peace. I hope I haven't hurt anyone." Quinn knew better than anyone how dangerous it could be to mess around with a new gift when you didn't know what it could do.

"There have been rumors of a new dreamwalker wreaking havoc in this world. I assumed it was you, but now I'm not so sure. If you've resisted the urge to meddle with the few dreamers you've encountered, then you are doing remarkably well."

"I don't have a clue what I'm doing."

"But you have good instincts." Navid smiled. "You should trust them."

"Is ... does a dreamwalker help people?" The temptation to

use his power was there, like it always was, but it was so much easier to ignore here.

Navid sighed as he sat back. "That's a complicated question."

"What does a dreamwalker do?"

"In simple terms, we were once the guides who helped dreamers travel safely back to the waking world. Before the Great War, all Immortals came here to rest. During the war, some with more talent for this place began to use it as a weapon, terrorizing dreamers as they slept. As the mortal population grew, they too came here. Many believed the mortals should have been extinguished rather than banished. Some dreamwalkers used their ability to attempt just that." Navid frowned at the unpleasant memory.

"The dreamworld is a sad, broken place, Quinn. It's nothing like it once was. Few have the gift anymore. Those that do often let the power go to their heads. Those like myself take the job more seriously. It is our responsibility to protect dreamers—Immortal and mortal alike."

"Protect them from what?" Quinn asked.

"Other dreamwalkers. Losing their way among the nightmares. This place can be dangerous. Those who die in their sleep ... more often than not, the death is due to a dreamwalker —or lack of a competent one. Sadly, those of us who have taken up the traditional role are far too few."

"You should know, I am an addict." Quinn hung his head in shame. "Most of my gifts are dangerous, heinous things I would rid myself of in an instant if I could."

"We are all addicts here, Quinn. It is the plight of the dreamwalker."

"You too?" Quinn wondered if this man could be the precedent he'd looked for all his life.

"I am." Navid nodded. "I know exactly what it means to

suffer from the addiction. It is why I can never stay here too long. I know my limits and I do not exceed them."

"You have no idea what it means to meet someone like you." Quinn leaned his elbows on his knees for support, letting his head slump forward. "To see a kind man your age who has managed to fight the addiction and keep his humanity. It is inspiring."

"I haven't always. I've stumbled. And when I do, I start over." Navid shrugged. "Believe it or not, but I find mortal AA meetings to be quite helpful. I learned a very long time ago how important it is to forgive myself for my weaker moments so I am able to be strong when it truly counts."

"When can we meet again?" Quinn asked. "I don't want to keep you here too long."

"I will come find you."

"Thank you." Quinn leaned back, staring at the sky. "It is peaceful here." He looked back down at his hands, seeing the bruises from the shackles that held him in the waking world. "If a man found himself in a bad situation in the waking world and retreated here for a break, would it save his mind from the torment? Enough for him to find his strength again?"

"Now you're thinking like a dreamwalker," Navid said. "We have all the time in the world to teach you how to navigate this place. That can come later. Find your respite here. That is how the dreamworld is going to save you from Soma. Come here. Rest. Recover. And when your punishment is over, you will return to Livia, not as the defeated boy she expects, but as a man ready to face his demons."

"She doesn't let me sleep much. I'm never really here long enough to rest."

"You are a dreamwalker, Quinn. A strong one. You do not need to sleep to come here."

"I don't?" Quinn asked in surprise.

"Let that be our first lesson before I leave you. You will have to work at it, but you simply need to reach a meditative state of mind to come here and stay in your dreamscape as long as you like."

"I can do that." Quinn nodded. "They'll put me in the white room soon. That will be my best chance."

"I will come find you when I can and we will have our lessons. I must leave now."

"Thank you, Navid." Quinn watched as Navid walked down the path. In an instant the dreamwalker was gone.

Quinn stayed in the forest for as long as he could, but with the familiar splash of water mixed with alcohol and acid, he was back in the waking world, his body on fire.

"You will stay here for as long as it takes to get it through your head, we own you," Michael sneered as he closed the door to Quinn's white prison.

With the echo of the slamming door, Quinn smiled. Last time he was sent to the white room, the sameness of it drove him mad. Day in, day out, nothing ever changed. White walls. White tile. White food. Everything bathed in fluorescent white light. But this time it would be his oasis.

It took him several attempts, but Quinn finally managed to enter the dreamworld while his body was awake and in a meditative state. He knew the routine of the white room quite well. Between his pitiful breakfast and dinner, he never saw a soul. That left him with the hours in between to escape to the dreamworld. He spent the majority of his days there now.

Quinn traveled the world, all within the safety of his own dreamscape. He only had to think of a place he'd like to visit and he was there. He explored the most beautiful forests and meadows with the most glorious colors he didn't even have a name for.

On the nights when his body rested, Quinn spent hours building a fortress of a library just for himself. It quickly became his home in the dreamworld. He reclined on a red leather sofa in the evenings and read his favorite books.

Each day he grew a little stronger than the day before as his mind healed from the stress of his time at Soma. He met with Navid often, but only for brief lessons.

Quinn was confident that when Livia brought him out of the white room, he would be ready to act. Ready to get himself, Santi and the others out of Soma for good.

CHAPTER 26

Sasha: Verumkai - The Chola Valley Temple

"*Verumkai* is hand-to-hand combat, using the forms and weapons we learned in the earlier phases of *kalaripayattu*. In addition to the student's individual gifts." Jayesh paced in front of Sasha's unseeing eyes. She listened, but didn't really hear. She didn't really care.

I want to go home.

"But there is a level of *verumkai* that is only taught to those students the mother deems worthy."

"Let me guess. It totally sucks. And I'm one of the lucky few." Sasha sighed.

"Pretty much." Jayesh sat down in front of her at their favorite meditation spot beside one of the natural fountains. He took her hands in his. His warm reassurance was comforting.

"I don't like seeing you like this, Sasha."

"I'm just tired. Please, tell me about our final phase of training."

"It will not be easy for either of us. You are so young...."

"Just tell me, Jay. I can take it. *Ankathari* was difficult, but I'm strong. I will find a way to get through *verumkai* as well."

"In addition to honing your grappling skills, you will be

learning the art of *marmas* manipulation. There are one-hundred-eight *marmas*, or pressure points, in the human body. Sixty-four of them are lethal. *Marmas* are used in the arts of healing, meditation and in yoga, as I'm sure you have experienced training with your mother. But they are also used in *kalaripayattu*. A master of *kalari* can use *marmas* to temporarily disable their opponents, or to kill when it becomes necessary."

"So we're going to focus on those lethal ones, right?" Sasha asked.

"You will learn and experience each of the one-hundred-eight *marmas*. Including the lethal ones."

"So you're going to kill me at least sixty-four times? Which means I will have to recover sixty-four times. And at the rate I heal, it means we are no closer to leaving this place than when we first arrived."

"Some lethal *marmas* kill instantly. Some offer a slower path to death. In those instances, I will try not to kill you." He gave her a tentative smile. "If you promise not to be a brat."

"Tell me how they work and we'll see." She returned his smile with a playful glare.

"*Marmas* are the vital pressure points found at specific junctures in the body. These areas are where the life force is believed to be located," Jayesh began. "The points are concentrated where the flesh, tendons, veins, arteries, bones and joints meet.

"In *kalaripayattu*, we are trained to attack using these points to our advantage. An advanced *kalari* master can disable or kill his opponent merely by touching the correct *marma* with just the right amount of pressure. However, this is taught only to the most trustworthy students."

"And those whose gifts are inclined for the assassin's trade."

"Don't let this make you cynical, Sasha. We will approach

this carefully. I will teach you the healing *marmas* right along with the painful ones so it is never more than you can bear."

"And how many times will I have to experience each of these *marmas?*"

"Only once. Just so you may know how it feels and what it does to your body. If you will be using the lethal *marmas* against an opponent, you will understand through firsthand experience how it feels."

"Then let's get started, shall we? The sooner we begin, the sooner we are done." She remembered saying the same thing her first day here. It felt like a lifetime ago.

"*Marma* points are grouped in three categories. *Sanakha* are those points found on the legs and feet. *Madhayamanga* are located along the torso, and *jatrurdhara* are found on the neck and head.

"The heart, forehead and throat are the most vulnerable areas of the body." Jayesh pointed to each area. "These *marmas* will cause the most damage. The arms and legs are less vulnerable to severe injury, but can still cause a great deal of pain to your opponent with the right manipulation."

"Show me."

"We don't have to start today."

"I can handle pain, Jayesh. The agony of being here is way worse than anything you're going to do to me."

"Give me your foot."

Sasha leaned back on her elbows in the grass and placed her foot in his lap. Jayesh looked as though he would like to be anywhere else in the world than sitting in the beautiful garden preparing to teach her such destructive things.

"I will not make you suffer any longer than you have to." He massaged the pad of her foot, splaying her toes in preparation for her first lesson of *verumkai.* "You will pay attention to every movement as I explain it and once you have experienced the pressure point for yourself today, you will do the same to me tomorrow. When you can perform them perfectly, we will move on."

"I have to hurt you too? This is barbaric, Jayesh." He was older and would recover much faster than she would, but it still didn't sit well with her that she would have to bring him pain. Kill him, even. Jayesh never talked about himself very much, but she got the sense that he had experienced enough pain in his three hundred years to last him an eternity.

"It is how it is done, Sasha. It will be nothing I haven't experienced before." He continued to massage her foot, coaxing her to relax.

"There are four *marmas* located in the foot. Here, just between your big toe and the second metatarsal." He pressed lightly on the spot at the base of her toe. "This is called the *kshipra* and it affects the heart and lungs. She relaxed involuntarily as he gently massaged the area. "See how I've stimulated the *marma* with gentle pressure?"

Sasha nodded. It felt nice for a brief moment until he increased the pressure, focusing on the point that was as small as the tip of a needle.

Her breath came in short gasps as her lungs refused to cooperate with their lifelong rhythm of expansion and contraction. She saw stars dancing in her peripheral vision, her lungs like huge boulders in her chest.

Jayesh released the pressure, returning to the gentle massage.

"If I were to strike this *marma* directly with maximum pressure, it would stop your heart. And here." His fingertips slid down to the pad of her foot. "At the juncture of the tendons where the plantar arteries are exposed is the *kulcha*. Watch what happens as I apply pressure."

Sasha placed her palms flat against the grass beneath her,

shaking as Jayesh pushed hard against the tender part of her foot. She gasped as her vision grew dark around the edges.

"I can't blind you with this *marma*, but I can directly affect your vision."

Sasha nodded, but didn't relax until her vision returned. "You can control all of that just with my foot?"

"There are two more." Jay's fingertips wandered down to the arch of her foot. "This is the *talhrdayam* point. It can affect the lungs similarly to the *kshipra* point, although this one will cause your lungs to contract, where *kshipra* will simply make it difficult to breathe."

With a flick of his thumb, Sasha's lungs began to spasm and she couldn't breathe at all. Her fingers sank into the grass beneath her palms. Her left lung collapsed and blood oozed between her lips when he released his hold on her foot.

Sasha curled on her side, choking as she fought to get her breath.

"Jay ... I can't ... breathe," she gasped, unable to fill her lungs.

"Relax, Sasha. You have a collapsed lung. It will heal on its own in a few hours."

Sasha closed her eyes and focused on her right lung, imagining it expanding and contracting, giving her the oxygen she needed while her left lung recovered. The sensation of not getting enough air soon passed.

"The final *marma* located in the foot is the *kurchashira*." His thumb found the center point just above her heel at the base of her arch. The pressure of his thumb made her uncomfortable.

"Are you ready, Sasha? This will cause muscle spasms along the sciatic nerve."

"Do it."

He held her foot steady and brought his thumb down on

the sensitive spot. Sasha felt something pop as heat spread up her leg, causing her muscles to spasm from her calf to her hip.

The pain chased all sense from her mind as she twisted her body, bringing her left foot up in a swift kick to his temple. But Jayesh caught her foot before she could strike him.

Sasha curled in on herself as her right leg spasmed out of control.

"Breathe." Jayesh applied small amounts of pressure to the *kurchashira* point until the nerve began to relax and the warmth receded. "Better?"

"Yes." She nodded, wiping the sweat from her brow as she lay on the ground, panting.

"You tried to kick me." He looked down at her with an amused smile.

"I meant to. It's really annoying the way you always seem to be one step ahead of me."

"Five steps, actually."

"Your gift?" she asked. She'd often wondered if he had some talent for seeing ahead.

"Only in battle. I'm always five steps ahead of everyone else. It makes me the best at what I do."

"And what is that, exactly?"

"International man of mystery." He winked.

"You've watched one too many spy movies."

"We'll do one more pressure point today, and then tomorrow you will perform each of these *marmas* on me to exact your revenge."

"This wasn't so bad," Sasha said as Jayesh stood, offering her his hand. "It wasn't a picnic at the mangrove forest, but it wasn't awful."

"We will always begin slowly, never taking it beyond what you can bear. For today, I simply want you to get a feel for how these vital pressure points can affect the body. It is not meant to give you pain for the sake of suffering, but so that you may understand better how the body functions and can use it to your advantage when it becomes necessary to protect yourself. *Marmas* should only be used in self-defense and only when our opponent gives us no other choice. A Chola assassin will always seek to kill quickly and mercifully with the blade first, but when all else fails, we use the lethal *marmas* with precision."

Sasha brushed the grass from her tunic and her hair. Her breath still uneasy. She was a bit of a mess from just these first four *marmas*.

And only a hundred and four left to go.

"Stand opposite me," Jayesh said, moving to face her. "I will strike you here." He pointed to the soft place just behind her ear. "The *vidhuram*."

She barely felt it when he brought the fleshy side of his palm down against the spot behind her ear. The instant he struck her, her chin lolled against her chest and she could no longer move her head.

"I've paralyzed the muscles used to support your head." He reached behind her to massage the area, bringing it back to life until she could finally lift her head again. "Good job today. That wasn't so bad."

"At this rate, we'll be here for months. Isn't there a crash course where we could blow through all these in a week? Just to get it done?"

"No. *Marma* manipulation is an art form and it takes time to master. This will not be easy, Sasha. I'm going to have to kill you. Many times. And recovery will take time, given your age."

"I hear a 'but' coming."

"But when it is over, your training will be nearly complete."

"I thought this was it. Once *verumkai* is done, we're out of here."

"Once this is behind us, you will be even more profoundly

altered than you are now. You will need time before you can return to your old life. Before either of us can go back to the real world. The final stage of *kalaripayattu* will be a time of healing. A way of coming to terms with who you are now. Our training is brutal and it can break something inside of you. Before the mother will release you, she needs to know you are healing up here." He brushed his palm across her temple.

"So after you all have made me kill my family, kill myself and pushed me so hard I no longer recognize myself, you want to put me back together again?"

"It is the only way you will come full circle."

"I know, but it's absurd. Tear me down to the studs only to build me back up again."

"Absurd? This is a chance to truly see yourself for who you are. You came to terms with that during *ankathari*. You have the chance to walk out of here a stronger, much more capable version of the lost, mouthy little girl who arrived here all those months ago. Don't be like me, angel. Don't waste this opportunity by not learning anything. I would hate to see you miss the true point."

Jayesh did his best to teach her slowly, letting Sasha experience several new *marmas* each day. They always began with something mild, like a momentary loss of hearing, followed by something more painful that usually involved some sort of muscle spasm. He could touch her wrist and give her seizure-like convulsions. To give her a break from anything painful, Jay would desensitize her by activating the *apastambha* point just below her breastbone. The respite was brief, but it helped her through the worst moments.

The first time he killed her, she didn't even see it coming.

He explained how the *amsa* would affect her brain. The next thing she knew, it was nine days later when she awoke in her dormitory, experiencing for the first time in her life what a hangover must feel like to a mortal after a week-long bender.

Her *verumkai* training resumed immediately when Jayesh showed her the *phana* point to alleviate the throbbing of her head.

She'd experienced death several times since then, but it never got easier.

Sasha reluctantly made her way along the well-worn path to the northwest pavilion. She trusted Jayesh to keep them moving forward, but each day got a little worse than the day before.

"Lay down," Jayesh said when she joined him in the gardens. "This one will be difficult, so let's get it out of the way first."

Panic rose in her throat. "Will it kill me?" The first time she died, it was instant. But with other marmas, she had suffered painful deaths that were more terrifying than anything she'd ever experienced. It gave her so much respect for mortals who approached their deathbeds with grace and dignity. For them, death was a part of life. For her, death was an anomaly and rarely final. Even knowing she would come back, the intensity of death affected her more each time.

"It shouldn't." Jayesh looked her in the eye. "This will give you a violent seizure, but if I can release the pressure in time, it will not kill you and we can move on after you have recovered from the shock."

Sasha settled back into the grass, gazing up at the sun high in the sky. They could practice anywhere, but they both preferred the gardens and the privacy it afforded them.

"Ready?" Jay peered down at her, his forehead furrowed in concentration and worry.

"Yes," she said, reaching up to smooth his brow. "I'll be fine."

"I know you will. You've taken this like a champ."

"When we get out of this place, you owe me a trip to Hawaii and about a month's worth of fruity drinks with pink umbrellas and a few roasted pigs."

"It's a deal." He smiled down at her. "Ready?"

"Let's do it."

"Close your eyes and follow the movement of my fingers along your skull. Here is the *simantakas*." He pressed against her forehead and along her hairline. "This one can affect your reality and your sanity as well as the blood supply to your brain. Here." His fingertips moved through her hair, sliding along the seams of her skull to the peak of her head. "This is the *adipati*. It affects the functions of the mind, the nervous system and, when under pressure, can cause an epileptic seizure."

His hands in her hair felt nice. After all the time they'd spent together, they shared a level of comfort and intimacy now. Sasha caught herself wondering what it might be like to have his hands on her when he wasn't teaching her about pressure points.

It's not fair to Quinn. She shouldn't be thinking about someone else. She owed him more loyalty than that. Especially after the way she'd left things with him.

But Sasha wasn't the same girl that had entered the Chola Valley more than two years ago. *Two years for me.* She couldn't fathom going back to her old life, picking it up like nothing had changed.

"Deep breaths. Let's try to get through this without further injury. Bite on this." Jay placed a strip of leather between her teeth as he pressed a knee to each of her shoulders to hold her steady.

With his palm gently at the nape of her neck, he struck the top of her head with the point of his knuckle.

Sasha exhaled. She'd expected it to hit her immediately. Confusion clouded her mind.

"What's going on?" she muttered around the leather strap in her mouth. "What's that awful smell?" It was like gasoline. She tried to sit up, but her arms twitched and her fingers curled against her chest as she convulsed.

The seizure hit her hard as her eyes rolled into the back of her head and she foamed at the mouth, her back arching and her feet jerking.

Jayesh rolled her onto her side, holding her steady and giving her a moment to experience the effects of the *adipati marma*.

What an awful way to die. She shrank away from her body, retreating to the safety of her mind, the pain growing distant and dim.

The sharp crack along the top of her head brought everything back into sharp relief. Her body trembled and jerked, every joint and muscle a tightened coil of tension.

"That's it, Sasha. Breathe." Jay's voice sounded like a warm haven of life, pulling her back from the darkness of death. "You did it." He smiled as he pried the leather from her teeth and rolled her back onto the grass. "Just breathe."

"I don't like dying," she murmured as a tear slid down her cheek. She turned away from Jayesh and curled up in a ball of misery.

"I know, angel. It's almost over." His gentle hand at the small of her back brought a surprising comfort.

"Feel the separation of the tendons?" Jayesh asked as Sasha ran her thumb down the back of his neck.

"Here?" she asked, settling on the small depression where his back muscles met his neck.

I could run my fingers across his body all day long.

"Yes. And what is it called?"

"Hmmm?"

"Focus, Sasha. What is this *marma* called?"

"Oh, right. *Sirmatrika*. It can affect the blood circulation from your heart to your brain and other organs."

"You've experienced the death associated with too little blood reaching your vital organs. Now it's your turn in the driver's seat. Just a quick stab of pressure with your index fingers should do it."

Sasha explored the length of his neck, settling her index fingers over the sensitive spot.

It confused her. How comfortable she was with him now. How familiar she was with his body after all their hours of training together. The last time she'd experienced such intimacy with another person, it was with Quinn.

I feel so guilty. Like I've betrayed him.

"Any time now, angel." His voice held a teasing tone that did pleasant things to her.

"I don't think I can do it, Jayesh," she whispered. She'd killed him once before. An accident when she wasn't able to restore the function of his lungs quickly enough. To do it on purpose.... She didn't think she had it in her.

"I'll be back with you by dinnertime." He reached for her hand over his shoulder. "Don't overthink it."

"It's just so ... mean."

"Think of it as retribution for all the times I've killed you. Remember the day I used the *guda marma* and didn't warn you that it would make you soil yourself?"

Sasha frowned at the humiliating memory and without further thought, brought her index fingers down with precision against the area where tendons met muscles. Jay's head drooped for a moment before he slid to the ground like a dead weight.

Only thirty-six left.

Chapter 27

Sasha: Summer - The Chola Valley Temple

"How many yards was that?" Sasha asked.

The monks were all lounging in the shade of their canopy, murmuring about Sasha's last shot with the sniper rifle she was finally getting to shoot just for fun.

With all three stages of *kalaripayattu* behind her, she had earned her title as an official Chola assassin, master of *kalari,* and was now enjoying her post-training reprieve. There was still a darkness inside her. She didn't think it would ever go away, but with each passing day, she was feeling a little more like herself. Maybe not her old self. That girl was dead. But she was figuring out who the new Sasha was and coming to terms with her.

"Over three thousand yards," Jayesh said, lowering his binoculars. "That's nearly two miles, Sasha." He beamed down at her. His eyes were clear and there was a lightness about him he hadn't had when they first arrived. She never asked what the mother wanted to teach him during his time in the valley, but whatever it was, he seemed to have learned his lesson too.

"The bullet went right through the steel plate and blew the ballistic gel to bits." He lay back down beside her on the mat.

"Armor-piercing rounds, baby." Sasha sighted down the scope to see the evidence of her last shot. "You know, if the Senate ever needs you to shoot up a steel plate at three thousand yards, I'm your girl."

"You know it's not going to be a practice target on the other end of that scope when this is real?" Jayesh said softly.

"I know." Sasha moved to trade places with him. "If I'm shooting magnetized ammo, I'll be okay. But real life-ending bullets are going to be a problem for me, Jay."

"I know, angel. We'll cross that bridge when we get there."

She knew he would do his best to keep that inevitable future from coming too soon, but ultimately it wouldn't be his choice when and where the Senate would call Sasha into active duty. She could only hope that when they did call on her, he would be the one leading her team.

"Take a selfie with me?" She rolled over and faced the camera toward them.

Jayesh leaned in close so they could both fit in the frame. "Where did you find a camera?" He wrapped his arm around her.

"It's Imogen's. She thought I might want to get a few mementos of my time here. Big smiles!" She grinned and snapped the photo.

"Seriously, it's my turn, Sasha." Jayesh pulled her away from the gun. "Stop hogging it."

Sasha watched him as he adjusted the scope and took his sweet time lining up the shot before he pulled the trigger. Her feelings for Jayesh were all twisted up with her feelings for the Chola temple, the mother, the Senate and her time away from her family. She cared a great deal for this man and counted him a lifelong friend. And if she were honest, she had more than just a little crush on him. *He is way too old,* she reminded herself.

"You're talking to me with those eyes again." He smiled.

"You're a terrible shot. Don't quit your day job." She gave him a playful shove.

"What? That was a clean hit. Did you see the way the bullet sailed right through the ballistics gel?"

"It's more fun when you blow it to smithereens."

"Flashy maybe, but a clean shot takes more precision."

"Good thing you're here to teach me," she said.

"I'm too old for you, Sasha."

"Agreed." She peered down over the cliff side where they'd perched the Barrett M107A1. "But I won't always be seventeen. And the two-hundred-seventy years between us won't always feel like it does now."

"Call me in two hundred years and it's a date," Jay said, lining up his next shot.

"It's a date." It felt odd, thinking of being with someone other than Quinn. She still couldn't wait for the day when she would see him again. And when she did, she hoped he would understand that she didn't think she could go back to the way they were before. She wasn't that girl anymore and she doubted very much if he was that same boy. "Promise me, Jayesh," Sasha said softly. "Promise me you won't wait that long to see me again?"

"You know we have to leave, Sasha," he said gently. "It's time."

"No. Not yet." She stared up at him.

A year ago, she would have given anything to leave the Chola Valley and never look back. But in the months since her training ended, she'd experienced some of the happiest times of her life here. Nearly three years had passed for Sasha during her time at the temple. It frightened her to think of returning to her old life, knowing for the rest of her family, it had only been six weeks. *How can I go back? How can I leave him?*

"I'm not ready." She shook her head stubbornly. "Imogen's not ready. She is still training with the mother."

"I don't want to leave either, angel. That's why I know it's time to go. Imogen needs to stay, but you need to leave."

"Come home with me? Just for a little while?"

"I can't. I have a job waiting for me."

"Africa." She nodded. His entire team was waiting for him to return so they could complete an important mission.

"When will I see you again?" Her chest ached at the answer she knew he would give.

"Hopefully never. I'll miss you, but I don't want you to have the life I've had."

She nodded, staring at her hands.

"I owe you some long overdue truth," Jayesh said. "I know I can trust you to never repeat this. To anyone."

"You have my word."

"While I do work for the Senate from time to time, they are not my true employer. I can't tell you much, so you're going to have to trust me. But I have orders to bring you in when this is done."

"Bring me in where?" Sasha took a hesitant breath.

"I can't tell you."

"Then why are you telling me anything?"

"It will be a cold day in hell before I betray you like that. I tried really hard to keep you at arm's length. But I can't do it. I won't do it. We have to get you home safely but I'm not sure how."

Sasha nodded. "Your team will be waiting for us the moment we walk out of this valley?"

"They have orders to take you on sight."

"What if we had help?" Sasha smiled. "You don't really think my mother would let us leave without someone to watch our backs?"

"Of course." Jay returned her smile. "She had you followed?"

"My uncle."

Jayesh stood and walked along the edge of the cliff, taking in the lay of the land in each direction. "We could leave the valley the hard way." He pointed to the hiking trails to the north. "But how would we find him?"

"He'll find us."

"How?"

"If I told you, I'd have to kill you," she said sweetly.

"We need weapons, just in case we run into my team. They'll know when we've left the valley and when they realize I'm avoiding them, they'll circle around and come for us."

"How will they know?"

"If I told you, I'd have to kill you." Jayesh shot her a grin.

"Imogen and I brought weapons with us."

"Of course you did. I would expect nothing less of the women of your family. You don't have any more sisters, do you? I'm officially boycotting the El Sadawii women; they are too much trouble."

"I'm the last one, but watch out for the Carmichael girl. She's got that El Sadawii spunk too." Sasha smiled at the thought that she might be seeing Allie soon. "When should we leave?" she asked. She wasn't ready, but if his team was lying in wait for her, she needed to get out of here.

"Tomorrow night."

"Will Imogen be safe when it's time for her to leave?"

"Once they realize I've left, they'll come for me. I'll lead them away from Imogen."

Sasha frowned. "You're going to be punished for helping me escape, aren't you?"

"No. The official story will be that you grew suspicious of

me and left the valley on your own. When I realized what you'd done, I followed but was too late. They'll buy it."

But she didn't buy it. He was lying. If he let her escape, he would be punished ... and Sasha wasn't going to let that happen.

CHAPTER 28

Quinn: Fall - The Dreamworld

"What are you saying, James?" Santi paced along the forest path under the canopy of ancient redwoods where Quinn had experienced his first lessons with Navid only a few weeks ago.

In the waking world, he and Santi were back in Livia's penthouse, recovering from their respective punishments. They spent their days training and their nights in the dreamworld.

And now he'd pulled James into his dreamscape too.

"You knew it was coming eventually." James shrugged. "It's not like there's anything I can do about it. Lennox has a few weeks left at Soma, at most. And hopefully her new owners will treat her well, considering what she is."

"She's a little girl, not a damaged product!" Santi balled her fists at her sides.

"Lennox knew it was only a matter of time before someone found out about her early Awakening. She's grown up here, guys. And when you grow up at Soma, you get used to the idea that you don't have a say in your own future. She'll be okay. There's a chance she might even earn her freedom one day."

Quinn glared at his friend. James could be a good guy

when he wanted. He had decency buried somewhere beneath the depravity this place had ingrained in him. But sometimes you had to dig deep to find the man he was supposed to be before Soma ruined him.

"We're not letting them sell her. It's not up for discussion," Quinn said.

"She was sold at Amrita, guys. It's a done deal," James said.

"We have to get her out of here." Santi shook her head stubbornly. "Like right now. We can't risk waiting any longer."

"What, you're going to walk out the front door tomorrow?" James folded his arms across his chest.

"Yeah. Exactly," Santi said after a long pause.

"What?" Quinn looked at her like she'd lost her mind.

"I have an idea," Santi said. "But we need James." Except James wasn't listening. His eyes held a faraway look, like he wasn't quite there with them.

"Give him a minute. He's seeing something," Quinn said.

"Nope. Didn't see nothing." James shook his head, backing away. "Just ... if you find a way to get Len out of here, don't ever look back. That kid deserves a good life." He shoved his hands in his pockets and took off along the path.

"Not so fast." Quinn followed him. With a brush of his hand against James's arm, he brought him back to the fallen log, shoving him down to sit. "What did you see?"

"I saw you walk out the front door with Livia. Just like Santi said. I don't know what it means."

"Santi, what are you thinking?" Quinn asked.

"Can I go now?" James tried to get up again. "I don't want to be involved."

"Stay right where you are." Quinn shoved him back down. "You're part of this friendship whether you want to be or not. If we get out, you're coming with us. If Santi has a plan, I want to hear it." But James gave him a look that said hoping was pointless. He was broken in a whole different kind of way.

"How much time do we have?" Santi asked. "Before her *owners* show up?"

"A few weeks. Maybe."

"Then we don't have much time to figure out our next move. So talk fast, Santi. What's your plan?" Quinn asked.

Santi paced back and forth in front of them, chewing on her thumbnail. "If we escape, Livia will just reel us back in. But what if we escaped with her?"

"What? Like trick her?" James scoffed. "She's not easily fooled, in case you haven't noticed."

"So we have to be convincing."

"What could we possibly say to get her to go along with us?" Quinn asked, ignoring James.

"It's risky. I've been thinking about it since Quinn dragged himself out of that tunnel in Cleveland. I was hoping we'd have more time to work out a better plan, but with Lennox's situation, we have to act now. Can we trust you, James?"

"If you really think you can get Lennox out of here, I'll keep my mouth shut."

"It's going to fall to you to get her out of here."

"No dice." James shook his head. "You've experienced how Livia pulls you back. You've met me, right? I am not strong enough to resist that. Hell, even you two couldn't do it, and you're way more motivated than me."

"She doesn't control your gift, so how can she pull you back?" Quinn asked.

"She owns me. She can pull me back by my Soma leash." He pointed to the brand on his arm. "She owns us all and for those of us who live here, she controls our brands. If we try to escape she can use the brand to pull us back. If she has control of one of your gifts, her pull is even stronger."

"I thought Ryan controlled the brands? It's his gift that makes them."

"And he passes his control to the owners. For us, that's Livia. If we're sold, she would pass ownership to the highest bidder, giving them that same kind of control. It's how some of us are able to go out into the world to do Soma's bidding. We come back because we are well-trained dogs who don't like the tug of the master's leash."

"So let's say we got her to take us out on another mission and we exhausted her ability?" Santi asked. "Theoretically, you could walk out the front door with Lennox and not look back, right?"

"There's a chance Ryan would be able to stop us." James ran his hands through his hair. "But if he were distracted too, it might work. Except for the hundreds of Coalition and Soma agents at Sterling Tower who would question why I was removing property from the building."

"But you can come and go however you like," Santi said. "You should be able to sneak her out."

"That's easier said than done," James muttered.

"We *will* come up with a plan, James," Santi said. "We're not leaving you or Lennox behind. We'll get Livia and her team occupied, and you'll get Len out of the building. Then you come meet us."

"Sure, no problem." James laughed.

"This is happening, James." Santi gave him a hard look. "We give you the chance to get her out and you take it. You hear me? You fail and you'll have to deal with me."

James nodded. "All right, I promise. If you two can pull this off, I'll get Lennox out of here."

"And what is our part in this?" Quinn asked, eager to hear what Santi had up her sleeve.

"Can you give me your absolute trust, Quinnton?"

"You have that in spades, Mina."

"Say that again when you hear the rest of my plan."

"I'm listening."

"You have to let her push you over the edge. Give in to your addiction and she'll break you."

"No." Quinn shook his head.

"Think about it before you say no. You succumb to the addiction and she'll think she's won. She'll have no reason to think you aren't completely hers."

"And she'll be right. That's ridiculous, Santi. If I lose control of my power … I won't be me anymore. I won't have a reason not to tell her whatever she wants to know. She'll go after my family."

"Exactly. She will break you and you will tell her everything she wants to know. All you have to do is trust me to take care of the rest. Can you do that?"

"I trust you. But I don't think you understand what you're asking me to do."

"When you tell her everything she's been dying to know about Allie, she's going to go after her and that's exactly what we want. The point is for us to escape. To do that we need help. We take the fight to your family and we get the help we need."

"You think if I let her attack my family that they'll win, take her captive and free us."

"I've never seen a family more well-connected and prepared than yours. She won't expect it. You all have resources I couldn't even fathom. You've turned Kelleys Island into an impenetrable fortress."

"There's one giant hole in your plan, Santi."

"What's that?"

"How do we know what I'll do once she breaks me? How do we know I won't tell her what we're planning?"

"When she breaks you, your gift is going to take over, right?"

"Yes, and that version of myself is a lunatic."

"A lunatic that will want to be a Soma slave?" she asked, her brow raised to make her point.

"No. He won't want to be under Livia's thumb any more than I do."

"You guys are talking like there's more than one Quinn in there." James rapped his knuckles against Quinn's head. "That's worrisome."

"You don't know the half of it," Quinn said. "That guy has been trying to take control since I was sixteen years old."

"Multiple personalities?"

"It's my power. It manifests as an alter ego. He wants the freedom to use my power his way and not mine. I keep him in check. What Santi is suggesting would mean letting him come out to play. And there is just no predicting what that asshole will do."

"So the question of the hour is, would crazy-Q play along with our plan?" James asked.

"You know him best, Quinn. But it doesn't sound like he'd blow the whistle on us if what he wants is freedom. He's been a prisoner inside you all his life. He's not going to want to trade one prison for another."

"Do you think you can reason with him?" James asked.

"If Livia pushes me into my addiction, I'll resist it. It's just in my blood. I'll hear the voice. He'll tempt me, like always. I would have time to reason with him, but there's no guarantee he'll go along with the plan."

"That's where you're going to have to trust me to do my part too," Santi said. "I'll make sure this goes our way."

"I trust you, Santi. I do. But I don't think I could come back to myself after that."

"We don't have time for your stubborn self-doubt, Quinnton. You really can't see it, can you?" She shoved him hard, pushing him down on the log beside James. "You're really that stupid?"

"Santi, I know what my limits are."

"No. You know what scares you," she accused. "Like a coward, you set your limits too low and you refuse to budge. But you are *not* a coward." She cut right through him with her glare. "You can do this, Quinn. You have strength unlike anything I've ever seen." Her voice softened as she knelt beside him. "You are one of the kindest men I've ever known—and you're hardly more than a boy. You have grace and humility. But you do not trust yourself. You let Livia break you and we'll beat her at her own game. And then you'll come back to me."

"How do we know that, Santi? How do we know I wouldn't just become the weapon she wants?"

"You failed once before, Quinn. When you came out of that tunnel, you failed. You won't fail again."

"I told you I had no idea when I turned back." It wasn't fair for her to throw that in his face now. It wasn't like her to be so cruel. "It wasn't a conscious choice to turn back."

"That's not when you failed." Her eyes blazed with fury. "When you realized you were back where you started, why didn't you turn around again? They couldn't get to you through that concrete wall. When I opened the door and went back to her, I was no longer in control of myself. I fought until the last second. But why did you walk out of that tunnel on your own?"

"I was at the end of my rope, Santi. I couldn't turn back and do it all over again. I opened the door and went back with my tail tucked between my legs because she controls me."

"Because you refused to fight, Quinn. You failed to escape because you refused to cross that line you set for yourself when you were sixteen years old. I know you. I know you sat in that tunnel and thought about pushing yourself. To keep going. But your fear of losing control is what stopped you. Len's life is on the line. If you won't risk this for yourself, will you risk it for her?"

"Santi ... I can try, but you don't know what you're asking me to do."

"No. There is no trying. You will do this and you will believe in yourself. You have to step across that line. Give in to the addiction and the madness of your gift. Let Livia think she has won. And then trust in yourself to come back from it. And you will, Quinnton Loukas, because I need you to come back to me."

"Santi, I know if anyone could bring me back it would be you. But I don't see how the rest of your plan is going to work."

"What does Livia want more than anything in this world?" Santi asked.

"Her demented father's approval," Quinn said.

"No. She breaks her back to give him what he wants, not for his approval, but to maintain some sort of peace with him and to keep her mother safe. I think she got this way because at one point all she wanted was to make Marcus proud, but that ship sailed a long time ago and he never noticed. So what does she want?"

"She wants out," James said. "Even more than we do."

"Exactly." Santi's eyes gleamed in triumph. "But she's trapped. He'll never let her go. He'd chase her to the ends of the earth."

"And if my family takes her captive, he'll come after them," Quinn said, still not liking her plan.

"That is a fight for another day. You can't tell me you would walk out of Soma and go back to your old life and forget the suffering that man brings? No, our families *will* bring an end to Marcus and all of Soma."

"Do you really think she'll fall for it?"

"What's the one thing Livia wants from you? The thing she is dying to get her hands on?"

"Allie. And she thinks I'm the key to getting her." Quinn sighed. "But I don't want to use my friend as bait to save my own ass."

"You don't have to. We're not going to give her what she wants. We're just going to tempt her with it. Then we walk out the front door with her and none of us ever come back."

Quinn started to see the merit of Santi's plan. "You're right. If I let her break me, she'll immediately go after Allie. But I can't take her to my home. Santi, I can't do it."

"You don't have to," James said quietly as he sketched furiously with a stick in the dirt at their feet. His eyes narrowed to slits, glowing like cat's eyes, and his voice sounded deceptively calm. "The heir will gather the Anchors under the blood moon. Her rage will bring death to her enemies the moment she comes into her inheritance."

"What is he babbling about?" Santi asked.

"Shhh. Let him draw." Quinn rose to stand behind James.

"It begins here," James whispered, pointing with his stick.

"What does?" Quinn watched James's robotic movements.

"The future. A new age begins this night." He thumped his drawing with a fist of triumph.

"Is he having a fit?" Santi whispered.

"He is speaking prophecy," Quinn said softly.

"Oh shit."

"She already sees. This *will* happen. The two will meet in a confluence. Then it will be up to the children of prophecy to lead us into this new era." James shook his head, his eyes widening as he came out of his prophetic haze.

"What does it mean?" Quinn asked.

"It means this will happen whether it's you pulling the strings or someone else," James said. "The events were set in motion a long time ago, but they solidified the moment you made the choice to open that tunnel door and come back to Livia. It *will* happen. So you might as well be the one driving this bus."

"But what does it mean? The blood moon? The heir? Anchors? What's a confluence? Who are the children of prophecy?" Quinn felt hopelessly inadequate, but Santi and James were looking to him for answers.

James shrugged. "I just draw it, man. I'm acting completely on instinct without a mentor to guide me. But I do know this is a reference to another prophecy ... I just don't know which one."

Quinn looked down at the drawing of a map. He saw a house at the end of a winding drive. A beach cottage along the lake. "The orchard," Quinn whispered, tracing the lines of the roughly sketched barn. "This is Imogen's house in New York."

"This confrontation you're talking about forcing between Livia and your family," James said. "It could happen in this place in just a few weeks. Your redheaded friend is already dreaming of it. She will figure it out and she'll react. Do nothing and it will still happen. But it will be somewhere else. Maybe in a few months, or even a few years. And it will most likely happen at your home. My prophetic gut tells me forcing this version now will yield the better outcome than waiting it out."

"Allie would help them prepare," Quinn murmured. It was all coming together despite his reservations. It could work. If he trusted himself enough. If he trusted Allie to figure it out in time.

"You can do this, Quinn," Santi whispered. "We'll lead

Livia there. She'll have absolutely no reason to suspect they might be prepared."

"When will this happen?"

"I see a blood moon every time I close my eyes," James said. "This is about so much more than your escape. It's about Livia and Allie coming to a head. It's going to happen no matter what you do. But you can use this to our advantage. The next blood moon is in two weeks."

"When we leave for New York, you get Lennox out of here and you two head for Cleveland as fast as you can," Quinn said. "If everything goes right, you'll never even feel the pull of your brands."

"How do I find you once we're there?"

"Go to the docks at Edgewater Park. Our sentries will find you."

"Are we doing this?" Santi asked.

"I think we have to," Quinn said. "When this is all over, I'm going to need you to pull me back. It's never easy for a broken Immortal to come back. It could take years until I'm myself again, but it's worth it to get us all out of here and put an end to this."

"We'll take it one moment at a time." Santi stared up at him, her touch a soothing balm to his racing heart. "One breath at a time." She took a step back, holding his hands.

"We better go," Quinn said. "We have a lot of planning to do."

"I trust you'll keep me in the loop on a need-to-know basis?" James kicked the dirt over his drawing and made his way along the path through the woods. He would wander into his own dreams and wake in the morning remembering every detail of their conversations here.

"We begin tomorrow," Santi said as she drifted back to her own dreamscape.

Quinn set off to his library to plan until it was time to wake. *I am not Livia's slave. I'm no one's slave.* It was time to take a risk. Lennox deserved a chance at life with a family that loved her. *If we can get Lennox out of here, I'm going to see to it she gets a family of her own.* And he had just the family in mind.

CHAPTER 29

Sasha: Summer - The Chola Valley

"Going somewhere?" Mother Raghavan asked, stepping from the shadows of the northern gatehouse. Jayesh and Sasha had made it through the temple and across the entire complex without seeing a single soul.

Of course she would know our plans. Sasha gave the mother a bow of respect.

"You don't miss anything." Jay smiled. "It is time, mother. Don't you agree?"

"It is time. But no one leaves my valley like a thief in the night." She whacked him with her cane. "Least of all you, dear boy. Come give Mother Raghavan a kiss."

"Thank you, mother." Jayesh bowed. "For everything." He bent to kiss her cheek.

"You have finally gotten the lesson this time, yes? You remember what must be done now?"

"Yes, mother. I will not be making the same old mistakes again. I will do the right thing."

"If you don't, I'll bring you back here as Brother Jayesh."

"Yes, ma'am." He pulled her into a bear hug and Mother Raghavan giggled like a young girl.

"And you, Sasha El Sadawii. I am proud of the work you've done here. But I don't want to see you in my valley again. You have important work to do, child. Go and do it, Senate be damned. Just remember no one expects you to be perfect except you and that hard head of yours." She tapped her cane against Sasha's forehead. "So forgive yourself for your mistakes. Learn from them and do better next time."

"I will, mother." Sasha bent to kiss the mother's cheek. "Thank you for everything you've taught me. You've changed me for the better."

"You changed yourself, dear girl. My valley is but a tool to help you do it. You best leave now. It's a long way through the mountains."

Sasha took Jayesh's hand as they passed through the outer gates and into the sweeping grasslands of the Chola Valley.

"Quiet," Sasha whispered as she crouched low along the hilltop in the growing darkness. Gen's weave of protection had grown hot over the last several minutes; the henna-like patterns burned as a warning that danger lurked just ahead of them.

"What?" Jayesh crept up beside her.

"A leopard and her three cubs." Sasha pointed through the darkness. "She's coming to see me, but she does not like you. I'm going to go meet her before she acts on any of her threats."

"Sasha, she could tear you to bits."

"She won't. She has a sick cub and she knows I can help her." Sasha took a few careful steps toward the momma cat with her sick baby clutched in her mouth. Two others scrambled up behind her. They were about three months old and the runt was going to die soon.

"Hey there, girl." Sasha held her hand out toward the

mother, letting the cat catch her scent. “I’m going to help your little one, okay?”

The leopard cut her eyes at Jayesh, where he stood crouched on the hillside.

“Don’t worry about him, he’s just scared of you.” Sasha reached for the cub with the injured hindquarters. She’d almost been a snack for some larger predator and the bites were infected. Sasha swept her hand along the cub’s back, helping her relax. “Jay, stay back. She’s in no mood for any sudden moves.”

“Be careful, Sasha.”

“Yes, I’m going to help you.” Sasha smiled at the cub’s curiosity. She was so tired and so sick, but she had a strong will to live. As Sasha reached for her power, the icy burn filled her chest, warming her palm as she settled the cat in her lap and stroked her back until she purred.

The momma leopard came to Sasha’s side and nudged her face with her velvet-soft nose, settling on her haunches to watch.

“You’re welcome,” Sasha whispered as she worked to heal the little one. The other cubs sat and watched with big eyes, chattering amongst themselves about the strange human. It seemed they were heading to the temple for help. It was known among the animals of this valley that the monks could be trusted. But the little one wouldn’t have made it that far. When the mother sensed Sasha nearby, she came to her for help.

“All better.” Sasha patted the mother’s head and scratched her ears. “She’ll be tired for a while, but she’ll live.”

The big cat let out a roar of approval and nudged Sasha’s shoulder in thanks.

“I’ll be okay,” she said. “It just makes me a little tired.”

Sasha watched as the mother bundled her three healthy little ones close and told them to leave the nice lady alone so she could rest. She didn't go far, but she retreated into the darkness to watch over Sasha and her "untrustworthy" friend.

"Let's go." Sasha stood on shaky limbs.

"That wiped you out. Are you okay?" Jay came to her side, taking her backpack and offering his arm for her to lean on. They'd left the temple hours ago, but the path through the mountains was treacherous.

"I'll be fine. I had to help them."

"That was the bravest thing I've ever seen anyone do."

"Let's keep going. The mom is going to watch our backs until we get out of here."

"I'll take the extra protection any day," Jay said as they continued along the steep path.

"When do you think we'll be out of reach of the mother's gift?"

"Any minute now."

Sasha clutched Jay's arm as he helped her up the path.

"Are you all right?" He glanced down at her.

"I will be after a good meal and some rest. The healing was a little beyond my ability. I can handle the occasional injured paw or broken wing, but that was pretty extensive damage."

"You shouldn't have risked it."

"I so didn't have a choice. She was going to eat you if I didn't help."

"*Me?* What did I do?"

"She didn't like your scent. She settled down after I agreed to help her. Before that she was making all sorts of threats. She's used to a different sort of human, I guess."

"We'll stop soon so you can rest."

Sasha followed him along the rocky path until the ground began to even out. One moment they crept through the growing darkness and the next they stood at the edge of a cliff, with the rising sun just making an appearance along the horizon.

Rolling green hills and dense forests spread out before them in every direction.

Sasha had anticipated having a moment to collect herself before she stepped back into her world. Now that she was back, fear nearly overwhelmed her. "I'm not ready." Sasha crashed to her knees.

"Yes you are, angel." Jay stooped beside her.

"We should keep moving." Sasha tried to stand up. "Aide will need some time to find us," she whispered. Liam would have noticed the moment she stepped out of the valley and would be getting word to Aide shortly.

"Rest a little while, Sasha. We have some time before my team will know where to look for us. You're going to need your strength."

Sasha fell asleep against his shoulder, exhausted.

CHAPTER 30

Quinn: Fall - Atlanta, Georgia

Quinn lay on the pristine white floor of Livia's private gym. Blood and sweat pooled beneath him, spoiling the effect of the brilliant white she always surrounded herself with.

"Get up," Livia barked.

But Quinn didn't move. He didn't care. Once he'd given himself permission to succumb to Livia and his addiction, it was easy to fall into the downward spiral that would lead to his doom. It was pretty much all he could think about.

Is Santi right? Can I really come back from this? He'd fought for so long, the idea that it was suddenly okay to give up that fight brought him a huge amount of relief. And a whole new list of worries.

Relinquishing control proved to be difficult. He'd always known what his limits were and he never wavered. Not until the last few days. Little by little, he was letting Livia push him further than ever before. It felt good, not caring. The voice came to him more often now, but it didn't scare him anymore. Succumbing to the addiction was always inevitable. Having it happen this way—as a choice—brought him some measure of comfort. At least his addiction would accomplish something good in the end. Freedom for Santi, Lennox and James. *They are worth the risk of letting this madness overcome me*

Madness? The voice mocked him. For two years, Quinn had suppressed that voice; thought he'd conquered everything it represented. And then he came to Soma and realized it was still there, simmering just below the surface, waiting for him to slip.

That's where we just don't see eye to eye, Quinn's gift said. *You see addiction and evil. We see our freedom.*

"Don't make me drag you to your feet, Quinn." Livia flexed her fingers, her knuckles bloody and bruised. "I guarantee you won't like it."

Quinn found himself wishing he could just stop feeling. Anything. It hurt too much. That was when he knew he was close. Livia would break him. And it would happen soon.

Please let it happen soon.

With a strong image of Santi in his mind—an image of her safe and happy with his family—Quinn slowly got to his feet. If she was happy, he could deal with whatever his future might hold. If that meant locking himself up in the crypt until he was fit to be around the people he loved, then he would willingly enter their most secure cell and close the door on himself. Not that crazy-Q would do that once he was in control.

Hells no.

Quinn's arms and legs trembled beneath him, but he stood, staring blankly ahead.

"Do I see a chink in the armor?" Livia mocked his weakness. "Shall I bring in one of the kids? Just to be sure?"

"I don't care anymore, Liv. Do what you want. We both know I have no choice."

"You're not the first to attempt escape, Quinn. No one ever escapes Soma, but the stubborn ones always try. It's the failure that often pushes them to their breaking point," she said softly. "To feel so close to freedom only to be pulled back—to be shown just how firmly you *belong* to someone else—it's been the final straw for many. You're so close, Quinn. One final push and you're mine."

"Whatever." Quinn swayed on his feet.

"Bring her in," Livia called to one of her minions.

Don't be Lennox. Don't be Lennox. Anyone but Lennox. He couldn't bear it. He couldn't look into those clear blue eyes and watch Livia use his power to drive her toward the brink of insanity and back again. Livia loved Lennox. He was sure of it, but he could never fathom how she could torture Len just to prove a point to him.

Don't be an idiot. Lennox let her thoughts drift to his mind. She knew how this had to go. He'd pulled her into the dreamworld, where they explained the plan to her.

You're too soft to hurt anyone on purpose. Least of all me. This is not your battle to win on your own, big guy. Let me do my part.

"Just get on with it." Quinn's voice sounded like gravel to his own ears.

Lennox screamed, clapping her hands over her ears to stop whatever torture Quinn's gift was giving her, but she couldn't escape it. Not when Livia was in control.

Yes! Finally, his gift rejoiced. Quinn could feel him stretching after a lifetime of confinement.

"Come on, Quinn, don't you have any fight left in you?" Livia shoved him with the toe of her boot. "You're making this too easy."

But he lay on the floor, staring blankly at the ceiling. He

felt numb. Len's screams no longer felt like a punch in the gut. He just genuinely didn't care.

Livia had his power raging inside of him now. He was hanging on by his fingertips.

It's okay, Quinn. Len's voice was weak and distant. *It's time to let go. You've been fighting for so long. Let someone else carry the burden for a while. We'll bring you back, you big ox.*

With a deep breath, Quinn stopped pushing back. For the first time in years he just ... let go. Livia's gift surged through him, shoving him across the metaphorical line he'd set for himself when he was sixteen years old. The sensation was euphoric. Like an addict taking a lethal dose of their favorite drug, Quinn fell down the rabbit hole.

"That's it, Quinn," Livia said. "Give in to it."

And he did. He could feel himself slipping away. The feeling was both terrifying and freeing at the same time. "Santi," he whispered, relinquishing the last shred of himself to the madness of his gift.

"Now I'm in charge," he muttered, a smile he didn't feel spread across his face.

Quinn opened his eyes and stared up at the ceiling. *No*, he moaned as his body moved without his permission.

"That's more like it." Livia smiled as he stood up. But she looked hesitant, as if she saw something in him that frightened her.

You did it, Liv. I'm a broken mess in here and a madman is in charge now. I hope you're ready to bring this bastard to heel.

"Do you know how *long* we've been dying to get out and stretch our legs?" Crazy-Quinn laughed, cracking his neck and shaking his hands. "*Man,* it feels good to be in control." He paced like a predator, eager to pounce on anything that moved.

"But you're not," Livia said.

"Semantics." Quinn shrugged.

"You're a little bit crazy, aren't you." She took a step back.

"Lady, we're *insane*!" He crossed the room and bent over Lennox. Her eyes glazed over, unblinking, as her tormentor examined the results of his power like a proud student. "Let's make her squeal some more." He reached for Lennox again.

Don't you dare touch her. Quinn itched to wrap his hands around the psychopath's neck, but he was locked inside the insanity of his own mind.

It's okay ... it's okay ... it's okay, Lennox murmured.

"Don't touch her." Livia grabbed his arm. "You do *nothing* without my permission."

"Buzzkill." Crazy-Quinn stood to his full height and wrenched his arm away from Livia, knocking her to the floor.

Livia seemed to get a clear picture of what she was dealing with now. She scrambled back to her feet, her eyes blazing with silvery fire. "Kneel." She pointed at the gym floor, pushing crazy-Q back into his place. Reminding him who was in control. He resisted, but in the end, Livia won the battle of wills, exerting the dominance of her gift to bring him to his knees.

"You know the kid's a telepath?" Quinn cackled like a maniac, still staring at Lennox like he wanted to devour her. "Kinda useless if you ask me. She only gets part of the conversation. Let us have another taste."

"Enough." Livia pulled a chair into the center of the room. "We have a few things to discuss. Questions you will answer." She sat down, keeping Quinn on his knees before her.

"I'm an open book, Liv, baby. Ask away. You're kinda hot when you go all dominatrix on us."

Don't be a douche, you idiot. But crazy-Quinn wasn't listening. Quinn wasn't even sure his alter ego could hear him anymore.

Oh, we're just ignoring you the same way you've ignored us for years.

Fine by me, but you know what we need to do to get out of this place, right?

We're up to speed.

And?

And we won't dish on the plan. But we're in control and once we're out of here, we make the decisions. Deal?

Deal.

"Let's be clear, crazy-Q," Livia said. "I'm in charge. You will answer my questions. Pull any bullshit and we go for round two. And you don't want me to break you twice."

"What you wanna know?" Quinn eased back on the floor, leaning on his elbow like he was having the time of his life.

"Tell me about your family first. Then we'll see if I believe you."

No. Quinn's heart clenched in fear.

Quinn, let it happen, Lennox said. *This is what we want.*

She was right. This was their plan. His only job was over now.

I believe in you, Quinn, Lennox whispered.

"Mom used to be a pirate and tops the Margrave's most-wanted list," crazy-Quinn blurted. "Dad's a wreck and kinda useless since he was in a Coalition prison for most of his life till Mom broke him out. Little brother's a pain in the ass, but he's a talented techie. You know that. He's practically the poster child for what Soma wants in their young Immortals."

"What exactly does Graham do?" Livia leaned in close, eager for the answer.

"He talks to machines or some shit like that. Put a computer in front of him and he could take over this place in an hour."

This was all going exactly as planned, but Quinn didn't

have a shred of control over what came out of his mouth. All his family's secrets would lay at Livia's feet the instant she asked.

"And Allie. Tell me about her?"

"She's like a homeless stray some friends took in last year. Didn't even know what she was till her Awakening hit her. She's an unknown."

"What is so significant about her?"

"Wouldn't you like to know?" He cackled at his own joke. "We weren't paying attention. She was into the other dude. She's crazy powerful but hasn't got the sense God gave dirt."

"I want to collect her. And you're going to lead me to her."

"What's in it for us?"

"Absolutely nothing," Livia said. "But you'll do it anyway. Tell me where I can find her."

"Kelleys Island, Ohio. But you can't step foot on the island without an engraved invitation from the Great Lakes Governor. It's protected. Even Allie doesn't realize how protected she is."

"So I'll grab her from school."

"Can't do it, Liv, babe. From the moment you took off with our buddy, Quinn, the other kids have been under constant supervision. You can't touch her. Not without our help." He gave her a manic grin that would have scared most people.

"And how do you propose to help?"

"Ask your resident prophet."

"My prophet?"

"James. You're so focused on modern gifts that you didn't realize you had a prophet right under your nose."

"There's not been a true prophet in centuries." Livia sat back in her chair. Quinn could see the wheels turning in her mind.

"He's been writing and drawing all sorts of prophecies about the redhead."

"Why? Why would a prophet have any interest in an insignificant girl?"

"Maybe she's not so insignificant," Quinn said. "She's powerful, Liv. We know you want her. Bad. You think we're one of the strongest of our generation? She has more power in her little finger than we can ever dream of owning. And she doesn't even know what to do with it. She'd be putty in your hands, baby."

"You're going to tell me exactly where she is and how I can get my hands on her."

"Piece of cake, princess." He winked. "You do what we say and she'll be yours. But we get to make her squeal first."

Quinn was surprised Livia hadn't hit him yet. But she seemed completely enthralled with the new information on Allie.

A huge part of Quinn still wanted to fight. To keep this psychotic version of himself from telling Livia all his secrets. But she was buying it, and that was the important thing. But there was another part of himself—a part that was tired beyond belief—that just didn't care.

It's okay, Quinn, Lennox said. *We got this....*

CHAPTER 31

Sasha: Summer - Outside The Chola Valley

Sasha woke to the scent of beef jerky.

"I knew that would wake you." Jayesh laughed.

"Did you just wave that under my nose?" She stretched her stiff muscles.

"Yep." He smiled, offering her a piece. "Food is typically the fastest way to get your attention."

"How long was I out?" She took a big bite of the jerky, hoping he had more. Using her healing power on the leopard cub had left her ravenous.

"Almost two hours."

"Aide should find us soon."

"My team will be heading for us by now."

"We should move to open ground." Sasha reached for her pack.

"We'll leave in a minute. I need to say something first." He grabbed her hands, easing her back against the tree where she'd slept.

"Don't," she whispered. "Don't say goodbye, Jayesh. Come with me?"

"I can't, angel. And I'm not saying goodbye. I need you to make me a promise first."

"Like what?"

"Go back to your life and try to be happy. Do whatever you can to help Quinn but do *not*, under any circumstances, go to Atlanta like you planned. I will help him if I can, but I cannot bear the thought of you ending up in that place. Not after everything you've been through."

"I can't make that promise, Jayesh. I'm so much more capable now than I was when I arrived. I know I can get him out of there."

"The moment you step into Sterling Tower, your life is forfeit. It is an impenetrable fortress with no way out. Not for someone like you—not even a Chola assassin. Promise me you will not step one foot in Atlanta."

"I won't. If you'll promise to come home with me and help me find a way to get him out. We could do it together."

"I would if I could, but I am needed in Africa."

"Then come find me when you get back? I will keep your promise if you will promise me that much."

"I will." Jayesh nodded as if in defeat.

"Then we have a deal," Sasha said. The hum of a chopper sounded in the distance. "We should get close enough to see if that's yours or mine."

"Let's head up the path. The forest isn't as dense toward the peak," Jayesh said.

Sasha followed him, laying low in the shadows in case the chopper wasn't her uncle.

"I don't recognize him," Jayesh said, crouching low at the edge of the woods. "Doesn't feel like one of mine."

"It's my uncle." Sasha recognized his familiar presence.

"Then we should head down the other side. There's a

grassy slope not too far from here," Jay said. "He'll never see us up here."

Sasha gauged the distance of the chopper against the dense forest between them and the clearing where Aide could land. They would have to hurry if they were going to make it before Aide circled the area and missed them.

"We only have one shot at this. If we miss him, my team will find us."

"Let's go." Sasha grabbed his hand and ran along the steep path down the other side of the mountain. Sasha was careful not to run faster than Jayesh. She didn't want to risk losing him. He was coming with her if she had to drag him onto the helicopter herself.

Imogen's weave of protection warmed her skin. "They're coming." She chanced a look over her shoulder. She couldn't see them yet, but the patterns along her body grew hotter with each breath she took.

As they broke through the trees and rushed the clearing, Sasha waved and shouted to draw Aide's attention.

"They're closing in." Jayesh watched over his shoulder.

"Yes! He's seen us," Sasha said. "He'll get here first."

Jayesh stood with his back to her, putting himself between Sasha and those who would take her. "Get ready!" he shouted over the roar of the helicopter blades.

As soon as Aide landed in the clearing, they ran.

"I'm not ready," Sasha cried over the sound of the blades. "Please, come with me, Jayesh. I can't leave you like this." She clutched his hand in an iron grip.

"It's time, angel. Go back to your life, and live a good one." He pulled her close, dropping a kiss on her forehead.

"You don't need to do this, Jay." She tugged him back toward the waiting helicopter. Aide stood crouched in the doorway, ready to pull her inside. "You don't need to go back to that life."

"People count on me. I have to go."

She saw his team breaking through the trees behind him.

"They're going to hurt you."

"Nothing will hurt me more than seeing them take you. Go!" He shoved her hard, but she held on to him, refusing to let go.

"Please, Sasha, you have to go."

Imogen's protective marks lit Sasha's body on fire as the patterns moved to break her hold on Jayesh. Sasha stumbled back.

"Get her out of here!" Jayesh turned to face his pursuers.

"No!" Sasha took a step toward him. But Aide pulled her back into the chopper. "Protect him!" Sasha screamed as her uncle flung her into the co-pilot's seat.

"Time to go." Aide took the pilot seat and lifted them into the air.

Sasha pressed her face against the window and watched as the leopard and every predator within her reach came to stand between Jayesh and his pursuers. Monkeys, mountain lions, panthers and even a tiger guarded him. She called the yak, the deer and even the elephants to stand with him. It was the only thing she could do for him now.

Sasha walked across the rocky shores of São Miguel in the Azores, the sound of clashing weapons carried on the warm breeze.

Less than twenty-four hours ago, she was shooting a sniper rifle with Jayesh, all thoughts of home far from her mind.

She watched as Allie and Aidan sparred along the rocky

jetty reaching into the sea. They seemed so young to her now after everything she'd been through. It suddenly occurred to her that her relationship with her brother might never be the same as it was before. He'd always treated her like a little sister that needed protecting. But she felt so much older now, like decades stood between them rather than weeks.

"Sasha!" Allie cried. Throwing down her practice sai, she charged up the jetty, hopping along the rocky path like she'd spent her life training on such terrain.

She's changed. Allie moved more confidently, but she carried a heavy burden on her shoulders. Sasha wasn't the only one who'd gone through something. *She's stronger than when I left.*

Aidan raced past Allie and slammed into Sasha first.

"I missed you," he whispered, holding her close. He held her at arm's length, studying her carefully. "Senate internship, my ass." He shook his head. "Tell me where you've been. I've been so worried."

Sasha smiled, and thinking of Jayesh she said, "I hope never to speak of such things with you, brother."

CHAPTER 32

Sasha: Fall - Kelleys Island Ohio

"My niece is seventeen." Liam slammed the bar bill on the table in front of the Immortal Sasha had come to meet. "Get out of my bar."

"Liam, I can take care of myself." Sasha sighed.

"Out. Of. My. Bar." His blue eyes sparkled with rage. "Jack is not the sort you should be hanging around with, Sasha."

"You didn't tell me *Liam* was your uncle." Jack leaned toward her. "We're just talking, sir. I'm not here to make trouble." Jack held his hands up in surrender. "She just has a few questions for me."

"Imogen's on her way to pick you up, Sasha. I suggest you make it quick." Liam stalked back behind the bar.

"That is one big Viking," Jack said nervously.

"Your report?" Sasha asked.

"Right. I don't really know what else to tell you. Jayesh just ... doesn't want to be found. I've done all I can do. The man is a ghost."

"Keep digging. He came back from Africa more than a month ago. There has to be some kind of trail."

"I told you, he left for Indonesia within days of returning to the States. He's gone, Sasha."

"He wouldn't do that unless something went wrong." She shook her head stubbornly. Jay had promised he would come find her when he returned from Africa. There was no way he wouldn't keep that promise.

"I do have something for you." Jack pulled an envelope from his coat pocket. "I found this in my car about a week ago. I don't know how it got there, but it's addressed to you."

Jack passed the note across the sticky table. Sasha recognized Jayesh's handwriting.

"Any news on Quinn?" Sasha slid the envelope into her purse, her hands trembling with the desire to rip into it right there.

"Nothing new. If you want my advice, go to Amrita. I hear it's coming to Cleveland later this month. You might find a fresh lead there, but be careful. It's a dangerous place. Don't go alone." Jack stood, tossing a few bills on the table to cover their drinks. "Good luck to you, Sasha."

"Thank you, Jack." Sasha sighed as she sat back and sipped her drink. Jack was the third man she'd worked with in the months since she returned to the real world. At first Sasha focused on diving back into her efforts to help Quinn, but as the weeks went by and there was still no sign of Jayesh, she began actively looking for him too.

Assimilating back into her life was just as difficult as Sasha had expected. She went through the motions each day. School. Basketball practice. Training. Homework. She did what was expected of her but she kept to herself, finding it impossible to return to the life of a seventeen-year-old.

Sasha's three years in the Chola Valley took place in the span of six short weeks. Going back to high school after that felt like some kind of cruel joke when she felt like a twenty-year-old master assassin.

"Why do I find myself throwing you out of my bar every time I turn around?" Liam took the seat Jack had just vacated.

"What can I say, Uncle Liam? Your bar caters to the kind of clientele I'm looking for."

"You know I'm better at this sort of work than any of the idiots you've hired. I wish you'd just come to me for whatever it is you're looking for."

"You'll just tell Dad."

"If it gets you out of my bar and away from creeps like Jack, then I'll keep your secret and tell you everything I know about Quinn."

"All right. You're hired." She leaned forward. "But this isn't about Quinn. Not entirely, although I'm going to hold you to your promise."

"If this isn't about Quinn, then what are you up to?"

"I'm looking for the man I trained with this summer." Sasha pulled the worn photo from her purse. The selfie she'd taken with Jayesh on their last afternoon before they left the valley. "His name is Jayesh Basu. He was supposed to come here as soon as he returned from Africa. But that was weeks ago."

"I see. I haven't crossed paths with Jayesh in a very long time."

"You know him?"

"Once upon a time I did. Let's hope he's changed since then." Liam set the picture down on the table. "Are you sure about this? Wouldn't it be best to leave him in the past and move on?"

"Unacceptable," Sasha said.

"Okay." He nodded. "I will put out some feelers and see what I find. I can see he cares about you." Liam frowned at the picture. "I wish to see you happy like that again."

"Thank you, Uncle Liam." Sasha reached for his hand.

"Are you sure he hasn't just ... gone on about his life?" Liam asked. "He is quite a lot older than you."

"This isn't about some silly summer romance. I can't expect you to understand what we went through together. But he made a promise he wouldn't break unless something went wrong."

"Very well." Liam nodded as he stood. "Wait here for Imogen, and for God's sake, don't talk to anyone else."

"I won't." Sasha lifted the envelope from her purse. Her heart raced at the sight of Jayesh's handwriting. She slipped her finger under the flap and tore into the letter. A single sheet of paper lay in her hands. She stared at the five little letters that broke her heart.

I lied.

It seemed Jayesh never intended to keep his promise. *So why should I keep mine?* Sasha decided right then that she would go to Amrita, look for new leads, and then she would head to Atlanta. It was time she took matters into her own hands.

"Sasha, this is becoming a habit," Imogen said as she marched across the bar. "Next time I'm bringing Mom with me."

"You of all people should know what this has been like for me. You know I don't feel seventeen anymore. Haven't for a long time."

"I know, sweetie." Imogen sat down across from her. "I really do. But coming to places like this, snooping around for clues about Quinn and Jayesh ... it's not healthy for you. Both of them would want you to focus on yourself now. Take the time to heal."

"And how's that working out taking your own advice?" Sasha glared at her sister. Imogen had returned just a few weeks after Sasha. But the moment she saw her sister's face, Sasha knew the time in the Chola Valley had taken its toll on Imogen. Since her return, Imogen threw herself into her role as head of security at Cliffton Academy, spending every moment she had as far away from her husband as she could. They were having problems. Lucien was much younger than Imogen. He'd had very little experience with the more ancient aspects of the Immortal world, so it was difficult for him to identify with what she'd been through.

"Not good." Imogen sighed. "It's easier said than done, isn't it?"

"Are you ever going to tell me what the mother needed five years to teach you?" Sasha leaned across the table.

"She was preparing me for something she sees looming ahead. Something that could affect all of us. I can't tell you more than that because I don't know. Whatever it is, it's not set in stone, but I am trying to protect Lucien. This thing. It will change him. He will suffer. It is best if I keep my distance until I know what we are dealing with. If I can keep this from touching him, I will."

"And have you told him any of this?"

"I can't. It's important that I keep this to myself. Although Mother Raghavan said I could share this much with you. She knew I would need someone to confide in. But you are dealing with enough. You don't need my issues weighing you down."

"You are my sister, Imogen El Sadawii. Anything that burdens you burdens me. I am always here for you, just as you were for me through these last difficult years."

"I'd forgotten how very hard it is to come back to the real world." Imogen frowned. "I am so sorry this happened to you, Sasha."

"It's okay. I'm dealing with it and one day it will get easier. For both of us." Sasha reached for her sister's hand, hating to see how much she was struggling. "We should probably go before Liam gets violent."

"Aren't you going to tell me about that?" Imogen gestured at the paper in Sasha's hand.

"This?" She glanced down at the note from Jayesh. "*This* is garbage." Sasha balled up the letter and crushed it in her fist. If Jayesh thought he could get rid of her that easily, he was dead wrong.

CHAPTER 33

Sasha: Fall, The New Moon - Kelleys Island

Sasha paced across her father's silent office, waiting for her mother to pick up the phone. It was the middle of the night and the rest of the family were in the common room, discussing a plan of action to deal with the threat Allie saw in her vision. A plan that left Sasha behind with the other kids.

"Mom, you're really going to make me sit here and do nothing?" Sasha asked as soon as her mother answered.

"Sweetheart, we can handle this," Naeemah said gently. "Thanks to Allie's warning we have time to prepare. You don't need to be here for this battle. You are too young."

"How can you say that after everything I've been through? I'm a Chola assassin, Mother. Not a child."

"You are still *my* child."

"But you let Darius fight with you. You know I feel closer to his age than the others."

"I do understand how frustrating this is for you, but I still think of you as my little girl. Give me time to learn to see you as you see yourself."

"What if we don't have time for that, Mom? What if this is

it? Allie just saw your *execution*! If you die, I will have to live with the knowledge that I could have helped."

"I'm so sorry, Sasha. Your father and I are about to fight for our lives. I can't be worried about my children. I need to know they are safe so I can come back to them in one piece."

"If anything happens to you and Dad, I'll never be able to forgive myself," Sasha whispered. "Please, Mom. Let me fight with you."

"You will stay in the underground with the others while we handle this threat. And that is my final word, Daughter."

"I love you, Mom. Don't ... don't die. I can't bear it."

"I love you too ... I should have protected you better," Naeemah whispered as she ended the call.

"I hate this!" Sasha threw her phone, shattering it against the door. She wasn't the girl they remembered, yet they all treated her as if nothing had changed.

"Why so screechy?" Aidan asked, peeking around the doorway. "You done throwing things?"

"I can't take this, Aidan." Sasha shook her head in frustration.

"That's why we're leaving. Now." He peered back down the hall, gesturing for her to follow. "The babysitters think we're holding vigil in the Yard. Grandma Nadira says it's the safest place for us while this thing is going down."

"Then how are we— Have you lost your mind? We're swimming out?" Sasha hissed as she followed him along the corridor to the Yard.

"It'll be cold, but it's the only way we can get out of here."

Sasha nodded. The far end of the Yard opened into a low, dark cave where an underground river surged into the lake. The stock room there was full of weapons and supplies for an emergency exit but anyone would be crazy to leave the underground that way. Or desperate.

"What do you know?" Sasha demanded. Aidan had a front-row seat to Allie's visions. "What isn't Allie saying?"

Aidan halted at the entrance to the Yard. "If we don't fight with Allie, people we love will die. So we're going."

"Good enough for me. Let's go."

"Get down!" Sasha called softly to the others, scrambling for cover behind a stand of oak trees. Their journey through the lake was terrifying ... and cold. Sasha had never been so cold in her life. But the closer they got to her sister's house the more focused Sasha became on the task ahead of them.

"What do you see?" Aidan ducked by her side.

"Someone's up ahead," she whispered.

"What should we do?" Graham asked as he and Chloe joined them.

Sasha waited for Aidan to give instructions. But he looked to her for answers.

"What? I've been paying attention since you got back," Aidan said. You're way more qualified to lead us than I am. What should we do?"

"Smell that?" she asked. "They're setting fires. We all know that's the Coalition's MO. This whole area is going to be ablaze soon. They'll want to box them in with fire. We need to get through before it's too late. Let's circle back to the car and take the old horse trail up to the back of the barn."

"Let's go," Aidan said.

"Stay close. We need to move fast," Sasha added.

They crept quietly back down the narrow dirt road. When they were out of earshot, Sasha picked up the pace. She darted past the cluster of cars parked along the path. This route would take longer but it should give them the chance to slip past the enemy's sentries. Allie didn't know who the enemy was, nor what they wanted. She only knew it was happening and she'd figured it out just in time to get them the help they needed.

But none of it made any sense to Sasha. She had been so focused on her own issues for so long that the news of this attack showed her just how little she'd been paying attention. She'd had no idea that Allie was even capable of having a vision as powerful as the one she'd seen about their family.

I'm a terrible friend. But she vowed to be a better one once they got through this night.

Sasha breathed a sigh of relief when she saw the barn through a haze of smoke.

"Let's get inside." They ran up the path in a crouch, making as little noise as possible.

Sasha took a last glance behind them as the others stepped inside the barn. The fire was getting closer. She could hear the mortals in the distance—the Coalition. They were backing away, letting the fires do their job for them. Sasha shuddered at the thought that her parents' funeral pyre might be burning at this very moment.

"This must be killing little bro, missing out on all the fun." The voice drifted to the back of the barn. Darius was going to be furious with them.

"Who's missing out?" Aidan asked as he stepped around the rusty old cider press.

Sasha wasn't in the mood for their drama. She had preparations to make. As the rest of the family led their attackers to the orchard, Sasha would take her shots from the hayloft.

Graham was busy with his drones and Chloe paced, working on her own mental preparation. Sasha gave her shoulder a gentle squeeze as she made her way around the barn, checking each window and door, evaluating the best areas that would give her adequate protection and a clear shot to key points across the orchard.

She remembered playing in the orchard as a kid. It was always a happy place—a fun trip every fall to go pick apples and make cider. Tonight it was a battleground, a fight for her family's lives. A fight she intended to win.

"All right, Allie. Let's do this. Tell us how this is going to go down." Darius called them all to the front of the barn.

"Chloe, I want you to stay away from the fight...." Allie's voice grew to a din in Sasha's ears. The coming battle weighed heavily on her mind. Her training had prepared her for this. Sasha was confident in her ability to fight, but she knew she had to set her emotions aside. If she had to kill to protect her family, she would.

"Put this on," Graham said, handing her a Bluetooth headset. "So we can all stay in touch."

Sasha nodded, sliding it into her pocket. She didn't want the distraction.

"Graham, when you see ... Quinn, you cannot react," Allie said. "Do not let him see you."

Quinn's here? Sasha's knees almost gave out. This wasn't just about saving her parents now. This was so much more than a random Coalition attack. If Quinn was with them, this was Soma. Just a month ago, at Amrita, Sasha and her friends had put the final pieces of the puzzle together. They always knew Livia was the head of the Fold, but that was just a front for Soma. A slave market. And now they were coming for her family. Sasha's hands tightened into fists at her side.

"Sasha," Allie said. "Quinn needs to see you. He *has* to see you."

Sasha's mind reeled and her pulse pounded in her ears as she caught bits and pieces of Allie's instructions.

"...Go find Liam and tell him to take you up to the gates...

Wait until you see Quinn on his own... Don't get too close... Come back here... When you see Quinn with Emma... Snap out of it when he hears your voice."

"Will we ... get him back?" Sasha cleared her mind, putting on her assassin's face.

"We'll try."

"There is no trying, Allie. This is the only chance we're going to get." Sasha would not let them fail. If Quinn was here, he was coming home tonight or she was going with him.

Leaving the others to their preparations, Sasha made her way across the orchard.

"Liam?" she called as she jogged along the path up to the gates.

"Sasha? What are you doing here?" His face turned so white he was almost translucent.

"No time. Allie says I have to be here so I'm here. You're supposed to take me up to the gates. Quinn will be with them."

Liam nodded, turning up the path at a jog. They crouched among the trees to wait.

"The first wave came through a few minutes ago. I don't know how, but they had a code to the gates. They're circling the house now," Liam said, pointing to the fires in the distance. "Nearly twenty. Mostly mortal."

"When he sees me, I have to lead him back to the orchard. You have to stay here."

"Sasha, I can't leave you unprotected," Liam protested.

"You know all about my training, Liam."

"I know you're capable, but I'm still not leaving you."

"I'm not the same girl who left here—not by a long shot. I'm a trained assassin, Liam. I think I can handle a trip back through the woods on my own."

"Please be careful, Sasha. Assassin or not, in my eyes you will always be my favorite little niece."

"I'm your only niece, Liam." She rolled her eyes.

"Well, I like you more than my idiot nephews." He grinned down at her.

"Oh my God," she whispered, pointing across the lawn. "Look."

The gates creaked open and a familiar figure stepped onto the driveway. If she hadn't seen it with her own eyes she would never have believed Quinn capable of such a betrayal. He'd entered the code. He was responsible for this.

"He's succumbed," Liam said softly. "This isn't the Quinn we know, Sasha. Be very careful with him. Until we know more, we have to treat him like the enemy."

"An enemy we intend to take captive." She nodded, waiting for the flood of Immortals and Coalition to pass through the gates. There were at least twenty people with Quinn, in addition to the twenty that came in the first wave. Half of them crept over the lawns toward the house in the distance. The other half drove through the gates, their vehicles idling, waiting for the first strike to begin.

As the caravan of vehicles crept forward, Sasha and Liam watched in silence. More fires dotted the lawn as the second group set up a base point along the hillside just out of sight of the house. This group seemed to be patiently waiting for the others to do the work while they stood by to take charge of the prisoners.

Sasha waited for the opportunity to get Quinn's attention as he closed the gate behind the last SUV.

She got her chance a few moments later when the fighting began up at the house. Sasha rushed out of the woods and onto the lawn, halting only steps away from him. He had his back turned to her.

"Quinn," she called softly, almost afraid to reach for him.

He turned slowly in the moonlight. Their eyes met and she smiled, taking a hesitant step toward him.

Don't get too close. Allie's warning sounded in her mind. But this was Quinn. He would never hurt her.

"It's just me," she said, reaching for his hand. "It's time to go home."

His eyes narrowed to slits as he smiled. But it wasn't the smile she remembered. Quinn lunged toward her—not in a help-me-escape way, but in an I'm-going-to-kill-you way.

"No...." Sasha turned and fled down the path back to the orchard. This was all too familiar for her. She'd killed that version of Quinn more than a hundred times. She refused to do it again. She glanced over her shoulder to make sure he'd followed. He was just steps behind her and getting closer.

As she entered the orchard, she dodged between the rows of trees, picking up her pace to lose him. She would get through to him, but she had to get her head on straight after the shock of seeing him so like the Quinn she'd fought during *ankathari*.

Sasha ducked into the barn, grabbing her bow, and hauled herself up to the hayloft where she could get the best vantage point. With her back against the wall, Sasha took a deep breath, settling back into the assassin's mindset where emotion had no place.

She could hear activity coming from the direction of the beach house. She darted to the open window at the side of the barn and arrived just in time to fire her first shot. She needed only a fraction of a second to engage with her gift. Her wooden arrow sailed through the trees, striking the mortal chasing her father up the rocky path. She aimed for flesh wounds or joints, hoping to slow them enough to give her family the advantage. She'd get serious about it if they got back up. Tonight, the assassin in her wouldn't be letting anyone get up a second time —not with her family on the line.

At the top of the path, Gregg and Emma turned to meet their attackers. Sasha watched as Allie met them, lunging for the man who'd followed them, but Allie hadn't seen the woman just behind him. Sasha put a lodestone arrow through the woman's head. She'd recover, but not tonight.

Sasha moved to the open hayloft door, scanning the scene below. The fight was coming to them. Sasha saw at least thirty people locked in battle across the orchard and the areas around it. But she couldn't spot Quinn anywhere.

Then she saw the woman standing at the opposite end of the orchard. Sasha had never seen her, but she knew this was Livia. All of this—Quinn, the attack, all of it—was Livia's doing, and Ming Lao was about to make her pay.

Sasha watched as Ming Lao stalked behind Livia, her long katana blade at the ready. Livia threw her sword up just in time as she turned to meet Ming's attack. Livia seemed to taunt her, but she was no match for Ming. Their swords clashed and Ming quickly drew first blood. Daniel circled the two, looking for an opening. Mother and son intended to exact justice for Quinn.

Sasha did a double take when she saw Quinn taking up the fight alongside Livia. *Helping* her. Fighting against his father and grandmother.

"He doesn't know what he's doing," Sasha murmured as Livia disappeared, only to appear again just out of Ming's reach. She was using Quinn's gift. The thought that she'd taken it from him—the one gift he was actually proud of—sickened her.

Sasha gripped her Chola blades and jumped from the hayloft, landing in a crouch on the ground below. In that moment she embraced her training, grateful for it. She charged down the rows of trees, mentally erecting a barrier between herself and her emotions. Quinn was coming home tonight whether he wanted to or not. And Livia would be lucky if she didn't end up scattered across this orchard in pieces.

Sasha ran past clusters of her family working together to fight the enemy. She dodged random strikes, wielding her blades with calculated precision. By the time she reached the end of the orchard, where Quinn and Livia faced Daniel and Ming Lao, her white blades dripped red with blood.

"This isn't you, son," Daniel said, trying to talk Quinn down.

"Quinn's not here." His eyes flickered with blue fire and his insane laughter chilled Sasha to the bone.

This wasn't the Quinn she knew, but he was in there somewhere. She could sense him struggling inside this creature that wore his face. If she could just get through to the real Quinn, she knew she could bring him out of this madness. But Sasha stumbled. The din of battle growing faint in her ears. She swayed on her feet, dizzy and confused as her breath came in short gasps. She ducked behind a gnarled apple tree. Her chest tightened, like a fist gripped her heart.

"Quinn?" She could feel the pull of his presence—the real Quinn. She felt it the way she always had, but seeing him again, after everything they'd been through, made it a thousand times stronger.

Her heart raced at the sight of him. Her chest burned and her peripheral vision burnished golden with the flames of the forest around them. She couldn't draw a breath, overwhelmed by her feelings for the boy she'd loved most of her life. Sasha's eyes filled with tears. Just when she thought she couldn't last another moment without a breath, air burst into her lungs, fresh and sweet when it should have been tainted with the smoke of the fires.

The echo of an unfamiliar heartbeat thrummed in her chest, filling her with strength.

CHAPTER 34

Quinn: Fall, The New Moon - Rural New York

"Quinnton Greggory Loukas!"

Quinn stirred like a bear waking from a long hibernation.

"Sasha?" He fought to open his eyes, struggling to recall his last memory.

No! This wasn't our deal! his gift raged.

Quinn felt a surge of strength coming from some outside source.

Sasha. Just the thought of her gave him clarity.

You will have to fight us!

Did you really think I would go quietly? Quinn reached for his power, grasping it by a thread. But it was enough. He wasn't going to lose this fight now. He wouldn't make that mistake again. Through all the years of resisting his power, refusing to use his gifts for fear of losing control, he'd given the voice of his madness too much power over him. *No more.*

We won't go back! crazy-Quinn screamed.

No! This is my life! Quinn growled. *I decide how and when to use my power. Not you. Never again. I am not afraid of you!*

You will always fear us! his gift hissed.

I am done letting my fears rule me. Quinn clawed his way

back, seizing control of his power and his life. *Go back to where you belong.*

Quinn took a deep breath to still his racing heart. He didn't know how it happened, but he was back. He could sense his gift huddling in the dark recesses of his mind, howling and enraged. The madness would be back. It was a part of him and it was time he accepted it.

Strength flooded his limbs. Feeling surged into fingertips he mentally flexed, like he hadn't thought to use them in a long time. He felt the pull of Sasha. More than just her calling his name ... she was calling him. His power. His mind. Everything. She needed him.

He blinked and the world exploded into chaos around him. Screams. Blood. Moonlight. Livia fought beside him, but he only had eyes for Sasha.

She stood at the center of a battlefield, crazy hair on end, blood and dirt on her face with fury in her eyes. She was both a terrifying sight and an image from a dream. He stumbled forward, afraid she was just a figment of his imagination.

"Snap the hell out of it!" Sasha pointed her dagger at him like she would filet him on the spot if he didn't lower his sword.

My sword? Livia's never given me a weapon. Livia. She broke him. His last memories crashed into him as he dropped the sword to his side. Unable to tear his eyes away from Sasha, he took another step toward her, ignoring Livia's order for him to return. The sharp tug of his leash didn't faze him. He felt stronger than he had in months, but his breath came fast and uneasy. Confusion overwhelmed him. His chest burned, sending his blood pumping through his body like liquid ice in his veins. The world tilted and Quinn feared he would pass out before he could draw his next breath. When his lungs filled with sweet air and his world righted again, everything was different. Sasha was his lifeline and he held onto her. His heart seemed to beat right out of his chest. His pulse raced alongside the gentle echo of another heartbeat. It gave him strength and calmed him in the midst of war.

Jin Jing's sudden roar pulled Quinn into the present. He held his hand up to shield his eyes from the smoke. It's the orchard. Just like James said. *And his grandmother was fighting Livia.*

Something monumental had passed between Quinn and Sasha. Something that would change them forever, but he had to focus. This was Santi's plan in action and he had some catching up to do.

Santi? Where is she? He scanned the rows of gnarled old apple trees for any sign of her. But the chaos overwhelmed him. His hands itched to fight, but he couldn't settle his mind on who the enemy was.

"Stay with me." Sasha stepped up beside him. "I'll will not leave your side until this is done."

Quinn nodded, a little unsettled by the cold look on her face. But the sound of Livia's laughter brought his attention back to the fight. She was the enemy.

The silver-fire in Livia's eyes flamed in fury, but the look on her face was one of panic. She was cornered. Quinn gazed around the orchard. Most of her team had fallen to his family, and those who remained were fleeing.

No, Livia! He watched in horror as Ming Lao fell to her knees at Livia's feet. It made no sense. Livia was alone and outnumbered. His father and grandparents had her trapped and his great-grandparents stood at the ready to help.

"Go, son!" Daniel cried, taking up the fight against Livia. He shoved Quinn and Sasha toward his great-grandparents, Ju Long and Lu Li.

He couldn't watch. His father was strong but Livia would exploit Daniel's limitations.

"Relax, Quinnton. You are home now," Ju Long whispered.

But he couldn't relax. He knew Livia. Quinn knew she wouldn't back down just because she was surrounded. He could see the power simmering in her eyes. She hadn't just wounded Ming Lao. She'd done something horrifying. He could sense it in the air. They all could and they each took a step back.

"No!" Quinn sobbed when it hit him. Ming Lao and Jin Jing regarded each other as strangers. Something unnatural and heinous had putrefied their Complement bond. Quinn could sense the decay.

"What have you done, Livia?" Quinn roared.

"Ming?" Jin cried as she dropped her sword, clutching her chest like she wanted to rip her heart from her body.

"Mom!" Chloe burst through the trees, flinging herself between her parents, boldly standing between them and Livia.

"Chloe?" Daniel moved to put himself between Livia and his little sister.

With a sickening thud Quinn would never forget, Livia's sword came crashing down, sending his father's hand and his sword to the dusty ground. Daniel stumbled, holding the bloody stump of his arm, trying to stay on his feet.

Quinn cried out in frustration, breaking his great-grandfather's grip. Livia had hurt Quinn so many times and he took it, but he refused to watch her hurt his family. He needed this nightmare to end. He wanted to go back to not feeling anything. *Not caring was better than this.*

"Don't let her win," Ju Long said. "She can sever their bond but she will never destroy this family."

"Quinn!"

"Santi!" He turned at the familiar voice, finding her standing among the shadows of the apple trees.

"Come, please, we have to get away. Remember the plan? Please come back to me?" she begged.

"You did it," he said softly, taking a step toward her.

"Let's go. While Livia is distracted." She reached for his hand.

Quinn gasped as his heart clenched in agony. He stared at Santi, but turned back to Sasha. The hurt and confusion on her face tore him up inside.

I'll never be enough for both of them. I'll always fall short.

"Listen to the girl, son," Ju Long said. "You and Sasha go with her now. We will deal with this threat. We have the upper hand."

"Santi?" Quinn took another step toward the girl he loved, aching at the pain he caused the other girl he loved just as much but in a different way.

"Yes. Remember James and Lennox? They'll be on their way to us soon. We did it. You did it!" Santi's smile overwhelmed him. He'd never seen her smile like that before. She was free. All they had to do was walk away, far from this place. But Sasha's pain caused him to hesitate. He wanted to tell her not to give up on him.

I still love you, Sasha. So much it hurts. But after all this time, somewhere along the way, his love for her had transformed into something he didn't understand. Rooted to the spot, he couldn't make a choice between the two most important people in his world.

He saw the hardness sweep through Sasha. The way her shoulders stiffened. Her face grew cold and unfeeling. This was not the Sasha he remembered. She'd changed. Like maybe he wasn't the only one who'd gone through hell and back.

Without a word, Sasha turned toward the barn ... right into the arms of another man.

"Jayesh?" Her voice warmed with hope and a hint of pain. The smile that lit her face rivaled the sun.

The man with the face tattoo watched Sasha with eyes starved for the sight of her. Jayesh had promised he would sever all ties with Sasha. Clearly she hadn't let him.

Santi's hand wrapped around Quinn's. It was a painful moment, watching Sasha cast a last glance over her shoulder at him. But when Jayesh turned and retreated back through the woods toward the house, Sasha followed, taking a piece of Quinn's heart with her.

"Oh, but I can do much worse, my dear Alexis." Livia's taunt pulled Quinn away from Sasha's retreating figure and back to the battle.

"Quinn, let's go. Please." Santi pulled his hand.

"I can't leave my family to clean up my mess," he said, turning to face Livia.

"Liv, don't do this," Quinn begged her to end this. "Please. We'll come back with you."

"No!" Chloe cried when Livia lunged toward Jin.

Quinn watched as Jin shoved his daughter behind him. Livia's sword flashed silver in the brilliant moonlight.

No longer Complements? Livia had always kept her own abilities close to the belt. While she knew every nuance of her slaves' individual gifts, the only thing Quinn knew she could do was hijack another's gift.

"She's severed their bond," he choked. Their Immortality lay within the Complement bond. If that bond no longer existed ... what would that mean for Jin and Ming's mortality?

Gunfire sounded just as Livia's sword arched toward Jin's chest. The bullet hit Livia's shoulder, but it was too late.

At the last moment, Ming Lao jumped in front of her husband. Livia's sword had sliced right through her heart.

"Momma!" Chloe shrieked, dropping to the ground beside her mother.

"It is best that one of them not survive this, child," Livia said, ruffling Chloe's hair. Then she gripped her shoulder where bloodstains bloomed across her white shirt and set off across the orchard.

Chloe's screams echoed in the sudden stillness of the night.

Quinn lunged to follow Livia.

"No, Quinn!" Santi pulled him back. "Let her go!"

He really wanted to believe in Livia. That she wasn't the monster she seemed to be. But nothing gave her the right to do what she'd just done. Cornered or not.

Livia joined Selena at the edge of the orchard, but Emma, Ju Long and Lu Li boxed them in. Michael waited for Livia along the orchard path to the gates, but seeing their predicament, he turned tail and ran.

Santi and Quinn's plan was a success. Livia wouldn't make it out of here a free woman—but it had cost his grandmother her life.

Quinn followed his mother, ignoring Santi's pleas as she trailed behind him. He drew his sword, focusing on the woman responsible for all of this.

"Get back, son. She's mine," Emma said.

"Listen to mommy," Livia taunted. "Shall we tell her of all the tortures you've experienced since you've been with me, Quinn?"

"You're outnumbered, Liv. Give it up." He cast a glance at Selena. She was busy with Ju Long and Lu Li. They were keeping her on her toes.

"I don't give up." Livia lunged her attack, stalking Emma

like prey. But Emma was ready for her, countering her advances like the blade master she was.

Livia and Emma circled each other.

"You'll never touch another hair on my son's head," Emma snarled. "I will soak this ground with your blood and dance on it."

The two women were well matched. But Livia was young and she surrounded herself with those even younger. Emma had over a thousand years of experience and wisdom on her side. And she fought with the fury only a mother could know. She wasn't going to lose this fight.

"Get my son out of here!" Emma shouted at Santi. The ground shook with the force of their blows as Emma moved in a blur, chasing Livia through the rows of trees. True to her word, Emma's sword carved Livia's flesh, spilling her blood all across the orchard.

"Quinn?" Santi whispered at his side.

"I can't leave my mother and my great-grandparents to fight on their own." But just as he turned to help Ju Long, his brand seared hot on his arm, forcing Quinn to drop his weapon. The tug of his leash brought him to his knees. Santi fell beside him as Ryan came to collect them.

Quinn searched the orchard for help. He wouldn't go back. Not when his plans had led to the death of his grandmother and all of this bloodshed. *No.* He refused to be a captive any longer.

"You're coming with me." Ryan hauled him to his feet.

"No! Let him go." Santi shoved him, scraping her nails across his face. "Go!" She shoved him again. "Turn tail and run like the coward you are," Santi sneered, "we're not coming with you. You're outnumbered?"

"I'll pull you back. You belong to Soma." Ryan watched as

Emma fought to bring Livia down. At the same moment, two Coalition joined Selena in her battle with Ju Long and Lu Li.

"No!" Quinn lunged to help his great-grandparents, but Ryan's held him back. "Please!"

The Coalition thugs had given Selena the opening she needed. With a touch of her gift, she drained Quinn's great-grandparents of their knowledge, dropping them to the ground when she was done with them. She'd make a fortune selling their priceless secrets.

In an instant, the Coalition moved in for the slaughter. Like the butchers they were, they ripped the Immortal's hearts from their chests and tossed them into the nearest fire like proud hunters discarding the offal from a fresh kill.

Selena took a step toward Livia, like the well-trained dog she was, but Livia wasn't her master. Marcus had given Selena enough freedom to make her own choices. With a smirk in Quinn's direction, she fled the orchard with her Coalition guards.

With a roar of misery, Quinn broke Ryan's hold. "Get out of here," Quinn said. "Before I make you pay for this."

Ryan cast a last glance at Livia, on her knees in the dirt, and followed Selena without a word.

Emma panted with fury. The effort of simply standing beside the woman who'd taken her son was too much for her. Quinn could see the coldness in his mother's eyes. She wanted to make Livia suffer.

"Mom," Quinn whispered. "She's not worth it."

The sound of her son's voice pulled her back. Emma raised her sword and brought the hilt down on Livia's head. The crack of her skull echoed in the silence around them as Livia slid to the ground in a boneless heap.

"I want to kill this woman!" Emma screamed in frustration.

"She should die for what she's done to my son and our family." She gasped with the intensity of her anger.

"Mom. Can we go home, please?" Quinn asked, his eyes glued to the gruesome sight of his great-grandparents lying still in the moonlight.

"Yes, we have to go," Naeemah said as she charged through the trees, coming from the direction of the gates. "If we're going to get out of here at all, we need to move now." She reached to pull the unconscious Livia across her shoulders. "Now, Emma. Get your sons and get out of here. I will see to our dead."

Emma grabbed Quinn's hand with a gentle squeeze and they were running through the trees, far away from the house, the orchard and the madness of the last hours.

Quinn pulled Santi behind him, hope stirring in his chest at the taste of freedom.

As they stood beside the row of cars his family had strategically placed in the woods for their quick escape, Quinn's brand erupted, lighting him on fire. Santi buckled under the intensity of the pull. The desire to return to Soma filled them both. Livia still had their power, but Ryan had taken ownership of their brands the moment she fell. He would see to it they returned. If he had the strength to make them obey.

"Quinn? What is it?" Emma demanded, searching him for the source of the pain.

"It's the Soma brand. They're calling us back," he gasped. "We won't be able to resist it."

Emma nodded. "I'm going to collar you both. It won't help with the pain, but it should dull your desire to return to Soma. Eventually, you'll be able to break the bond of the brand. But you're going to have to outlast it." Taking a set of magnetized collars from her hip, she placed one around his throat with a look in her eye that said she would never let him go.

"Do you mind?" Emma asked Santi.

"It's okay. It won't be long," Quinn said.

Santi nodded, closing her eyes as Emma clasped the collar around her throat.

"Quinn?" Daniel stumbled to the car, clutching Graham for support.

"Dad. I'm so sorry. I—"

Quinn's father wrapped his one good arm around his son.

"Don't ever apologize." Daniel's face paled as he clutched the bloody stump of his arm against his chest.

"Let's get our boys home," Emma said softly as she helped Daniel into the front seat.

"Quinn!" Graham slammed into his brother's chest.

"Little man, it's good to see you." Quinn cried, holding Graham tight. "But if you ever go anywhere near Soma again, I will personally nail your feet to the bottom of the lake."

Graham helped Quinn and Santi into the back seat and a moment later, they were speeding along the dirt roads that ran along the backside of the property.

"Welcome back, bro," Graham said softly as Quinn's body erupted in agony, the pull of the Soma brand chasing all thought from his mind.

Chapter 35

Sasha: Fall, The New Moon - Rural New York

"Jayesh?" Sasha charged through the trees and came to an abrupt halt at the edge of the lawn. "Gen?" She shrank back into the shadows cast by the blood red moon, high overhead now. The lawn in front of her sister's home swarmed with the fleeing enemy. Voices shouted as Livia's people rushed to secure their captives. This was the Coalition. Livia's backup. At the center of all their activity, Imogen and her Complement, Lucien, were collared and waiting on their knees beside a roaring fire. Jayesh stood over them, brandishing a blade and barking out orders. A woman led Sasha's cousin Dean by the collar she'd placed around his neck, shoving him into the caged back of one of their vehicles.

Sasha couldn't breathe. Had they just traded Dean's life for Quinn's? There was no way she was going to stand by and watch her sister and brother-in-law die in place of their parents. And she sure as hell wasn't going to let Jayesh be the one to do it.

Sasha stepped into the circle of light, heedless of the Coalition agents scrambling to leave. "Jayesh. What are you doing?"

she demanded as she stalked across the lawn to her sister's side. "You can't do this."

"Sasha, no," Imogen said gently. "You have to leave me here, sweetie. It will be okay. This is what Mother Raghavan was preparing me for."

"You knew this was coming?" Lucien took his wife's hand.

"I knew you and I were headed for a difficult time." Her eyes shone bright in the moonlight.

"That's why you've pushed me away since your return," Lucien said.

"I was trying to distance myself from you. Hoping to save you from this."

"Please let them go, Jayesh," Sasha whispered.

"I can't. There are too many eyes watching me."

"Go Sasha," Imogen said. "We will survive this. Jayesh, get her out of here!"

Arms pulled Sasha back, dragging her to her knees beside her sister.

"Wait," Jayesh said. "I'll do it." He took the collar from the Coalition woman. His voice was hard, showing no trace of the careful mentor Sasha had come to admire. Or of the man she was falling for. The enormity of his betrayal broke her heart.

"Leave us," Jay commanded.

The mortal woman released Sasha but she forced Imogen and Lucien to their feet. "Be quick about it." She shot Sasha a glare as she shoved her captives toward the waiting van.

"No! You can't, Jayesh. She's my sister!" Sasha lunged after them, but Jayesh held her back.

"No, Sasha."

"Don't do this." Tears rolled down her face. "Take me instead. Let them go and I'll come quietly."

Jay turned her to face him, keeping a firm grip on her arms. The cold look in his eyes grew warm as he stared at her. "I need you to trust me, angel," he said softly. "I will not let them execute Imogen and her husband, but they're going to have to come with me. For now. I have a job to do."

"No, Jayesh." She couldn't fight the tears. "I know what this means now." She reached to cup his face, brushing her thumb over the tattoo. The lines were old and faded, but she'd recognized the symbol at Amrita and knew it was the same as his tattoo. The ouroboros snake, biting its tail, just like the Soma brand. The symbol marked Jayesh a slave. "Come with me now and you can be free."

"I'll never be free of the master who tugs my leash." He closed his eyes, bringing his hand up to hers.

He was so defeated, she wondered how she'd never realized. He hid it well. A broken Immortal was a dangerous and unfeeling weapon. Immortals like Jayesh spent their lives following the orders of the one who'd done the breaking. But there was a spark of the real Jayesh in there. She'd seen it.

"Go now. While they're not looking. I'll see your family isn't taken to the prisons. That's the best I can do for them. But if you don't go now, I'm going to have to bring you with me, and I'll die before I see you with the Soma brand."

"Jayesh. I can't leave you. Not like this. Not again." Sasha clutched his shoulders, trying to drag him away with her.

"Don't." He took both of her hands in his. "Go back to your life. Go back to Quinn. Your family has won this battle and I've got to get our people out of here while I can."

They both flinched as a blood-curdling scream filled the night and the horizon flickered with a golden green light.

"Allie?" Sasha gasped.

"You've got to go, angel." Jayesh pulled her into a tight hug, pressing a kiss to her forehead. "Now, please."

"Come with me. Please, Jay. My family can protect you."

"I am the only one who can keep Imogen safe. If I stay here

with you, the one who owns me will come for me. I can't have him anywhere near you or your family. Forget about me, Sasha."

The trucks and SUVs began to pull back down the drive, taking her sister with them.

"Get in the car, Jay," Selena said, pulling up beside him. "Bring the girl in this time and you might win back the favor you lost when you let her go the first time."

"Run, Sasha. Please." Jayesh shoved her hard.

Sasha stumbled backward and then she was running through the trees, her body shaking with sobs she couldn't control. How many times were the people she loved going to be ripped away from her?

CHAPTER 36

Quinn: Fall, The New Moon - Kelleys Island

"You don't have to do this," George said. "The pull of your brands seems to have subsided. I see no need to secure either of you in the crypt."

"I think we've outlasted Ryan for now, but he will try again," Quinn said. He was just grateful to be home and with family. George technically wasn't family, but he was Aidan's brother-in-law and that made him family in Quinn's mind.

The long drive home from New York was excruciating for both Santi and Quinn, but with the growing distance between themselves and Ryan, the intensity of the desire to return to Soma was fading.

"Each time he tries to lure you in and you outlast him, the brand's influence will fade, as will the mark itself," George explained.

"So I don't have to live the rest of my life with this ugly reminder?" Santi glanced down at the slightly faded Soma brand on her wrist.

"You are both strong enough to fight the control of the brand, so for you it will fade. Others might not be so lucky."

"Thank you, George," Quinn said, stepping into the crypt cell with Santi.

"I don't like seeing you behind bars, Quinn." George shook his head sadly. "Not after all you two have been through."

"It's okay," Santi said.

"Until I feel like I'm truly in control of my power, I'll feel better behind bars," Quinn insisted.

"It's been so long since I've been able to use my power without permission. I just don't think either of us trusts ourselves yet," Santi added.

"Well, don't tell Seamas I'm the one who locked you up," George said. "My husband would have my hide and I'd like to have a peaceful night when all of this is over. You are free to go whenever you like. All you have to do is ask and we'll let you right out." He closed the gate to their shared cell with a clang.

George had just secured Livia in a highly magnetized cell, ending her control over them and anyone else as soon as she stepped inside. But Santi and Quinn still didn't feel fully in possession of their power and suspected they needed to wait it out for her residual influence to fade completely.

"What can you two tell me about a young Immortal man traveling with a little girl?" George asked, glancing down at his phone. "Our sentries found them at the docks and they're asking for you."

"James and Lennox!" Santi cried. "Please bring them here. They're our friends."

"The girl suffered an early Awakening," Quinn said. "She's an amazing kid, but she grew up in Soma and never had a family."

"She has one now." George smiled. "At least as far as Seamas is concerned. He's the one who found them. I can't believe it, but my husband is now a father. He bonded with her the moment he laid eyes on her tonight. I'm not sure she's reciprocated yet, but it's been an eventful night."

"Thank God. That's just what she needs!" Santi smiled. "Thank you so much."

"I'm anxious to meet her," George said. "For years we've been talking about adopting, but it was never a good time. I just can't imagine what she's been through. What all of you have been through."

"She'll have what she needs now," Quinn said. "Seamas will know better than anyone how to help her recover."

"What about James?" Santi asked.

"He's not really a kid, but he could definitely use some parenting," Quinn said. "Or some brothers to beat some sense into him."

"He will have a home here," George said. "He can stay with Scott and Darius in the loft for the time being."

"And my family?" Santi asked.

"We need to get Santi's family out of Atlanta as soon as possible," Quinn said. "I know that's asking a lot, but I promised. I—"

"Don't worry, son. We'll take care of it," George said. "You two just get some rest, and don't worry about a thing. Now I'm going to go meet my potential new daughter, but I'll be back to check on you in a bit."

Quinn paced the cell after George left, trying to shake off the uneasy feeling that something was missing.

"How are you ... yourself?" Santi finally asked. She bit her lip nervously.

"Sasha. I think. Something about seeing her again snapped me out of it." He stopped beside the cot where Santi sat.

"I'm glad." She hesitantly grabbed his hand. "We're free." Her smile was just as hesitant.

"Funny thought considering we're in a prison cell." He

crouched in front of her, taking both her hands in his. "What happened after she broke me? How did the Coalition become involved?"

"That was something we hadn't counted on. I'm so sorry, Quinn." Her eyes filled with tears. "I wouldn't have taken such a risk with your family if I'd known she was going to come against them with such a force." She shook her head. "I'm so sorry about your grandmother and Ju Long and Lu Li. Our freedom wasn't worth the cost of their lives."

"Shhh, Mina, it's not your fault." He moved to sit beside her on the cot.

"It was my plan." She leaned into him.

"No one could have anticipated that would happen. We knew we were taking a risk." If it was anyone's fault, it was Quinn's. He didn't want her blaming herself for things that were out of her control.

"I think Livia was afraid of you," Santi whispered. "She couldn't seem to control you or predict what you would do. She called in her team and a legion of the Coalition just to be sure she would have the numbers on her side. After she forced James to tell her what he knew of Allie's whereabouts from his prophecies, she was like a woman possessed."

"Was I that awful?" He wasn't sure if he even wanted to know what his madness had done.

"It wasn't you, Quinn. Your madness was a little more than we expected." She shivered.

"Did I—Did I hurt you?" He wrapped his arm around her, pulling her close to his side.

"No. But it wasn't like I thought. You were so insane. Nothing like the person you are in here." She tapped his chest with her fingertips.

"I've conquered him before. I can do it again, but he'll always be there, lurking inside of me."

"He's not you, Quinn. You know that, don't you?"

"I know." He nodded. "He is part of me, but he doesn't rule me. I can't let him dictate how I use my power."

"We get to shape who we become, Quinnton. We get to decide who we want to be. Not our batshit crazy gifts."

"You're right." He smiled.

"Listen, now that we're out.... You don't owe me anything." Her fingertips trailed across his jaw.

"I owe you everything, Mina." He kissed her fingertips.

"What about Sasha? I can feel this enormous thing you have with her. I can sense the bond. I don't understand it, but it's bigger than me—"

"No, Santi. I don't know what this is. But I know it doesn't change the way I feel about you. I want to be wherever you are."

"We have a few ... guests." Gregg's voice drifted from the crypt entrance.

"Allie?" Quinn stood, crossing the cell to the barred entrance.

"Quinn?" She rushed over to him, reaching for the bars. "Why is he in a cell?"

She looked like hell. Blood and dirt smeared her face, like she'd cried bloody tears. Her red hair was a rat's nest on top of her head, but she was beautiful. His friend. His family.

"It's not safe for us to be with the family yet," Quinn said. "I won't trust myself until I'm in full control of my power again."

"He asked us to put them here," Gregg explained.

"It's a long story, Allie. But I'm glad to see you." He reached through the bars to clasp her hands.

"I'm so sorry, Quinn. It should have been me."

But he was so grateful it wasn't Allie in his place. Not that she couldn't have survived it, but he suspected Allie was way more important to their future than he was.

"I'm so glad it wasn't you. It was better this way." He gestured over his shoulder to Santi, sitting quietly on the bed in the corner of the cell. He couldn't imagine his life without her now.

Looking at Allie, Quinn knew she was headed for a confrontation with Livia. He glanced toward the door leading to Livia's cell, grateful he wouldn't be there when it happened. "Just ... don't judge her too harshly, Allie," Quinn said. "She's a heinous bitch, but she's had a hard life. She's never really had a choice." He knew that now. Livia's father made her into a weapon and never gave her a chance to be the person she wanted to be. She was a reluctant weapon. She didn't know how to be anything else.

"Who?" Allie asked.

"Livia," Gregg said. "She's here. We couldn't risk letting her escape this time."

"Take me to her, please?" Allie's voice rang with a confidence Quinn had never heard from her before.

"Are you sure?" Gregg asked.

"Yes."

"She's in a pissy mood, as you can probably imagine. And she's not thrilled with you."

"I bet not." Allie heaved a huge sigh as she followed Gregg into another room where the cell bars practically hummed with magnetic energy.

Quinn caught a glimpse of Livia pacing her cell in a fury. He met her eyes just for a second and thought he saw her smile.

"Oh good, you brought the brat."

CHAPTER 37

Sasha: Fall, The New Moon - Kelleys Island

Sasha paced the length of the common room. The steady thump of her heart felt out of rhythm, like each beat held a faint echo. In the hour since she arrived home safely, she still hadn't recovered from the rush of battle. Something was missing. Like a detail she couldn't quite remember.

When Sasha had returned to the orchard after leaving Jayesh, she was a wreck, but pulled herself together when she found her mother gathering up their dead. Sasha watched in horror as Jin and Chloe laid Ming Lao in the back of the SUV. She could sense the wrongness shrouding Jin like a sickness and realized Ming Lao wouldn't be rising again. Sasha moved to help Naeemah bring Ju Long and Lu Li to rest beside their daughter. Chloe crawled in beside her mother's body, holding her hand and staring with vacant, dry eyes. There was something vaguely terrifying about the look on Chloe's face.

There was no room in the vehicle for Sasha so she slid behind the wheel of one of the remaining cars. She sat in a daze, half of her wanting to follow Jayesh. The other half pulled her toward Quinn like a beacon.

Sasha stopped her pacing at the sound of a weary step coming up from the crypt.

"Sasha?" Allie's voice sounded haunted.

"I heard you coming. What do you know? I just got back." Sasha's nervous babble tumbled out of her mouth.

"I was going to ask you the same thing."

"Have you seen him?" She was going to throttle Allie if she didn't start talking.

"Quinn? Yes. He's fine."

"Where is he?" Her eyes were starved for the sight of him. She needed to see him.

"He asked them to lock him up in the crypt. He's still not himself. Livia had some kind of hold on him. She was using his gifts."

"She took them?" Sasha's stomach heaved at the thought that she'd stripped him of his gifts.

"No. It seems she can piggyback onto a gift without actually stealing it. He was in bad shape, but you broke him out of it, Sash. You did it. You brought him home. I don't think we could have gotten through to him any other way."

"Then what is *this*?" She threw her hands up in frustration, her eyes bright with unshed tears. Quinn was home. Her was here and he needed her. She could sense his anxiety.

"Calm down. Let's sit," Allie said. "What are you talking about?"

"I can *feel* him, Allie. Like I can feel his heart beating in my chest. Something happened out there when we saw each other."

Allie paled in the dim light of the common room. "Have you talked to Naeemah?" she asked hesitantly.

"No, I haven't seen anyone since I got back."

"Who did you ride home with?"

"I drove home alone. I followed Mom."

“Where is everyone? Where’s Aidan?” Allie asked.

“I think Aidan's with Emma trying to treat Daniel’s severed hand.” She’d heard his screams when they returned. Naeemah rushed off to help, leaving Sasha behind to wait and wonder about Quinn. *Is he okay?* She could hear herself babbling but she had no idea what she was saying. Her mind and body were so attuned to Quinn, she couldn’t register anything else.

Allie grabbed her hands. “Deep breaths, Sash. You’ve been alone for hours, not knowing what this is?” Allie wrapped her arms around her. “Just breathe; it’s all going to be okay. But I need you to calm down. Focus on me. Let everything else go.”

The tension finally left Sasha’s shoulders and it hit her. There was something vastly different about Allie. Something in her presence—her bearing—had changed. She could feel her brother’s aura blending with Allie’s.

Sasha pulled away, staring at her friend in disbelief. “What *is* this bullshit? You too? With Darius?” *And not Aidan?*

Allie nodded. “Let’s go find your dad. You need to see Quinn, and Gregg needs to explain this to you both.”

Allie pulled her up from the couch, but Sasha felt numb. This was what she’d always wanted, right? To be with Quinn for real. Her mind told her this couldn’t be the Complement bond, but her body told her differently. *Why do I feel like this is the last thing I want?*

“I always wondered if Quinn might be my Complement,” Sasha whispered as they headed down to the crypt. “But it never felt right. I love him. I’d be proud if he were. It's just never worked; but this feels very ... Complementy.” *And very much not what I want. I still love him. But so much has changed. With Jayesh.... How can I have feelings for two people?*

“Quinn is a huge part of who you are.” Allie pushed on the door leading to Quinn’s cell, but it was locked. She knocked and waited.

Sasha could sense him on the other side of that door. He was upset. He needed her. "I'm going to break it down." Sasha moved to kick the door. She was desperate to set her eyes on Quinn at last. After all this time, they were about to come full circle.

Chapter 38

Quinn: Fall, The New Moon - Kelleys Island

"Let her in, Darius," Quinn said. "Sasha's coming through that door one way or another." He gripped the edge of the cot, his body attuned to Sasha's distress.

"Well, this is about to get messy." Darius glanced at Santi as he opened the door before Sasha could kick it in.

Sasha rushed past him. "Open the cell," she demanded.

"Sasha?" Quinn leapt to his feet. "I missed you." He reached through the bars, his heart racing at the sight of her.

"Get him out of there!" Sasha's eyes blazed with blue fury.

"It's not safe, Sash," Quinn said. "I need a few days in here—"

"You will *not* hurt me. You don't have it in you. Now get him out of there." Sasha glared at Darius.

"Will do." Darius moved to unlock the cell.

Before Quinn could take a step out, Sasha ran in and threw her arms around him, locking her legs around his waist. His heart surged into his throat the second he touched her. *Finally, I'm home.* His arms slid around her, familiar and comfortable as he inhaled the scent of her hair.

They clung to each other. After so much time, Quinn still

felt like Sasha made his world right. The thought should have alarmed him. He was pretty sure he was hopelessly in love with Santi, but Sasha was home. She was ... Sasha.

"Who is she?" Sasha asked as her gaze fell on Santi.

Please understand, Sash. "This is my ... girlfriend, Santi," Quinn said carefully. He met Santi's gaze, begging her to understand even though he couldn't explain how he could love them both at the same time.

"Hi," Santi said softly. "He forgot to tell me you were beyond gorgeous." The hint of pain in her voice knifed right through him.

How can I get through this without hurting either of them?

Sasha slowly slipped out of Quinn's arms and stared up at him. A little piece of his heart broke at what he saw there. She was no longer the girl he'd grown up with. No longer his childhood sweetheart. They'd both moved on and become different people, set on different paths now.

So what are we to each other?

"You have a *girlfriend*? You've been off in some kind of prison camp, have obviously been through hell, and you come back with a *girlfriend*? While I've spent the last eight months *dying* inside, you've been hooking up?" She gave him a shove and Quinn stumbled back.

Anger is good. I can deal with angry Sasha. That's our thing anyway. I just can't deal with hurt Sasha.

"Sasha, it's not going to change whatever this bond is we have now," Quinn said.

"Wow, she's pretty feisty. I like her," Santi said.

Sasha shot her a glare that could have melted glass. "I—"

"Can we argue later, Sash?" Quinn asked. "Right now, I'm just really happy to see you." He reached to cup her face. The gesture was so familiar. He'd done it a thousand times—with

Santi and with Sasha, and he could tell Santi didn't like it. At all.

Caught between two strong-willed women. This wasn't going to be easy.

"Come on, you two," Darius said. "Santi ... uh, you should probably stay here."

"Fine by me; I'm exhausted. It's been a really long ... year." She stretched out on the bed with a yawn.

Quinn met her gaze and she smiled. They were okay. *We'll be okay.*

He trembled beside Sasha as they Followed Allie and Darius through the hallways of their childhood home. The memories of this place were distant to him now. He would need to explain that to Sasha soon. She had to understand how that night at the ball felt like a million years ago to him now.

"It's okay. You're home now," she whispered. "Life isn't going to go back to the way it was before. We're not those people anymore, Quinn." She squeezed his hand. "But we can build a new future. A new normal."

Quinn breathed a sigh of relief. *She gets it.* He took a moment to really look at her. There was a hardness about her that wasn't there before. Sasha was as changed as he was.

"What's this?" Gregg met them at the door to his office, the phone halfway to his ear.

"Sorry, Dad," Darius said.

"You've got to be kidding me." Gregg's jaw dropped. "You too?"

"I sense lots of group Syntrophos classes in our near future," Darius said.

"We're going to go." Allie pulled Darius toward the door. "We'll talk tomorrow, Sash."

"What's a Syntrophos?" Quinn asked.

CHAPTER 39

Sasha: Fall, The New Moon - Kelleys Island

"Say something, Da," Sasha said.

Gregg stood at the bar in his office, staring into the amber liquid in his glass. He glanced up at her, his eyes filled with sadness.

"I should have seen this coming. This explains everything I've watched you two struggle with in your relationship." He sighed as he crossed the room to sit in his worn leather chair. "I should have recognized it and prepared you for it."

"What does this bond mean, Gregg?" Quinn asked. "In all my studies, I've never heard of a Syntrophos bond."

"Quinn, you have loved my daughter since the moment you met her," Gregg said. "And you've been torn apart for eight months. I can imagine how gut-wrenching that has been for you both. Especially with not understanding the nature of the relationship that has been building between you for years. And I don't think either of you realizes how long those eight months have been for the other, nor what you've been through in that time."

"How could you possibly know about Michael?" Quinn asked.

"He attacked Aidan tonight," Gregg said.

"Aidan?" Sasha jumped to her feet, worried something terrible had happened to her brother.

"He's fine. We were able to save him in time but we've taken Michael prisoner. He won't be hurting anyone with his gift ever again."

"What did this man do to you?" Sasha glanced at Quinn. There was no doubt he was different. Older somehow. *Has this time away been more than it seems for him too?*

"The first three months at Soma were a nightmare." Quinn sighed. "Michael was one of the 'trainers' there. His psychological gift made those three months feel like five years of torture." Quinn turned to Sasha and took her hand. "In my mind, I feel like I've been away from you for nearly six years, Sasha. That last night at the ball ... it's a distant memory for me." His voice trembled with regret.

"It's been nearly four years for me," she whispered, squeezing his hand gently. She couldn't imagine the torment he'd suffered. How difficult it likely was for him when he realized those years didn't actually happen.

"How?" Quinn gasped.

"The Senate sent me away to train as a Chola assassin. I was gone for six weeks, but time moves slowly in the Chola Valley. To me it was three years. Three very long years."

"The Chola Valley? I've read about that place. Sasha, the training there is brutal." Quinn pulled her into his arms and held her. "I'm so sorry," he whispered.

"It seems we've both had a very long eight months." Sasha buried her head in the crook of his neck, inhaling the scent of him like a childhood memory.

"I'm so sorry about Santi. I never wanted to spring that on you so suddenly." Quinn pulled away.

"I understand. You go through something like that with

someone and it changes you both." Sasha couldn't fault him for moving on.

"Jayesh?" Quinn asked.

"Yes. Maybe. I don't know," she whispered. "He's not free."

"He is a good man."

"You know him?" Her eyes widened in surprise.

"We've met." Quinn smiled.

"You've both suffered more than any of us will ever know or understand," Gregg said. "But you're home now and it's time for some healing. Learning to cope with the Syntrophos bond will be difficult, but I suspect it will also be an immense relief to you."

"What is it, Da?" Sasha asked. "It feels so much like I imagine the Complement bond to be."

"But there was no choice," Quinn added. "It just happened."

"Aye, that's the way of the Syntrophos bond. It tends to build under the surface for a time before it comes upon you like a storm. The Syntrophos bond began with the earliest queens of Indriell. The queen's council was made up of the Syntrophos, who were the heads of their noble houses. They acted as her council, but they were also her army."

"So it's a battle bond?" Quinn asked.

"In a way, yes." Gregg nodded.

"That would explain why we are more successful as sparring partners than as romantic partners," Sasha said. But Quinn was so much more to her than just a right hand in battle.

"We've often suspected that Sasha has a genetic link to Indriell nobility," Gregg said. "With her hair threaded with gold, and the strength of her power and talent, if Indriell still stood today, she would likely have grown up as the companion to the first princess. Eventually she would have become the first of the queen's council. A woman like that would have had a strong Syntrophos standing by her side and the two would have taken charge of the queen's royal council."

"But what does it mean for us? Indriell no longer exists, so what does a Syntrophos do?" Sasha asked.

"Today, the remaining Syntrophos keep it hidden. You will need to learn to mask the bond you share so it cannot be detected. The Senate can *never* know about your bond, Sasha. They are just waiting for a reason to take you away from us. If they discover you and Quinn are a bonded Syntrophos, they will take you both."

"Then learning to mask this bond will be a priority," Quinn said. "I will never again let anyone take my freedom—from me or from Sasha. It's not an option."

"The Syntrophos bond is an intimate thing," Gregg said. "It will rarely make sense to anyone outside of it. And until one of you bonds with your Complement, we won't know which one of you is the anchor."

"Anchor?" Sasha asked.

"The Syntrophos bond involves three people. The Anchor is the glue that holds you all together. The Anchor will have a Syntrophos and a Complement who will be closely linked as well. The Anchor's Syntrophos and Complement will often be each other's best friend and their worst enemy. The Anchor will feel torn between their love for both. Like he or she isn't enough. Until the third wheel, so to speak, bonds with their own Complement, the relationship can be extremely rocky for all involved. Jealousy will always be a part of the bond. When the fourth joins you, he or she will bring a balance to the relationship but they will never be part of it. The fourth is destined to sit on the sidelines of the bond."

"So this bond would explain why we love each other so much, but no matter how much we want it, the relationship never works." Sasha could almost feel her worldview changing.

"It will take years for you two to come to terms with what this bond means for you," Gregg said. "Only you will ever be able to define what you mean to each other. We always categorize the people in our lives. Family, friend, lover, enemy. A Syntrophos doesn't fit into any of those boxes."

Quinn nodded, a small smile beginning to light his face. "That explains a lot."

Sasha felt the first stirrings of relief and she was so happy to see Quinn's similar reaction.

"The only love you will ever know that supersedes what you two have now will be with your Complements. The Syntrophos bond is a very different kind of love, but it is still love. You will feel the need to express your love in a physical way—and I don't mean sex. I like to think of myself as a modern man, but I'm not having that conversation with my daughter."

"Dad!" Sasha groaned, mortified.

"I'm glad to see I can still embarrass you." He smiled. "You grew up during your time away, Sasha. I wasn't ready for that. And I'm not ready for this either. For the Syntrophos who aren't bonded with a Complement, it is very easy to let that love become a romantic relationship, as you two have attempted time and again. The way you gravitate toward each other in a physical way will never go away. You'll always feel the need to touch. Your romantic partners will never understand that, but your Complements will in time. That's where the jealousy will come in. But at its core, the Syntrophos bond is a very innocent kind of love."

"So ... loving two people at the same time is inevitable?" Quinn asked.

"Aye." Gregg nodded. "And you've no need to beat yourself up about it."

"I will do my best not to come between you and Santi," Sasha said softly. "But it won't be easy." Her eyes clouded with tears. She didn't want to share him. Not now that she finally had him back. But at the same time she could understand how torn Quinn was feeling. In a sense, she felt like she'd finally gotten her heart back, but there was a little piece of her that was with Jayesh. She had no idea what her future would hold with him, but she owed it to him to find out.

"And I will do my best to explain to her how much you mean to me," Quinn said.

"We will spend a great deal of time over the coming weeks discussing the Syntrophos bond. We will bring Santi into those lessons if you'd like," Gregg said.

"Thank you." Quinn nodded.

"Wait," Sasha said. "Allie and *Darius*?"

"Aye." Gregg smiled. "Allie and Darius too."

"That's ... unexpected." Sasha giggled. "I'm sorry, I don't mean to laugh." But she suddenly found the thought of Allie at the center of so much boy drama absolutely hilarious.

"Poor Aidan." Quinn laughed, slipping his hand around hers.

"Poor Darius." Gregg grinned.

"She's going to drown them both in the lake." Sasha threw her head back and laughed. It felt good to laugh. It felt good to finally understand her feelings for Quinn and how he would always be one of the most important people in her life. Knowing that would never change made it easier to think of him with someone else—easier to think of herself with someone else.

Jayesh.

Epilogue

Livia: Fall, The New Moon - Kelleys Island

"Oh good, you brought the brat." Livia paced the length of her cell. It was the only way she could mask the panic she was feeling.

How did I get myself into this? Marcus is going to slaughter these people. And it's all my fault.

Livia turned, setting her eyes on the girl who was the source of all her trouble. Allie met her gaze with defiance. This was not the same girl Livia had met eight months ago. That girl had been a shadow. A child who hadn't yet come into her own. *She's found her footing since then.*

"Do you know why you're looking for me?" Allie asked, her voice clear as a bell.

"Of course. But I won't be telling any of you that." Livia looked Allie up and down, scouring her face for clues. *What is it about this girl? What am I missing?* She was certainly powerful, and if Livia's suspicions were correct, Allie was also very important. But there was something more—something Livia hadn't figured out yet.

"Not the reason your boss wants me. Do you know why *you*

are so intrigued by me? Why time and again you come looking for me?"

"What do you know?" Livia paced as close to the magnetic bars as she dared.

"You're my sister."

Of all the things the girl could have said, this was not what Livia expected.

"Not possible." Livia reached for the necklace at her throat. The memories that had plagued her for years came back to her now. Memories of another life. Another family. Livia had a life once. A life before Marcus.

"Of course ... *Alivia*," Gregg whispered. "I haven't thought of her in more than a century." He stared at Livia like she was a missing piece of his family. "Do you remember when you were taken?" he asked. "You were so young. I can't imagine you could remember much of your natural mother and father."

"I was adopted. I'm no natural born." But the vague memories and dreams that tormented her sleep were proof that what he said was true. What had Marcus robbed her of? What might her life have been like if he'd never taken her from her ... family?

"You remember a woman with hair like mine, don't you? You said it the moment you laid eyes on me in that warehouse last year when I was the one behind bars. I remember her too, just vaguely."

"The necklace ... let me see it," Livia demanded.

Allie tugged a chain from under her coat and held it in the light.

Livia did the same, removing a long chain tucked under her jacket. The pendants were nearly identical. The serpentine figure around Livia's necklace was more clearly an ouroboros than Allie's, but the pendants were eerily similar. And eerily like the Soma brand, except the serpent curved into a figure eight rather than a circle.

Allie's mortal mother, Lily, had given Livia the necklace when she'd visited her in New Zealand more than eighteen months ago. Along with a story that didn't seem quite right. That trip was the catalyst that started all of this—Livia's obsession with Allie.

Livia hadn't discovered the answers she sought that day, only more questions. Questions that led her back to Allie again a year later.

"It makes no difference." Livia lifted her chin. She couldn't let these people see how shaken she was. "I was raised by the man I call father. That is all that matters." Livia turned her back to them. She couldn't look into Allie's eyes for another second. She was too ashamed of all she had done. There was no way this girl could ever understand that Livia did it all to keep her mother safe.

Do I really have a sister? A little sister that needs more protection than she realizes?

"I don't know you. I don't know who you work for. I don't know anything about you, but you're my sister," Allie said.

Livia closed her eyes, swallowing back her emotions just as she'd been taught all her life.

"She isn't worth the effort, little one," the big blond man said. He was right.

"She's my sister," Allie insisted.

"You saw what she did to Ming and Jin?" he said.

Livia wished she could take it back. Her gift was an abomination, but it was the thing Marcus loved most about her—her ability to sever the Complement bond. It made her physically ill every time she used it. Taking a life that way ... ruining another life at the same time ... it was unbearable.

"She broke their Complement bond. And to make it even

more unnecessarily tragic, she murdered Ming Lao in front of their daughter."

"To be fair, I was aiming for the other one." Livia whirled around, masking her fear with defiance. "It's usually easier for the woman to survive without her Complement, especially when she has natural children. I was trying to be nice." Livia let as much venom and sarcasm into her voice as she could.

Allie's eyes crackled with green fire and rage, her fists clenching at her sides like she wanted to wrap her hands around Livia's throat.

"Little *sister*." Livia sneered. "What a joke. I'll get out of this hellhole of yours and, so help me, I will take you with me. I'll break you just like I did your buddy Quinn. I'll wear your gifts like a cloak and then I'll hand you over to my father. He's been looking for you for thousands of years."

The hurt on the girl's face told Livia she'd won. She didn't need Allie thinking they could be real sisters. It wouldn't be safe for her.

"That's enough for tonight," Gregg said.

"What will you do with her?" Allie asked as she turned to leave.

"She will be treated kindly, but we can't let her go. Not yet."

"I-I'll come see you again," Allie said.

Please don't. I don't think I can bear it. She couldn't bear the hope surging within her. Hope that she could ever actually have a family of her own.

"Don't bother. Go live your little charmed life and forget about me."

Allie whirled around with a look that could make the ground quiver, and marched right up to the magnetized bars like they didn't faze her. "I don't know anything about what you've been through, Livia. But you don't know shit about me and what I've been through either. You and I can be enemies, or we can learn to work together, filling in the gaps for each other. There's a lot I could tell you about our parents. It's up to you which way this will go. You can bend or you can break, but something tells me you're too strong and too smart to break. I know I am."

With that, her little sister turned and left.

Livia watched her go, feeling a sense of pride for the sister she'd never known. Marcus would come for Livia, and when he found Allie, he would discover what he'd been looking for since the moment he'd discovered that damned prophecy.

I have to protect her from him. And Livia knew the best way to do that was to get as far away from the girl as she possibly could.

"Would you just go, Allie?" Livia paced across her cell, trying not to let the girl get under her skin any more than she already had. Allie insisted on visiting every day. For the last four months Livia had both dreaded and looked forward to her sister's visits. She really wanted to hate her—part of her did. But the other part of her saw how special her little sister was. *She's so powerful and so humble about it.* Allie reminded her a lot of Lennox. A prime example of how the people Livia cared about always got hurt. If it weren't for Quinn and Santi taking matters into their own hands, Lennox would be well on her way to her new owners by now. Instead, she had a new family of her own with a full life ahead of her.

Livia wanted to resent Allie for the life she'd had and the family that loved her. For all the things Livia never had. But there was still so much she didn't understand. Things her instincts told her she didn't want to know.

"If you'll just listen, I can tell you what I know about our parents. There are things you need to know."

"How many times do I have to tell you I don't want to know?" Livia turned on Allie, her palms itching to use her power, but the magnetized cell left her helpless.

"You must have so many questions," Allie insisted.

"Get out." Livia pointed to the entrance of her cell. "Before I rip every strand of that ridiculous hair from your head and hang you with it!"

"Fine! And people say I'm stubborn." Allie stalked from the room, clanging the bars shut behind her.

Livia crossed the room to the fully stocked bar and poured herself a drink. Liam had brought in everything she could possibly need, turning the cold prison cell into a richly appointed cave. He treated her well—better than she deserved. She didn't know what was worse—being held captive against her will after all the years of doing it to other people—or having a kind jailor.

If she were honest, Livia was relieved to be away from Soma and all of her responsibilities there. This place was quiet and comfortable. In a ridiculous way, she almost felt free. If it weren't for the separation from her power, she would gladly stay here and rot.

"She's just trying to get to know her sister."

Livia turned at the sound of a familiar voice.

"I should have known you'd end up being behind all of this."

Livia wasn't as surprised as she probably should have been to find the last queen of Indriell entering her cell. She'd known Alísun all her life as her father's most prized captive. For most of that time, she didn't really understand who the ancient was. She came to realize it in time and hated her father for it. Alísun was regal and powerful. She deserved his respect and admiration.

"You can't really blame me for escaping, can you? Now that the tables have turned on you, surely you must understand?" Alísun stood at the center of the room, watching Livia intently. Her long blond hair had faded almost entirely to silver and she'd aged during her years in captivity. The stress of the constant torment took a toll on her. But she was still beautiful, and radiated a strength and vitality Livia couldn't fathom in one so old. She was a queen to be reckoned with.

"Of course I understand the desire to escape. It still doesn't change the fact that I've always had a job to do, with no choice but to do it. You were friends with my mother. You know everything I've ever done was to keep her safe."

"Porcia has always been capable of taking care of herself. She never needed you to do it for her."

"She's also so blinded by her love for my father that she can't see him for the monster he is."

"She sees," Alísun said as she took a seat on the leather sofa. "But she loves him anyway. And it torments her. That's why she let me go."

"I know." Livia sighed, taking the seat opposite the queen. "And she'll take whatever punishment he gives."

"You don't know, do you?" Alísun leaned forward, her silvery gray eyes darkening with the dim glow of her power. No matter how hard Marcus tried to sever her power, the magnetic sickness never took the queen completely. "Porcia and I escaped together. She is no longer under your father's control. She left him."

"What?" Livia shot to her feet. "This whole time? He's been refusing to let Mother have visitors as punishment for helping you escape."

"He's been lying to you, dear. That should come as no surprise. That's all Marcus knows how to do."

Livia sank back to her seat, her hands shaking with fury.

"He is a monster. I'm glad she's rid of him." But it cut Livia to the core to think her mother had left her behind. "Where is she? Is she here?"

"She is safe. You have nothing to worry about."

"I need to see her."

"She needs to disappear for a while. Let Marcus exhaust his attempts to find her. She will come find you when the dust settles."

"You mean once you all figure out if I can be trusted?" Livia clenched her fists in frustration.

"Can you blame us? You are his right hand. We have no idea where your loyalties truly lie. Until we know that for sure, you will have to stay here."

"How could you think I would be loyal to him?"

"Your actions, dear. The way you've pursued Allie every chance you've had. You knew who she was and you sought to deliver her to your father. We have to take that threat seriously."

"That is not what happened." Livia leaned forward. "You of all people know how much I *loathe* him."

"I want to believe that you've only ever done his bidding to keep your mother safe. Trust me, I want to believe that more than anyone," Alísun said.

"I didn't know she was my sister. I only suspected she was the child you spoke of in your prophecy." Livia glared at her. "I was trying to protect her. To get to her before Marcus realized he was looking for a boy when he should be looking for a girl. If he gets his hands on her...."

"Good girl. You figured it out." Alísun smiled. "I recorded that prophecy myself, back when we used to have scribes for that sort of thing. Changed a few of the details so it wouldn't be clear without the assistance of the prophet who spoke it." Alísun stood and crossed the room to pour herself a drink, and refilled Livia's empty glass. "That's what your father has been trying to torture out of me for over a thousand years." Alísun handed Livia a fresh bourbon.

"And you never cracked." Livia often wondered how Alísun had survived for as long as she had without succumbing to Marcus's will. But the ancients had a power the younger generations could never truly understand.

"Marcus has never had much respect for women. That was one detail I knew he wouldn't question." Alísun returned to her seat, knocking back the amber liquid with a grimace. "I knew he would never stop to consider that one of the most powerful and most important Immortals ever born could possibly be a woman."

"It's never crossed his mind."

"He must think he's getting close to tracking down the *boy*."

"He's been obsessed with him for the last decade," Livia said.

"Marcus believes the boy is Greggory's son, Aidan," the queen said. "We must continue to let him think that."

"The boy will need protection," Livia said. "Marcus will lose his patience soon and he will act on his suspicions."

"Aidan is protected. More than he could possibly realize. His parents have sent him to a school in Germany with a horde of security to guard him. He will not return until it is safe."

"And you will provide Allie the same protection?"

"We will keep them both safe. Safe and separate. The true prophecy speaks of them as one. She is the child born of the Indriell line. She is the key, but Aidan is her equal in every way. He is just as integral to our future as she is. But they are young. They do not need to know everything yet."

"So we protect them both?" Livia chewed her bottom lip, thinking it wasn't enough. If anyone knew the lengths Marcus would go to reach Allie and Aidan, it was Livia. They needed to take every possible precaution. "They should be kept down here, far away from Marcus's reach."

"They deserve to have a childhood. Neither of them has had much of one as it is. We will protect them, but we will also give them a chance at life."

"Do you trust me now?" Livia asked.

"I do." Alísun nodded.

"Can I leave this cage?"

"Not yet. You need to win over our hosts. Talk to Liam. Let him get to know the real you and in time you will be free of this place."

"It's no more than I deserve." Livia sighed.

"This is your one and only chance, Livia. This is your chance to make a change and become the kind of woman we all know you are on the inside. It speaks volumes about your character that four of your former slaves have stepped forward to speak on your behalf."

"All of them? Even Quinn?"

"Quinn has been the most adamant in his belief that you can be rehabilitated if only given the chance."

Livia didn't even know what to say to that. The thought that they would all speak for her ... after all she'd done to them ... it was too much.

"You know, when Marcus took you from your family ... it was a horrible thing to do to a child." A tear slid down Alísun's face. "Our children are our greatest joys in our long lives. But I was secretly grateful. He kept you close. Let me see you—my beautiful granddaughter."

"No." Livia sucked in a breath. "That's not possible." She squeezed her eyes shut tight, not wanting to believe it. "When you said Allie was born of the Indriell line ... I thought you meant in some sort of remote way."

"You are blood sisters. My natural granddaughters. Direct descendants of the first queen. Allie is my heir only because she is more powerful than you despite being a second-born child. But do not think for one moment that you are any less important than she is. You will play an important role in future events. You will be her champion. But it is up to you to decide if you will take on that role. You can have a bright future if you learn to shrug off the horrors of your past and leave Marcus behind. He was never your father. Your father loves you. Has thought of you every single day of your life."

"No. I don't want to hear this. It's time for you to leave." Livia gestured for the queen to leave. She didn't want think about what any of this meant.

"It is time for you to face who your family is, Alivia," Alísun said softly, reaching across the coffee table for her granddaughter's hand.

Livia shook her head. "Do not call me that. Please." She'd heard echoes of that name in her dreams. Long-forgotten memories that never made any sense to her. Flashes of silvery blond hair like Alísun's and vivid red hair like Allie's. Green eyes. Silver eyes—like the ones staring at her now. Memories of the family she'd been torn from.

"It is your name. It is the name my daughter Kassandre gave you when you were born of her body."

"No." Livia shook her head, fumbling with the cut-glass tumbler in her hand. Anything to avoid the queen's penetrating gaze. "I didn't know. I swear," Livia whispered.

"We know." The queen's voice was full of pain and sympathy.

"Does Allie know?" Livia finally met her grandmother's gaze.

"That your parents are Ashar and Kassandre? Yes, she knows. It's what she's been trying to tell you. What you've been refusing to see."

"No." Livia dropped her gaze again, tears falling on her hands. "Does she *know*?"

"Know what, Alivia? Say it. It will help."

Livia lifted her head, tears blurring her vision and burning her throat. "Does my sister know I killed our mother?"

How can Allie forgive Livia? Will they ever be sisters in truth?.
Find out soon in
Heir (Immortals of Indriell Book 4)

But before **Heir** releases, check out **Assignment (An Immortals of Indriell Novella)** Available now!

About Melissa A. Craven

Melissa A. Craven (the "A" stands for Ann—in case you were wondering) writes Young Adult Fantasy with crossover appeal to other genres and audiences of all ages. She believes in stories that make you think and she loves twisty plots, and playing with foreshadowing, leaving clues and hints for the careful reader. She draws inspiration from her background in architecture and interior design to help her with the small details in world building and scene settings. Melissa is also the indie manager and a staff reviewer at YABooksCentral.com. You can follow her reviews and her contributions to the YABC blog at the link below. And if you love Sweet Romance and Contemporary Fiction, you can find Melissa's books in those genres under her pen name, Ann Maree Craven.

Join Melissa's Underground on Facebook
Follow Melissa on YA Books Central
Melissaacraven.com

facebook.com/MelissaACravenAuthor
twitter.com/melissaacraven
instagram.com/melissaacraven
bookbub.com/authors/melissa-a-craven

Acknowledgments

Words cannot express how grateful I am to my family. I could not have done this without the love and support of my sister, Angela. A special thanks to my mother, Debby, who is the only one who will still talk to me about my book without rolling her eyes. And to my awesome dad, David, for giving me his very special gift of sarcasm.

To the one who shall remain nameless, thank you for your countless hours of acting as my sounding board. I literally could not have done this without you. To Jenny, thank you for your support and enthusiasm! To my beta readers, thank you for your valuable input. To Sandhya Semendy, I cannot thank you enough for your help getting Sasha's experiences in the Chloa Valley just right. You provided an enormous amount of inspiration. To Alexandria Palama, thank you for giving Santi an authentic voice and just the right amount of Latina sass!

Chase Night, of Story Tamers, you are a tough critic, but the best editor I've worked with in a long time. Your feedback is always appreciated. And Robin Schroffel, thank you for your grammar expertise! And to Zoe Shtorm and Daqri Combs for the amazing cover art! To the wonderful indie author community, you offer the most amazing support system. I definitely couldn't do this without you. A big thank you to all my readers and fans. I hope you love Quinn and Sasha's story as much as I do. Finally, I thank God for the constant reminder that I am doing what I'm supposed to be doing. Over the past years, circumstances *always* bring me back to writing—my favorite thing to do in the whole world.

www.ingramcontent.com/pod-product-compliance
Lightning Source LLC
Chambersburg PA
CBHW021944200826
50139CB00064B/75/J
* 9 7 8 1 9 7 0 0 5 2 1 2 1 *